UNBROKEN HOPE

A Novel
Michael Wells

ISBN: 979-8-9947730-1-7

Copyright © 2026 Michael Wells

This book is a work of fiction. Any references to historical events, real people, or real locales are used fictitiously. Other names, characters, places, and incidents are products of the author's imagination, and any resemblance to actual events or locales or persons, living or dead, is entirely coincidental.

All rights reserved, including the right to reproduce this book or portions thereof in any form whatsoever.

This book is dedicated to my mom, Barbara. She instilled in me a love of reading and went through so much in her life.

To my children Lauren, Ryan, and Grant. They constantly remind me of the wonders of youth.

And especially to my best friend, my wife, Dede. She has graced me with her common sense, good humor, and steadfast love.

Prologue

Oklahoma of the 1930s was dry and raw. It left grown men jamming back tears and women staring dully with unfocused eyes. There was nothing anyone could do to stop the carnage on the land. Children played, but their sandbox was simply the corner of their bedroom where the winds relentlessly puddled sand through every pore of the weather-beaten shacks.

Oklahomans bragged they were tough. That these hard times would not beat them. It was brave and stupid. Inside, fear gnawed at them. No money. Not enough to eat. Little water to drink. They were ghosts, dust covering them from head to foot. Dust so thick even a bath wouldn't clean them. They tied bandanas around their noses and mouths to no avail. Nothing would stop the onslaught. The land, long their friend, had turned against them. They couldn't believe that tomorrow would be as bad as yesterday. And yet it was. They placed their trust in God, and he rewarded their faith with a hot, laughing wind and blasting sand that gouged the eyes and gagged the throat.

It was a cursed land into which my mother, Barbara, was born. Even though she lived there for less than four years, it impacted her life more than she could ever know.

My mother never knew her history, so this is pretty much a work of fiction. Some of the people in this book existed, but not how they are portrayed here. This is her story, if only it would have happened this way.

PART I
HOME

"I am certain that after the dust of centuries has passed over our cities, we, too, will be remembered not for victories or defeats in battles or in politics, but for our contribution to the human spirit."

John Fitzgerald Kennedy

Chapter 1

Wind. Rain. Too much of one and too little of the other. The land scarred by both. The land required hard work, but it had spit out crops. Farmers who knew no better had stretched the land's womb to breaking. The land had been there last year, and it would be there tomorrow. So the farmers farmed. That's what they do. They scraped the land, ripped its skin, tore its heart out. Sucked the life out of it.

At one time the land had been good. Abundant rains had made sure of that. Grandfathers had staked their claims during the great land rush, and the land had been in the farmers' hands ever since. The land was theirs, so the land was everything.

The family needed the land to eat and to survive. The land *had* been good to them. Not even five years earlier the farmers had made a killing on wheat. Wheat prices were high, and the land simply couldn't be held back. It poured out wheat like an everlasting geyser of golden grain. And the farmers farmed it and farmed it and farmed it. They farmed it so hard that they didn't really see what they were doing to the breast that fed them. Or maybe they saw it, but they needed what the land could give them so badly, they ignored it. No matter. One year wheat was king and then the rains stopped, and the kingdom lay in ruin.

No rain meant no wheat. Not that it mattered much thanks to the ruination of the economy. It had started with the stock market crash of '29, and had led to successful businessmen selling pencils on street corners to make a dime. No one had any money, so no one could really buy much wheat.

Then the winds came, stripping off the precious layers of topsoil and spewing soil into massive violent clouds. Pushing the suffocating dust into the towns, down the throats, and finally into the hearts of every man and woman. "It'll be better next year!" the farmers would exclaim. They believed it simply because they could say it. They borrowed money against their farms to survive to that next, better year. But the next year came, and it wasn't better. It was worse. And the year after that was worse than the year before, and the farmers knew not what to do, but borrow more money. Next year would *certainly* be better.

Five years - no crops. No food to eat or sell. The banks wanted their money for the loans, but the farmers had nothing to give them. The land had broken them.

And then the flyers appeared. Nailed to telephone poles and handed around outside after church.

800 Orange Pickers Wanted in California!

Chapter 2

"It's 1937 and it's been goin' on too long, Erma!" Clay Stanley stammered. "I leave in the next two days, and I can make Californie by May. There should still be plenty of jobs picking oranges." He held up the green and orange flyer.

Erma glanced at the flyer and then stared at him, a man who over the past three years of little food had turned from wiry to walking skeleton. His dark brown hair and stubble of whiskers were dull. He wiped his hands on the front of dirty overalls. His bandana, ever at the ready around his neck, was pulled down as he talked to her. She held a small child, a girl. She looked down at her, just two years old.

"Barbara Jean, you hear that, yor Daddy is gonna leave us," she whispered to the child. The child didn't know that Clay was not her father.

"Oh Erma! Don't be scarun the baby. I ain't leavin ya forever. Soons I get work, I'll send for y'all. I promise."

Erma stared him down. Then as tears welled up she sat down. Clay stood there staring, dumbfounded.

"Erma, honey, now don't go cryin. That ain't gonna help."

Erma was wearing a print housecoat. Her apron was frayed at the corners, and she was pushing the corner of it into the baby's mouth to comfort her. Erma was a solidly built woman with a pretty face. Her dark blond hair set off her blue eyes perfectly. She had a turned-up nose dotted with caramel-colored freckles.

"But w…w…w…warwee gonna go?" Erma mouthed between sobs. "I jus gotta stay here! This is muh –muh – muh home."

"But you know you cain't, we've done been kicked out, and asides we ain't got nuthin left here. We done sold ever goddam thing!!"

This made Erma cry even harder. The baby, Barbara Jean, cried in sympathy with her mother. "I said whar will we go?" she shouted emphatically, with a stamp of her foot.

"I tole you, you'll stay with your sis and Jimmie at their place. It's already been worked out. They don't mind. Jimmie bought hisself a little time with the bank. Just enough time to give em some breathing room. Jest as soon as I get me a job out in Californie, I'll send for ya. And you cain come ridin in on a train, all in high style!"

Erma's sister, Mamie, and her husband, Jimmie Driggers, lived about ten miles away on the edge of Oklahoma City. Mamie and Erma had both been born in Wayne County in southern Illinois not far from where Illinois, Tennessee, and Kentucky meet. Mamie had drifted to the southwest when their parents had moved to New Mexico. It was in New Mexico that Mamie met Jimmie, a tall good-looking Texan. She and Jimmie had eloped and moved back to Texas where they had lived for a while. They later moved to Oklahoma City and had been there about five years.

"I cain't put Mamie out again. I stayed with them for close to a year when I first came here. Why cain't we stay here?" Erma complained.

Clay motioned around the room. "We been through this, Erma!" Clay shouted in exasperation. "What's here for ya? Eh? Nothing! The bank has taken it! We ain't got nothing and nothing is what we're gonna keep n lest I can get some money comin in soon, an Californie is our best hope of makin that happen!"

Barbara Jean had been looking on wide-eyed. The child wasn't scared, because she was used to this type of talk. But she was getting tired. She stared outside as the sun could be seen setting through the open window. Her mama rocked her gently, involuntarily. The rocking motion had been a part of Erma's movements since she had given birth almost three years previously. The rocking was present even when the child was asleep on her pallet, and Erma was just standing. She didn't even realize she was doing it. The child's eyes grew increasingly heavy.

"Erma, put the baby down an les go outside. Looks like the dust is takin a break," Clay said gently.

Erma laid the child gently on her flat mattress. The girl quickly rolled on her side with her thumb slipping into her mouth.

Erma walked toward the door, grazing her finger on the rough wooden table they used to eat on. Her finger left a small dust cloud in its wake.

"My Gawd in heaven," Erma whispered. "Look at this dust! I just cleaned this table not two hours ago."

"Fergit the table, honey," Clay said and walked outside. Erma followed him.

Clay immediately squatted down in the yard. He absent-mindedly began sifting the dirt through his hands. He then grabbed a handful and held it out to her.

"Kin you believe this? This used to be goddam good, rich topsoil. Now it's more of a beach than a farm." The sand sifted through his fingers, and he hung his head on the verge of tears.

Erma moved quickly to him and cradled his head against her stomach. The sobs erupted from them both.

"I'm so sorry Erma. You have to admit that when we first met things was lots better. I had this farm and wheat was selling. Gosh it wasn't even that long ago. Now look at us." He struggled with the next words, "W…we's poor!"

Erma stared at the man who wasn't her husband nor even fiancé. He was someone that she lived with and loved, but she had no ownership of him. He was a good man, but at the moment there was nothing more to say. Neither of them were spring chickens, as the saying goes. Clay was 35 and Erma, 31.

She had been born Erma Venita Wells and she grew up in Illinois. She had married Lawrence Owen in Illinois two days before Christmas, 1923. She was 18 and considered by the law to be a minor, so her mother and father had to sign their approval on her marriage license. Her parents stood at her side at the pitiful little civil ceremony. A year later her parents were living in New Mexico and she and Lawrence were still in Illinois..

Lawrence had stood alone at the wedding. He had been 22 and was a farmer just like his daddy and his daddy's daddy. But he had always wanted to be a barber. He had a dream of owning his own barbershop. Erma and Lawrence had wanted children, and she had become pregnant three times from 1924 through 1929. The first pregnancy ended in a miscarriage in the third month. The second went a little further, but not much, when it too ended in a miscarriage. The third went full term, but the little baby boy was stillborn. They named him William Lawrence Owen, II, after his father and buried him in the family cemetery where the two unnamed fetuses lay. It took Erma all the energy she had to keep her wits about her after that. It all became too much for both of them.

She had considered leaving Lawrence in late 1929, after having caught him in the middle of an affair. She had walked in on them after a shortened three-day visit to her sister, Myra, who lived two counties over. Erma was stunned but was determined to work things out with

Unbroken Hope

Lawrence. Despite what he had done, she still loved him. For awhile it worked, but it was clear his that mind and heart were elsewhere. After awhile she filed for and obtained a divorce. However, she still loved him and stayed on in Illinois, trying to think of ways to win him back. He married the hussy in 1932, and even still, she was sure she could win him back. And she had come close when she somehow got him alone on a cold night in November of '33. One thing led to another that night, and she lost her "virginity" again to him. She had been no virgin, and he certainly was no gentleman. Once a scoundrel, always one. Lawrence went back to his wife. In early 1934, Erma discovered she was pregnant. Shamed by it all, pregnant and unmarried, Erma escaped Illinois to live with her sister, Mamie, in Oklahoma City. She assumed that she would miscarry, because that was her lot, so she didn't worry much about being pregnant.

She met Clay while she was pregnant, and he didn't seem to mind her delicate state at all. She assured Clay not to worry about the baby, because she never carried one full-term. So, they had a fun and freeing time experimenting with sexual techniques with no fear of her becoming pregnant. A time that they both enjoyed immensely.

On August 10th, 1934, the big surprise arrived. Barbara Jean Owen sprang into the world. Full of life. Erma had wept tears of joy, but she also knew in her heart this would be her only child and thus protected the baby with all her might. Clay seemed happy, but Erma knew he couldn't love the child like a real father would.

As their past surrounded them in their thoughts, Erma and Clay stared daggers into the ground.

"Poor ain't the word for what we are, Clay," Erma said quietly.

"I know! That's why I have to leave!"

"Then take us with you!" Erma said, looking Clay straight in the face. "I am here with *you*! By *your* side, and this is where *I* need to be."

He shook his head. "That ain't gonna work, Erma. I'm going to give the house back to the bank. They want it, and they can have it."

Erma looked at the shack Clay had referred to as a house and laughed. "Tain't much of a house, but it is our'n."

Clay glanced at the house and smiled. He changed tactics. "Listen, Erma, do you think I like any of this?" Clay stammered. "My daddy left me this farm. He staked his claim to it during the land rush. It's been good land until the rains stopped. Twarn't nothing any of us did wrong. I'm jest hoping Californie will be a whole lot better!"

Erma knew the family history about the farm, but she was resolute in her decision. "We're coming with ya, Clay," Erma said firmly. "And I ain't gonna hear no more about it."

"Awright then," Clay said, resigned to her temperament. "I was gonna hitchhike out to Californie so you'd have the Ford to get around, but I'll get her fixed up, and we'll leave day after tomorrow. Is that awright with you?"

Erma walked over and stood on her tippy toes and kissed his cheek. "That's jus fine with me. Thankyee" she whispered. "Now let's get to bed, cuz we got us lots a work to do in the mornin."

"There's jest one thing. What are we gonna do for money?" Clay asked.

Erma walked inside and, in a moment, came back with a small coffee can. She opened the can, and she held it out for him to look inside. At the bottom was a roll of money and some scattered coins.

"I been squirlin this away. About a hunert and ten dollars. Knew we were going to need it."

Unbroken Hope

Clay was puzzled. "A hunert and ten! You bin keeping this from me?" he asked meekly.

"Yep, sold the jewelry my mama left me a while back. Didn't get near what it was worth, but at least it's somethin. So, do you think it'll be enough?

"Should be. It's a ton a money! But even if it ain't, it'll have to be, won't it? Mayhaps I can find some work along the way."

The next morning, Erma rose before Clay. He snored merrily along, curled into a ball. Erma looked over at the baby. She would be waking soon. Erma began fixing a meager breakfast of mush. It wasn't much, but they needed to save all the food they could for the trip. Who knew what was going to happen or what they might need?

By the time Clay rose, the sun was coming up, and Barbara Jean was sitting on a chair at the table, messily spooning mush into her mouth.

Clay stepped outside and peed off the front porch. He came back in stretching. "Gonna be a hot one today."

"Here, eat this," Erma said, handing him a bowl of mush. "We got lots to do today. We ain't got much here to sell. We done sold most of it already. The Ford won't hold much of it anyways." She looked out at the car sitting in the yard.

The Ford was a 1927 Model A sedan that Clay had purchased used in 1930. His crop of wheat had done well that year, and he had splurged and paid $200 for the car. The factory color on the car had been maroon, but over the years, the color had faded and now could barely be seen due to the layer of dust on it. With the haul from the wheat, he had also been able to buy 10 laying chickens, two pigs (a male and a female), and a milk cow. They had all served him well. Several years earlier, the chickens quit laying because they couldn't get enough to eat, so the small family ate them one at a time. The pigs had given birth two times. The most recent time was a couple of months previously. The birth yielded one baby. The father had died just after the conception, and the mother had died not long after the piglet weaned, so emaciated she was. The sow hadn't provided much meat. The piglet quickly grew into a sturdy young shoat.

"I think we take the tent, sleeping bags, some cooking pots, and clothes. Oh, an a course a few toys for the baby. We can jus leave what's left of the furniture or could try to sell it."

"I'll go into the city this morning and see if anyone wants to buy anything. Pretty sure no one will, though. I'll leave just as soon as I'm done eating. You stay here and start packing things up. I'll get some oil for the car and change it this afternoon. I'll fill her up with gas too."

"You need some of the money for that?"

"Nah, I got a little bit. Should be enough," as he closed the door behind him.

Erma could hear the car start and pull away. She busied herself for the rest of the morning, cleaning and packing. She thought she would be torn about what to take. It turned out, she didn't have that many items to choose from, so the choices were simple.

Clay wasn't back by ten, and she was little surprised she hadn't seen him. But she had plenty to do. The couple had one remaining chicken and the young shoat left. She decided she better butcher both. She could fry the chicken. They could have that for dinner. The shoat, she could salt down. They had a small keg that would hold it perfectly. The meat would no doubt come in handy.

By four o'clock, the shoat was salted, and the chicken plucked, cut up and ready for the frying pan, and still no sign of Clay. They had no telephone, so all she could do was fret about his absence.

Then, finally, a cloud of dust came moving up the road, the Model A. Her heart settled down as she saw Clay behind the wheel.

She came running out of the house, furious.

Unbroken Hope

Clay climbed from behind the wheel and immediately held his hand up, knowing her temper.

"Hole on a second, honey. before you go rippin my head off."

"Hole on a second, my foot!" glared Erma. "Where in the world've you been? I figured you'd be back by noon at the very latest."

"I know. I know. I tried as hard as I could to get someone to buy the furniture. Thought I had it sold, and the deal fell through. That was one of the things that took so long."

He then reached into the car and brought out two large loaves of bread and a couple of cans. "I also had to wait in the bread line at the church. Thought this stuff might come in handy."

Erma grabbed the goods and hugged them. "They shore will."

"And stopped I by your sister's and tole her we were pulling up stakes. Jimmie and her are coming over early tomorrow to say goodbye."

"Oh, well that makes sense and thanks for that. I didn't know how I was gonna say goodbye," Erma said, the wind slowly seeping from her sails. "Well, I got everything packed up. Even slaughtered and salted the shoat, and I'm fixin to fry our last chicken for dinner. We'll have biscuits with it if that's awright?

"Sounds good! I'm mighty hungry. I'll change the oil while you fix the chicken. That work for ya?"

Erma had already turned to the house and waved over her shoulder. "It does. Should take about an hour so you have plenty of time."

While Erma cooked the chicken and biscuits, Barbara Jean played with a rag doll on the dusty floor. Erma had tried to keep up with the dust, but eventually it got the best of her. So, she reduced the times she swept and dusted each day to two, and that was just as much a losing battle as sweeping every hour had been.

By the time the chicken was done, Erma could hear the water pump handle outside being worked and knew Clay was washing up. He came inside wiping the water off his hands on his overalls. Men, Erma thought, they wash their hands only to wipe them on dirty overalls. She would never understand it, but she loved him all the same. He was a good man and had provided well for this family. That is, until God and the world got the better of him. But he had no fault in any of that.

"Boy, that smells good! I was getting a little sick of mush!" he said with a laugh.

"Well, enjoy it while you can, dear. Maybe the last we get for a while."

The little family of three sat at the table preparing for their meal. They bowed their heads and offered up the simple grace they had taught the child. Barbara Jean looked from her mother to her "father" and mouthed the words, "God is great. God is good. Let us thank him. For our food. Amen"

The family dug in, and before long, every piece of chicken and every biscuit was devoured, leaving only a small stack of bones.

"Twarn't much of a chicken, kinda scrawny, but it sure tasted good, Erma."

Erma stood to clear the table. "Thanks. Glad you liked it."

"Awright, show me what you got packed today," Clay said as he stood.

For the next hour, Erma showed what she had packed and where everything was. Somewhere in the middle of this the baby dozed off and was put to bed. When Erma's work had finally passed inspection, Clay said, "Looks good. I guess we should go to bed. We'll want to get an early start in the mornin."

Chapter 3

With no alarm clock or rooster to awaken her, Erma could have slept till noon. She had been lost in a wonderful dream. She was in California and was sitting in the wonderful sun on a wonderful broad porch attached to a wonderfully beautiful house. Somewhere in the dream she knew the wonderful house belonged to Clay and her. A nice cool, wonderful breeze enveloped her as she sipped wonderfully tasting orange juice from a wonderful crystal glass. It was all so... wonderful! In her dream, Clay wasn't on the porch with her. He had just gotten up to drive into town. She could hear the car starting.

Except the starting car wasn't in her dream. It was starting in real life. She bolted upright and felt in the bed next to her. Clay was missing. She jumped up out of bed just in time to see the headlights flash through the small room and the car go jolting up the road in fits and starts.

She ran to the front door and flung it open. "Clay!" She screamed after the car to no avail. "Clay," she said again, though this time softer. She glanced back inside and saw a note on the table. The open coffee can sat beside it. She picked it up.

Dear Erma,

I'm sorry about all of this. But you didn't want to take no for an answer, so I had to leave without you. Don't worry, Mamie and Jimmie will be coming to *get you about 8 or so. I will bring you and the baby out to California just as soon as I can. I <u>will</u> write to you at your sister's.*

I Love You,

Clay

PS - I took half the money.

Erma read the letter twice and still couldn't believe it. She was so angry she trembled. She could feel her temper bubbling up inside herself. This time, she had nothing and/or nobody to take it out on. So, she dumped the money out of the can and threw the can across the room. It startled the baby awake, and she began to cry. This made Erma even madder. She looked around the room for something else to throw, but there was nothing. Virtually everything had been sold or packed. Then her eyes lit on Clay's family Bible resting on the lone table. Sitting there, it made her furious. How can a man who deserts his family have a family Bible? She thought. Erma ran to the Bible and began ripping out pages and flinging them into the air. As she did, she laughed and cried all at the same time. This terrified Barbara Jean, who didn't know what was happening. She simply wailed louder, and the louder she wailed, the more intense the Bible page ripping became. Finally, Erma realized how futile her anger was, and she calmed down and looked over at the young child. She bent over, picked her up, and began soothing her with soft, cooing noises. She and the baby held on to one another in a puddle of Bible pages.

At her feet, Erma could see the scattered pages of the Bible. She knelt down and picked up two of the sheets, which were the first two pages of the Bible. She studied them. There, on the pages, was the family tree carefully filled in by four generations of the Stanley family. About two-thirds of the way down was Clay's name, Clayton Vernon Stanley, her name, Erma Venita Wells, and her daughter's name, Barbara Jean Owen weren't even in the Bible. They were not a part of Clay's family. Erma started to cry again. How had her life come to this?

"Knock, knock," someone said softly at the open door. Erma turned with a start. It was Jimmie Driggers, her sister's husband. He stood meekly staring in. His wife, Mamie, stood silently by his side. Erma had not heard them drive up. She stared out at them, not registering at first who it was. It was Mamie that moved first. She looked down at the pool of Bible pages and sighed.

"Oh, you poor thing," she said as she rushed to comfort Erma and the baby. She took the baby and then put an arm around Erma's shoulders. "I thought you would take this poorly."

"What am I gonna do?" Erma beseeched them. "What am I gonna do?" saying it a second time forlornly. Then she broke down, sobbing.

"You're going to come stay with us. That is what you're going to do, you and Barbara Jean. And we'll just figure this out." Mamie said with a soft pat on the shoulder.

"He left. He just up and left!" Erma said through her tears.

It was then that Jimmie stepped forward. "He had to go, Erma. But he'll send for ya. He stopped by yesterday. He's got a real good plan."

"A good plan, huh? So good he couldn't share it with me?" Erma spat out. Right now, she wanted nothing to do with the deserter.

"Now, honey," Jimmie said ineffectually. "He knowd you wouldn't go along with him leaving without you. But you gotta see he was right. You couldn't be traipsin halfway across the country with a baby. For right now, you're better off with us. He'll send for ya or come back and get ya, you'll see."

"Let's get your things and the baby's too," Mamie said calmly. She, like so many of her neighbors, had seen and been through a lot. No one had been spared some level of heartache. "What things would you like to take, dear?

Erma walked to the stack of packed goods she had prepared yesterday. She noticed the tent and a sleeping bag were missing. But the keg containing the shoat was still there.

"If you have room, I would like to take it all," she said and then softly added, "for safekeeping. Plus, there is some food there."

There was so little that it took only a few minutes to load it. Erma looked around the inside of her dusty two-room home. It hadn't been much, but it had been hers. She would miss it. Oh well, she thought, it will be better in California. She closed the front door and got into the back seat of her brother-in-law's blue '28 Dodge Brothers sedan.

The ride to Jimmie and Mamie's was a quiet one. Erma didn't feel like talking, and the baby just stared at her aunt and uncle. She had begun forming words about six months earlier, but her vocabulary consisted mostly of mama and daddy. So, she just stared straight ahead.

They arrived at Jimmie and Mamie's little house. It was about the same as Erma's, though a little bit bigger. It had two bedrooms and a small common area that combined a kitchen and living room. Jimmie hustled Erma's things onto the porch.

"Erma, you think your things will be alright out here for tonight?"

Erma shrugged as if to say she didn't care what he did with them. "Well, may wanna bring that thar shoat in," as she motioned toward the keg. "Coyotes might smell it an tear into it."

"Well, talk of that shoat is makin me hungry. You hungry, dear?" Mamie said. We've got some tomatoes and bread I could make you a tomato sandwich if you want."

Again, Erma just shrugged.

"OK, well, I'll make you one. If you don't eat it, then I will. What about the baby? She must be hungry!"

Unbroken Hope

"Hungwee!" Barbara Jean exclaimed. Erma was stunned by the new word.

Mamie laughed. "I will make you a tomato sandwich too, Sugarpie." She poked the baby lightly in the tummy.

Erma went back to staring off. She seemed completely exhausted by her recent ordeal.

The dust was just as thick in Mamie's house as Erma's. It was funny how, after a while, you simply didn't notice it that much. There hadn't been a dust storm in over a month, but the dust kept trickling in.

Mamie went to making sandwiches. She was a plain woman with straight brown hair and a crooked nose. She and Erma shared bright blue eyes. She had a great smile that warmed anyone who met her. Before all the troubles, she had gained a little bit of fat around the middle, but over the past three years, all of that had vanished. Jimmie and Mamie were childless, for reasons they didn't understand, but as the economy continued to plunge and food became more and more scarce, they were plain happy they had no little mouths to feed.

"Where'd you get the tomatoes?" Erma asked absently.

"Jimmie traded em for some car parts he had stashed away. Those parts sure came in handy!"

"Yeah, thank God Dodges are popular!" Jimmie chirped in.

The three adults and the baby gathered around Jimmie and Mamie's little table and ate the sandwiches in silence. In the middle of the meager lunch, Barbara Jean began to nod off.

"Maybe, she could use a little nap," Mamie said as she gathered the young girl in her arms. She took her and laid her on the bed and came back to the kitchen.

"Erma, you haven't eaten a thing. We can't waste food, and you need to keep your strength up."

"Oh, what's the use?" Erma croaked.

"Plenty's the use," Jimmie said. Then to Mamie, "Maybe she might want to lie down too??"

"Jimmie, that ain't such a bad idea," Mamie said. "Come on, Erma, let's go lie down. I'll save your sandwich for later."

Erma stood at Mamie's urging and sleepwalked into the second bedroom, where she collapsed on the bed. She was dead asleep before her head hit the pillow.

Mamie crept from the bedroom, closing the door behind her.

"Poor thing," she said softly to Jimmie. "All of this is really too much for her."

Jimmie nodded in agreement.

Not a peep emerged from the bedrooms. The time flew by until it was dark, and still nothing from the bedrooms. When it was time for Jimmie and Mamie to go to bed, they moved Barbara Jean in with her mother. Neither moved a muscle.

Jimmie and Mamie turned in.

Once they were in bed, Mamie turned to Jimmie and asked softly, "Do you think he'll send for her?"

"Why sure he will," Jimmie answered incredulously. "Don't you think so?"

"I honestly don't know. But I do hope so. I surely do hope so. I'm not so sure how we're going to feed her, though. We barely have enough for ourselves."

"We'll figure a way," Jimmie said sorrowfully. "We always do."

CHAPTER 4

It was very early morning the following day and Erma sat in the Greyhound bus station. Barbara Jean sat on her lap. The baby was content sitting and people watching. Erma's bags sat at her feet. She was holding Clay's goodbye letter.

Erma saw them coming from a ways off. She had been expecting them. It was Jimmie and Mamie. "Erma, you scared the bejeesus outta us, sneaking out in the middle of the night, leaving like that." Mamie said.

"How'd you know I'd be here?"

"Where else would you be? You can't walk to California!" Mamie retorted." How in the world did you get here, honey?"

"I hitch-hiked."

"You hitch-hiked!" Mamie exclaimed. "With the baby! That is too dangerous!"

"We got here awright!" Erma said stubbornly.

"But where exactly are you going?" Jimmie asked.

"Got me a ticket to Los Angeles," Erma said straight-faced, holding the ticket up. "I have to find Clay. Our family needs to be together. There is nothin here for us, and I don't wanna be a burden on you two."

Jimmie looked at Mamie and then back at Erma.

"Would you talk some sense into her, Mamie?" Jimmie said with exasperation.

Mamie sat down next to Erma.

"Erma, honey, you can't go to California. California is gigantic, and you don't even know where Clay is."

"We'll find him. I know we can. I'm just not staying here. My mind is made up."

"But how much money you got?" Jimmie asked. "It's going to take a lot of money. Where will you stay once you get there?"

"I'll figure something out, don't you worry about that."

Mamie took Erma's hand. "But what about the baby?" she asked softly. "You have her to worry about."

Erma grabbed her hand back, "You let me worry about her. We'll be jus fine."

"But you don't know no one out in California," Mamie objected. "This is plain crazy!"

"Again, let me worry about that. I got a plan."

"You've got a plan, huh?" Mamie shouted. "What's your plan? To drag poor Barbara Jean all the way out there? To put her through God knows what? To <u>not</u> find her father? Can't you see it is impossible?"

It's not," Erma pleaded. "I've got faith and I got hope. I know I can find him."

"How?" Jimmie interceded. "Do you even know where he's going?"

"He said he was heading to San Bernardino," Erma admitted.

"But that can change," Jimmie said. "Out there, things change."

Mamie decided to change her tactic. "Erma, Jimmie asked how much money you got?"

"Thirty-seven dollars."

"Thirty-seven! How you going to live on thirty-seven dollars once you get there?" Mamie implored.

"How am I gonna live here on thirty-seven dollars without being a mooch on you?" Erma shot back.

"You're not a mooch. You're family," said Jimmie calmly.

Erma thought for a moment and then reached over and held Jimmie's hand.

"I preciate that Jimmie," Erma said tenderly. "I really do."

Mamie reached out for the letter and pointed to it in Erma's left hand. "May I see that?" she asked.

Erma held it back initially, then proffered it forward. Mamie read the short note quickly.

"See, he says he'll write you here with us," Mamie said. "That's a good thing. You need to wait to hear from him so you know where to go. Can't you see that?"

Erma took the letter back. Folded it and put it back in her pocket.

"I awready bought my ticket, eighteen bucks," she said glumly.

"I think we can get them to give your money back," Mamie said kindly. "Come home, Erma." She reached down and took the baby. Erma stood and meekly followed them out of the bus station. Jimmie grabbed Erma's single battered suitcase. One of the latches was broken, causing the bag to bulge at the seams. It contained everything important that she owned in the world. Her entire life could be summed up in that one battered and dirty bag. Jimmie headed off with her ticket to get a refund.

She climbed into the back of the Dodge, and when Jimmie came back, he handed her the eighteen dollars, put the bag on the seat next to her, and started the Dodge up. She rode silently for a while, thinking about what Mamie had said about what she would do for money in California. She knew in her heart that the fifty-five dollars she now possessed would hardly be enough. So she would have to figure out another way to get there besides buying a bus ticket.

"Do you think he will write?" she asked softly.

"What's that, honey?" Mamie asked, turning to look at her. Mamie had the baby in her lap and had been playing with her by letting her pull her index finger and rocking her around gently. The baby was still focused on the finger while Mamie listened.

"Do you really think Clay will write?"

"Why, yes, I do. He said he would, and so he will. Clay is a man of his word."

"Why'd he have to run out on me in the middle of the night, though?"

"He just knew you weren't gonna let him go without you," Jimmie interjected.

"I probly wouldn't have," Erma agreed. "But I sure wish he'd of woken me up to say goodbye and to kiss the baby."

Mamie just nodded, having nothing more to add. The threesome rode on in silence.

"How you gonna feed us?" Erma finally asked. "You barely got enuff for you two."

Jimmie tightened his grip on the steering wheel and rubbed his chin. "Now you don't go worrying about that, Erma. We'll figure it out one ways or nother.

"Well, you got to promise me one thing," Erma said.

"What's that?" Jimmie asked.

"You cain't be starving yorselves just to feed us, I need to pull my weight."

"Fair deal," Jimmie said quickly. "We'll figur it out, I promise you.

Unbroken Hope

The car pulled up in front of the house. A billow of dust followed in its wake. The three adults and one child sat in the car. Barbara Jean carefully studied each of the adults. "Daddy?" she finally said.

"Daddy's not here, baby," Erma said.

"Daddy?" the child repeated.

Chapter 5

US Route 66 was the ant trail to the picnic blanket. The farmer ants started from as far east as Arkansas and as far north as Nebraska. The farmer ants moved slowly but were steadily attracted to the sweet smell of work. The sugar that guided the ants was a trail of paper flyers.

Flyers were posted on telephone poles and shop windows, anywhere there was an empty space. They could be found fluttering down Main Street. For hundreds of miles the flyers could be found. They were torn from those same phone poles and shop windows by greedy little ant hands. On street corners and feed lots, a flyer was dragged from a back pocket and discussed intensely. The flyers begged for hard working farmer ants to rush to the Promised Land.

The flyers were stuffed in ant pockets. The flyers were passed around at campsites and service stations. Every ant on the road knew about the flyers. Hell, the flyers were the reason the ants were on the road to begin with. The flyers screamed for help. Worker ants were needed, and the farms were just waiting for them!

The flyers were hope and hope is a glorious thing, and maybe an ant only has hope.

The flyers were a beacon pointing the way to the picnic blanket filled with food for the taking. One had only to get there. To California.

And so the farmer ants set out. They walked and drove broken-down jalopies. Farmer ant families with their entire life's processions loaded in creaky old trucks. Trucks that sagged in the middle and tires that bulged under the load. Trucks so full that farmer ant families with more than three or four had to lie on top of one another. The trucks didn't look like they could make it 10 miles, let alone the almost 1400 miles for the trek. Steam poured from radiators, and baby ants screamed in discomfort. And yet the farmer ants kept coming. Urged on by seeing more and more flyers, the ants never dreamed they would be out of luck by the time they reached the picnic. It was hope that drove them.

What the farmer ants didn't know, couldn't know, was that California had become very good at crushing the hearts of all sorts of ants. California had lured hundreds of thousands of gold-seeking ants from around the world to the gold fields less than a hundred years earlier. Most ended up poorer than when they arrived.

Chinese ants almost single-handedly built Leland Stanford's great Central Pacific Railroad through much of northern California. This railroad, when joined by the golden spike with the Union Pacific Railroad, linked the nation from ocean to ocean. Chinese ants did the work when virtually no one else would. And yet when the railway was completed, the Chinese ants were told they were no longer needed or wanted in California.

Of course, farmer ants didn't know any of this, and even if they had, they would have ignored it. Could the farmer ants overcome California? They believed they could because they had hope, and, you see, *hope* is a mighty powerful thing.

Chapter 6

Clay had driven for the better part of two hours before he could relax. He felt terrible leaving Erma and the baby, but there wasn't anything he could do about it. Erma could be mighty stubborn, and he just couldn't risk her coming with him. He had a plan and he knew it would work.

He figured if he could average forty miles an hour, he could make four hundred miles a day. He could make California in less than four days. He could be working inside a week!

He had fifty-five dollars. He would buy a loaf of bread at the next store he came to and a jar of peanut butter. He could eat peanut butter sandwiches for the next four days and drink nothing but water when he stopped to fill up with gas.

The challenge was making the forty miles an hour. The roads were clogged! He couldn't believe how many people were on the roads. He had been forced to stop over ten times since he had left the farm. Cars and trucks were broken down, and he felt terrible that he couldn't help the families. But farmers knew their way around the handle part of a wrench and could fix pretty much anything mechanical. The problem they would run into was parts. If they needed a part that they didn't have, they would play hell trying to find it. The one thing he knew was he didn't have any spare parts for them. The ones he did have were for his Ford, and he couldn't spare any of them. His goal, his single-minded goal, was to make California, and he was prepared to do whatever it took to do just that.

Clay had a beat-up old map that showed him where to go. He knew the route was easy, just follow US 66 right into California. So, getting there was the easy part. The hard part was finding out what to do once he got there. The good news was that he had the flyer to help with that part. He would simply drive into California and head to Burkey Farms outside San Bernardino, just like the flyer said.

He was making pretty good time. He figured he would make the Texas line in another hour or so. Then on to Shamrock, and he thought he had enough gas to do just that. He figured he would stop for gas, buy his sandwich fixings, and then put in a couple more hours before camping for the night.

Even though he was surrounded by tons of people, it was a lonely drive with no one to talk to. Clay was a friendly sort, and he enjoyed jaw-boning with other folks very much. But there was no one to talk to here, and so he drove on. Each mile driven made him one mile closer to his goal.

As he drove along, he passed people walking and pulling children in wagons. People crammed into old, broken-down cars. One family had a mule hooked up behind their car and was going ever so slowly on the side of the road. When Clay got to them, the driver waved him around. Clay didn't have a clue how long it would take them to get to where they were going, dragging the mule along. Maybe they were going to try and sell it. Hell, he thought, they may have to eat it! He waved, but the people didn't wave back. They had looks of dead seriousness on their faces. The children didn't play but rode along in silence.

Most everyone was heading west, and it slowed his pace to a crawl. He had not seen a car going in the opposite way in over two hours. He felt guilty being the only one in his car, but he wasn't going to take anyone with him… at least not yet.

The car had no radio, so Clay whistled as he drove. He whistled to amuse himself, and he whistled to keep himself awake. The time crawled by, but then so did the miles. Clay kept whistling.

It took him five hours longer than he thought it would, but he whistled himself clear to the Texas state line. When he got there, he pulled into the inspection station.

"Where ya headed?" The agent asked brusquely.

"To California," Clay replied with a broad smile.

"Yeah, you and everyone else," the agent said, bored. "Carrying any fruits or vegetables?"

"No sir."

"OK, then move along. Welcome to Texas, but keep moving. We don't tolerate vagrants here in Texas."

"But…" Clay started to question the agent, but thought better of it and moved down the road.

At a snail's pace, he eventually drove by a *Welcome to Shamrock, Texas* sign. The population read 3,740. Shamrock wasn't much to look at as he drove through the town. He moved slowly past some broken-down buildings. Down a side street, he saw three workers repairing the road. Parked beside them was a WPA truck. The WPA, or Work Projects Administration, was a federal government program aimed at putting people to work while improving the streets, roads, and other infrastructure. Clay had seen these crews in Oklahoma City but had never been able to land a job on one.

He looked around as he drove on. Many of the small storefronts were closed and looked abandoned. One shop was open, and a woman was hopelessly trying to clear the dust from the sidewalk in front. Her broom pushed the dust, but the dry wind kept forcing the dust back, fighting her every sweep.

He drove on, finally pulling into a service station across from a small grocery store. Perfect, he thought. I can get gas and then go across and get some food.

He pulled in front of a pump and was getting out when a grizzled old man came limping over to the car. The old man wore surprisingly clean coveralls, but his hair looked tousled and filthy.

"You got money?" the old man demanded.

"Yeah, sure I do!" Clay said, incensed. "What do you think I am…a bum?!"

"I don't know what you are, let me see it. The money." The old man certainly had no manners.

Clay fished in his pocket and produced his small roll of bills.

"OK, how much gas to do you want?"

"Well, I don't rightly know. I don't know how much I need."

"Well, you got to pay in advance." The old man said with a sneer.

"OK, why not give me two dollars' worth to start," Clay said, peeling off two bucks and handing them to the old guy. "At twenty-two cents a gallon, that'll buy me close to ten gallons.

"That's right." The old man had softened a bit once he had seen Clay had money. The old man screwed off the gas cap, which was located in front of the windshield. He pumped the two dollars' worth, which filled the tank.

"Anything else?" the attendant asked.

"I think that'll do it," Clay said and then asked. "Oh, you got any water?"

"I do. It will cost you though. Water's scarce around here."

"OK, how much?"

"Twenty cents a gallon."

"Twenty cents! That's as much as the gas!"

"Tole you it was rare around here. Want it or not?"

"OK, I'll take a gallon. I got a jug."

The old man filled the jug, and Clay paid him with two dimes.

"Why you got to be so mean?" Clay asked sheepishly.

The old man sidled up to Clay and smiled a Jack-O-Lantern smile with three front teeth missing. "Sorry about that," the old man said. "Been stiffed more than once over gas. Too many people need too much gas, and no one has any money. They're desperate. Once you put the gas in, it's hard to get back out without siphonin it. Had to siphon a couple of times, cuz there was no money to be had. Pure desperation. That's what it is."

"Oh," was all Clay could think to say. "Is it OK if I park my car over there?" Clay pointed to a bare spot by the road. "I got to go get me some grub at that store."

"Sure, no problem, and I won't even charge you to park there!" the old man grinned his toothless smile.

"Well, thanks for that!" Clay said with a smile.

Clay moved the car and got out. He locked the car and quickly hustled into the store.

A bell on the door rang, alerting the owner someone had entered. A curtain behind the counter was pushed aside. A short, attractive woman came in and stood behind the counter. Clay could see what looked like living quarters behind the curtain. Clay had a hard time making out how old she was. She looked about forty, but Clay had learned that hard times put a lot of age on people. She could have been as young as twenty-five.

"Hello," she said cautiously as she sized Clay up. He reached in his pocket and pulled out the roll of bills.

"I got money," he said as he held the roll aloft."

"Well, I don't see that much these days." The woman said with a smile. She had warmed up knowing Clay was going to be a paying customer. "Whatchya need?"

"Bread and peanut butter," Clay said stoically.

"Bread is over there," the woman said, pointing. "And the peanut butter is down that aisle."

Clay grabbed a loaf of Wonder sliced bread. It was wrapped in wax paper with the ends folded over. The package had a white background with red, yellow, and blue circles that looked like balloons. Clay looked at the package with amusement. He quickly grabbed a wide-mouthed glass jar of Skippy peanut butter and went back to the counter and laid his purchase down.

"That be all?" the woman asked, clearly disappointed that Clay wasn't buying more.

"It sure will ma'am. Sorry I ain't buying more. I only got this little bit of money to last me till I get work. I'm going to…"

"I know, California," the woman finished his sentence for him. "I probably should go myself. Can't hardly make a dime in this hole here."

"It's bad isn't it?" Clay said. "Government says things are getting better, though."

"The government!" the woman spat out. "It's the same ole blather coming out of them. Two years ago, they said things were getting better. Better? Better! They got worse. Them fellas in Washington don't have a clue what's going on out here! We're starving, that's what! We're starvin!" The woman broke down a little and then composed herself. The curtain pulled aside, and a boy of about seven peered out.

"You awright, Mama?" the boy asked.

Unbroken Hope

The woman turned toward the boy. "Right as rain, Charlie. I'll be back in a minute."

Clay looked at the boy. "Right handsome boy you got there ma'am. I got me a daughter back in Oklahoma."

"You left her?"

"I did. Pained me to do it too. But I had no choice. Left her mom and her with her mama's sister. They'll be OK til I can bring them out to me."

"My Peter left for California over a year ago. Ain't heard a peep from him since he left. Don't know whether he is alive or dead. All I got now is Charlie and this blamed store, and this store ain't good for much. Can barely keep it stocked. And what I got I cain't sell. That peanut butter you got there has been on the shelf for close to three months. No one has any money. We used to offer credit to folks here abouts. Had to quit doing it cuz no one could pay their bill."

"You live back there?" Clay pointed behind the curtain.

"We do." The woman said proudly. "Lost the house right after Peter left. Bank took it. So, I fixed up the stock room to live in. That will be nine cents for the bread and twenty-four cents for the quart of Skippy."

"Say, do you sell postcards?"

The woman nodded, "And stamps," she added. "Over there." She pointed to a corner rack.

Clay took off for the rack.

"Postcards are a penny and stamps a penny." She called after him

Clay grabbed a postcard and came back to the counter. She handed him a stamp.

"Here's thirty-five cents. That make us square?"

"It sure does," the woman said with a smile.

"You have a pen?"

She handed him a pencil.

Clay scribbled some notes on the back of the card and addressed it. He stuck the stamp on it. "Could you make sure this gets mailed, please?"

The woman took the postcard. "I sure will."

"Thanks!"

Clay stood awkwardly there a moment and then said, "Well, I better hit the road. It was sure nice talkin to ya."

He turned toward the door and then turned back to her. "I'm Clay, by the way."

"Sarah." The woman said, holding her hand out.

Clay took her hand and warmly shook it.

"Well, you take care now, Sarah."

"I will, and you be careful out on that road, Clay, and if you run into my man, Peter, send him home to us will ya?"

Chapter 7

Clay moved on down the road. The car was running well, and he was making time, not good time, but time all the same. The line of cars and people walking clogged everything up. He would go about five hundred feet and then come to an abrupt standstill. Then about ten miles outside of Shamrock, the car started sputtering and came to a stop. Clay was able to push it onto the side of the road with the help of a couple of people who'd been walking.

He pulled up the hood and looked at the engine. The two men who had helped him push looked with him. "Whattya reckon it is?" one of them said.

"If I had to guess, bad gas. I just filled up back aways. Didn't have any problem before that," Clay answered. "But's getting dark and I ain't gonna be doin anything with it tonight. I'll deal with it in the mornin."

Clay rose just as the sun was coming up. He recalled how the Model A had sputtered one last time before the engine fell silent. The old car, with its cracked paint and worn leather seats, had never given him trouble like this before. He tried to start it again. The engine struggled to start and faltered again as soon as he hit the gas.

He popped the hood with a grunt, the old latch squealing in protest, and stepped back. The engine looked mostly fine - dusty, sure, but nothing out of the ordinary. Still, the smell of burnt oil and something foreign lingered in the air. He pulled the cap off the gas tank and took a cautious sniff, confirming his suspicion. The unmistakable odor of kerosene mixed with gasoline hung around.

Kerosene! The thought hit him like a freight train. It was the only explanation that made sense. He'd seen this before, but it had been years. A mix of kerosene and gasoline could cause an engine to sputter, backfire, or simply refuse to run. If someone had added kerosene to the gas, the Model A wouldn't have a chance. It was an old trick to stretch the gas. That crooked old man! Had to be!

Clay cursed under his breath. He knew he had to drain the tank, but that wasn't going to be a quick fix. It was a pain, but he had no choice. What a way to start this trip off, as if he didn't have enough trouble!

He walked over to the rear of the car and started pulling the toolbox from the trunk. Wrenches, screwdrivers, and a few old rags. He had never been a mechanic, but after years of tinkering with the Model A, he'd learned how to get by.

First, he needed to siphon the gas out. He pulled the siphon hose from the toolbox, checked the end for cracks, and slipped it into the gas tank. The process was slow, but after a few minutes, the gas started to flow - brownish, with a slight sheen on top. He grimaced. Kerosene, all right. It ran out on the ground.

After he drained what was left in the tank, Clay checked the fuel lines. He would need good, fresh gas to clean the lines.

He looked around at the slow-moving cars. He asked several of the drivers if he could buy a gallon of gas from them. Finally, the fourth driver he asked had a gallon to spare and sold it to him for two dollars. It was highway robbery, but Clay wasn't going anywhere without it. They transferred it to an empty jug Clay found.

Then he went back to the fuel lines. They weren't clogged, but they'd likely been contaminated with the bad gas. He loosened the lines one by one, running a bit of fresh gasoline through them to flush out the bad stuff.

Next came the carburetor. He unbolted the carb and set it on the ground. A few quick twists of the wrench, and the top came off. Inside, it was clear the kerosene had started to leave a residue - a thick, sticky sludge that didn't belong. He wiped it clean with a rag, making sure everything was as smooth as it could be.

By now, his hands were slick with oil and grime, but he didn't mind. The day was beginning to warm, and the smell of gasoline and kerosene mixed with the musty scent of the open countryside reminded him of the years he'd spent as a boy, watching his father work on cars in the backyard.

With the carburetor cleaned and reassembled, he carefully reattached it to the engine and bolted everything back into place. The tank was ready to be refilled with fresh gas. As he poured the remainder of the gallon of gasoline into the tank, he could almost feel the Model A's engine sigh in relief. He'd done his part—now it was time to see if the old girl would run.

Clay slid behind the wheel and turned the key. The engine coughed twice and then roared to life. He grinned, wiping his hands on his pants as the purr of the Model A filled the air.

The road stretched ahead, ready to take him to California. For now, he was just thankful to be back on track, the broken-down car nothing more than a memory, but a painful one at that. It had taken him almost all day to get the car to run, and he still needed gas. Hopefully, there was a station close by.

The attendant, a lanky man named Earl, judging from the embroidered name on his shirt, was leaning on the pump, chewing on a toothpick, his expression unreadable. The station was still relatively new, and the gas pumps stood like sentinels, glass cylinders atop of metal cases. Proud in their own quiet way.

"Need a fill-up?" Earl asked without looking up, his voice flat.

Clay nodded as he got out of the car. "Yep, that' be good."

The older man shrugged, turned, grabbed a handle, and pumped. The gas flowed up into the glass cylinder. Then, Earl put the fill hose in the car's tank and turned the valve. Gravity went to work, and the gas flowed into the tank.

"Plenty of folks drive by, not many stop," Earl said.

"No money," Clay said flatly.

"You got that right. Well, that does it.

The glass cylinder was empty. Clay paid Earl, adjusted the cap on his head, and climbed into his car. The sun was nearly gone now, painting the sky in shades of purple and orange. It took him a little while to work his way into the crowded flow of cars on the road.

He continued to be amazed by just how many people were on the road. After driving half an hour, he pulled over to the side. He was a long way from the New Mexico line. He pulled out his fixings and made himself a peanut butter sandwich for dinner. He got out and sat down under a tree. An impromptu picnic. The early evening was nice, no clouds, and thankfully, no dust. The peanut butter was thick and stuck to the roof of his mouth, but it tasted good. He washed it down with slugs from the gallon water jug. He lamented his lost time. but vowed to try and make it up.

"Say, mister, you wouldn't happen to have any food to spare, would ya?"

A young teenage boy came strolling out of the shadows up behind Clay, who whipped around to confront the teen.

"I haven't eaten in over four days," the teen continued.

"How old are you, boy?" Clay asked.

"Fourteen," the boy replied.

"Where are your folks?

"Dead"

"Dead? Whaddya mean dead?"

"They died about a year ago."

"How'd they die?" Clay was now curious.

"Not sure. They both took real sick. Had high fevers and such. Had no money for a doctor or medicine. Then they just died. Sheriff came over and hauled em off. Had a funeral at the church. Buried them at the church cemetery."

Clay listened, stunned, and then said, "What's your name, son?"

"Archibald… Archie that is."

"You want a peanut butter sandwich, Archie?" Clay said with a smile.

"Yes, sir," Archie said softly.

Clay made up the sandwich and invited the boy to sit. The boy tore into the sandwich, and it was gone in three bites.

"I'd offer you another un, Archie, but I got to make things last." Clay felt somewhat embarrassed in not being able to offer the boy more. "Where are you living?" Clay asked. "You got any kinfolk around?

"I ain't got no relatives or nothin. It's just me. They took me to this orphan home after Ma and Pa died, but it was horrible. I ran away.

Now, I camp out in the woods. I made me up a little lean-to, and I got a sleeping bag. I try to catch fish and rabbits, but they gotten kinda scarce lately."

"Well, I figured I would sleep here tonight. You're welcome to stay. Should be a nice mild night."

"Thank you kindly, I might just do that. What did you say your name was?"

"The name is Clay Stanley. I came from Oklahoma City and am headed to Californie. Pleased to meet you, Archie." Clay extended his hand and shook Archie's formally. They grinned back at each other. Clay had taken an immediate liking to the boy.

"Clay, I'll be right back," Archie said as he jumped up.

"Where ya going?"

"To go get my sleeping bag. It's just back over there a little bit."

The boy went running off and, in less than two minutes, was back with his sleeping bag. It was dirty, well-worn, threadbare. Archie spread it on the ground not far from where Clay was spreading his.

"Should be a warm night tonight," Clay said. "Don't think we'll need a fire."

"Just as well," Archie said. "They'll run you off if they think you're squattin. They would see the fire and run ya off."

Clay settled down on his sleeping bag and faced Archie, who was relaxing back. His legs were crossed, his hands interlocked behind his neck. Archie's clothes were filthy. His hair was the color of rust, and he had a big smile pasted on his face.

"What are you smiling about?" Clay asked.

"Oh, nothing, really. It's just nice to be able to be around someone. It's been a while."

"How long?"

"Since my folks died. After the funeral, they grabbed me up. But I wasn't gonna stay. I took to the woods. I was so mad."

Clay listened, as Archie continued.

"I was so mad at God," then he paused, thinking about what he had just said. "Do you think it's OK to get mad at God?" Archie asked. He looked eager to hear the answer.

"Well, you know, Archie, that there is a very good question. I have to say I've had my fair share of getting mad at God."

"You have?"

"Why sure. When the rains quit coming, and I couldn't get anything to come up out of the ground, I got good and mad at God. I tried to bargain with him. You know I would tell him that I would go to church every Sunday if he would just let it rain a little every week."

Archie nodded. It seemed he had been trying his share of bargaining as well.

"It didn't work though," Clay continued. "I don't think God is much of a bargainer. It pretty much seems like it is his way or nothin. I tried everythin from bargainin, prayin, even screamin, nothing worked. The rains never came."

"Think he even listens?" Archie mumbled.

"Well, I suppose he does for some people. Never seemed to listen much to me."

"Maybe he listens to a preacher man!" Archie exclaimed.

"Maybe, he does. But I knew a preacher back home that gave it all up after things hadn't gotten better for a few years. Said even Job didn't have to put up with the nonsense God was pulling with this here drought."

Archie listened wide-eyed. Clay wasn't sure how to proceed, so he asked. "Say, you want another sandwich?"

"Sure!" Archie said hungrily.

While Clay made the sandwich with a very thin layer of peanut butter, Archie talked. "Do you even think that God is out there?"

"Well, ya know, I've given that very thing some thought too, and I wish I had an answer for ya."

"Well, I think God is there, but I don't think he is some old guy in a long robe with a long gray beard."

"You don't?" Clay asked.

"Nah, I know the Bible says he made Adam and Eve in his own likeness, but I'm not really sure that's true. In fact, I'm pretty sure Adam and Eve is just a story!"

"You don't say," Archie had gotten Clay's attention. Clay handed Archie his sandwich. Archie took a bite and continued his theological musings with a full mouth.

"Mmm-hmmm. If Adam and Eve were real, then they were the first man and woman. Then we all came from them, right?

"That's right."

"Well then, when Adam and Eve had Cain and Able, where did the girls come from for them to marry?"

"Good question," pondered Clay.

Archie continued. "The only way it could have worked was for Adam and Eve to have more kids, and if that is the case, they would have had to marry their sisters, yuk!"

Clay hadn't thought about it before.

"So you can see God didn't think that one out too well, did he?"

Clay laughed, "No, I guess not."

Clay liked the kid. He had been through a lot but still kept his wits about him.

"Say," Clay asked, "How would you like to go to Californie with me? I could use the company?" He might be making a mistake, but he didn't think so.

Unbroken Hope

"Well, there ain't nothing holding me here, but I ain't got no money."

"That's OK, I think I got enough, cuz you can work can't ya?"

Archie nodded. "I can pick cotton and vegetables, and fruit. That's what I done on my folks' place."

Clay looked sternly at him, "And you ain't lying to me about your folks. No family atall, right?"

"Honest Injun, Clay. I am all alone, no brothers or sisters, and my ma and pa are dead. I swear."

"Awright then, it is settled. Let's get some shut-eye, and we'll be off in the morning."

"Oh boy, I can't wait!" Archie sounded like a kid on the night before Christmas.

Chapter 8

Land doesn't know who owns it, and it certainly doesn't care who owns it. Land is land and it will yield up its fruit, or not, to whomever knows how to urge it in the right direction. Bankers aren't farmers, and so the mysteries of the land remain just that to them…mysteries. Bankers think they own the land simply because they can take a piece of paper away from the man who farmed it.

Money isn't the root of all evil. Man is. Money is just the tool that man uses to inflict evil. Money is attracted to money. People with money attract money, and people with money always want *more* money. Bankers are people with money.

People without money need money, and so they figure out ways to get it. One way to get it is to risk land that your granddaddy left to you. Land that is your home. Land that feeds your family. You need the money because, without the money, there is no seed from which to grow things. Without the money, you have no tools with which to plant and harvest. Without the money, your family might starve until harvest time. And so, you make a deal with the devil. You agree to put up your land with a promise to pay back a loan. A loan that is more like a millstone around your neck. But you do it anyway because you need the money, and heck, the crops will come in this year.

Except they don't. And now your kids can't eat because there are no crops, and still the damn bank wants its payment. You string the bank along, convincing them to wait for payment. You use every excuse, except they aren't excuses. They are truth. For a while, the bank believes you. Of course you are racking up late payment fees, but you don't care. You must hang on to the farm. The farm is your world, what would you do without the farm?

You hear rumors.

The bank just took Stan's farm! How can they do that? That farm has been in his family for a hundred years!

The bank just sold the McMillan place to a big corporation out of Chicago. They bulldozed the house down!

The bank don't care. But the bank is US! Our neighbors run the bank. The bank don't care. We don't care.

Chapter 9

Barbara Jean was sitting on the front porch swing. She liked sitting there in the early evening.

"Whatcha doing baby girl?" Erma said poking the little girl as she sat down next to her. She rocked gently back and forth.

The girl looked, smiled and said, "mommy." She then waved, although it was backward as if she were waving at herself. Erma laughed.

"Come here and sit on my lap," Erma said gently tugging the little one closer to her. Barbara Jean climbed up on Erma's lap facing her mom. Erma took hold of the little girl's arms and began to gently pull on them. Barbara got into the rhythm of things and began leaning backward as Erma held on to her for safety. Barbara would rock further and further back. She would laugh each time she went a little further.

"Moe! Moe!" Barbara would shout gleefully with each rock backward.

Soon the screen door clattered shut, and Mamie came out carrying a bowl of fresh-picked green beans and sat next to her sister.

"Hey sis!" she said.

"Hey," Erma said, absentmindedly focused on Barbara Jean playing. "She loves doing this. Funny how the simplest things will keep a child happy."

"Got these beans from our lil pitiful garden. It's the last of em. Ain't much, help me snap em?"

Erma put the baby down, reached into the bowl, and began to break the beans in half.

"I need to talk to you," Mamie said.

"You sound so serious."

"Oh, no, this is good news, although it could bring some trouble on us," Mamie said, patting Erma's hand. "Jimmie got a job!"

"A job! Why that is wonderful! What is he doing?"

"He'll be driving a tractor for the new corporate farm out in Midwest City," Mamie said, a little dispirited.

"You don't seem happy about that, Mamie. It's a job!"

"It's a job awright, and we certainly need it, and he's gonna take it. But I don't have to like it. That farm he will work at is made up of farms that ten different families owned. The banks threw them off the property."

"That seems like the way it is these days," Erma replied sorrowfully. "You're right, but we don't need to like it. So, when does he start?"

"He started this morning, pays pretty good too."

"But how does this big farm company plan on getting any crops out of the land?"

"They ain't even gonna try. They get paid by our government to turn crops over into the soil. They ain't much in terms of crops, but it's food. Everyone can use food these days. They gonna turn the whole thing into a cattle ranch. Government is paying up to sixteen dollars a head to ship em up north and feed the hungry in the big cities. It's all the government now. This big corporation figures to make a killing on it. Jimmie is just along for the ride."

"How long does he figure to have a job?"

"Not sure of that. Could be a few days, but he's hopin to catch on with the cattle ranch. They gonna need good men, and Jimmie knows his way around cattle."

"Where in the world will they get water? Ain't much around here. Everythin has dried up."

"Plannin on truckin it in. The one thing the corporation has is money, and they can afford to buy water. Also plannin on diggin deeper wells for water."

Erma reflected on that for a bit.

"Where'd they get the cattle?"

"They're buying up everything they can. Good or bad. Rumor is the government will pay them for every head. Folks are desperate so they're sellin them, every one they own."

"Hmm," Erma sniffed. She wasn't impressed. "Well, so long as Jimmie has a job, I guess that's all that matters."

The two women finished up the beans in short order…there were so few. Mamie stood, stretched, and started inside.

"Reckon I'll clean for a bit, not sure why, but it's something to do." She said as she opened the screen door.

"I'll help," Erma said as she stood. "Barbara Jean, you stay out here and play for a while, OK, Baby?"

The young girl looked up at her mother. She had been playing with her foot. Not much in the way of toys. She made a cooing sound.

The women went to work on the house. They dragged up rugs and took them outside and beat them. Dust came pouring out in thick plumes. Once the rugs were beaten, they tackled the floors. They swept, and then on their hands and knees, they scrubbed the floors. The work was hot, but they didn't mind it. It was spring, and the weather had thus far cooperated in terms of a cool temperature if not in terms of rain.

There hadn't been a dust storm in over a month, so they were optimistic that things could stay clean for a while.

But both women remembered Black Sunday - April 14, 1935. That afternoon, a gigantic cloud swept across the Great Plains. 1000 miles long with howling winds...speeds up to 100 miles per hour. A dank, black cloud obliterated everything in its path. Hundreds of thousands of tons of dust were torn from the ground of the dry, abused farmland.

Erma and Mamie had been used to dust, but they had never seen anything like that day. Erma had huddled inside with Clay, gripping her eight-month-old baby. Bandanas didn't help her breathe, and she feared for her child's life. She later compared it to the Red Sea closing in on the children of Israel ... it got so dark that you couldn't see your hand before your face, you couldn't see nobody in the room! It was like midnight in the middle of the day.

For now, the skies were peaceful, but things could change in a heartbeat.

The women put their cleaning equipment away just as they heard a truck pulling up in front of the house. They heard the truck door slam and then heavy boots stamping out the dust on the front porch. Jimmie came busting in the front door with Barbara Jean in his arms.

"Look who I found!" Jimmie exclaimed.

The young girl squealed with delight. Jimmie nuzzled her neck, which caused her to squeal even more. He put the child down and moved over to peck his wife on the cheek.

"How did it go on your first day?" Mamie asked.

"Pretty good," Jimmie replied. "They tole us what their plans are." He moved over to the sink and washed his hands.

"Well?" Mamie said impatiently.

"Hold on a minute, can't a feller get cleaned up a bit?"

Unbroken Hope

Mamie bit her tongue and waited for Jimmie to dry his hands. She stood there tapping her foot.

"OK. The plan is to plow everything under and replant it with prairie grass. I guess prairie grass don't need a whole lot of water. That is what the cattle will graze on, I reckon."

"So they *are* doing cattle. You think they'll keep you on?" Mamie asked.

"Gracious woman, it's only the first day," Jimmie exclaimed, frustrated. "I think I got as good a chance as the next guy, I'll tell ya that."

Jimmie walked to the table and sat down. "What's for dinner?"

"Green beans and corn bread, it's all we got." Mamie replied.

"Well, my first paycheck comes day after tomorrow. Won't be much, but it should be enough to buy a little food."

Mamie set plates of green beans on the table, and they all began to dig in. In between bites of cornbread, Jimmie went for his back pocket.

"Almost forgot. I stopped by the post office. They had this here postcard for ya Erma. It's from Clay.

Erma leapt on Jimmie, grabbed the card, and quickly read it.

"This is all he wrote!" she despaired. "Don't say nothing!"

"Well, he made it as far as Shamrock, we know that. That card was mailed a couple of days ago. So he's making good time."

"Shamrock, that isn't that far. He better hurry up and git there, I cain't wait forever!"

Chapter 10

Archie and Clay had made slow progress since they hooked up. The car had run well since the kerosene incident. What slowed them was *all of the people*! If anything the road had gotten more crowded the closer they got to California. It had taken them three days to drive across New Mexico, as they were able to make around a hundred miles a day. But then they really slowed down when they hit Arizona. At this rate, Clay thought, it'll take another week or more to get there, and we're gonna miss the orange picking.

Clay had decided to hold off mailing another postcard to Erma until they got to Flagstaff. He could imagine her reading it and admiring the picture of the Grand Canyon, but he couldn't spare the money for the card or the stamp.

He couldn't wait to get to California. But what lay ahead was a lot of unknowns. One of the things he dreaded the most was waiting for him ahead. The drive across the Mojave Desert and Death Valley. Those words made him cringe.

They had camped out under a spread of mesquite trees near Williams, Arizona, and they weren't alone. There were some thirty cars scattered about as if pushed by the wind. Families with children and single men camping side by side. They had eaten a community meal of stone soup with everyone. Stone soup started with a giant pot of water (or even two or three) and several stones. Then everyone added ingredients they had to the pot. The result was never the same. Archie and Clay had been starving, and while the soup hadn't been much, it had sure tasted good.

A young boy had been coughing through much of supper. He had been listless, and his mother mentioned that he seemed to have a pretty bad fever. The other women consoled her, offering different ideas of what could be done. The consensus was there wasn't much to be done but to just let the flu or whatever it was run its course. The child, in the meantime, continued to cough violently.

After supper, the men had gathered around. They passed tobacco to those that didn't have any and lit up hand-rolled cigarettes and battered old pipes. Clay and Archie didn't smoke, so they passed the bag of tobacco along. The group had grown steadily over the last several days. They all traveled at different speeds, so the mix of people had varied from rest spot to rest spot. Clay had been in a hurry and thus didn't want to wait for stragglers. Archie was content to do whatever.

No one really could remember any names, so they were called by an identifying trait. For example, Slim was doing most of the talking.

"We're headin directly to Bakersfield. We heard they was lookin for about a thousand pickers," Slim said, as he blew smoke in a ring around his head. He was tall and gawky with a brown fuzz of hair. His teeth as well as his clothes were stained and rough-looking.

"We're headin further north," a small wisp of a man, whom they referred to as Shorty, offered. "Most everyone will be looking for work just as soon as they hit the border. I figure my luck will be better if we go further in before everyone can get there."

A man with a pipe between his teeth snorted a laugh, "I don't think you'll have to worry about beating anybody, everybody is already there. There ain't no work there. It is all a pipe dream!" He finished with another snort.

Unbroken Hope

"What are you talking about, buddy?" Shorty said, pulling a flyer from his back pocket. "This here paper says they need plenty of pickers and I aim to be one of them!" He held the wrinkled and torn document up for all to see. Others in the group nodded in agreement.

"Well, I know what that paper says," the snorter snapped back. "But I'm here to tell you there ain't enough work out in California to keep you fed."

Clay listened and then couldn't contain himself. "Well, what do *you* know? We're all going out there to get work!"

"I been there." The snorter said flatly. "I'm going back home myself. Had enough of it. The farms don't need the number of people pouring in and there have been fights. A thousand men showed up for eighty jobs. Fistfights break out. The farms offer one rate of pay, but when they find out how many men they have to choose from, they lower it. Pretty much you're scrambling around, and even if you get a job, it doesn't pay enough to live off of." He delivered a final snort to punctuate his comments.

Clay had no comeback to that except, "Well, I reckon I'll just go see for myself."

The other men nodded in agreement, but they all remained silent.

The silence grew uncomfortable, and one by one, each of the men wandered off to turn in. They all had a long day ahead of them the next day.

When Archie and Clay had returned to their bedrolls, Archie asked, "Do you think that feller knew what he was talkin about, Clay?"

Clay thought about it for a moment and said, "Archie, I don't rightly know. But what I do know is we have nothing behind us, so we better go find out for ourselves what we've got in front of us."

Archie looked at Clay. He didn't seem frightened by the prospect. "Well, sounds good to me. I ain't got nothing on either end of this run. What do we have to lose?"

"You're surely right there. Well, I guess I'll turn in," Clay said as he snuggled into his sleeping bag. The nights were cold out here, and he was glad he had brought a good bedroll.

He quickly fell asleep.

The scream jolted him awake. It was disorienting, and he sat bolt upright in his sleeping bag. "What the…" he said groggily.

A woman was screaming hysterically, "Do something! Do something! He aint' breathin!"

Clay struggled out of bed and ran to the woman who was stroking her young son's face. He was the boy who had been coughing so violently earlier.

"Oh, do something," she said, rocking him back and forth. It seemed to be the only thing she could say.

"Here, let me take him," a kindly older woman offered, and the mother handed the child over to her. The older woman gently touched the child's face and rested him on the ground. She listened to his chest.

"I'm sorry," she said at last. "He's gone, but he's with Jesus now."

"With Jesus!" the woman screamed. "No! No! No! He can't be gone. The little feller just needs some rest. That's all." She was wailing now. She grabbed for him and hugged him to her chest, rocking him.

The group of people looked on sorrowfully as the woman continued to wail a haunting cry of anguish. It broke Clay's heart, and it made him think of Erma and Barbara Jean. He walked off weeping gently to himself. When he approached his camp, Archie was sitting up.

"What happened?"

"You know that young boy that was coughing through supper?"

Archie nodded.

"He died," Clay said gently as he hung his head.

Archie stared off, and slowly, silently, tears began to roll down his cheek.

Clay lay in his bedroll for what seemed like forever. He could not get the kid out of his head. He couldn't have just up and died. Could he?

In the bedroll next to him, he could hear Archie sobbing. A hollowness crept into his chest. He missed Erma, and he was scared he would get to California with nothing awaiting him. He feared he would fail Erma and the baby. Tears slowly rolled down his cheeks. He was crying for himself, and Erma, and Barbara Jean. For a life lost in despair. He cried for a child that had died in the middle of nowhere on the side of the road. Hell, he didn't even know the kid's name. His parents, so panicky in the dead-end life they had been dealt, had dragged him and his brothers and sisters halfway across the country to try and make a better life. How had it come to all of this? How?

He wiped his eyes in the dark and started to calculate how much money he had left. Nineteen dollars and twenty-seven cents, and Archie had nothing. Not much, but enough to buy gas and a little food until they could find jobs. But he vowed he would spend a small part of his cash and send a telegram to Erma the next chance he got. It might cost as much as fifty of his cents, but he figured he just had to do it. That made him feel a little better. Finally, sleep swept over him like a wave.

"Clay? Wake up!" Archie was jostling him awake.

"Huh?" Clay mumbled, sitting upright. It was morning. "What's going on, Archie?" He looked around; it was early morning.

"They're having a funeral for that little boy," Archie said. "I thought we should…we might ought to go."

Clay stood upright, rubbing the sleep from his eyes. "Sure is early for a funeral, but I'll bet they want to move on down the road. So…Yep, you're right, we might ought to go."

Clay and Archie moved over about 300 feet to a small group gathered near a large tree. The tree's branches had dried-looking leaves, but it seemed it was the closest thing to shade they had around these parts.

The men stood around, hats in hand, not knowing what to do with themselves. This was mostly a woman's domain, and they let them have it. The women were comforting the mother. A deep hole had been dug, and the boy's body had been wrapped in his bedroll. The body rested to the side of the grave.

Clay and Archie removed their hats and stood in the outer ring of the group. They bowed their heads as a tall Negro man started to speak. It seemed odd to Clay that the group had asked a Negro to say the blessings.

"I been asked to speak cuz people knowd I was a preacher in another life." He spoke in a crystal clear, deep voice.

In another day and place, a black preacher would have never been asked to say the blessing over a white boy, especially in West Texas. But these were strange times.

The men began to shuffle their feet in the dirt. Small clouds of dust whipped around their cuffs. The mother cried gently as several of the women tried to comfort her. Her husband stood stolidly and silently by her side. His grief-stricken face was held together by the strongest of wills. A face of granite. He struggled to hold the tears back and finally cleared his throat in an effort to gain control.

The preacher continued, "I didn't really know the boy. Fred was his name. I figure none of you knew him much either. But from what his folks said, he was a good boy. Saint Mathew wrote, But Jesus said, Suffer little children, and forbid them not, to come unto me: for of such is the kingdom of heaven. And I can't argue with that much. In times like this, we can only hold on to the fact that he's with Jesus now. It doesn't give us who are struggling here on earth much peace, but at least it's something to hold onto."

He then nodded for two of the men to lower the boy into the grave.

"As we lay young Fred to his final rest, I offer him up to you, gentle Jesus. Keep and hold him close to your heart. I'll close with this thought from Luke, neither can they die any more: for they are equal unto the angels; and are the children of God, being the children of the resurrection."

He raised his hand up over the grave and made the sign of the cross.

"Ashes to ashes. Dust to dust. Amen."

The attendees mumbled an amen and then moved over to console the grieving parents once more. Two of the men started to shovel dirt into the grave. A board had been found for a grave marker. The boy's name and dates of birth and death had been carved into it.

There was no wake. So, the crowd moved back to their individual campsites.

"I figure it's time for us to move along, Archie," said Clay as he rolled up his bedroll. "Next town we come to that has a telegraph office, I'm going to need to send a telegram home."

Archie just nodded. The men silently packed the car and drove out of the camp saying goodbye to not one soul.

Chapter 11

Erma was about at the end of her rope. It was so *boring* living with Mamie and Jimmie! She had helped Mamie do all the housework, worked in the pitiful garden, mended everyone's clothes. She didn't have enough to do. Jimmie was never around, as he was taking as many hours as the ranch would give him. And that was a good thing, they needed the money desperately. The money bought food.

She and Mamie were sitting on the porch. Erma was trying to read a book she had found in the house, but she wasn't making much progress with it. Mamie stared off watching Barbara Jean playing in the dirt. Finally, Mamie got up and went over to the child. Barbara Jean was pushing a small object around in the dirt as if it was a small car. She was making motor sounds with her mouth.

'What's you got there, honey?" Mamie asked the child.

The girl looked up and raised her hand up to her aunt to show her the "toy" she was playing with. She slowly opened her hand to reveal a dead Brown-banded cockroach. Mamie gasped and knocked the bug out of the girl's hand. She then quickly ground the dead bug into the dirt.

'Oh, nasty honey!" Mamie said.

Barbara just stared up at her and then looked down at her crushed "toy".

"What is it?" Erma asked from the porch.

Mamie laughed, "Our little girl here was pushing around a dead cockroach for a toy!"

Erma got up and went to the child. "Oh, Baby, what am I going to do with you?"

The child began to put her hand in her mouth.

Erma swatted it away. "No, not in your mouth. Yucky! Let's go wash your hands."

She moved to the hand pump and ran water over the child's hands. She soaped them up and then rinsed.

She was just finishing up drying them when Mamie said, "Looks like someone is coming up the road."

The two women stared down the road, shielding their eyes from the glare of the sun.

"Wonder who it is?" Erma inquired blankly. Mamie just shrugged. The two women watched silently as the car moved along, trailing a gigantic cloud of dust raised from the dirt road.

"Why, it's old man Pruitt's truck," Mamie finally said.

The two watched as a black Chevrolet panel truck pulled into the yard. On the side of the truck was lettered:

Pruitt's General Store

A young man of about seventeen or eighteen climbed out of the truck. He was dressed in dungarees and a work shirt. His closely cropped brown hair was combed to the side. He was a handsome boy, one the girls had all swooned over in high school. He worked in his father's general store part-time after school and on weekends. The women moved toward him.

"Well, howdy, Wade. How are you? How's yor mama and daddy?" Mamie asked.

"I'm just fine, ma'am, and my folks are too." He then turned to Erma. "Hey, Miz Erma, I got a telegram for ya."

The general store also operated the local telegraph office on the outskirts of Oklahoma City. Wade had become a pretty good telegraph operator when he was available. This earned him and the store a good deal of extra cash, which it needed. He handed the envelope to Erma.

They all stood there awkwardly for a minute or so, saying nothing. Then Wade took the hint.

"Well, I've got to run. Have a nice day, ladies!" he said heartily. He climbed into the truck and was gone in short fashion, leaving the women in his wake of dust.

Erma stared at the envelope. It was addressed to her. She turned it over to examine it and then turned it back to see her name again on the front.

"Ain't never got a telegram afore. I'm afraid to open it; it's gotta be bad news from Clay. Or maybe something happened to im!"

"Well, you'll never know until you read it. Go on, Erma," Mamie cooed gently.

Erma slowly opened the envelope and removed the telegram. She read the words and then re-read them silently to herself. Her lips mouthed the words.

"So what does it say, Erma?" Mamie demanded. Erma said nothing. Mamie took the envelope from Erma's hand and read it.

```
    MADE  IT  THROUGH  Williams,  Arizona  YESTERDAY -
(STOP)- CAMPED LAST NIGHT WITH A SMALL GROUP AND YOUNG BOY
DIED OF FLU -(STOP)- MISS YOU BAD -(STOP)- SHOULD GET TO
SAN BERNARDINO IN THREE DAYS -(STOP)- WILL WRITE THEN -
(STOP)- LOVE YOU - CLAY,

Williams, Arizona  US
```

Mamie handed the telegram back to Erma, who grasped it to her breast.

"Where the heck is Williams?" Erma asked.

"I don't know," Mamie answered simply. "But we can find out. You up for a walk?"

"Where we going?"

"Over to the Franks' house. Daniel Frank's got all sorts of books. He went to college. Fat lot of good that does him now, but I bet he'll know exactly where Williams is."

"What happens if he ain't home?"

"He'll be home alright. He ain't got a job and no car!" Mamie, said with a short guffaw.

It took the women about half an hour to get ready for the short walk to the Franks' home and another forty-five minutes to walk there. They took turns carrying the baby when she refused to walk, which was often. It was fairly hard work, but at least the walk gave them something to do.

"What are you two doing all the way over here in the middle of that day?" Amanda Frank hollered at them when she spotted them coming up the road. She moved toward them. When she reached them, she eased the young toddler into her own arms, relieving Erma of the weight.

"My goodness, she's getting big!" Amanda exclaimed. "Won't be able to carry her like that for very much more! Come on up on the porch and rest your dawgs!"

"Cain't really carry her that good now!" Erma exclaimed with a laugh.

The women sat down, and Amanda brought them each a glass of water, which they selfishly gulped down.

"More?" Amanda asked.

"Not right now, Amanda," Mamie offered. "Maybe in a bit, eh, Erma?"

Erma just nodded.

"What brings you over our way?" Amanda inquired.

"We were hoping to see, Dan. Is he around?" Mamie asked.

"He is," Amanda responded. She had a puzzled look on her face, but stood and yelled through the screen door into the house. "Dan!" She called. No answer. "Daniel?" she repeated.

Dan's footsteps could be heard moving toward the porch. "Yeah, honey," he said as he stepped outside.

"We have company," Amanda said. "I'd invite you all in, but it's cooler out here."

Erma could tell that the coolness on the porch wasn't the only reason keeping them from going inside. Like so many people, Amanda was no doubt embarrassed by how little they had left inside. They probably had to sell it off in exchange for food. Her expression couldn't hide that simple truth.

"Oh...oh, hi, Mamie!" Dan said as he stepped over and pecked Mamie on the cheek. "How's Jimmie? Heard he took a job at that new cattle ranch!"

"Yes, he did. He's doing real good there. Dan, you remember my sister, Erma, and her daughter, Barbara."

Daniel stepped forward, took Erma's hand, and shook it gracefully.

"Nice to see you again, Dan," Erma said.

"The pleasure is all mine, Erma," he replied. He then tickled the child under the chin. Barbara Jean didn't react as she stared intently at the man.

"That there's my daughter, Barbara Jean," Erma said with a smile.

Dan motioned to his wife to pass the baby over. He held the small child up and stared into her eyes. After a moment, he grinned and said to the child, "Well, it is a right pleasure to make your acquaintance there, Miss Barbara Jean." He gently tossed the child up slightly, and she cooed with pleasure.

"What a joy," Dan said as he handed the girl back to Amanda.

Dan Frank was as tall and thin as Amanda was short and wide. Mamie often pondered how Amanda could keep so much weight on in the face of so little food around. She guessed it was just one of the Lord's great mysteries.

After the pleasantries, Amanda offered, "Dan, they came to see you."

"Me!" Dan chortled. "Well, what can I do for you?"

"It's Erma here that needs the help," Mamie said.

"Well, let's sit down and see what this is all about," Dan offered gently.

Erma removed the telegram and handed it to him, and he proceeded to read it. He looked up and then quickly re-read it. He folded the telegram and handed it back to Erma. She held the telegram in her lap. while Barbara Jean sat quietly.

"I had heard your husband had headed off to California."

"He has done that," Erma replied. "And it seems like he's been gone a year."

The foursome all nodded in agreement to that comment.

"Here's my question for you," Erma continued. "Do you know where Williams, Arizona, is? It says on the telegram that was where it was sent from."

Dan scratched his chin while he thought. "I'm not sure, but we can find out. I'll be right back." He then dashed into the house.

They could hear him rummaging around, then they heard him say, "Ah, here it is."

He came back straight away. He was carrying a folded map. He sat down and unfolded the map. There was a big Rand McNally logo in the corner. Dan found what he was looking for on the map. He put the map on the porch in a direction that Erma could see it, and then he knelt across from her.

Erma could see it was a road map of the United States. Dan plopped his thin finger down just a little west of Oklahoma City.

"Here's where we are," he said with authority. He then began to trace along Route 66 with his finger. "Route sixty-six is the main road that runs clear to California. Here's where Clay sent his telegram, Williams, Arizona."

His finger came to rest on a point in western Arizona just south of the Grand Canyon. He then continued to move it along the route toward San Bernardino, California.

"It looks like Clay has a little under four hundred miles to go."

Erma stared at the map thoughtfully. "So, you think he was about right on how much longer it would take?" she asked.

"What did he say, three days?"

Erma nodded.

"I'm not sure how many miles they are making a day, but he should easily be able to cover that in three days." Dan acknowledged.

Erma leaned toward the map and traced her finger over their route. She nuzzled up to Barbara Jean's ear and whispered, "This is the direction your daddy took. He's right here." She pointed to Williams on the map.

For the next several hours, they all visited, getting caught up on the current events of their lives. But Erma's mind kept coming back to the issue of when she would be leaving for California. She felt like she was going to bust if she had to sit around here much longer. Clay better hurry and get some sorta job!

When it came time to leave, Erma asked Dan if she could borrow the map for a while.

"Sure thing, Erma," he replied. "No need to get it back either, we're not going anywhere soon." He smiled.

Erma and Mamie made it home not long after that. It was just on the verge of getting dark. Erma fed Barbara Jean a quick dinner of leftover cornbread and put her to bed,

She then turned to Mamie. She held up the map.

"This was a really good idea, going to Dan. It made me feel lots better."

Mamie reached over and patted Erma on her arm. "I'm glad," she said with a smile.

Erma yawned. "I guess I'll go to bed too." Then, after a long pause. "Night."

"Night. I'm gonna wait up for Jimmie"

Erma changed into her night clothes and climbed into bed. Her sleeping daughter's breath, a slight snore, as she snuggled beside her. She heard Jimmie come in through the front door and could hear her sister and her husband whispering.

She clutched the road map. It was her link to Clay. How long before he sent for her? God only knew. She clung the map to her chest and was soon fast asleep.

Chapter 12

The bird soared high above the desert road. If she had any amount of real intelligence, she would have known she was a red-tailed hawk. But she didn't know that about herself. She swooped and glided on the air currents. Her eyes, almost ten times more powerful than a man's, could pick up almost microscopic movements in the desert below.

Life on the edge of the desert was tough for all concerned. Plant life struggled and those that survived were the heartiest of all. Desert tortoises hibernated much of the year, the winter often times being too cold and the summer much too hot. They could dine on the plants when they lumbered out to feed. They moved so slowly it was as if the sun was melting their feet into the sand.

And the hawk saw it all. The hawk could see the slow movement of the humans' cars along the roadway. The waves of heat rose from the road. She swirled on the air streams while keenly watching the road. Then she saw what looked like an opportunity. A car had run over a baby jack rabbit. The rabbit was no bigger than a large rat, but the hawk spied it. It would make a good dinner, if she could just get to it. The stream of cars was steady and offered little breaks.

The hawk floated to the dusty side of the road. She eyed the dead rabbit. Thus far, the cars had mercifully missed running over the rabbit a second or third time. The hawk looked back and forth, looking for an opening to hustle in and snatch the meal. The cars were relentless.

Finally, there was a break in the line of cars, and the hawk made its move. She glided in and swooped the broken animal up in her talons. The rabbit's leg broke off in the bird's claws, but the remainder of the rabbit stayed glued to the road. Just as the hawk cleared the road. A car crushed the rabbit's remains into the hot asphalt. The hawk escaped with the leg as its meager dinner. As she tore into it, the hawk stared at what remained of the rabbit as car after car smashed it further and further, burying it into the road.

She looked up the road as a string of cars slowly crept by.

Chapter 13

A light mist drifted down from the sky. Clay was deep in sleep, but the light rain ran in rivulets down his nose. He touched his face in his sleep as if to shoo a ticklish fly away. He then jumped up, fully awake.

"It's raining!" he shouted at Archie. Then looking around, "Though it ain't much of a rain!"

Archie sat up, bleary-eyed. He rubbed his hands over his face, then looked at the water coating his hands, "It shore is!"

Clay grabbed his sleeping bag, which was getting wet from the slight rain. "Guess we better roll these up and get them in the car before they get soaked."

Archie quickly got to his feet, gathered his bedroll and shoved it into the back seat of the car.

The men had made slow progress over the past three days, passing through Arizona at a tortoise's pace. They had parked the night before after a long drive, pulling in alone, but after surveying the area that morning, they saw that a number of campers had followed them in.

"Jest twenty-five miles to the Californie border, Archie." Clay said excitedly. "Been quite a ride! Eh?"

"It shore has. I cain't wait to get to San Bernadoodo? Bernadaado? What is it?'

"San Bernardino. Burkey Farms is where we're headed," Clay said as he looked up just as the clouds parted and the rain stopped. "Well, that rain shore didn't last long." He removed the worn-out handbill from his pocket. He rubbed as if a talisman, folded it gently, and put it back.

"Archie, bring me the road map."

Archie went to the car and gathered a crumpled map. Clay took the map and spread it out on the ground.

"We're here," his hand pointing to an area on the map. "Farnconia was where we just went through last night. We're headin to Needles. But we gotta head through the desert. That may be a bit rough on the car. We need to make sure we have extra water, so the car don't overheat." He looked at Archie. Archie didn't seem too concerned.

"So we hit Needles, then Barstow, and then down into San Bernardino. It's only about 300 miles. We could make it by late this afternoon, with any luck. If these dang people would just get out of our way!"

Clay threw Archie a piece of bread and some jerky. "There's your breakfast. Let's get packed up and on the road."

The men silently packed the car and were just pulling out, when a dusty old Model T pulled in from the road. It was clear that the car had been coming from the direction of California. The man driving looked to be about 40. He had an old ball cap perched on his head. He waved at Clay. The people surrounding Clay and Archie came over to see what was going on.

"You heading to California?"

"Yep"

"Well, I can save you the trouble." The man said stoically. "They've blocked the borders. No one is going in."

"What'd you say?!" Clay stammered. "That cain't be right!"

Murmuring erupted in the surrounding crowd.

"It is! Here read for yourself."

Unbroken Hope

The man flipped the front section of a newspaper, the Los Angeles Herald Express.

Clay read the story out loud,

Indigent transients heading for California today were warned by H. A. Carleton, director of the Federal Transient Service, to stay away. Thousands of penniless families from other states have literally overrun California. Carleton estimated the influx at 1,000 a day.

Despite some protests, the officers turned back hundreds of railroad-fare evaders, hitchhikers, and families, in loaded-down trucks and cars. The migrants were offered a choice of leaving California or serving a 180-day jail term with hard labor.

"See?" the man in the car said as Clay handed him back his paper. "We were turned back. They ain't letting anyone in, unless you can prove you have a job waiting for you, or that you live there already."

Clay collapsed on the fender of the car. "My Gawd…what are we gonna do? I ain't got nothing to go back to."

"Neither do we pardner. But we's going back to it all the same." The man inched the car forward. "Good luck to you," he said with a wave and drove off.

Archie took a deep breath and slowly exhaled. "What *are* we gonna do?" he asked meekly.

"I don't rightly know, but movin forward is better than movin backward, I know that much."

Clay smiled at Archie and motioned him to get in the car. He started the engine, and they started moving toward whatever awaited them.

Chapter 14

Three days passed like a snail methodically picking the next leaf to munch on. If Erma was about ready to blow when she received Clay's telegram, those magic words from him helped calm her down. At least for the three days. She imagined Clay moving through the deserts of Southern California and then coming up over a rise to reveal its beautiful farmland. She could almost see it. Fertile land, with trees fully loaded with their cargo of oranges waiting to be picked. She could almost smell the air. Sweet, fragrant.

She kept herself as busy as she could by helping Mamie keep the house clean. On the second day after the telegram, a dust storm rolled in. Erma wouldn't have believed another could hit. How could there be any more dust left to blow around?!

When she and Mamie saw it coming, they did what they always did. They grabbed rags and dish towels and tried to seal the windows. But just as always, the dust was so fine it still found ways to get inside. Jimmie was working when it hit, so of course, Mamie was worried about his safety.

"I don't know what we'd do if something happened to him," Mamie fretted.

"Nothin is gonna happen to Jimmie, Sis." Erma said, consolingly patting her sister's arm. But she too shuddered at the thought.

The wind continued to howl, but as if Jimmie had read their thoughts, the women could hear him stamping his boots on the porch.

The door crept open, and then with a rush, Jimmie was inside, slamming the door behind him.

Jimmie's job had been a godsend, and he was happy to have it. It put food on the table and a little leftover to save for a rainy day. Even though rainy days were in short supply.

Jimmie came into the room and pulled his bandana down from his mouth. His face was covered with dirt, and his eyes squinted. He took the bandana to the water pump, washed it out, and then wiped his face with the wet rag. He took particular care with his eyes. He wished he had a pair of goggles, but once the storms started a few years ago, they were impossible to come by. He poured himself a glass of water, swished the dirty water around in his mouth, and spit it out.

"Durn!" Jimmie said in disgust, "That ain't hardly water there's so much grit in it."

"Here, baby, it's just dust in the glass," Mamie said as she took the glass and carefully cleaned it, filling it halfway. "Here."

Jimmie took the glass and drained it. "Thanks, darlin, that's better!"

It was amazing that the hand pump brought water up at all. Jimmie and Mamie had been blessed with a deep well, one of the few around. It provided a good source of water, but of course, it could not be used in the fields as there was no way to deliver it. For the crops, they needed rain. Of course, they also didn't know how long the well water might last.

Jimmie sat down at the table and motioned for Mamie to sit on his lap. Mamie readily complied, and Jimmie gave her a sweet kiss. His arms firmly encircled her waist while Mamie hugged his neck fiercely. Erma stood and watched, a little embarrassed to be a witness to a tender moment between husband and wife. She looked off, trying to blend into the woodwork.

Mamie leaned back and asked, "How was work?"

"It was OK," Jimmie said with a frown. "The new foreman arrived today. We had a big meeting. Everyone was there, including the corporate big cheeses. The foreman's name is Bill Percy, and he's pretty much a hard case."

"What do you mean?" Erma interjected.

"Well, they brought him out from, if you can you believe it…California," he laughed. "He managed a big operation out there."

"Californie!" Erma and Mamie exclaimed at the same time.

"Yeah. Can you believe it? Anyways, he stood up at the meeting and went on and on about how things were going to change, and if we didn't like it, there were plenty of others waiting for our jobs. And those men from the corporation just stood around grinning at him, nodding their heads in agreement."

"So, did he have a plan?" Mamie asked.

"Sure, he did. About what we figured. They're gonna try to put cattle on the land. Government is backing them, so even if it fails, they will make money out of it. You know how these big corporations are. Have my doubts, though, if it will even work."

Mamie climbed off his lap and went to look in on Barbara Jean, who, still asleep, had her thumb firmly inserted in her mouth. She turned to Jimmie and said tentatively, "Did they say how long you could expect work?"

"No, it didn't come up, but they made pretty clear we ought to be down on our hands and knees thanking them for the work we have."

Mamie went to her husband and brushed his cheek with her hand. "Well, it's true. Work is hard to come by, and we *are* thankful."

Jimmie abruptly stood up. "I know that. And I am thankful. I just don't like the way they present it like they're God and we should bow and scrape to them at every turn." He then sat down heavily in the chair, put his elbows on the table, and held his head up with his hands cupping his chin.

"I know. I know," was all Mamie could think of to say.

The next day, Jimmie went off to work, and the women stayed home trying to make the best of things.

The day after that, Jimmie went to work, and the women waited for him.

This went on for five days.

As each day passed, Erma fretted more and more with no word from Clay. On the eighth day after the telegram arrived, Erma blew her top. She was drying the breakfast dishes and putting them away. Mamie knew Erma's dark moods and stood warily watching, not having anything to say. Sometimes, Erma just needed to blow off some steam, and her hair trigger would be assuaged for a while. Mamie was just moving toward Erma when she heard footsteps on the front porch.

"Wonder who that is?" she said to Erma. The women looked at each other.

It didn't take long to find out as Jimmie came through the front door. Mamie was shocked and knew by the look on his face that he wasn't bringing good news.

Mamie went running to him. "Honey, what happened?"

Jimmie was almost in tears, "They fired me!"

Suddenly, the sound of shattering glass cut through the air. Jimmie and Mami jumped, startled. They then quickly turned toward Erma, who had thrown a glass into the sink. She was in total rage. She had cut her hand on the glass. Blood was flying everywhere. Erma broke down sobbing.

Mamie jumped into action. "Here, dear, let me see that." Jimmie came over to investigate as well. "Oh, it doesn't look too bad. Just some blood," Jimmie said.

Unbroken Hope

"Jimmie, go get me that box of band-aids," Mamie said, and slowly rinsed the cut under the pump faucet.

Jimmie returned with the first aid supplies, and Mamie motioned for him to sit down. She expertly and quickly applied first aid to Erma's hand. "There, that should do it. It was just a small nick," Mamie said, closing the band-aid box. Soon, the three of them were sitting down across from one another at the little table.

Mamie now turned her attention to her husband. "Jimmie, honey, tell me what happened?"

Jimmie stared at her for what seemed like an eternity, as if not comprehending her request. He then blew out a gigantic sigh. "Well, I thought things were coming along pretty good. We were making good progress clearing off the land. The company had brought in big water trucks. We had plowed everything up. And water was going to be laid down to control the dust."

He paused, "Think I could have some water?" He asked meekly.

Erma got up and brought him a glass. He quickly drained it. The women stared at him, waiting for him to continue.

"We were just getting ready to start the day," Jimmie continued. "The boss came in and said to hold up a minute. He had an announcement. He said that there had been a change of plans and they wouldn't need most of us after all. He said to just wait, and he would get back with each of us to tell us our fate. It didn't take long. I was the first to be told I was let go. I gathered my stuff, and here I am."

Mamie just stared and then slowly started weeping. She knew the significance of this. Weeping gave way to sobbing, which soon gave way to wailing. Her grief knew no bounds. She cried as if she had lost a child. Jimmie tried to comfort her, to little avail. He was in shock himself.

Erma stood stunned. She moved toward where Barbara Jean was sleeping. She stopped to put a hand on each of Mamie's and Jimmie's heads. But she said nothing. She moved to Barbara Jean and lay down beside her. She said nothing for the rest of the day. She slept through the day and through the night.

When she awakened, it was still dark. She could hear the soft breathing of her sister and her husband as they slept in the next room. She knew she would need to act. They had been barely making it with Jimmie's salary. Now, there was no way she could allow them to keep her afloat.

She had to do something.

Where in the heck was Clay, and why had he not written? He should be in San Bernardino by now. Where the heck was he?

She had to do something.

She could not stay here one more day, but she really didn't know what to do. She had kept a good portion of the small bit of savings she had when she came here. Jimmie and Mami had refused to take any of it at first but were forced to take some of it eventually. She now had forty-nine dollars and some change, which wasn't going to be enough to do anything. But…

She had to do something.

Chapter 15

Clay felt that his telegram was a good thing. When he sent it a week ago, he had felt better, connecting to Erma and what he was trying to do. He felt things were moving along.

Until they weren't.

The Model A had been running just fine until it wasn't. It had blown its radiator, a terrible omen with the desert looming ahead of them. It had taken Clay the past week to find someone who could rod the radiator out so he could get the car running again. He and Archie had pulled the radiator, and Clay walked it over to the repairman while Archie stayed with the car. It had been a week of pure hell and had taken several of Clay's last dollars. They were running dreadfully low on cash. He knew Erma would be blowing her stack, but there was nothing he could do about it from here. At least he and Archie were moving now.

As they got closer to the California border, Clay knew something was up. At Kingman, Arizona, the traffic had slowed, and there were many cars heading toward them, going away from California. In all their days of travel, they came across so very few traveling in the opposite direction. Clay knew in his heart that the man in the Model T had been right. They were turning back people at the border.

Judging from his map, Clay knew Needles lay at the California-Arizona border. It was about an hour or so ahead at normal speed. But now they were lucky to hit twenty miles an hour. At this rate, it would be many hours before they hit the California state line. Traffic was stop-

and-go. Ahead was a line of cars stretching as far as Clay could see. They would move forward a car length and then come to a dead stop.

"We sure ain't getting very far," Archie said, frustrated.

Clay understood the impatience. He was about ready to explode himself. "I know, Archie...I know." That was all he could muster.

A car going back east stopped. Clay's window was down as was the other driver's.

'Might as well turn around right where you are. They are not letting anyone through." The man behind the wheel shouted. His rig was weighted down with all his family's life possessions. His wife tried to eek out a smile, but it was beyond her. Two kids, a boy and girl, looking to be around ten or so, stared dully at Clay. Everyone in the car looked thoroughly and totally discouraged. The dingy windows cast a deathly pall over the entire family.

"They letting *anybody* through?" Clay asked.

"Not that I can tell. It's the end of the line, Buddy."

"Whatchya gonna do? Where you gonna go?" Clay asked mildly.

"Hell, if I know," the man said through gritted teeth. It was obviously taking every bit of strength he had to hold back the tears. The car behind him started honking. Irritated, the man waved over his shoulder. "Why are they in such a goddam hurry? To get back to what? To nothing, that's what!" He then extended his middle finger to the car behind him. He nodded at Clay and moved on down the road.

Clay looked over at Archie, who was crying. It hit him hard, seeing the young man silently weeping, his bottom lip quivering, trying to put up a brave front. Oh God, Clay thought, what have I done?

The brutal sun beat down on the line of cars as they crept forward. Cars kept coming from the opposite direction. Many of those drivers just shook their heads as they passed. Some stopped and offered little in the way of encouragement.

Unbroken Hope

After about four hours, Clay could see a way station head. It looked like this was it. There were two lanes next to a small building going through what looked sort of like a guard post. He could see two officers, one in each lane. Near the side behind the building, he could see about ten black and white police cars. It was obvious these men meant business. He continued to inch forward, saying a prayer with every foot taken. Ahead, the officers were pointing for the cars to make U-turns and head back the way they had come.

Finally, he reached the building. A stout police officer motioned him to roll forward. The officer had a sour face as if he had just eaten a lemon. His disposition was no better. Past the building, the lanes ahead were blocked by two black and white Ford Model A California Highway Patrol vehicles.

"Where ya headed?" the officer asked.

"San Bernardino," Clay replied with a smile.

"You got work there?"

"Why yes, yes, I believe I do," Clay said.

"You got some proof?"

"Uh-huh," Clay said as he reached into his pocket. "I've got this," pulling out the flyer he had carried since Oklahoma.

"Oh, you have this, eh?" The cop said as he took the paper. He looked at it. "Say, boys!" he hollered to his fellow officers. "He's got some paperwork!" as he waved the flyer at them. They all laughed. He looked at Clay and smirked.

Clay just stared back while the cop pointed to a small table. On the table was a stack of the same flyer with a rock on top of it. "You ain't got paperwork. You got hoodwinked." The cop said with a laugh. "You can just turn around right here and go back to where you came from." The cop motioned ahead and then whipped his hand with finger raised in a big circle over his head.

"And…and if we don't want to?" Clay stammered defiantly.

"That's what they're here for." The cop motioned over his shoulder to the waiting police force.

"But you don't understand, we ain't got nothin to go back to." Archie chimed in. Clay looked over at him and smiled. The boy had showed some courage.

"I don't give two hoots in a holler," the cop replied, his hand coming to rest on the butt of the gun at his waist. He was a short man, and his uniform looked too big for him. Like many short men, he came across with an attitude.

"What's the hold-up?" A man wearing a straw hat and a checkered shirt said from behind Clay.

Clay turned to see six men standing there, and could see their open doors down the line of cars. He could also see the scared faces of family members in the first two cars. Eight or nine cars back stood a man and a woman, on each side of the brown Model T, shading their eyes from the sun.

The cop stared him down and looked back again at his compatriots and then back at Clay. His hand slowly pulled the gun from the holster at his side. Two of the waiting officers brought up shotguns. Everyone was poised on a razor's edge of tension.

"You gonna turn around or what?" the cop addressed Clay.

Clay just stared at him. Then the cop addressed the crowd.

"You might as well just turn around, we are not letting any of you filthy Okies in," the cop yelled. "No one wants you here. There are no jobs for you here."

"Why don't you let us find out for ourselves?" the straw-hatted man behind Clay challenged. "You cain't stop us from coming over. We're Americans, and we have a right to go wherever we want in our own country!"

Unbroken Hope

"That's right!" screamed a second man, fat and balding, dressed in coveralls, standing beside him.

By now, a group of about 30 was gathered around. They started murmuring amongst themselves. "They cain't do it" and "We have our rights" were among the things being said.

The group of cops started to move forward, joining the short leader. Clay looked from the leader to the cops and then back to the group of travelers. He held up his hands as in surrender.

"Look," he said. "We don't want any trouble. We just want to go peaceably. We're just looking for work. Trying to feed our families."

The short cop stepped up to him, eyeing him. He sniffed the air. "Phew!" he exclaimed and then turned to his cohorts. "Can you smell that?" Then to Clay, "Don't you Okies know how to take a bath? You stink!"

His gang of cops laughed at the comments and then turned back to the crowd. The lead cop was just getting warmed up.

"What makes you think we want any of you here. You all smell like you been laying down with pigs. You smell like pig shit. Think you're pigs?" A pause and then, "Eh, boy? Here, little pig! Soo—eee!! Here piggy, piggy."

The cop laughed hard, and his friends joined in. "I think it is time for you folks to move along. There is nothing for you here." A tall, lanky officer then spoke out.

"And I think it is time for us to stay!" Straw Hat screamed at him and plopped himself straight down in the road, sitting Indian style. The others joined in gathering around him, sitting on the hot tarmac of the road. "We ain't leaving til you let us through!" Straw Hat yelled through clenched teeth.

Clay and Archie have been watching this, not sure what to do. They wanted to join the protesting people sitting in the road, but they also didn't want to make matters worse. By now, more travelers had joined the fracas, and the group is numbering better than a hundred, well outnumbering the highway patrolmen.

The head cop stared at Straw Hat, seething. He pushed by Clay and Archie and stood over the seated man.

"Get up," the cop snarled at Straw Hat.

"No," Straw Hat said stubbornly.

The cop looked across at the group of people. "I am ordering you all to go back to your cars."

"No!" came the choired reply.

"We ain't moving," Straw Hat said, motivated by his support.

The cop slowly stepped toward him and pointed his gun at him. "I'm telling you to get back in your car and get out of here. You are about to do something you are going to regret."

"What are you going to do, shoot all of us?" Straw Hat said, spitting the words out.

The cop stepped forward and pressed the barrel of the gun to Straw Hat's forehead. "No, I'll just shoot *you*!" He pulled the trigger back.

Straw Hat sat calmly and stared at him. "Do you think this scares me. I ain't got nothing to go home to. You'd be doing me a favor pulling that trigger. So, go ahead and do it."

The crowd gasped a collective breath as they could see that the cop was struggling with what to do next.

"Hey, Billy!" The tall, lanky cop bellowed out. "Just hold on a minute. I'm getting on the radio to see what headquarters wants us to do."

Billy pressed the revolver against Straw Hat's head as if trying to decide if he should blow his brains out or not. Finally, reason took over as he pressed the barrel harder and then relinquished and holstered the weapon. The barrel had left an angry red spot on Straw Hat's forehead.

Unbroken Hope

Clay breathed a sigh of relief. They were at a standstill for now. But what was going to happen? What did headquarters want done? He moved to Archie and put his hand on his shoulder. He nudged him to the car, and both slid into the front seat.

Billy walked confidently toward Clay and leaned in the window. The sun glinted off the badge pinned to his left chest. It flashed in Clay's eyes, and he winced a bit.

"Where are *you* going?" the cop sneered.

Clay was astonished by the question. He stammered, "You said to turn around. That is what I'm fixin to do. I don't want any trouble."

"Son, trouble is what you already got."

The cop wasn't much older than Clay, so the 'son' struck him as funny. But he didn't say anything. He just choked back a chortle.

"You think something's funny?"

Clay just stared at him.

"Well, do ya, BOY?!"

"Nnnn, no sir, I don't."

The cop eyed him. "You just stay put for the time being. We have to deal with these, these," He struggled for the right word. "These Okies." He spit out the words as if they left a bad taste in his mouth.

"Hey, Billy!" The tall, lanky cop called back. "I couldn't raise headquarters on the radio. It looks like we're it for the time being."

Billy turned to the group. "You all wait right there." He walked back to his compadres, and they huddled. Clay could see Billy talking animatedly to the others but couldn't make out what was being said. The nine remaining highway patrolmen were offering some suggestions. A couple of them were shaking their heads. Then just as quickly as they had huddled, they were climbing into their cars and went screaming off down the highway into the desert. The group sitting in the road was left alone.

Clay and Archie got out of the car and approached Straw Hat. "What in the world happened?" Clay asked to no one in particular.

"Durned if I know," Straw Hat exclaimed. "And I don't care. I'm getting out of here!"

Everyone climbed in their cars and came across the state line of California unimpeded.

Clay was stunned by the sudden turn of their fortunes. "Can you beat that?" he said to Archie.

"What do you think changed their minds?" Archie asked.

"Not sure I know, but judging from the look of those patrolmen's faces, they didn't want no part of trodden on another man while he was down."

Clay and Archie drove on for about half an hour, and then Clay stopped the car. He got out and fell to his knees. Archie joined him. Clay looked to the heavens. Archie bowed his head.

"Thank you, Lord, for bringing us safely here to Californie. We promise to live up to your will. Now, please guide us on what we should do next."

Clay looked to the sky. Fluffy, white clouds drifted past, set against a brilliant blue. No rain here. Of course, this was the desert, so no one ever expects rain.

PART II
INTO PARADISE

"Do Re Mi
California is a Garden of Eden, a paradise to live in or see,
But believe it or not, you won't find it so hot
If you ain't got the Do Re Mi"
Woody Guthrie

Chapter 16

They worked the fields. Cold weather, hot weather. Rain. Sun. They picked the crops. They worked long rows, carrying bags too heavy for two men to lift, but one managed.

They had labored for decades. As far back as 1900. Taking the jobs no one else wanted.

Hundreds of thousands of them. Spicks, Braceros, Field Rats, Brown Tractors. None of the names were kind. But they didn't care, they still worked hard. They moved from farm to farm doing what was asked with no complaints.

They took their directions in English and replied in a mix of Spanish and English. They spoke only Spanish in the fields. They didn't make much money, but it was certainly better than what they made at home.

Tijuana, Mexicali, San Luis, Nogales, Juarez - Mexican border towns that had provided an endless supply of workers. And so, they had come.

They had discovered what many had dreamed about. California. The Land of Milk and Honey. Abundancia - Abundance. Blessed with a temperate climate and long growing seasons, its fields could yield a limitless variety of crops.

Whatever the ground brought forth, they were waiting to pick it. They moved with the crops. They had been doing it for years. They knew the rhythms of the land. They had long-earned relationships with the farms. The farmers knew them, and they worked hard to continue to keep that trust. They moved like swarms of locusts devouring the fruit and vegetables and storing them in bags and boxes. Their yield was sent off to places like Monterey, where the canning companies stood ready to package up the yield, making it ready for sale.

They were hardworking. They were family-oriented. They were dedicated. They were Mexicans.

But a new storm was brewing. A storm called the Great Depression. And hundreds of thousands of these loyal workers were going to feel its impact.

As the Great Depression took a toll on the nation's economy, the Mexicans became targets for discrimination and removal. Federal government officials claimed that Mexicans made up most of the California unemployed. White trade unions claimed that Mexicans were taking jobs that should go to white men. So, depending on who you listened to, the Mexicans were either too unemployed or employed too much!

The Depression had made things bad for the Mexicans. But it was going to get a whole lot worse. The Okies were coming.

Chapter 17

"Mama?"
No reply.
"Mama?"
Still no reply.

Barbara Jean was tugging on her mother's skirt. Erma stood staring out the window above the sink. It was early morning and white billowy clouds hung in a bright blue sky. Erma was watching the interchange between Mamie and Jimmie as they stood in the yard. The window was open so she could hear their murmurings, but they were talking just low enough she couldn't make out what they were saying.

But she really didn't need to hear what they were saying to know what they were talking about. They were talking about her and the plight she had put them in. Jimmie loved Mamie so much and he was as kind a man as Erma had ever met. He would never put Erma and Barbara Jean out. He loved Mamie that much. Mamie stood in the yard listening intently to Jimmie. She was twisting the ties to her apron nervously. Erma could tell that her sister was upset.

It was obvious both were worried sick. It had been four days since Jimmie had lost his job. The little bit of money that they had squirreled away was dwindling at a high rate of speed. Erma had done everything in her power to help conserve it. She was eating hardly anything. She had lost a lot of weight since Clay had left. She was down to skin and bones on her short frame. Thank God the well had not run dry, so they still had water.

Any extra food she had, she made sure Barbara Jean got. She nestled tidbits under the ridge of her plate to sneak to the young girl after the table was cleared. Mamie caught her once and admonished her, telling her that she had to eat to keep her own strength up or she wasn't going to do anyone any good. And yet Barbara Jean still went to bed hungry. She had become weaker as the days wore on. Often, she would cry herself to sleep. The sobs were wracking Erma's heart.

So, Mamie and Jimmie spent more and more time in the yard. Discussing the same things over and over again. Erma had tried to tell them that they would be better off without her here. But they pointed out that she had nowhere to go. A point she could not argue with. But the more time they spent outside, the worse Erma felt. She needed to come up with a plan and she needed one fast. And then it came to her. She went and got the Rand McNally map Dan had given her and she studied it.

She was still poring over it when Mamie and Jimmie came inside.

"What ya doin, honey?," Mamie asked her.

"Jest thinkin, really," Erma replied. She then took a deep breath. "I need you two to sit down and listen to me."

Mamie could see the level of seriousness in her sister's eye. She looked at Jimmie, and they both grabbed chairs by the table.

"We're gonna leave," Erma said flatly.

Jimmie and Mamie exhaled heavily, almost at the same time.

"Now, honey, we've been through this. The best thing for you and Barbara Jean is to just sit tight."

"No!" Erma declared. "I've sat as tight as I'm a gonna." She pounded her fist on the table and then continued.

"Look, I cain't keep spongin off you. It is hard enough for the two of you to get by. You do not need any more mouths to feed. I have a plan, but I need yor help."

She leaned forward conspiratorially. Her sister and her husband leaned forward, taking the bait.

"OK, Erma," Jimmie said, we're listening.

Erma had to give him credit. At least this time, he was willing to listen. She grabbed her map.

"Lookee here," Erma said as she spread the map on the table. Both Jimmie and Mamie stood and came behind Erma.

"See these lines here," Erma said, pointing at solid lines. "These are roads. See, Route 66, right here." She pointed to the heading that read US 66. "But these dotted lines are railroad lines. See?" She pointed to a dotted line that said Southern Pacific Railroad in very fine print. She then pointed to another set that said Gallup Railroad.

"You're not thinking about hoboing it out to California in a rail car!" Mamie exclaimed.

"That is exactly what I'm thinkin. And I can do it too!"

"Erma!" Mamie shouted, standing up.

Jimmie grabbed Mamie and sat her back down. "Let her finish, Mamie."

"Jimmie, you ain't considerin lettin her do it, are you?

"I ain't considerin nothin. I'm jest listenin." Jimmie said quietly to his wife. "Go on, Erma."

Erma was a bit flustered. She didn't really think she would get even this far with the two of them.

"Well, I haven't thought it completely through yet. My plan still needs a little work, but here's what I been thinkin."

She paused for effect and to see how her words were sitting with her sister and her husband.

"Can we sit down, so I can explain my plan?" Erma looked pleadingly at Mamie.

Mamie sat down and crossed her arms across her chest. Obviously, she was skeptical. Jimmie sat down casually on the edge of the table.

"OK, Erma," Jimmie whispered. "The floor is yours. Or should I say table" he said with a smile.

Erma cleared her throat. She hadn't been certain she would get this far. "Ok, then," she stammered. "Here goes nothin."

Mamie snorted, "Let's hope you got something better than nothin!"

"I do. I do. Let me jest do this my way. OK?"

Mamie uncrossed her arms. She could tell Erma was determined to see this conversation through. She nodded at Erma to continue.

Erma nervously spread the creases from the worn map. "Like I said, these here lines are the railroad lines. See, they go clear into Los Angeles...but before they get there, they go through San Bernardino. Tha's where..."

"That is where Clay is heading, we know," Jimmie said as he looked at the map. "But the Southern Pacific line ain't anywhere around here. See it does cross in the Texas panhandle, but that's about it. How ya going to get there?"

"Well, I thought about that," Erma said encouragingly. "Didn't you tell me ole Roy Raleigh used to work for the railroads? I could talk to him. He don't live far from here, does he? Maybe he could help?"

Mamie looked at Jimmie, who shrugged. "Maybe he can talk some sense into her," she said flatly.

"I want to go talk to him now," Erma demanded. "If'n you won't take me, I suppose I can walk."

Mamie laughed, "You don't even know where he lives!"

"And you probably wouldn't tell me either," Erma sulked.

"Oh, don't get yor self all tied up in knots. We'll take you alright. Jus like Jimmie said, hopefully he'll talk some sense into you!"

Unbroken Hope

In a little over an hour, Erma, Mamie, Jimmie, and Barbara Jean were all sitting on Roy's front porch. At 78, he was a widower. His weathered face showed the hardships he had endured throughout his life. His eyes were sorrowful, but his mouth gave away his natural playful nature with a big grin. Dressed in clean overalls over a white shirt, Roy looked much like the retired farmer he was.

"You say what?" The old man's mouth had fallen open after Erma shared her plan. "You some sort of fool or something?"

Erma stared daggers into him. She waited, and he waited.

"Hm," he finally said. "Well, are you?"

Erma was squeezing her hands so tight that they were turning white. She clenched her teeth and looked to Mamie for help.

Mamie turned to Roy and said, "Roy, I know it sounds crazy, and me and Jimmie do not support it, but can you please jes answer her questions? I think she will see what a fool's errand this is gonna be."

Roy sighed heavily. "OK, Erma tell me again what you're wanting to do."

"I need to get to Californie. Clay is already there. I just need to get there. I cain't stay here no more. I cain't hitch, and I thought the train would be the quickest way. But I cain't buy a ticket, not enough money, so I need to…"

"You need to jump a train, is what you're trying to say. And you're planning on doing it with this here small child?" He snorted. "Woman, you are plumb crazy. That's what you are! Why don't you just take the bus?"

"I tried that already. It still don't leave me enough money for when I get to Californie."

"Well, hell, hitchhiking would be safer than trying to jump a train. You're just plumb crazy!"

Erma sat back and stared, then she attacked. "Well, I cannot jes sit here and do nothing! This poor man, Jimmie here cain't do for his wife *and* me *and* my child... it ain't fair to him!"

"Listen to me," Roy interrupted, "Riding the rails is too dangerous. The railroad companies hire security guards. They're called Bulls. The Bulls' job is to keep hoboes, which is what you would be by the way...a hobo, off the trains. So, you couldn't just go to a railroad yard and climb on. Most hobos will hide along the tracks outside the yard. They'll run along the train as it gains speed, grab hold, and jump into an open boxcar. It's a tall jump and one not easily done. Sometimes, they miss. Many have lost their legs or their lives. When the train reaches its destination, you then have to jump off before a new set of Bulls arrests you or, worse, beats you up."

He stopped and looked at Erma, then asked incredulously, "You planning on doing that with a baby in your arms? It would be suicide, I tell ya!"

Erma, who hadn't considered all the challenges, sat stoically for a moment as tears welled up. "Oh my God," she finally stammered. "Is there no end to this?' She wailed. She looked to her sister and then at Jimmie, finally back at Roy.

Barbara Jean had been watching and then crawled onto Erma's lap and touched at the tears on her face. "Mama, sad?" the little girl asked in her rudimentary language.

Erma grabbed up the child in a bear hug, "No, little girl. Mama ain't sad no more. Mama's mad!"

Chapter 18

"I can see you're determined," Roy finally said. "So here is what I can tell you if you are bound and determined to do this."

Erma leaned forward listening intently to Roy.

"Safety is a big deal on the railroad. It is real easy to get good and hurt. You are made of soft, breakable stuff, while railroad equipment is made of very hard, very heavy, unbendable stuff. A rolling boxcar won't even flinch as it quietly rolls right over you in a sneaky surprise."

Roy paused for emphasis.

"Don't walk on the tracks. Don't cross under couplers or cars. And watch for cars rolling quietly through the yard. You need to be careful out there. As I said before, the Bulls are your enemy. A sure way to get caught by a Bull is by being stupid."

Erma was now eager to hear more. "What do you think I should bring with me?"

"Keep everything dark, dark clothes, dark pack, dark sleeping bag or blanket. That'll make it harder to get caught as you blunder around the train yards. You'll be walking a lot and throwing your pack on and off of trains, so pack small and light - under 25 pounds. If you have something in your pack that can break, it will. Leave your valuables at home." He stopped and looked at Barbara Jean.

"You consider her valuable?" Roy asked.

"She's coming with me!"

'OK, and I can see that!" Roy exclaimed. "You need to think about keeping her and you warm. You may end up in an open car in the middle of the night with a 60-mile-an-hour wind blowing in your face. Your clothes and your sleeping bag should keep you warm, comfortable, and dry. If you're cold and wet, you're going to be miserable."

'I'm not even sure where I could catch a train," Erma said meekly.

"The Gallup Railroad has branches clear to California. But you'll have to switch trains. Find a local freight yard. The closest one is down in Norman. That aint' too far. There'll be a train leaving or coming through there eventually. When you get out into the country, try looking for train yards in the forgotten part of town, the part of town with all the rough neighborhoods. The yard is usually near big industry, maybe near a river or port. It may be hard to know when to switch trains. You need to pay keen attention to landmarks, signs, even others traveling with you."

Roy took a breath and then forged ahead.

"In order of preference, you want to ride in open boxcars, or on the rear platform of a grainer or hopper."

"Is that all, Roy?" Erma asked.

"No, but that's all I know to tell you. If you are going to do this, you will need to learn fast. There ain't much room for mistakes. Oh, there is one more thing."

Erma leaned forward again as Roy stood up, bent over, and looked her right in the eyes.

"Don't forget to bring your patience. Freight-hopping involves as much walking and waiting as actual riding. You spend most of your time waiting for information, waiting for a train, waiting for your train to get underway, waiting, waiting, waiting. For this, you'll need to be flexible and patient. Your safety and your child's should be at the top of your noggin," Roy said while he tapped Erma's head with his index finger. "So, don't take shortcuts to save time. Ever! Got it?"

Erma nodded. Her head was spinning. She really hadn't thought through the practicalities of the situation.

Unbroken Hope

Roy suddenly reached out and grabbed her on each side of her jaw, squeezing her cheeks together. "I don't think you do. You been sitting here noddin your head like I was telling you how to plan a picnic. Well, this ain't no picnic, woman!" He continued to squeeze for emphasis. "These trains are dangerous. One wrong move…" he paused "and blooey!" Erma jumped, startled. It's all over for you and your girl here. Trains are very unforgiving."

He studied her. She stared back with steely eyes. "You done?" she squeezed out between pressed lips.

"Yeah, I am," he released her face. Erma rubbed her cheeks and mouth.

"That hurt," she mumbled.

"Not as much as a train is gonna," Roy spit out.

Erma and Roy stared at each for what seemed an eternity.

Jimmie finally asked, "So Erma, you ain't gonna do this blame fool thing are ya? It's too dangerous!"

Erma looked at Jimmie, then Mamie, and finally Roy. 'I…I don't rightly know…right now!"

She then stood straight up and held her hand out to shake Roy's. "Roy, you have certainly given me a lot of food for thought. Thank you."

"You are most welcome, Erma. Please don't do this."

"I will consider that, Roy. You can trust me on that." Then she turned to Jimmie. "I think we can go now. I do believe we have taken up too much of Roy's time."

She moved toward the door as Mamie and Jimmie said their goodbyes. Just as she reached the door Erma turned for a final question of Roy. "Roy, you think it's **possible** for me to do this?"

"It does seem like you are one determined woman," Roy answered. "I don't know if you can make it or not. But the odds are certainly stacked aggin you. If you do *do* this, please be careful."

Erma had nothing to add so she marched to Jimmie's car.

Chapter 19

Once Clay and Archie had made it through the California border, Clay thought it would be easier going. He was surprised how wrong he could be. Time on the road had dragged by. It seemed like he had sent that telegram to Erma a month ago, but it had only been ten days ago.

He knew that Erma was no doubt beside herself with worry. But there was not anything he could do about that now. All he could do was forge along. And so, he and Archie headed on into San Bernardino. His map showed it to be under 200 miles. So, they still had at least six hours of driving. Six very long hours and perhaps double that with as much traffic as they were moving through.

It was about four in the afternoon, and Clay felt like a fresh start in the morning would do both of them good. Praise God, the car hadn't given them a lick of trouble since the radiator busted. Many others they had passed on the way hadn't been so lucky. They passed families standing near smoking cars with blown motors and leaking radiators. Many had flat, bald tires too worn to even be repaired. Clay had felt bad turning a blind eye to the many who begged him to stop. But there had been nothing he was going to be able to do to help. It made his heart ache though.

"Archie, whaddya say we pull over for the night? Looks like there is a whole group of campers up ahead. We could bed down with them. Maybe see what's what." Clay said, leaning toward Archie.

Archie simply stared ahead, "Sounds good to me, Clay. I could use a break from this seat!" He leaned over and rubbed his butt. "I don't think that ole Henry Ford had long trips in mind when he built this here Model A."

Clay just laughed and looked for a place to pull in. "How we fixed for food?"

Archie rummaged in the back seat and pulled out a jar of peanut butter, about a third full, and a quarter loaf of bread. "We got this much!" Ain't much, but it'll do. We still have quite a bit of water!"

Clay looked at the jar, "Well, that'll do tonight. We're gonna need gas in the morning, and we'll stop and buy some more peanut butter and bread unless we can find something else for less!"

"There's a spot!" Archie exclaimed, pointing at a clearing. "Looks like there's a stream over there!"

"Great!" Clay said with a smile. "I could sure use a wash up!"

Clay parked the car, the men secured their belongings and walked to the bank of the stream. There was a small group of people splashing in a muddy little stream. Six men, five women, and four kids.

Clay nodded at two of the men, "How do ya do?" he said. He knelt down, scooped water in his hands, and splashed his face, letting out a satisfied moan in the process. "Boy, does that feel good!"

"Ain't much in the way of water," snorted a leathered-looking man with a droopy moustache and long, greasy hair.

"Well, at least it's wet," Clay responded, then a second later "Where y'all from?"

"I'm from Arkansas. Name's Henry, Henry Grove…people call me Hank though.

"Pleased to make your acquaintance," Clay said. "I'm Clay Stanley. This heres…" motioning to Archie, "Archie…" Clay paused for a moment pondering something. "I'll be damned," he said, as he turned to Archie and started to laugh. "Archie, I don't even know your last name! Ain't that a shame? I been travlin with ya for the past two weeks!"

"Ain't nothing, Clay. It's Simpson," and he extended his hand with a laugh, "Pleaze ta meet ya!" Clay grinned back and shook it with both hands.

Archie then turned to Hank and extended his right hand. "Archie Simpson, good to see ya, Hank." As the men shook.

Hank then nodded at the second man, who looked somewhat like a vulture, his large head sloping over his hunched shoulders. Tall and gangly. He stepped forward, shaking hands with both Clay and Archie. "Harry Musgrave," was all he said, and then stepped back behind Hank.

The men continued to wash in the slow-moving stream. The children splashed a little bit downstream, laughing and giggling. The women gathered in a clutch, whispering to one another.

"That's my wife, the one with the red hair," Hank said, motioning to the woman. "Name's Maud. My little un is the boy, Jed."

"My wife is the other un, name's June," Harry added. "I got two kids, the girls…Sally and Jenny."

"I got a wife and little girl myself," Clay added, fudging on the married part. "They's back home."

"Where that be?" Harry asked

"Oklahoma. Outside OKC."

The men all nod, knowing the grief that had driven them all to this very spot.

The group was quiet for the longest time.

Finally, Clay broke the silence. "So, you think we'll find work?"

Hank scratched a stick in circles in the dirt. "Honestly, I don't rightly know! We got them blamed flyers. You got those?'

Clay removed his wadded flyer from a pocket and waved it aloft. "Says go to San Bernardino."

"Well, I'll be switched," Hank stammered, "ours says Fresno!" He grabbed the flyer from Clay's hand. "Different company too!"

"Whend you get yours?" Archie asked.

"Right afore we left. A week or so ago."

"Not the company, eh?" Clay stated, not so much a question. "Maybe we all head to San Bernardino first and see what is what. It's closer. We can always move on to Fresno, or maybe they'll tell us where to go."

The men all nodded in agreement.

In the morning, they set out for San Bernardino.

Chapter 20

Erma tossed and turned most of the night.

When the four of them had gotten back home, Jimmie and Mamie wouldn't let it alone. They argued every point they could think of. The one that stuck the most, was how she was going to be able to find Clay. California is a mighty big state, Jimmie had argued, and he was right. It was then that she came up with a plan. She told them that when she got to a small town, with a telegraph office, she would spend the night there and would send a one-word note of greetings to Clay. This would help save money. The telegram would state the town from which it had originated. This way, if they heard from Clay, they could send her updates of his approximate location. Once she got to San Bernardino, she would let them know where she was. They could pass the word on to Clay. Or they could tell her where he was.

Erma looked out the window. She had no idea what time it was. Finally, she snuck out of bed, trying not to wake Barbara Jean. She quietly closed the door behind her and sat in the rocker in the living room. Lost in thought, time passed slowly. She looked up at a noise as Mamie quietly closed her bedroom door. She motioned Erma to join her on the porch.

The two sisters sat quietly on the porch watching as the sun broke its way over the horizon. Mamie put her hand gently on Erma's wrist.

"You know I love ya, sis, don't ya?"

Erma nodded.

"You know I would do anything for ya?"

Again, a nod.

"Then I'm beggin ya, don't do this!" The look of pain and worry was clearly etched on Mamie's face.

Erma looked soulfully at her sister, searching for the words. She thought back on themselves as little girls. Mamie had always been the braver of the two. Mamie had always had a little daredevil in her. Erma could remember that Mamie was always first to take up a dare. She never even needed to be taken to the double dog dare stage. Unafraid of heights, she would walk doggedly on the tops of fences precariously balancing herself. Laughing when Erma, almost in tears, would beg for her to get down. Yes, Mamie had been the brave one. Now it was Erma's turn.

Erma looked down and began picking at her thumbnail. "I was jus thinking about when we were kids," Erma said, still focused on her thumb. "We had a purty good childhood, wouldn't ya say?'

Mamie stared at her sister, thinking back, and nodded. "Yeah, I reckon we did."

"Member that time, that dog got in the henhouse. Ma was fit to be tied. We could hear the chickens a squallin, and the dog barkin. But there weren't much Ma could do. She started beatin on the hen house with a broom. Member how she looked. like a crazy woman?" Erma started to laugh. The memory was vivid, and she could see her mother, hair all askew, screaming for the dog to get out while flailing her arms and swinging the unwieldy broom.

Mamie started to laugh along. "The more Mama hit the henhouse, the louder the ruckus inside got, and the madder Mama got."

"Then you member Pa comin out? Takin in the whole scene." Erma managed to eke out between laughs. "You'd a thought Ma was just beatin a rug!"

Unbroken Hope

Mamie cackled out, "Yeah. And Pa sa.." she couldn't finish, she was so doubled up with laughter. "...Pa said..." and she still couldn't finish, the laughter was getting the better of her.

Erma finished for her, "Pa said, whatchya doing Ma?" Then she erupted with even more laughter. "I can remember the look on his face!"

It took a minute or two for the women to regain their composure, and then, they would look at each other and bust out laughing again. Finally, the laughing gave way to the seriousness of the situation.

Erma went back to picking at her thumb. "I want Jimmie to take me and the baby down to Norman to the rail yard there," she said quietly.

Mamie opened her mouth to protest.

Erma raised her hand, placing it over Mamie's mouth. "Shush! Do not say a word. My mind is made up."

Mamie studied her sister's face and could see the resolution written over it. She grasped Erma's hand gently, moving it away from her mouth but continuing to hold it. "I can see that, but please just leave the baby. No sense risking her life."

"No! She's comin with me. I ain't leavin without her. You two can either help me or not. But I AM going. And I'm ready to go now, just as soon as Jimmie gets up."

Erma reminded her sister about her telegram plan, and that appeased her a little.

Just then, the bedroom door opened a crack, Jimmie stepped out, rubbing sleep from his eyes. "What are two up to?" He asked sleepily.

"She's goin," Mamie said, trying desperately to hold back the tears.

"Now, Erma, that there's a fool's errand," Jimmie said as he realized the implication of Mamie's statement. He then stared at Erma, waiting for a reply.

"That just might be, Jimmie Driggers!" Erma flared. "But it ain't eny more foolish than sittiin around here waitin for rain. Which you been doin for years and which is just about the last thing that's gonna happen."

Jimmie flopped down next to Mamie and stared at the floor.

"Jimmie, here's what I need for you to do for me," Erma said, softening a little toward her brother-in-law. "I need you to run us into Norman to the rail yard."

"When?" Jimmie asked, and then something dawned on him, "What do you mean us?"

"Me n the baby."

"Erma!" Jimmie squealed.

Erma held her hand up and shook her head, which ended that part of the conversation.

"This morning." Erma continued.

"You're leaving this morning? It's still dark!"

"If I don't go now, I might not never go. I got my courage up. And I want to get there while it's still dark, so I can sort of take a look at how things work there."

Jimmie looked over at his wife who simply shrugged. "I've said all I could," Mamie finally said.

Erma stood and went back to get what little she was taking with her. It didn't take long. She came back with her knapsack containing a blanket, a change of clothes for her and Barbara Jean, and a few pieces of fruit that she had scavenged. She stood silently in front of Jimmie.

"You mean now!" Jimmie stammered. "Well, I got to get some clothes on."

"Me too," Mamie added. "I'm coming with yawl."

The ride to Norman was a quiet one. Every now and then, either Jimmie or Mamie would inquire whether Erma had thought about this or that with her plan.

Unbroken Hope

Erma rode quietly in the backseat, not offering much in the way of commentary back. She knew opening her mouth would cause a new cascade of concerned comments. She reached over and swept Barbara Jean's hair from her eyes. The girl's thumb was securely seated in her mouth. Her large blue eyes surveyed her relatives. It was hard to know what she was thinking.

Nearing the rail yard, Jimmie stopped the car and turned to Erma. "Where do you want us to drop you?"

Erma peered out the window. The yard was quiet with a few trains sitting on the rails.

She got out of the car on the driver's side. "Here's good," she said as she grabbed her child, hauling her from the back seat. Mamie came around the back of the car carrying a small bag.

"Here, take this."

"What is it?" Erma asked.

"Some food," Mamie whispered, struggling with tears.

Erma tried to hand the bag back, but Mamie stood with her arms crossed, shaking her head, no.

Erma opened the bag, looked in, and took out a well-worn twenty-dollar bill. "Twenty dollars! I can't take this!" Erma exclaimed. "You are going to need it!"

"Not as much as you," Mamie said quietly. "You take it, Erma, or I swear Jimmie and me are going to hog tie you and never let you go. Those are my terms!"

Erma dropped the bag to her side, closing the money in her fist.. Mamie reached out and grabbed her in a bear hug. The two sisters started to bawl. They rocked back and forth, refusing to let the other go. Erma slipped the money into Mamie's coat pocket.

"You better let us know where you are, like you said you were going to," Mamie whispered quietly in Erma's ear as they continued to hug.

"I will," Erma blubbered.

"And if y'all end up dying out there, I'm gonna kill you," Mamie added with a smile. She grabbed Erma again in a tight hug.

Finally, the pity party broke up. Jimmie reached for Erma while Mamie picked up Barbara Jean, giving her a gigantic hug. "You watch out for your Mama, little girl, OK?" The girl quietly nodded, thumb still firmly planted.

"OK, Jimmie. Let's go." Mami said, then abruptly turned and climbed into the car. Jimmie gave Erma a look as if to plead, please reconsider! Then they were off in a cloud of dust.

Chapter 21

Steam drove the first big wheels along the track. It was steam that allowed the country to close in on itself with the continental railroad. Eventually the railroad was a web of tracks owned by a variety of companies. Many had colorful nicknames such All Tramps Sent Free (Atchison, Topeka & Santa Fe), Aunt Mary (Southern Pacific), and Uncle Pete (Union Pacific).

Regardless of its funny nickname, the railroad meant a way to the west. Many paid for its use, but there were some who did not. In short, the reach of the iron horse meant freedom to many.

Steam gave way to diesel. The engines were big and powerful. They could pull over a hundred cars, more than 125 tons of freight. Some of it human cargo, including those looking to escape their lives.

Bum! Tramp! Hobo!

All one and the same? But No.

A hobo is not a bum.

Hobos work when they can and do not take advantage of others.

A bum is just that, a bum, and a blight on society.

Bums stay in one place until they are run off.

Hobos leave a place *before* they are run off.

It has been said that soldiers coming back from the Civil War said they were "homeward bound," perhaps shortened to "hobo."

Latin "homo bonus" means "good man," so "hobo".

Migratory farm workers were known as "hoe boys." The first hobos?

It's anyone's guess.

For as long as there have been railcars, the hobo has preferred them as his means of transportation.

The Hobo Code of Ethics:

Decide your own life. Don't let another person run or rule you.

Keep yourself clean and behave well.

Respect the local law and railroad operators.

Don't get "stupid drunk," – you just make it harder for the next hobo.

Don't be greedy with handouts - another hobo may need them in the future.

Don't cause problems in a train yard.

The last one is the most important.

Don't cause problems in a train yard.

If you do it causes headaches for everyone.

Chapter 22

Erma watched Jimmie's Dodge drive away. It was still dark so she couldn't see inside the car. She pictured Mamie reaching in her pocket and finding the twenty dollars and sitting bolt upright, wiping tears from her eyes. The thought made Erma weepy, and tears began to form. She looked down at her daughter. The girl was looking up at her.

"Mama sad?" Barbara Jean asked.

That made Erma cry more. She couldn't answer, only nodded her head. Get a hold of yourself, she thought. Wiping the tears away with the back of her hand, Erma knelt and surveyed the train yard.

"See them trains over there, Barbara Jean?" Erma said as she pointed to a long line of flat cars and box cars. "We're gonna get on one of those cars."

"How?" The little girl asked. The question, one simple word, had gigantic implications to Erma.

"I don't rightly know. But we're gonna figure it out."

The train yard was quiet. Erma could see two men smoking on the far side. Tall lights were spotted around the yard, casting large shadows. There seemed to be two trains. The flatcars on both were fully laden, so Erma assumed the boxcars would be ready to go as well. One train faced due West while the other faced northeast. The west-facing train was the furthest away.

Figures, Erma thought. The one I need is the hardest to get to.

"Ready to go little girl?" Erma whispered to the child who only nodded her head. Erma grabbed the child's hand and moved in a large arc around the yard, heading toward the diesel engine. She could make out a smallish clump of bushes about 300 feet in front of the engine. The outgrowth was fairly near the tracks. Erma thought that would be a good place to keep an eye on things. Her plan was to wait for the prime opportunity to climb on board a boxcar.

Erma swept Barbara Jean up in her arms and made a run for the clump of bushes. As she ran, she kept looking to her right to see if anyone saw her. The coast seemed clear, and her legs kept pumping. The child in her arms got heavier with every step. By the time she reached the bushes, her chest seemed about to burst. She crept in behind the bushes, pushing air into her lungs. Taking big gasps of air, she slammed herself to the ground.

"You OK?" she said to Barbara Jean, gently placing her hands on each of the child's cheeks.

"Uh-huh," the child calmly replied. "You ok?"

Erma spit a little laugh, "Yes, baby. I am."

The two rested and waited. Erma decided to take a survey of her resources. She reached into her bra and removed a folded wad of cash. Counting it, she found that she still had the forty-nine dollars to get her to California. *That isn't too bad*, she thought, *particularly if we can ride for free. Saving money on the bus ticket had been a good idea. If it comes down to it, I can always buy a bus ticket on the road.*

She opened her knapsack and pulled out the food she had brought, a half a loaf of bread and four apples. She then opened the bag Mamie had given her, and inside were two more apples, some wrapped cornbread, and a couple of pieces of jerky. It was pitiful, but it would have to do until they could get to someplace where they could get more food. She had her and her baby's birth certificate and a pitiful supply of three pairs of underwear for each of them, one change of clothes for each, and the map Dan had given her. That rounded out her worldly possessions.

Putting everything back in place, she turned to study the train yard again. But before she knew it, she and the child were fast asleep.

It was the noise of the engineer firing up one of the big diesel engines that woke her up. She looked up, dazed for a moment, not realizing where she was. Durn, she thought, didn't get enough sleep last night.

She had fallen asleep using her bag as a pillow. It had come on her so fast she hadn't even realized it. She peeked down at Barbara Jean, who was just now rustling awake.

"Morning, baby girl," Erma cooed. "You need to go potty? Cuz I sure do."

The girl had been raised with an outhouse and going outdoors, so she was easily able to do her business behind the bushes, using soft leaves as toilet paper. Erma followed suit.

Settled back, Erma whispered, "Hungry?"

The child nodded. Erma took out two apples, and they chewed quietly on them as Erma studied the yard. Much had changed in the amount of time she had been asleep. She couldn't honestly say how long that had been. It had been dark when she passed out. Now the sun was well up into the sky. She figured it must be about eight or so. The good news was neither train had left. But, with the sun out, she feared she had missed her window to board. Everyone would see her. And the yard was alive with men! It looked like they were checking tie downs on the flat cars and inspecting the interior of the boxcars. Two men to each train. They meticulously walked the line of cars, tapping on flatcars and opening and closing boxcar doors. Probably, it was a good thing she hadn't tried to board before now, as they no doubt would have found her hidden in a boxcar.

She noticed that the men periodically would run into a door that would not close easily. They left those slightly ajar. That might be my luck, Erma thought. I don't think I could budge one of them doors.

She was determined to try and be inside out of the weather. While the flatcars would be easier to climb aboard, she would be exposed to the elements. That was something she would rather not risk with Barbara Jean in tow.

Although not a patient person, she knew she needed to wait for the right opportunity, and it finally came.

"Baby," she whispered to Barbara Jean, "you think you can race me to that train?" Erma knew it would be almost impossible for her to carry the knapsack, bag of food, and the child that great distance.

"Uh-huh"

"That's good."

Erma grabbed up her belongings and waited for the men to get to the far end of the line.

Finally, she said, "OK, let's race!"

The small girl churned her legs as fast as they could go, but she still wasn't very fast. Erma quickly passed. She headed to an open door about 200 feet ahead. She reached it and turned to see Barbara Jean running to beat the band. She touched her Mom as she came running in, huffing and puffing. Erma threw the bag and knapsack down and swooped the girl up and set her up in the boxcar. The floor of the boxcar was almost up to Erma's shoulder, so it was quite a feat to get the girl that high.

Now she looked around for steps she could use to hoist herself in. She could find nothing, and the floor was too high for her to hoist her own body up. She tried and tried to lift herself up. She simply didn't have the strength. She looked around and could find no way to get into the car. Erma started to panic.

Then the train started to move.

Unbroken Hope

Oh MY GOD!, Erma thought. The train was picking up speed. Erma was easily able to keep up at first.

"Mama?" Barbara Jean bawled. "Mama!!"

The train edged even faster and Erma struggled to keep up.

"Baby!" Erma shouted. "You need to jump. Mama will catch you!"

The girl stood at the edge of the platform, closed her eyes, and flung herself into space. Erma was amazed at just how brave she was. She had not said she was scared. She did not hesitate. The girl's momentum knocked Erma into the dirt. But she didn't care.

Erma hugged the little girl tightly. "I am so proud of you, Barbara Jean. You are such a big girl.

"Hey! Hey, you!" A man was running toward them from the far end of the train.

Erma started to get up and run, and then thought better of it. She waited for the man to come puffing up to her.

"What in tarnation are you doing, woman?" he wheezed. "Ain't you got no sense?"

"We're trying to get to California," Erma said proudly, still on the ground, her face almost touching his workman's boots. Then she looked up into his face and struggled to her feet.

The man was tall with a large stomach. Even when Erma stood up, she was looking up at the man's face. He had a multiple-day stubble of beard. His eyes were deep-set and emerald green. He wore a tan cowboy hat, and sweat had crusted a thick swath around the hat band. His chambray work shirt was clean, but his jeans were dirty.

"Well, this is a darn fool way to do it. Don't you know you could go to jail for this? What's your name, anyway?"

"Erma Owen."

"Well, Erma Owen, let's go over to the office. We should talk about this."

"Coffee?" the man asked when they had reached the office.

"No, thank you," Erma politely replied.

The man poured himself a cup. He held the cup up, "You sure?"

Erma nodded.

"My name is Fred Barley. I run the yard here, Mrs. Owen. What's your girl's name?"

"Barbara Jean."

The man looked down at the child and smiled. "Cute kid," he said.

"Thank you," Erma replied for Barbara Jean.

"Now, like I said, I run the yard here, and we can't have people getting on our trains. First off, it's very dangerous, and secondly, they're our trains, and we're not set up to haul passengers."

Erma said nothing, only nodded. She wasn't sure if he was going to turn her over to the Sheriff's Department.

As if he could read her mind, Fred Barley said dryly, "You know I could call in the sheriff."

"Oh, no, please don't do that," Erma begged. "Pleeeeeze!"

She broke down and cried. But this was more than crying. It was wailing. Wailing for her lost family. Wailing for her lost life. Wailing as if it would solve all her problems. But it did no good, her problems were still firmly in place as the wailing slowed to sobs and then finally to sniffles.

"I, uh, I'm, suh, suh, suh, so sorry, Mr. Barley," Erma said through sniffles. Tears had run down and streaked her face. Her nose was running.

Unbroken Hope

Barley handed her a handkerchief. Erma nodded thanks and wiped her eyes and nose. She tried to hand it back, but he motioned for her to keep it.

"Sadly, tears ain't gonna change this situation. Can you tell me what's going on?"

Erma then related her entire story. It was a story all too familiar to Barley. He had heard many similar stories, and they all had broken his heart. He was a compassionate man, and his heart ached for Erma. But he also had a job, which was something not many could say. A job he could ill afford to lose, and his bosses wanted no one jumping their trains.

Barley leaned back and sipped his coffee. He didn't want to turn her in, but he knew she was a very determined woman. She had to be. Who would subject her young child to all of this unless she *was* determined?

Or crazy?

Chapter 23

The drive into San Bernardino had not been as bad as Clay had feared. They had a little caravan going so that if anybody broke down, there would be someone to help. Harry, in his broken-down Model T truck, led the way. It was hard to miss, loaded down as it was with kids and odds and ends of furniture.

Of course, the dread of arriving and finding no work gnawed at everyone.

Clay would never forget his first sight of the town. The caravan had pulled off the road to take it all in.

Nestled south of the San Bernardino Mountains and west of the lower desert, Clay could see the town laid out before him, surrounded by thousands of acres of trees. Clay assumed they were orange trees. The town had a few shops that looked to be doing business. A gas station stood on the edge of town. He could even make out a hotel, though he knew he didn't have the money to stay there. There was a steady stream of people on the streets. It looked like the current economic woes hadn't even touched them. People were going about their usual business. The town was a beautiful and wondrous sight.

Harry signaled to them that he was moving on. And so they headed into town.

As they drove slowly down Main Street, people stopped and stared at the six-car procession. Many frowned. Some scowled. Nobody looked welcoming.

They drove clean through the town when they came to a low, wood-sided building. The white paint was faded, though the shingled roof seemed to be holding up well. Signs hung advertising Union Gasoline and other automotive products. Words painted on the side indicated it also had groceries. Two cylindrical gas pumps stood proudly out front, their tall glass domes gleaming in the sun. This was Jennings Service Station, a town fixture.

Harry pulled to the side of the building, and the five other cars pulled in beside him.

"Reckon, I'll go in and see what they know," Harry said as he got out of the truck. "You want to go with me, Clay? The rest of you might best stay out here for now, don't want to overwhelm em."

Clay nodded to Harry and Archie and then followed Harry into the store.

"Howdy," Harry said in a friendly tone. "Sure is warm out there."

"Yep," said a dour-looking man of about forty behind the counter. He had a clean plaid shirt on and was slowly working a plug of tobacco. He had a spit can on the counter and hefted a wad of spit into it. "What do ya Okies want?"

"Sir, we're lookin for Burkey Farms. It's supposed to be around here somewheres."

"It is. Further out yonder," the man said as he pointed further out of town. "Let me guess, looking to pick oranges?"

"Why yes, that's right!" Clay chimed in. He reached in his pocket to pull out the flyer. "We have this..."

"You can save your breath. You might as well use that to wipe your ass, for all the good it'll do ya. Burkey ain't hiring no more. They're all picked out. Nothing left."

"What you say?" Harry mumbled.

"You boys are about two weeks late. If I had to guess, we had about three thousand people drift through looking to fill about fifty jobs. It had been first-come, first-served. Burky made out, though. They were able to get real cheap labor. I heard they had started at ten bits per hundred pounds. But there were so many clamoring for a job that they finally wheedled the people down to two bits per hundred. And the people who got the jobs were happy to get them!"

Harry and Clay looked at each other. "Two bits? Twenty-five cents!" Clay exclaimed, "Nobody can live on that! Where the hell we supposed to go, now?" Clay asked to no one in particular. "You know of anyone else hiring?" he finally asked the man behind the counter.

"Nope. But there is a tent city on the way to Burkey. I hear they got running water, showers, and food. All courtesy of Uncle Sam. You might start there."

Harry and Clay looked at each other, their spirits buoyed.

"But I'd hurry if I were you, our State Legislature is fixing to close all the camps."

"But even if the Feds are involved?" Clay asked.

"Yeah, not sure how far it will go. But make sure you understand one thing. You boys aren't welcome here. I know that you have been playing hell just to survive, but California ain't the land of milk and honey like you dreamed about. People are fighting over what few jobs there is. Including people who have lived here their whole lives! They ain't about to give that up to a bunch of strangers."

"Well, thanks for the information, sir." Harry said with a light bow and headed for the door, Clay close on his heels.

"You all be careful out there." The man shouted after them. Clay and Harry turned to face him. "We're not mean people here, but times is tough for everybody."

Clay and Harry simply nodded and exited the store.

"What'd they say?" Hank asked. The faces of the group showed the angst of the unknown.

"It's not good," Clay voiced. "There is no work here."

"Did they know where we might find some?" Hank asked.

"Nope. But supposedly, there is a tent city down the road. It was set up by our Federal Government. Has water, showers, and food. I say we head there."

"Maybe they will have an idea of where we can go next," Harry added.

"How you all fixed for gas?" Clay asked.

The group all agreed that it would be best to fill up here. Clay thought Mr. Jennings would appreciate the business.

And he did.

Chapter 24

Erma and Barbara Jean sat very still. They were both afraid to utter a word. Barley stared at them, making all very uncomfortable.

"I'm not sure what I'm supposed to do with you," he said flatly.

Erma didn't think his question required her to reply so she stayed mum, wringing her hands.

"So, what do you think I should do?" Barley finally asked.

Erma shrugged. "How should I know!" she stammered. "You could just let me go. I didn't hurt no one."

Barley seemed to consider it. "Hmmm. Yeah. And you would be trying to get on the next train. Either here or somewhere else."

Erma didn't argue with him, as she knew there was no doubt what she would try to do if he let her go.

Barley checked his watch. "Well, it's too late for breakfast, but I suppose the diner is open for lunch. You two hungry?"

Erma didn't even need to think about it. She was starving, and she knew Barbara Jean needed some food in her. Barbara Jean nodded her head up and down in the affirmative. Erma didn't answer.

"Tell you what," Barley continued. "Let me take you to lunch in town. The diner is only about ten minutes from here. We can talk about this over a nice bite to eat."

"We ain't got no money," Erma said quietly.

"It's on me!"

"No, we cain't do that."

"I insist, unless of course you'd like to try the meals at the jail," he said with a wink.

Ten minutes later, Erma and Barbara Jean were sitting across from Barley at a small table in Eloise's Diner.

The diner was typical of what you might expect, a long counter with stools facing it. Dotting the landscape of the counter were salt and pepper shakers, ketchup, and condiment bottles.

A girl who looked sixteen ambled over with menus. She had her longish brown hair tied back in a ponytail. She was wearing a pink waitress uniform with a grease spot near her right shoulder. Her apron had a pocket, and Erma could see her order book peeking out. Her name badge said Helen.

Putting the menus on the table, she said, "Hi Fred. How are you today?"

"Just fine, Helen. Just fine. This here is Erma and her daughter," Barley searched for the girl's name and came up empty.

"Barbara, Barbara Jean," Erma chimed in.

"Pleased to meet both of you," Helen replied with a smile. She then looked quizzically at Barley, wondering who the two were.

"Oh," Fred said. "They're just passing through. Thought I would show them some good ole Norman hospitality and treat them to lunch.

"Uh-huh," Helen said with a knowing grin. "I'll give you folks a minute to look over the menu." She walked away and made herself busy wiping the counter, but still within earshot, being a nosy girl.

Erma perused the menu and said, "You din't have to treat us."

"Oh I insist, Erma. Please order anything you like."

Erma was so hungry that - if God himself popped up in front of me, he would look like a loaf of bread—as her daddy used to say. She took Barley at his word about paying.

"Thank you kindly, Mr. Barley. I don't think I'll never be able to repay ya."

"I ain't asking for repayment. Jus doing what Jesus taught us to do. Help the needy and you sure do look needy."

Erma bowed her head humbly. "Well, thank you all the same, Mr. Barley." She still wasn't sure what he was going to do about her.

Helen came back over. "You decided?"

Erma nodded.

Barley motioned for her to order first with a tilt of his head toward Helen.

"I'll have the meatloaf, with mashed taters and green beans, and Barbara can have," Erma looked back at the menu, puzzled about what to order for the small child, as the portions seemed so large.

Helen sensed the problem. "We can put together a plate with a fried chicken leg and mashed potatoes if you'd like."

"That'd be perfect! We'll also have two glasses of water too, please."

"I'll take my usual, Helen," Barley piped in as he patted his abundant stomach.

"Yes, sir," Helen replied. "Chicken fried steak with mashed potatoes and cream gravy and corn on the cob. Apple cobbler for dessert and coffee?"

"Of course. That'll do it, Helen. Thanks!"

Helen grabbed up the menus and hurried off to put the order in.

Once she was out of earshot, Barley asked, "So, tell me why do you want to get to California?"

"As I told you, my man, Clay went out ahead to look for work."

"And you don't want to wait here…why?"

"Look around you, there is nothing here. I was staying with my sister, and we were doing fine until her husband lost his job. They will be losin their small farm any day. There is no way they can keep it. And they certainly did not need two more mouths to feed!"

Barley nodded knowingly. "Well, you know I can't let you get back on board the train. And I know that is what you will try to do, if not here, then somewhere up ahead."

Erma said nothing. She just stared at her lap. Silence gripped the table.

Helen brought two glasses of water and a cup of coffee and told them their food would be out shortly.

Barley sighed and expelled a big burst of air. "Ok, I've got an idea, but it is going to require you to be further into debt to me. Can you deal with that?"

"Depends on what you mean," Erma replied doubtfully.

Just then, Helen appeared with their meals.

"My, that was fast!" Erma exclaimed.

"We aim to please," Helen said with a laugh.

"Looks good," Barley chimed in. "Thanks, Helen."

Erma looked down at Barbara Jean and asked if she wanted to say the blessing.

The girl nodded and started with "God is great…" She finished, though neither Barley nor Erma could really hear her.

"That is very good, Barbara," Barley said with a smile.

"Jean," Barbara Jean added.

Barley was at first confused, and then he got it. "You are absolutely right. Jean…Barbara Jean."

Barbara Jean smiled at him.

"Tink ou," Barbara Jean said, grinning back.

"So dig in," Barley added, motioning to Erma's fork.

Both Erma and Barbara Jean chowed down like farmhands. Food was flying into their mouths as fast as they could shovel it in.

Unbroken Hope

Barley had barely taken five bites while Erma was half through her gigantic portion.

"Whoa! Slow down, Erma, that food ain't going anywhere anytime soon," Barley said with a chortle.

Erma set her fork down and took a deep breath. "Sorry," she whispered. "Didn't realize I was that hungry!" She leaned forward with her elbows on the table. "You were saying you might have a plan?"

"Well, I said I couldn't let you get on one of our trains, but that doesn't mean you can't get on a bus."

Erma looked down dejected. "I done tole ya, I don't have enough money for bus fare cuz then there would be no money left over once I get to California."

"I know," Barley said, holding his hand up in a stop gesture. "I'll buy your bus ticket. Barbara here gets to travel for free, due to her age."

Erma was stunned. "You'll what?"

"I'll buy your bus tickets."

"Now, why would you do that?"

"Because you have no other options. You clearly need the help, and as I said a minute ago, it's what our Lord Jesus Christ would want me to do."

Erma sat back, stunned. She then began to eat the remainder of her lunch while she thought about Barley's offer.

Barley went back to his lunch as well.

"But there is some bad news," he continued between bites.

"Oh?

"You will only get as far as the California border. I have it on very good authority that California officials have closed off entry to anyone that can't prove they live there or have a job waiting there for them. Honestly, I will be surprised if your man even *made* it through."

Suddenly, Erma lost her appetite. She began pushing her food around. Even though she could not believe she had a tear left, her eyes began to swell. She took out Barley's handkerchief and dabbed at her eyes.

"But," Barley continued, "if you think you have a way through all of that, I can spot you a ticket to Williams, Arizona ."

Williams, Arizona ! Erma thought. I know exactly where that is. "I'll take you up on that!" she said with a smile. She would figure out what would come next after the generosity of this kind man.

Chapter 25

The tent city was set up right where Mr. Jennings had told them. The caravan drove on the road out of town until they came to a smallish sign directing them down a dirt road. Half a mile down, they came to a lean-to shed. A sign read:

San Bernardino Migrant Camp
-Operated by Volunteers-

Just like at Jenning's Service Station, Harry and Clay elected themselves as spokesmen for the group. No one objected. They stepped up onto a shallow porch in front of the lean-to. Inside, they could see two tables with forms and papers in piles on top. On the wall was a chart drawn on a blackboard. **Work Details** was the header above the chart. There was a bulletin board with **Jobs.**

Centered at the top. There were no jobs listed.

Sitting on a chair was a young man with a shock of unruly, dirty blonde hair. He had brown eyes and was clean-shaven. His clothes were clean, which was more than Clay could say about his own.

"You boys traveling together?" the young man asked.

Harry and Clay looked at each other, then back to the young man. "I reckon we are. We got six cars and 18 people, six of them kids." Harry answered.

Uh-hm," the young man answered through a whistle. "Don't know if we have the room for that many!" He reached behind him and grabbed up a clipboard from a table.

As he looked over the top sheet, he said without looking up, "Name's Tom Wilson. People call me Tommy."

"Harry Musgrave," Harry said, stepping forward, extending a hand. Tommy just ignored it, studying his sheet.

Harry looked down at his hand, then quickly pulled it back and put it in his pocket.

"Yep. We had a couple of families pull out last night. We can take 4 cars." Tommy said.

"Four!" Clay stammered. Surely you can fit a couple more in."

"Sorry. No can do. We're over capacity as it is. We just don't have enough food or water to go around for the families we got here."

Harry and Clay looked at each other, stunned.

"You see, this isn't a Federal Camp like some of the others around the state. This camp was set up by volunteers cuz they could see the plight you all were in. I got four slots. Take them of leave them."

"We were told this was a federal camp," Clay said.

"Nope" was the simple reply.

"We're going to need to talk to our group," Harry mumbled.

"Go ahead," Tommy replied. "I ain't goin nowhere."

The men headed back to the cars, where the group was anxiously waiting on news.

"They can only take four of us," Harry said in disgust.

"Four! Well that still leaves us with fourteen people!" Hank roared.

"No, he didn't mean four people. He meant four cars, four families." Clay clarified.

"So, we have some things to consider," Harry calmly said. "Who should stay? Who should go? Or should we just stay together?"

"I think we need to figure out who should stay," said Pat, a short man with a slight Irish accent. Clay had not talked with him the entire trip.

Unbroken Hope

"We have the youngest children, so I think we should be one of the families to stay!" A thin woman, Joan, said softly.

"Well, I'll bet you do!" Hank echoed back. "We have my elderly mother."

Once the floodgates of discussion opened, everyone was clamoring over why they should be one of the families to stay at the camp.

As the discussion raged and anger began to float to the top, Clay motioned Archie to the side.

"I think we need to back out of this. We ain't got no kids, no old people with us. We can do for ourselves." Clay whispered. Archie could barely hear him over the group's rising level of protestations.

"I agree, Clay," Archie replied.

"OK, but I want to check on one thing, before we do this."

Clay started back to the lean-to.

"Where do you think you're going?" Hank hollered.

"Before we decide, I need to ask our friend in here something."

Clay quickly stepped into the lean-to and just as quickly stepped out. He then motioned Archie to meet him at the group.

"I got a proposal for y'all. I jes proposed to Tommy in there, if Archie and I dropped out, if somewhere he could fit all five of your families. He said yes. So, Archie and I will leave you all to it."

"Oh my gosh," Harry said, extending his hand in friendship. "That was an awfully nice thing to do."

"Wadn't nothin," Clay replied. "Happy to do it. Tommy said go on in and get registered."

Clay and Archie backed away to the Model A and watched as the men stepped in the lean-to. They hopped into the car and drove away in a cloud of dust.

"Where we going to go now?" Archie asked.

Clay smiled. "Well, Tommy told me that he had just gotten an order in for two laborers at a nearby farm. He was so impressed with us giving up our places that he gave me the job sheet." Clay pulled the sheet from his short pocket.

"I guess good deeds can be rewarded, sometimes," Archie said with a grin.

Clay and Archie headed out.

"Let me see the paper," Russ Tompkins said as he held his hand out. Tompkins was the foreman at Burkey Farms. Clay complied and handed him the sheet he had been given at the camp. Burkey Farms! That was the place he had been looking for!

Tompkins studied it quietly. "OK, if you're good enough for Tommy, you're good enough for me. Both of you are in good health?"

Clay and Archie both nodded. They said nothing for fear of saying the wrong thing.

"It's just manual labor," Tompkins continued. "We're laying pipe from a new well to the house. Probably take about a week. I guess you know your way around a shovel?"

Both nodded again.

"Don't say much, do ya?"

"We jus don't want to say the wrong thing. We really need the job."

Tompkins snorted, "You and everyone else. OK it's a little late in the day to get started. But here's the deal. We pay two dollars a day for ten-hour days. We have room for you in the bunk house, and we'll give you three squares a day."

Clay felt like he had died and gone to heaven.

Unbroken Hope

Tompkins continued, "As I said, we figure about a week's worth of work, two weeks tops, to get all of the work done. I can't guarantee you anything beyond that."

"Sounds fine to us," Clay responded.

"He don't say much, does he?" Tompkins nodded toward Archie.

"Ain't got much to say, I reckon," Archie replied good-naturedly.

"I guess you don't," Tompkins, chuckled. "Well, you two boys will be working with our three regular hands. They should be coming in real soon. Come with me, and I'll get you settled in."

The walk to the bunk house afforded Clay his first look at the property. A large two-story white clapboard farmhouse sat on the edge of the farmyard. Its two dormers overlooked the property. A wrap-around porch contained six worn-looking wooden rocking chairs. Several smaller outbuildings, some would call sheds, were scattered about. A large red barn sat west of the house. Clay could see a couple of milk cows and three horses in stalls. A couple of small goats wandered the grounds, as did multiple chickens. Three pigs were in a wet sty at the side of the barn. A hog wire fence contained them. Overall, the farm looked prosperous, particularly when you compared it to back home! It was still amazing to him that they had wound up at the place listed on his flyer. What a world, he thought.

The bunkhouse was an unpainted building sided with long horizontal boards. It offered a deep porch one step above ground level. Stepping inside, Clay could see a large table with chairs sitting in the middle of the room. The walls were lined with eight bunk beds.

"Any bed that doesn't have sheets and blankets on it is yours for the taking. Sheets and blankets are kept over yonder in that cupboard." Tompkins stated flatly. "We're up at 4:30. Breakfast at 5, working 5:30 until 11:30, break for dinner, then back to it at 12. We clean up around 4 and supper is at 5. The rest of the time is yours. Meals will be waiting for you on the front porch of the big house. Bring them back here to eat. Got all that?"

"Yes, sir," Clay said, and Archie mimicked it.

"The boys should be back anytime. You two go ahead and get settled. I will let you introduce yourselves to them. They'll show you the ropes."

Then Tompkins left, slamming the door behind him.

"Let's get our kits out of the car, Archie, and get ready to meet the boys," Clay said with a smile. He hadn't felt this good in years.

The three farmhands made it back to the bunk house right after Clay and Archie had made up their bunks. They had washed up in the yard, and their faces and hands were still dripping from the clean-up activity.

Archie was the first to look up when they entered. "Hey!" he said enthusiastically. He stepped toward the lead man and held his hand out. "I'm Archie!"

The man wiped his hand on his britches and shook Archie's extended hand. "Bill…Bill Meadows."

"This here is, Clay," Archie said, introducing his partner. The two men shook.

"Pleased to meet ya," Clay said.

"These two boys are Ralph Earle and Lonnie Blaire." All of the men shook and nodded their pleasure to meet each other's company.

"You boys get cleaned up?" Bill asked. "Supper is waiting for us to pick up on the porch of the big house in five minutes."

"I reckon we're as cleaned up as we're gonna be," Clay said good-naturedly.

"Well then, let's go. They will be waiting on us, and they won't like it."

Unbroken Hope

The five men stomped out of the house and made the walk to the porch of the big white farmhouse. They grabbed their supper and brought it back to the bunkhouse.

"So, where you boys from?" Ralph asked.

"I'm from just west of Oklahoma City," Clay replied

"And I'm further west of there, in Texas. Where are yawl from?" Archie offered.

Nebraska, around Lincoln," Bill replied.

"Kansas City, Kansas," Lonnie chimed in.

"And I'm from Modesto, a bit north of here," Ralph said with a grin. He had an infectious smile, although his teeth were very yellow and stained.

All three of the hands were about the same height and could have almost been triplets; they looked so much alike. They even dressed alike. Dark brown work pants and tan long-sleeve shirts.

"Anybody ever tell you that you three look like brothers?" Archie asked.

Lonnie laughed a big, hearty laugh. "All the time. But we never even knew each other till we met here."

Everyone continues to shovel food in while asking the random question now and then. The three permanent hands made Clay and Archie feel right at home.

After the supper was devoured, the men sat back and lit up cigarettes. Clay and Archie didn't smoke, so they just sat back and watched as the men jabbed and teased at each other.

Lonnie said, "You don't know it yet, but Bill here may be the laziest worker you ever seen." He guffawed.

I'm lazy!" Bill shouted back. "Why, you're so lazy you're always looking around for someone to wipe your butt!"

The men all laughed at that.

Lonnie snapped back, "Maybe I am lazy, but it's the lazy people who invented the wheel and the bicycle because they didn't like walking or carrying things!"

The men chuckled at that. A lull overtook the conversation as the men continued to smoke.

"Say," Clay interjected. "Can you tell us what we're going to be doing tomorrow?"

"The same thing that you will be doing the day after tomorrow and the day after that. Digging a trench." Ralph chimed in.

"Make sure you get some good work gloves from the tool shed. By the time we're through tomorrow, your hands will be glad they got em," Bill added.

"We just finished digging a well. To find water, it was about six hundred feet from the house," Lonnie said. "The boss wants a pipe run to a new windmill and storage tank, and from there, a pipe run to the main house. They plan on having gravity feed the water into the house. That's where we come in. We will be burying that pipe two feet down below the frost line. Because, believe it or not, it can get down to freezing in the winter here. Don't want frozen line!"

"So, we'll dig the trench first, then lay the pipe, then cover the pipe after we check for leaks," Bill added.

Clay and Archie just nodded.

The next day, Clay found himself on the working end of a shovel. The sun beat down on him. All five men were shoveling to beat the band. The digging on the hard pan was tough going. Bill would swing a pick ax to help soften the soil, and then the men would take turns pulling the soil up and placing it to the right of the working trench. They had been at it for three hours and had about fifteen feet of finished trench to show for it. At this rate, Clay couldn't see how they would be able to complete the work in two weeks, like they had been told. But I guess we'll see. Longer would certainly be good, he thought. Good solid work.

'Let's take a water break," Lonnie said, and the men needed no encouragement. They walked to the Lister bag, a canvas bag containing water and hanging in the center of a tripod. Tin cups were sitting next to the bag, and each man grabbed one up.

The men quickly gulped down a cup of water and just as quickly refilled it.

"So," Clay asked. "Where can I send a telegram?" I need to get word back home as to where I am."

"Oh, that's easy," Ralph said. "Just write down what you want sent. Someone goes into town every day. Pay the money, and they will make sure it is sent."

Clay started composing the telegram in his head when he heard the news.

CHAPTER 26

As the bus pulled into the Williams, Arizona station, Erma was dozing with Barbara Jean's head in her lap. Barley had made good on his promise to buy the bus tickets, but Erma wheedled him into giving her his address so she could send money when she was able to repay.

It had been a long ride from Norman. They stopped in virtually every town along the way. They dropped off passengers and picked new ones up. The bus stayed fairly full for the entire trip.

When they purchased their tickets, the Greyhound agent told them they were only able to go as far west as Williams. This confirmed what Barley had already told her. The border to California was indeed closed. The agent reiterated this. So, no tickets were available to Los Angeles, let alone San Bernardino.

It was dark as the bus pulled into its stall. Erma nudged Barbara Jean awake, and the little girl sat up and strained to look out through the window.

"Is still dark," she mumbled.

"Yes, it is, baby," Erma said with a smile, patting her daughter's hair. "But this is as far as we go."

"We see Daddy, now?" the girl said excitedly.

"No, not yet. We still have a ways to go."

"Oh," was all she said.

Erma gathered their belongings, took Barbara Jean by the hand, and led her off the bus.

As they entered the terminal, Erma looked at a gigantic clock on the wall above the ticket office.

"Whew! Five-thirty in the morning. There's a coffee shop over yonder. Let's see if we can get us some breakfast!"

The woman and child squeezed together on one side of the booth.

When the waitress came, they placed their order, and Erma asked her if there was a telegraph office nearby. Fortunately, it was housed in the bus station. Erma made a note that she would send Mamie a telegram letting her know where she was just as soon as they were done eating. She hoped and prayed that Mamie had gotten word from Clay.

"Mama, what dat?" Barbara Jean asked, pointing to an object on the counter.

"Well, I don't rightly know, Baby Girl."

Erma studied it. It looked like an oversized jar, with round objects floating in it.

"What's that?" Erma asked the waitress when she came over. She pointed at the jar.

"Oh, those? Those are pickled eggs."

"Pickled eggs?" Erma had never heard of such a thing.

"Yes, ma'am. They are real good. Hard-boiled and pickled in a pickling brine. Lots of people love em."

Erma looked at Barbara Jean and scrunched her nose up in a funny expression of disgust. Barbara Jean simply laughed.

"Say, would it be alright to leave my little girl here for a minute? I need to go send that telegram."

The coffee shop was empty, and Erma felt safe leaving Barbara Jean.

"Oh, sure," the waitress replied. "I'll keep an eye on her. No problem."

"Thanks," Erma said as she hustled off with her purse.

Unbroken Hope

She wasn't gone ten minutes. She was carrying a copy of her telegram, and she read it to Barbara Jean, who had been waiting patiently for her to return.

"In Williams, Arizona. Will check back at the telegram office tomorrow."

She folded the paper and placed it in her purse.

The waitress came and sat down across from Erma after cleaning the table.

"You get your telegram sent?" The waitress asked

"I shore did," Erma replied. "Thanks for showing me whar it was. Shore made things easy."

No bother at all," the waitress said with a smile. "My name's Trudy by the way."

"I'm Erma, and this here's Barbara Jean. Very nice to meet you."

"Sure thing. You seem to be a long way from home."

"You said a mouthful thar," Erma said. "We come in on the bus from Norman, Oklahoma. 'Twas a brutal ride, but it beat jumping a train!"

"Jumping a train! Are you plum crazy with that little girl?"

Erma brought Trudy up to speed on what had transpired over the past week. Just talking about it all exhausted Erma.

"That is quite a story!"

Erma nodded, then asked, "Say, is there a cheap place for us to stay the night?"

"How cheap?"

"Pretty cheap. Don't have much money."

"How does a dollar sound?"

"That sounds wonderful! Whar is it?"

"It's with me! I get off in another thirty minutes. My place is just around the corner."

"Oh, I couldn't do that!" Erma protested.

"Why not! I've got the room, and I need the money."

Erma looked doubtful. This was the second person in the last two days who had shown her kindness.

"Aright then," Erma said somewhat dubiously. "I promise we won't be no bother. Ah, one other thing, you think I might be able to stay two, maybe three nights? I want to wait to see if I get a telegram back from my sister."

"Oh, sure," Trudy said. "A dollar a night sure helps me, so the longer the better."

As Trudy unlocked the door to her apartment, Erma studied her. She was maybe five years younger than Erma. Still wearing her waitress getup, she had the eyes of someone who had witnessed a fair amount of pain. There was sadness in them.

"Home sweet home," Trudy said, as she swung the door open.

Holding Barbara Jean's hand, Erma cautiously entered. It looked to be a one-bedroom place. The living room contained a worn-out sofa and two beat-up upholstered chairs. The kitchen had a small wooden table and two unmatched chairs. The kitchen furniture had been painted white at some point in time, but it was hard to tell from all the chips in the finish.

"It may be small, but it does have its own bathroom! Which is almost unheard of in this neighborhood. Most people in apartments like this are sharing."

"Heck, sharing a bathroom wouldn'tna bothered us none. Back home, we jus have an ole outhouse. No real indoor plumbing 'cept a pump at the kitchen sink," Erma said, looking around. "Where do you want us?"

"I was thinking you and your girl would take my bed and I would sleep here on the sofa."

"Oh no, I cain't kick you outta yor bed!" Erma exclaimed.

"You aren't. It's just for a few nights, and besides, you're paying. So, you get the royal treatment. If you consider this royal!" Trudy laughed as she motioned around the room.

"Well, OK then, so long as you don't mind."

"It is no problem for me. Why don't you get your things into the bedroom? Maybe you want to freshen up a bit. That sounds like it was one long bus ride. Once you're cleaned up and you got Barbara Jean there down for the night, I would like to hear more of what you been through."

Erma opened her purse while Trudy was finishing. "I can certainly do that. Here is the three dollars afore I forget. For three nights," Erma said, holding the three ones out.

"Oh, I wouldn't have let you forget," Trudy said with a smile. "Now go ahead and get yourselves settled. Would you like some tea?

"That shore sounds nice, Trudy. I won't be longer than two shakes of a lamb's tail."

Once Erma and Barbara Jean had cleaned up, it didn't take the little girl two minutes to fall into a deep sleep in Trudy's bed. Soon, Erma found herself sitting across from Trudy, sipping a cup of tea. It had been so long since she had had tea that it was a pleasant and sumptuous surprise.

"So," Trudy started in. "Tell me *all* of your story."

Erma did.

Chapter 27

The telegram read:

```
Got a telegram from Clay
He's got work at Burkey Farms in San Bernardino
Stop
Has a couple of weeks of work
Stop
He said wait to come
Stop
Will send for you
Stop
Love, Mamie
Full Stop
```

Erma read it three times as she stood in the telegraph office.

Burkey Farms, she thought. The name on the flyer. He had done it! San Bernardino! Clay had made it! She couldn't wait to get there. She grabbed Barbara by the hand and marched over to the coffee shop. There were no customers inside.

"Hey Trudy!" she said, waving at Trudy to come over. "I got a telegram back from Mamie. Clay made it!" She thrust the paper in front of Trudy, who read it.

"That's terrific, Erma!" Trudy exclaimed, obviously excited for her newfound friend.

"I'm gonna need to get going," Erma said, heading for the door.

"Whoa, hold on a minute," Trudy said, grabbing her by the arm. "Come sit down. Let's talk about your plan."

The women sat down. Barbara Jean had been watching the exchange.

"Mama, dwink?" the girl asked.

"Sure, baby," Trudy chirped in. Would ya like a little milk?"

"Uh-ha," the child said with a nod.

Trudy came back with a small glass of milk and set it on the table. "Here ya go, Sweetie."

Barbara Jean carefully hoisted the glass and took a sip.

"Yum."

"Go on," Trudy then said to Erma. "Do you have a plan?

"Well, no, not much of one anyway. I still have a good bit of money left. I could buy another bus ticket, but I wouldn't be able to get through."

Trudy listened. Erma couldn't believe how close the two had gotten in only two days. It felt like she had known her forever.

"Well, I might have an idea," Trudy offered cautiously.

Erma waited a beat, then realized Trudy was waiting to see if she was interested in hearing her thoughts. "Go on," she finally said.

"I got a friend, Paul, who's a long-haul truck driver. He works for Chambers Transfer out of Phoenix. And he makes runs between here and Southern California every couple of weeks. I was thinking maybe he would let you hitch a ride with him."

"Do you think he would?" Erma asked, excited by the idea.

"No harm asking I guess."

"How do we getta hole of im?

"Oh, when he's in town, he comes in here all the time. I think he's kinda sweet on me." Trudy answered with a grin. "He's doing some local stuff and will probably be coming in here for supper tonight. I'll ask him if he could do me this favor."

"Les go, Mama," Barbara Jean pulled on Erma's hand. "I wanna see horthie!"

Erma looked down at the child, puzzled, and then looked quizzically at Trudy, finally figuring it out.

"Horthie? Huh? You mean horsie," Erma said with a laugh. "Where's the horsie, Baby Girl?"

"It dare," the girl pointed through the window, and sure enough, a young colored man was riding a chestnut horse right down the middle of Main Street.

Erma laughed as she looked over at Trudy, who had a big smile pasted on her face. "OK, little girl. Let's go see the man on the horse." And the two left the coffee shop.

As Erma approached the horse, she couldn't believe her good fortune. First, Mr. Barley had been so nice in buying her the tickets to get this far. Then Trudy had offered up her home for next to nothing. Finally, it seemed that she might have a way to California that wouldn't cost her anything. Maybe, things were beginning to turn her way!

She picked Barbara Jean up so she could pet the horse. The girl shied away slightly but put her hand out to touch the horse's mane.

"It's a nice horse, Baby Girl," Erma cooed. The rider just smiled at them. His white teeth gleamed in his dark face. "Thank you for letting us pet him," Erma said.

"No problem, ma'am," the rider said, tipping his cowboy hat. "You all have a nice day, now."

The rider guided the horse away, leaving the two of them to watch it go. It was a simple exchange, but it made Erma feel good. She couldn't wait to hear if Trudy was able to get her a ride to California.

Michael Wells

Erma was waiting anxiously when Trudy made it home. She had almost gone to the coffee shop, but held off.

"Well?" Erma asked, but she could tell by Trudy's expression that she didn't have good news.

"I talked to Paul. It's not good, Erma." Trudy said with a frown.

"He doesn't have a run for another two weeks, and even if he had one now, he said the company is cracking down on carrying anyone with him. Seems like a lot of the drivers have been helping folks get to California. I know you got your hopes up, and I'm sorry I started it."

"Don't you fret none," Erma said. "I'll figure another way.

The two women sat in silence. As hard as she tried, Erma couldn't think of another way. But she knew she would have to sort this out. Maybe an idea would come to her in the morning. She would have to get word to Clay.

Chapter 28

Sweat poured down Clay's forehead, stinging his eyes. The bandana tied around his head was little help controlling the cascade. Clay was no stranger to hard work, but the last several days had been brutal. Working from sunup to sundown, the men had made good progress. Clay and Archie were not in a big hurry to complete the project, because that would mean the end of the paychecks. The three regulars kept the pace up. They had no fear of being released once this job was done, so Clay and Archie were forced to pace themselves with them.

The job was monotonous. Throwing spadesful of dirt outside the trench, Clay allowed his mind to wander back to better times in Oklahoma. A time when the rains came and kept the crops lush. It was a time of plenty. Boy, he longed for those times again.

They had a trench dug about fifty feet long and they were getting ready to lay the first run of galvanized pipe. Ralph had been working with a ten-foot run, threading a coupling on to it. It required pipe dope, a thick caulk-like paste to be smeared on the threads. Then using a pipe wrench, Ralph tightened the connector for a watertight fit. It was messy, meticulous work, but a long run of pipe was made up of shorter pieces that had to be coupled together.

The first pipe had been laid in at the well head. The pipe had been run to a windmill, which would pump the water into a large holding tank. The holding tank would then let gravity feed the water into the second section pipe that headed toward the house and out to the fields. The old well had been an ordeal. It had dried up, so a new one had to be drilled. Also, a new windmill and holding tank to replace the old one was required. The Burkeys, who owned the farm, weren't poor. But the cost of the well and equipment had set them back pretty good. Without water, the farm failed. Clay knew that song, music, and verse. Whatever water God didn't provide with rain had to come from the well. When the original well began to fail, the new plan had been put in place.

"Hey, Archie!" Ralph hollered. "Give me a hand with this length of pipe!"

"Sure thing, Mr. Ralph!" Archie cried out on the run.

Clay had to give it to Archie. He was sure a hard worker and Clay had told him how proud he was of him. Archie had just beamed when the words had come out of Clay's mouth.

Archie and Ralph maneuvered the pipe. Archie held it as Ralph threaded it onto the coupling.

"That's it! We made it to the windmill," Ralph said proudly. "Next stop is the holding tank and then on to the house."

The men stood back and admired their work. Tompkins, the foreman, had been standing by and had been happy to see the progress.

"Ok, boys, it's 2:30, no sense starting the next length. Take the rest of the day off!" Tompkins said magnanimously. "With pay! You earned it!"

"Wow!" Archie exclaimed. "Clay, how about that? We got almost 3 hours till supper."

Tompkins laughed, "If you want to go into town, I'm heading in. We should still make it back before supper. Don't have time to get cleaned up, though. You'll have to go as you are."

All five of the men took him up on his offer, riding in the back of one of the farm's trucks.

As they rattled into town, the truck kicked up quite a dust storm. The dust shrouded the men in a deep fog. "Reminds me of home!" Clay said with a laugh. "Sure does," Archie joined in.

Unbroken Hope

The men hopped off the truck almost before it could come to a stop on Main Street.

"Where's the telegraph office?" Clay shouted to Tompkins.

"Down yonder," Tompkins pointed to a smallish storefront with a Western Union sign hanging out front.

"Say, you don't have a telegram waiting for me, do you?" Clay said as he entered the office. "Name's Stanley. Clay Stanley."

A middle-aged woman with brown shoulder-length hair stared at him. She had a frown on her face as she scanned her memory for recent wires. She was wearing blue jeans and a buttoned light blue shirt. Her sleeves were rolled up. Clay found it odd, a woman wearing blue jeans.

"I think we got something here for you," the woman said as she turned to her files.

Clay's heart leapt.

"Here it is," the woman said as she pulled a short piece of paper from the file. "It's from a Mamie Driggers in Oklahoma. You know her I guess?"

"I reckon I do, she's my wife's sister," Clay said casually, as he took the paper from the woman.

"Ain't much of a telegram," the woman said smugly.

Clay read it aloud, "She's on her way to you. Full Stop."

Clay read again his mouth moving with every word.

"No, no, no!" Clay spit out in anguish. "She cain't be coming here. Not yet. That blamed, fool woman!"

He headed out the door, leaving the woman staring in his wake.

"You get a telegram?" Archie asked.

Clay handed it to him, not saying a word.

Archie read it. "Huh? She's coming? When will she be here? Where's she going to stay?" He turned the paper over as if the answer to those questions would be on the back.

"Heck if I know the answer to any of those questions, Archie," Clay said dejectedly. "Mamie sent the telegram yesterday. But she doesn't say how far along Erma is. I reckon we just need to go back to the farm and do the work we been hired to do and worry about what she's doing later."

On the ride back to the farm, Clay turned the telegram over and over in his hand. Reading it and re-reading it. No further answers came to him. He kept to himself, wallowing in a sullen mood. He was excited at the prospect of seeing Erma and Barbara Jean again. But he knew he was not ready for them. He hadn't been able to save much in the few days he had been working.

He'd just have to figure it out, he thought, and folded the telegram and put it in his pocket.

"Damn fool woman," he mumbled. Archie just looked at him quizzically.

Chapter 29

Erma grabbed Barbara's hand and made a run for the train.

It hadn't taken her long to figure out that the quickest way to California was going back to her original idea, the train. But her first attempt had opened her eyes. She wasn't going to try to get on a train while it was moving. She was going to find a train that was sitting still, which allowed plenty of time for her and Barbara to get onboard safely.

She had asked around town regarding the local train yard and the head code number to look for. This would tell her where the train was headed.

She had set out for the Williams train yard, arrived in the late afternoon, and kept an eye on things. Near dusk, a west-bound train with a head code that indicated it was going to Los Angeles rolled in. Just the train she was looking for.

Some of the cargo was unloaded, and new cargo put in its place. By ten that night, the foreman yelled out for everyone to go on home. "She's going out in the morning at five," he hollered. "Be here by 4:30."

Perfect, Erma thought as she watched the men scatter. She waited a while to make sure everyone had left, and now here she was, running for an open boxcar. She had spied a stack of wooden apple boxes just to the side, so she swooped one up. She had thought about getting two boxes and throwing one onboard to help her get off when the train stopped, but had tossed that idea away. She would worry about getting off when the time came. Scooping up her daughter, she placed the girl in the boxcar opening and threw her knapsack up. Then, using the apple box as a step, she climbed into the boxcar. As she raised up, she was able to kick the apple box slightly away. Hopefully, no one will notice it, she thought.

Inside the car was full of crates. This was a good thing as it allowed her to make her way along one wall and hide. The crates gave her good shielding. Prying eyes looking in wouldn't be able to see her.

She and Barbara made a nest for themselves, using the knapsack as a pillow. The two stowaways were soon fast asleep.

A gigantic "BLAM!" shook the car. It startled Erma awake. What little light that had been coming in the car earlier was now completely gone. Erma realized that it was the boxcar door being slammed closed which had awakened her.

"It awright, Mama?" Barbara Jean asked. She seemed calm enough.

"Yeah, baby," Erma answered. "That was just them closing the door. We should be moving right shortly."

She had no more than said this than the train started to shake and move forward. Erma's heart rose, and she knew they were on their way.

Time crept by. Erma had no means to know what time it was, nor where they were. She knew this particular train was making stops in Needles and then San Bernardino, where she was going to get off. Based on her look at the road map, she knew San Bernardino was less than 400 miles from Williams. With any luck, it would take maybe ten or twelve hours to get there. Of course, she didn't know if there would be any more stops along the way and how long each stop would take.

She and Barbara Jean dozed and took little sips of water from a small milk bottle in the knapsack. Mostly, it was sheer boredom. The boredom was broken up by taking potty breaks. They did their business in a far corner. She felt bad about leaving it there, but there was little she could do about it.

Periodically, Barbara Jean would ask how much longer before they got there, but in general, the ride went smoothly. Erma thought it might have been about three hours when she felt the train starting to slow down. The clacking on the tracks got slower, and she could hear the squeal of brakes. Finally, the train came to a stop.

It wasn't long before the door opened and light came pouring in.

"OK, boys!" Someone shouted. This one has the first two rows coming off. Everything else stays. Nothing new will go in its place, so this car's going to be a little light leaving Kingman."

Kingman! Erma thought. If she recollected right, Kingman was a little over a hundred miles west of Williams. Needles should be next!

Erma nudged Barbara Jean to move deeper into the car and away from where the men would be working. With grunts and groans, Erma could tell that the men had started the unloading process. She could hear hand trucks being used and wooden crates scraping along the boxcar floor. Occasionally, she would hear someone say things like, "No, not that one!" or "There are two over here." But in general, the men made quick work out of emptying the cargo.

She peeked around the corner of a crate to see the last of the men jump from the train. They hadn't been gone more than ten minutes when she heard a rustling by the door. She took a peek. A man of about thirty was hauling his way up onto the train. He had set his bindle on the floor and then jumped up effortlessly. His bindle was a sack connected to a long stick. The stick was typically slung over a shoulder to carry belongings in the sack. He looked like he was traveling real light.

She studied the man. He was thin and wiry. He had longish, unkempt brown hair. His beard was neatly trimmed, but his eyebrows weren't. They were unruly as all get out. His clothes seemed reasonably clean for a person that lived on the road. This man is an honest-to-god hobo, Erma thought to herself.

The man headed to the opposite end of the car, and Erma headed back to her little cave. Barbara Jean started to talk, but Erma quickly put a hand over her mouth and gave a soft, stern "shhh!" the girls's eyes widened. Her mother had never done this before.

"This car is ready to go?" a man's voice came from outside the car. Down the line, the return was, "Yep, you can close her up." The door slammed, encasing Erma in darkness and trapped her inside with a stranger.

Erma still had her hand clamped on Barbara Jean's mouth. She slowly let loose. A puzzled look overcame her daughter's face. "Mama?" the girl said.

"Shhhh! I said," hissed Erma. The girl shuddered.

The train was still sitting still, and with no movement and no noise of the rails, Erma couldn't tell if the man had heard them or not.

The train began to move, and Erma breathed a sigh of relief. She laid back and let the movement of the train lull her to sleep.

Erma was in the middle of a fine dream. She was with Clay, and he was saying, "What do we have here?" Except it wasn't Clay's voice. She forced one eye open, and the thin hobo was glaring down on her. She jumped to her elbows with a start, shielding Barbara Jean from the man.

"I ain't gonna hurt ya none, little lady," the man said through a grin. "Jus relax."

The man's words were gentle enough, but the leering look in his eye made her very nervous. She skittered away from him on her butt, dragging her daughter with her.

The man just laughed, "Where ya goin? There ain't much more room thar."

Unbroken Hope

Erma could feel that the man was right. She had gone as far as she could... the wall and a crate blocked her way.

"Could...could you just move away a bit?" Erma said, shooing him back with her hand. The man's clothes might have been fairly clean, but he stank to high heaven. Now, Erma knew she didn't smell like any bed of roses, but he smelled like a manure heap.

The man backed up a step. "Say, whydn't you come out toward the door where there's more light? No sense sitting here in the dark."

Erma just stared out at him, not moving.

"I ain't gonna bite," he said casually. "I promise."

Chapter 30

Clay had spent a restless night. He tossed and turned worrying about what to do with Erma coming. When the breakfast bell rang, he was already dressed and headed out to eat. Archie joined him.

"Watchya gonna do?" Archie whispered as they moved across the yard toward breakfast.

"About?" Clay asked crossly.

"About Erma,"

"Well dang, Archie, I just found out. I don't rightly know. We'll just have to see whenever she gets here. Maybe I can talk Tompkins into letting her stay, at least until we finish the job."

Archie looked dubiously at him, shaking his head. "I sure hope they do, but I don't reckon they will."

Clay kicked the dirt, "Well goddam it, Archie! I don't really know what I should do! Right now, I'm just going to do the work that they asked us to do." He stared down at Archie.

"OK, ok, Clay. I know. I was jus wonderin." Archie said, looking like a scolded puppy.

All the other workers were already seated when Clay and Archie, with full plates, sat down at the long wooden table.

Everyone sat in silence, contemplating the day ahead. The only sound was the singing of forks on plates and murmurs of how good the grub was.

Clay spotted Tompkins and hurried, shoveling the rest of his breakfast down. Grabbing his empty plate he mumbled to Archie,

"There's Tompkins, reckon I need to go talk to him" He scraped his plate off into a garbage can and placed it in a sudsy bucket of water.

"Uh, Mr. Tompkins, have a word with ya?"

Tompkins nodded and crossed his arms to listen.

"I uh, jus got a telegram yesterday from my woman back in Oklahoma. Appears she's headin out here."

"OK, so what do you want me to do about it?"

"Well, I never wanted her to come yet, but she did anyway. Erma's strong-headed like that."

"I'm married to one of those, too," Tompkins said with a smile.

Clay took that as a good sign as he chuckled. "Well, I was hoping she might be able to stay here until we finish up."

"I thought that might be where you were headed with this," Tompkins replied thoughtfully. "When is she due here?"

I don't rightly know, sir. I would say within the next few days, a week tops."

Tompkins shook his head. "Clay, I'm sorry, but we got no place for her to stay. We just ain't set up that way."

"Well, couldn't we…"

Tompkins held his hand up to silence him.

"No, it just ain't going to work. Now that has to be the end of it."

"Okay, sir. Thanks for listening to me," Clay said, looking down at his hands and wringing his hat.

Tompkins nodded as Clay moved away.

"What'd he say?" Archie asked gingerly.

"Said it wouldn't work for her to stay here."

"Geez, Clay, whatchya gonna do now?"

Before Clay could answer, they were ushered outside to begin the day's work.

Unbroken Hope

The sun was beating heat waves as the sweat trickled down Clay's back. The men had made good progress, having laid four runs of pipe in a little over ninety minutes, when they hit a snag.

Trenching along, the men hit a buried tree trunk. The tree, an old oak, had been cut down below the surface of the ground. The men hadn't seen it prior to trenching. The remaining stump was about two feet in diameter.

"Well, dang!" roared Ralph. "Don't that beat all. Want we should go around it?"

"Nah," Tompkins said as he bent over to examine things. "We can dig around it and yank it out of the ground." He then turned to Archie. "Archie, go over to the barn and bring the truck back."

Archie headed off at a run.

"Boys, dig down around that stump until we can get under a root."

By the time Archie had returned with the truck, a good-sized hole had been dug around the stump, exposing a large root. They had tunneled under the root. Tompkins went to the bed of the truck and lifted out a large, thick, rusty chain. "Give me a hand with this, boys."

Ralph and Clay grabbed hold of the chain and lugged it to the stump.

"Loop it under the root and wrap her around," Tompkins said, pointing the way. "Archie, back the truck in here." He continued, pointing to where he wanted the truck, and Archie complied.

"Hook that end of the chain up under the axle," Tompkins continued to shout orders. Once the chain was in place, Tompkins ordered Ralph behind the wheel.

"Ok, Ralph," Tompkins yelled. "Take the slack out of the chain. You boys better move on over to the side." Motioning for Clay and Bill to move in front of the truck. "Archie, move down there behind the stump." He pointed where he wanted Archie positioned. "Let me know if you see it moving."

Tompkins moved over to the truck window. "Now, when I tell you, I want you to floor it. It's gonna take everything this old truck has to yank that stump loose."

Ralph nodded and waited for the signal.

"Okay, Ralph. Hit it!"

Ralph popped the clutch, and the rear tires started to spin, trying to gain traction. The chain groaned against the pull of the stump. The stump moved precious little.

"Stop, Ralph!" The truck eased back down.

"Clay, Bill, Archie, go dig some more around those roots. We need to get them freed up a bit more."

Archie and Clay jumped on the shovels, eager to comply. Soon, more of the stump was exposed.

"Let's try again," Tompkins said eagerly. He motioned for the men to step back.

"Ok, Ralph, give it the gun!"

The tires began to spin, and the truck groaned. Smoke poured off the back tires as they dug into the dirt. It finally looked like the truck was going to win the battle with the stump.

Suddenly, there came a loud metallic WHUMP!. When Archie thought back on the event, he could hardly tell what happened.

He heard the loud noise and then a massive cracking sound as the root and chain broke loose. Out of the corner of his eye, he saw them hurtling through the air. Then he saw Clay collapse with a heavy thud. It was then he realized the root had smashed into Clay's head.

"Clay!" Archie screamed as he went running to his fallen friend. "Clay! Clay! You alright?" Archie could not make out his friend's condition. Clay lay slumped. The chain still attached to the tree root lay on top of him.

Tompkins quickly moved to the scene. "OK, boys, move that root gently." The men gradually lifted it from Clay's head and chest.

As the root was gently lifted away, Archie could see his friend's head had been caved in. His eyes stared vacantly ahead.

"Clay?" Archie said, stunned. "Clay?" he turned to Tompkins. "Is he dead?"

Tompkins said nothing as he felt for a pulse. Archie knelt by his friend and sobbed.

"His heart's still beating," Tompkins yelled. "We best get him to the hospital!

The men gingerly placed Clay in the pickup bed. Archie hopped in beside him, holding his head. "Everything's gonna be OK, Clay," Archie whispered in Clay's ear. "You hold on. We're getting you to the hospital."

The truck roared off in a cloud of dust with Tompkins at the wheel.

The ride was bumpy, and Archie tried to keep Clay's head from being jostled too much.

On the ride there, something clicked inside Clay's brain, and he began thrashing around in a seizure, though he wasn't lucid.

Archie continued to hold him as he yelled out in a panicked voice to Tompkins, who was driving, "Hurry!! I don't know what's going on with him!!!"

Tompkins looked through the rear window to see Archie shaking like a leaf. It was clear he was barely holding back his emotions. He stared at Tompkins helplessly. Tompkins tried to coax more speed out of the old truck, but she was going as fast as she could.

The truck came swooping into the hospital lot, and Tompkins jumped, looking for someone to help.

"Hey! Got an injured man here," Tompkins yelled at a nurse standing near the entrance. "Where do I take him?"

She came running over and looked in the bed. She climbed up and checked Clay's pulse.

She looked sadly at Archie and then Tompkins. "I am so sorry, but he didn't make it."

Tompkins looked at Archie. A tear slowly coursed its way down the young man's cheek.

"Jeez," Archie whispered softly.

Chapter 31

Erma looked suspiciously at him. He was dressed in suit pants and a worn leather jacket. A button down shirt, that Erma assumed had once been white but was now a light gray and had a large stain in the middle of the shirt. His brown hair was swept back and his bearded face showed years of worry. His eyes were brown and had a dark intensity about them. She guessed him to be somewhere in his late thirties.

The man waited for Erma to size him up and then with a tip of his dirty, crumpled fedora, he whispered, hoarsely, "Name's Claude Jones."

He was handsome but not in a movie star way. He had dimples when he smiled and a mouthful of very straight, very white teeth. Erma wondered how he kept them so white. Her own teeth had taken a beating, with the lack of a meaningful way to brush. She unconsciously reached for her mouth as she thought about teeth.

Claude reached into his knapsack, "Would you like an apple?" he asked softly, holding a small green apple toward Barbara Jean.

Barbara Jean looked at her mother. "Go ahead, baby, it's okay," Erma said to her child with a nod. She then turned toward the man, "I'm Erma Owen. This here's Barbara Jean."

"It's nice to meet ya, Ma'am," Claude said with a nod, taking his hat off. "Nice to meet you, too, Missy," he said with a smile toward the child. Barbara Jean just stared back at him as she struggled to bite down on the apple.

Claude sensed her struggle and took a small pocketknife from his front pants pocket. "Here, maybe I can help you." He held out his hand,

and the young girl put the apple in it. He began to slice off small pieces and handed them to her. She took them and quickly started eating them. She was wolfing them down as fast as he could slice them.

"Whoa!" he said with a chuckle. "You better slow down!" then looking at Erma, "She's pretty hungry, eh?"

"She is," Erma agreed. "I think she's going through a growth spurt. And there ain't been much to eat."

Claude continued to feed the child as Erma watched. "So, what's your story?" Claude asked Erma with a questioning glance.

Erma shared her sad story up to that point. "And, where in California ya headed?" Claude asked once Erma's story had been conveyed.

"San Bernardino,"

"Ah, good ole San Berdoo. And you think you will find Clay there?"

"I do. He sent my sister a telegram telling her where he is."

Barbara Jean finished eating the apple and came over and sat on Erma's lap. Erma was sitting on a short crate while Claude stood looking down on them. He moved a second crate over and sat.

"Whew, that feels good. Been walking quite a way. Was sure glad when I came across the train yard. Thankfully, it was headin to California."

"Where you from, Claude?" Erma asked quietly.

"Oh, here and about. Most recently was in Phoenix. Not much there though, so I thought I would head out to California."

The talk slowed down as the two found little to discuss after the basics. Erma yawned. "I reckon I'm gonna take my little un back over yonder to try and get some sleep.

"You do that. I may do the same.'

Unbroken Hope

Erma carried the child to a corner. There was nothing soft to lie on, so she tried to get comfortable on the wooden floor of the boxcar. She used her knapsack as a pillow and rested Barbara Jean's head on her chest. The child barely moved as she snored softly. Erma, herself, was soon fast asleep.

As the train chugged along, Erma was gently rocked into a deep slumber, when suddenly the train lurched, causing Erma to bolt straight upright. "Wha?" she mumbled. She looked around. At some point, Barbara Jean had moved a short distance away and still lay asleep with her back to her.

She then looked over and discovered Claude was sitting on the floor a foot or so away, just staring at her.

"What're you doing?" Erma asked indignantly.

"Just looking at you."

"And why would you be doing that?"

"Cuz, I like the way you look."

Erma was starting to get the heebie-jeebies. "Well, just stop it! And move away. Over there." She waved the man back.

"Okay, okay. I can take a hint." Claude said as he moved back to his seat on the crate. But he continued to stare. He looked over at the sleeping child. "She's pretty tired."

"Yes, she is. This has been hard on her." Erma was now nervous at the unwanted attention Claude was paying her.

Claude moved back down to the floor. He moved so close that Erma could smell his breath. Surprisingly, it smelled like mint.

"You sure have pretty eyes, Erma. Kinda the color of the sky."

"Thanks," Erma didn't want to offer him anything more.

Claude reached out and brushed her cheek. "My gosh, your skin is soft."

Erma shuddered, "Please don't do that."

"Do what?"

"Touch me."

"Oh, I think you might like a little touch now and again," Claude said as he rubbed the top of her arm. "Don't that feel good?"

Erma pulled her arm away and slid backward. "Please don't." She looked over at the sleeping child, wanting her to wake up to provide a needed distraction, and at the same time, praying she'd stay asleep so she would not witness what Erma was fearful would happen next.

Claude slid on the floor toward her. "Now don't do that, I ain't gonna hurt ya." He quickly grabbed Erma's arm and forcibly pulled her toward himself. He simultaneously grabbed her left breast and gave it a firm squeeze.

"Owww!" Erma said, "Stop it. That hurt!" She tried to move further, but her back was up against tall cargo boxes.

Claude leaned into her and hissed. "How's about a little kiss. We're going to be in here for a while, might as well make the time go by a little faster."

Erma shook her head from side to side, "Nooo," she whispered. "Please just let me be."

"Hmm," He leaned in and licked her neck. "Don't think so."

Erma glanced nervously at her daughter and made a split-second decision to try to save her from a frightening experience. Erma remembered what Roy Raleigh had told her about the difference between hobos and bums, and Claude was no hobo...just a bottom-feedin bum.

Erma said, "Ok, I can see you're not gonna take no for an answer. Can we at least move away from my daughter, so we don't scare her?"

Claude jumped to his feet and dragged Erma up with him. "Les go back there," he said, motioning to the far side of the car. "There's room back behind them crates."

Unbroken Hope

Erma's mind was whirling as she tried to come up with some way to extricate herself from the situation.

Just then, the car took a gigantic lurch, rocking the floor and knocking Claude's legs out from under him. Erma pushed him, and he hit his head on the corner of a crate. It was enough to stun him, but it didn't knock him out.

He shook his head, trying to clear it. And Erma stomped on the side of it as hard as she could. He slumped to the floor.

Erma bent over to see if he was still breathing. He was. Now what was she to do? Thinking fast, she looked around for something to tie him up with. There was no rope or anything else that would work. Then a brainstorm hit. She struggled to turn him over. Fishing in his pocket, she came out with the pocketknife. Opening it, she felt its sharpness. This will do, she thought.

She went to work cutting long strips from Claude's pants. Soon, she had sturdy strips that she used to hog tie him. There, she thought, that should hold him.

"Wha y doin, Mama?"

She whirled to see her child standing behind her.

"Shhh, baby. He's a bad man, and I tied him up so he couldn't get at us."

She grabbed the child and settled down on the floor, holding her, waiting for Claude to awaken.

It didn't take long.

He struggled awake not realizing what was going on. He worked at the bindings. "Woman!!" he roared. "You need to let me go! Now!"

"Ain't happenin," Erma said quietly. Barbara Jean, scared, began to cry. Erma touched her arm to reassure her.

"I said now!" He continued to work at the bindings. But they weren't budging, and the harder he struggled, the madder he got. "Goddam it!"

"You need to just be quiet. Your fuss is gonna get us caught, if you ain't careful."

"You think I give two shits about that, right now?"

"I figure we got a couple more hours till we make San Bernardino. We'll get off there, and then you can be on your way."

"I'll kill you for this, bitch!"

"I'm sure you will," Erma responded sarcastically.

Erma was good to her word. She and Barbara Jean got off the train as soon as it hit the train yard. She left Claude hog-tied. Hopefully, someone would find him eventually. She just hoped it would be before he died of thirst and hunger.

Chapter 32

The work had been hard. The crew was short one man since Clay had died. So, Archie had to step up the pace. The sweat poured off him. He stopped to mop his brow and squinted into the sun. Up the road a car was coming, a plume of dust dragging out behind it.

"Looks like we might have company," Archie shouted to no one in particular.

He walked over to Tompkins and Ralph, and the threesome watched as the car pulled into the front yard. A woman and a small child exited the car. She leaned back to say something through the driver's window.

"This has to be Erma," Archie said. "You mind if I go see to her?"

Tompkins nodded.

"You're Erma," Archie said matter-of-factly, as he cautiously approached her.

The woman nodded. "I am, and this here is Barbara Jean."

"I'm Archie," he said, as he crumpled his hat in wringing hands.

The woman looked around. "Clay's here... ain't he?"

Archie was struck dumb.

"Yes, he was here," Archie said as he saw Mrs. Burkey coming toward Erma. Mrs. Burkey was a stout woman of about fifty years. Her gray hair was tied back in a ponytail, and she wore a house dress covered by a print apron.

Barbara Jean stared at her, speechless.

"I'm Judith Burkey" she said, holding her hand out to shake. "My husband and I own this place."

"OK," Erma said as she reached out to grasp Mrs. Burkey's hand. "I'm Erma Stanley. That is my daughter, Barbara Jean." Even though Clay and she were not husband and wife, Erma felt it best not to disclose that. "You said he was here. Where is he now?"

Mrs. Burkey examined Erma's face, trying to see how well she would take the news.

"I'm afraid there is no easy way to say this. Clay died. Day before yesterday."

"Wha?" Erma stammered. The world began to spin, and she felt herself losing grip on reality. She swooned, and Archie was there to catch her.

"Bring her inside, Archie."

"Yessum."

Archie swung the woman into his arms as Mrs. Burkey took Barbara Jean by the hand. She led the procession up the steps and into the house.

"Lay her down on the sofa, Archie. Then you can go."

Archie complied and backed out of the room. Mrs. Burkey disappeared in the kitchen as Barbara Jean sat quietly in an overstuffed chair. Mrs. Burkey quickly returned with a glass of water for Erma and a rather large cookie for her daughter.

"You like cookies, Barbara Jean?" The girl nodded, took it, and started eating greedily.

Mrs. Burkey sat and waited for Erma to come around. Slowly, Erma opened her eyes and sat up.

"Here, drink this," the woman said, handing the glass toward Erma. "It will do you good."

"Thank you," Erma said, taking the glass and taking several sips. She looked over at Barbara Jean, who was nibbling on her cookie but not missing a thing.

Unbroken Hope

"It was a terrible accident. The boys were trying to pull a stump up, and the chain got away from them and hit Clay in the head. They rushed him to the hospital, but he didn't make it," she said bluntly, and then added as an afterthought, "....sadly."

Erma quietly weighed this. She didn't say a word.

"Clay had told us that you were coming."

"Mm hm," was all Erma could muster. Tears slowly streamed down her cheeks. She began to shake and then burst into sobs and then wails. She tried desperately to hold back the tide of emotions. Her daughter, half-eaten cookie in hand, eased over and wrapped her arm around Erma's leg. Erma reached down, gently rested her hand on the girl's head, and began to slowly rub it.

Mrs. Burkey stepped toward Erma and sat down. She patted her arm. Erma fell into an embrace with the comforting woman. The two stayed put for several minutes with tears streaming down two sets of cheeks, and one woman wailing.

Slowly, the weeping began to subside.

"Where's Clay's body?" Erma meekly asked.

"I expect he's still at the hospital."

"Do you think I can see 'im?

"I don't see why not. We can give you a ride to the hospital. By the way, how did you get here?"

"The old-fashioned way," Erma said, making a fist and extending her thumb and motioning in the universal hitchhiking sign.

Mrs. Burkey chuckled. "Now, let's get you down to the hospital. Leave Barbara Jean here, I'll get Missy, my housemaid, to watch after her."

The drive to Ramona Hospital was uneventful. Erma sat silently, staring out the window as Mrs. Burkey drove a fairly new Ford sedan.

As they pulled into the parking lot, the hospital stood before them. A white stucco building with an orange Spanish barrel tile roof. It didn't look particularly big.

"This is the only hospital we got," Mrs. Burkey said. "And darn lucky we have it. Bank took it over in thirty-two. Bunch of doctors formed the Ramona Hospital Association, donating over $40,000 to buy the hospital back from the bank. And here she stands. Only hospital for many miles. We're lucky we live pretty close."

"Though I suppose it didn't do poor Clay any good," Erma added.

"No, no, it didn't." Mrs. Burkey replied sadly.

The two women were greeted at the front desk by a stern-looking nurse in a white uniform, her starched nurse's cap perched on her head.

"May I help you?"

"I'm Judith Burkey from over at Burkey Farms. We brought in a man who was injured a few days ago. He died on the way here. We wanted to know if you still had his body?"

Erma shivered when she heard the word "died".

"I remember. I think he was taken to the county coroner at the sheriff's office. Let me check. What was his name?"

"Clay Stanley."

She nodded, then stood up and walked down the hall.

"I'll be right back," she shouted over her shoulder.

She was gone about ten minutes, which seemed like hours to Erma.

"Yep. They took him over to the coroner. Let me see if he's still there."

She looked at a chart and quickly found the number. She dialed. "Hey, Joe. Lilly over at Ramona."

She paused to listen, "Oh. I'm doing fine."

"You still have a Clay Stanley over there."

Again, she listened as she uh-huhed at several different places in the conversation.

"Ok, thanks, Joe." And hung up.

"He's been buried."

"What!!!" Erma exclaimed. "So soon!

"Yes, ma'am. Sorry. Joe said they had no room, so he was interred this morning.

"You have to be kidding. How do I even know if it's Clay?"

"Joe did say they kept some of his personal effects. Maybe you can tell from them?"

"Come on, hon. I'll take her to the coroner's office," Mrs. Burkey said, as she gently guided Erma to the door. "The coroner's office is just down the street.

The walk to the coroner's office had been short. Erma collected Clay's effects, and they confirmed that it was indeed *really* him and that he was *really* dead. This led them to the local cemetery, where they found his grave marked with a temporary headstone. It only had his name and date of death, but not his date of birth.

Erma threw herself to the ground, grabbing the little wooden marker. "Oh, Clay!" was all she could say. She felt like bawling. Screaming to the sky at a deaf God. But she was so bone weary, nothing became of it. She just shrank down and hugged the marker.

Soon, Mrs. Burkey set her hand on her shoulder. "Come on now, dear, it's time to go."

On the ride home, Erma sat quietly. Mrs. Burkey left her to ride in silence.

When they got back to the farm, Erma was escorted to a bed where she promptly fell asleep on top of the covers.

Chapter 33

It was mild, and the hills of California wore their coat of green as if the rain had helped them forgive years of drought. In much of the central valley, many of the orchards stood with fruit heavy and ripe, the workers bent low, their hands finding the earth in steady rhythm, like a song that had no words. It was a land built for peace, it seemed - a land of men who lived in sunlight, and though the dust of the past still clung to the corners of the cities, the sunlight had a way of making it all look new, as if the land itself had a kind of amnesia.

In the towns - Salinas, Fresno, Santa Maria - the people went about their days without much thought to what was beyond their hills, beyond their roads. The newspapers, the radios, and the dusty sidewalks were filled with the hum of things that mattered to them: the prices of tomatoes, the war of words between the governor and the legislature, the struggles of the unions trying to keep the factories fair. There were whispers about strikes, about people losing their homes, but it was the kind of worry that could be washed away by a cool breeze or a sweet summer evening.

No one paid too much attention to Europe. It was just a place on the other side of the world, a place where strange men in strange uniforms talked in strange tongues, and what did that have to do with the land of plenty?

Yet, even as the people went about their lives - hauling bushels of peaches to the packing houses or gathering eggs from the chickens - there was *something* in the air, a tension, a vibration too subtle to grasp but there nonetheless. It wasn't in the eyes of the men who sweated in the fields, but in the way they looked at each other, in the way they talked about the coming harvest or the price of grain. It was the sound of a thing that was coming, something that they couldn't name, but could sense. For in the flickering shadows of their calm, distant lives, there was the muffled thunder of Europe - a storm that no one in California cared to hear.

When the radio cracked and hissed in the corner of a diner, a man would pause, looking up as the voices from a faraway place drifted in, but his hands never stopped working the till, never stopped stirring the pot of stew. The voices would talk of Hitler, of Mussolini, of men marching across borders, of planes in the sky that would drop bombs on cities, of the slow tightening of a noose. But none of the men in the room cared too much. The only war they knew was the one between the dust and the rain. The only conflict that mattered was whether the crops would yield, whether the water would stay, or whether the land would continue to provide.

The women, too, moved as though nothing could touch them. They hung their clothes on the lines and looked out toward the hills, where the breeze was kind, where the soil was rich, and where nothing could seem to go wrong. The days were spent on chores, on gossip, on the small happenings that filled up the space between dawn and dusk. They'd listen to the radio sometimes, too, and heard the names of countries they couldn't place, or the sound of air sirens over cities they would never visit, but they were just words, like a song played in a foreign tongue. They never bothered to ask the questions that rose in the back of their minds, because they were too busy with the things that had to be done now.

But if you listened close enough, really close, you could hear the deep hum beneath the everyday noise. You could hear the shuffle of German soldiers' boots marching, the soft sound of planes cutting through the sky. It was in the radio broadcasts that people would leave

Unbroken Hope

on for background noise, as much a part of the air as the fog rolling in from the ocean, or the buzz of bees over wildflowers. There were talks of soldiers, of barricades, of borders closing like locked doors. And yet, none of it felt real to the men working in California. It was just a faraway thing,

They had learned, through all their years, that a man only needed to know what was in his hands, what was in his life, for everything else was out of reach. The earth gave, and it took, but in the end, it was all a man or a woman could do to keep their balance.

And yet, if they had listened closer, they might have heard the fire creeping ever nearer - quiet, at first, like the shadow of a storm on a hot afternoon, a thing that couldn't be named, but could still be felt in the air. And though they didn't know it yet, the world they had built would be rocked by a storm that had been brewing long before they had learned to listen. But for now, the air was sweet, the land was still golden, and the people of California went about their lives, unaware.

And they had their own problems.

Chapter 34

Almost three years had passed. Barbara Jean shot up like corn in a warm Nebraska field. The Burkeys had been kind to Erma and her child. They allowed her to stay on, and she helped run the farm. She had grown up on a farm and so she knew that hard-scrabble way of life. She never shirked a job and, in fact, had come up with several ideas to streamline the operation. Barbara Jean liked to feed the chickens and was a happy child.

Erma had kept her sister, Mamie, informed of what was going on in California. In her weekly letters, she had urged her and Jimmie to join them. But they had declined, saying things were turning around on the farm. They had their first real crop in years, and it looked like things were getting better.

Erma also wrote Trudy in Williams, Arizona, on a regular basis. They formed as tight a friendship as two women could through the mail.

Archie, who was just fourteen when he and Clay had come to the farm, was allowed to stay on as well. He developed into a good hand and earned his keep. Mrs. Burkey had taken a shine to the young man.

Mrs. Burkey, the name Erma called her when they first met, evolved into Judith and then finally Judy. Barbara Jean looked up to her as the grandmother she never had. She learned to call her Gammy. Slowly, the mother and child felt as if they were an important part of the family.

Mr. Burkey, who became Clem, was a man of few words. His gruff exterior always collapsed in on itself whenever he laid eyes on Barbara Jean.

The Burkeys were without children. Erma had learned that Judy had lost three children in miscarriages, and then, finally, she failed to conceive entirely. The Burkeys looked upon Erma and Barbara Jean as the child and grandchild they never had.

Erma and Judy sat on the front porch, sipping water. It was one of the short breaks they took throughout the day. Erma marveled at the California weather. She watched Barbara Jean play in the yard.

"She sure is big for a six-year-old," Judy commented.

"Ya think?" Erma replied.

Judy chuckled, "Well, I don't really know. I don't have anything to compare her to!"

The two women sat companionably for a while, and then Judy offered, "She should be starting kindergarten in the fall."

"I know," Erma replied. "I'm not sure how she'll take to it."

"She'll be fine," Judy said. "We should get her enrolled next week."

The women went back to their sitting, not a word between them until Erma finally said, "Vince is coming over later. That all right?"

"Sure it is, hon. You know we like Vince."

Erma thought back on how she and Vince had met.

Vince was Vincent Rose. Erma had met him six months ago. He had been looking at a package of spinach seed at the local feed store when he asked Erma about it.

'You know anythin 'bout grown spinach?" he had said with a deep voice. Then with a laugh, "I ain't much of a farmer!"

Erma had taken the package of seed and showed him the back of the bag.

"The good news is it says here all you need to know!" Erma had replied and then read from the package, "Spinach plants form a deep taproot; for best growth, loosen the soil at least 1 foot deep before planting. Spinach seed doesn't store well, so buy fresh seeds every year.

Unbroken Hope

Sow them one-half inch deep and two inches apart in beds or rows. If the weather isn't extremely cold, seeds will germinate in five to nine days."

"Well, that doesn't sound too bad," Vince had said with a smile. "Thanks. Name is Vince Rose." It came with a tip of his dirty straw hat. He was dressed in bib overalls, but he didn't look like he belonged in them. It seemed to Erma that he looked more like a banker or a lawyer.

"I'm Erma Owen. It is nice to meet you."

"Where ya from, Erma?"

"Near Oklahoma City. Came out here like just about everyone else!"

"I'm from Colorado."

"Colorado! I ain't run into no one from Colorado!" Erma squealed.

Vince laughed in a good-natured way. Erma liked his dimples. His hair was hidden by his hat, but his green eyes pierced into her heart. If she hadn't known better, she would have thought it was love at first sight.

Vince must have felt the same. He looked down and then shyly asked, "You wouldn't mind ah having a cup of coffee with me, would ya, Erma?"

"Well, no, I wouldn't mind that at all."

And so, that was how it all started. Coffee led to dates. Vince took to Barbara Jean right from the get-go. Said he had always wanted a little girl. Soon, the three of them were going on picnics or just hanging around on the Burkey Farm.

"Here he comes, now," Judy said, pulling Erma out of her thoughts.

Erma looked up, and she could see Vince's black Chevy barreling up the dirt road with a giant plume of dust trailing behind. Pulling up, he climbed out of the truck, slamming the car door behind him.

"Hey, Judy!" he said with a smile, as he jumped up the stairs and onto the porch.

"Hey, yourself, Vince," Judy replied good-naturedly.

He moved over to Erma and put his hands on her knees, "Hey to you too, beautiful." He said, giving her a peck on the cheek.

"Vince! Vince! I missed you, too!"

Vince whirled to see Barbara Jean running at a full gallop toward him. She leapt into his arms.

"I missed you, too, punkin." She kissed him full on the mouth. "Wow! That was quite a kiss. I guess you did miss me!"

It warmed Erma's heart to see her child reacting so positively to this man. Barbara Jean had no recollection of Clay, which Erma thought was a good thing. Afterall he was not her father. Although Judy never knew the truth. She assumed that Clay had been Erma's husband and Barbara was their daughter. She had never asked, and Erma didn't volunteer anything. Vince also only knew that Clay had died, leaving Erma with a small child.

"Say, Erma," Vince said as he plopped down next to her. "I got something to ask ya."

"And that is?"

"Well, I got some good news first. I got a job in Los Angeles as an auto mechanic. A buddy of mine, who has been out there for a while, wrote me this letter about the job."

"That is good news, Vince," Erma replied warily as she read the letter. "So, what's the question?"

"Will you marry me?"

Unbroken Hope

Judy's hand flew to her mouth as she leaned back in shock. Erma looked at Judy and then back at Vince and then down at Barbara Jean and then back at Vince and then back at Judy.

"Don't look at me," Judy said with a laugh.

"Vince, what brought all this on?" Erma asked in a curious tone.

"Oh, I don't know. Just seemed like the time was right, and I wanted Judy to hear it along with Barbara Jean, so there would be witnesses to it as I ain't got no ring."

Erma sat back, stunned, her hand to her chest. She was speechless.

"Well, waddya say?" Vince asked anxiously.

Erma looked again at Judy, who nodded gently at her.

'Well, I say...YES!" Erma grabbed Vince by the neck and pulled him in for a kiss.

Vince swept her up in a hug and kissed her back. Judy leaned back and laughed. Barbara Jean couldn't figure out what all the excitement was about.

"What is it, Mama?"

Erma scooped the girl up. "Vince here is gonna be yor Daddy!"

Erma stood at the window of Judy's living room, staring out at the vast horizon. The sun was beginning to dip below the skyline, casting long shadows across the street. Her hands were tightly clasped in front of her, a mix of excitement and fear swirling in her chest. The proposal from Vince still echoed in her mind. He had asked her to marry him, to build a life with him in Los Angeles. It was everything she had ever wanted. Yet, now she had to face the painful reality of leaving Judy and everything that had been her anchor for so long.

"Mom, are you okay?" Barbara Jean's soft voice broke through Erma's thoughts. The young girl was standing in the doorway, her wide blue eyes filled with concern. Erma forced a smile, wiping away a stray tear.

"I'm fine, sweetie. Just thinking."

"About Vince?" Barbara Jean asked, taking a cautious step forward.

Erma nodded, swallowing the lump in her throat. She had promised her daughter they would stay with Judy for as long as they needed, and yet here she was, about to leave. To start fresh with Vince. The thought both exhilarated and scared her.

"Mama," Barbara Jean said again, "Are we really going to Los Angeles?"

Erma turned to face her daughter, kneeling down so they were eye to eye. "Yes, darling. We are. Vince got a job at an auto garage, and we're going to go with him. We'll have a new home, new adventures. All of us."

Barbara Jean bit her lip, clearly trying to process the news. "But... what about Gammy?"

The mention of Judy's name made Erma's heart ache. Judy had been more than just a friend to her. She had been a lifeline when everything else in Erma's life had felt uncertain. And now, she would be the one left behind.

Erma pulled the girl into a tight hug. "I know it's hard, sweetheart. I know. But Gammy will always be part of our family. We'll come back to visit, and we'll write. You'll see her again. We ain't moving to the moon!"

Barbara Jean nodded against her mother's shoulder, but Erma could feel the hesitation, the sadness settling in.

Erma heard some footsteps and turned to see Judy standing in the doorway from the kitchen, her face lighting up with a smile as soon as she saw Erma. But the joy faded slightly. Erma could see the unspoken question in Judy's eyes. She knew something was up.

"Erma?" Judy's voice was soft, concerned. "Is everything okay?"

Erma stepped back, gesturing for Judy to come in.

"Can we talk?" Erma asked quietly.

Judy came into the living room, where Barbara Jean was now sitting on the couch. The girl seemed content, but Erma could see her eyes darting between the two women, sensing the tension in the room.

Erma took a deep breath before speaking, her voice barely above a whisper. "Judy, I'm scared of leavin you an Clem."

Judy froze, her eyes widening. "What?"

Erma nodded, her gaze falling to the floor. "Well, we *are* moving to Los Angeles. After everythin you done for us, it seems like a mighty poor way to pay ya'll back."

The words hung in the air like a weight, and Erma could feel the tears start to well up in her eyes. She didn't want to hurt Judy. She couldn't imagine her life without her, but this was a chance for something new, something better for Barbara Jean. And yet, leaving Judy felt like leaving a piece of her heart behind.

Judy's eyes glistened with unshed tears as she stepped closer. With her voice trembling, she reached out and embraced Erma. "Erma…I am so happy for you. And I can't imagine this place without you. But…"

Erma felt a sob rising in her chest, but she fought it back. She stepped forward, reaching out to take Judy's hands in hers. "I know, Judy. I know. But Vince and I… we've been through so much. And he wants us to be with him. I don't know what else to do. It's what's best for us. For Barbara. You see that, don't ya?"

Judy's hands tightened around Erma's, but her voice was barely a whisper. "I do. I know it's what's best for you. But it's so hard. I love you, Erma. And I love Barbara Jean. I've watched you both grow, and I don't know how I'll let go."

Erma's tears finally broke free, but she quickly wiped them away. "I don't want to let go, either. But we're not disappearing. We'll be back to visit, and you can come see us too!, You're always gonna be part of our family. Nothing changes that. I will never, ever be able to repay you for all the kindness you have shown us. You literally saved my life."

Judy nodded, but the sadness in her eyes was unmistakable. She pulled Erma into another hug, holding her tightly as if to keep her close for just a moment longer. "Erma, it was our pleasure. I'll miss you so much," she whispered.

"I'll miss you too, more than words can say," Erma replied, her voice muffled against Judy's shoulder. "But you're always going to be with me, Judy. Always."

Barbara Jean stood up slowly, walking over to where the two women were hugging. She reached up, tugging on Judy's sleeve. "Gammy," she said softly, "You can still come visit us, right? And we can send you postcards and pictures?"

Judy smiled through her tears, kneeling down to pull Barbara into her arms. "Of course, sweetheart. I'll come visit as often as I can. And I'll never stop thinking about you."

The three of them stood there, wrapped in a bittersweet moment of love and loss. For Erma, the future was uncertain, but she knew one thing for sure: no matter where she went, Judy would always be a part of her life, a part of her heart.

The last of the boxes were in - Erma's tattered recipe books, that she had collected over the past few years, tied up with string, Vince's

Unbroken Hope

guitar with its cracked neck, and a couple of suitcases that had seen better years. Clem offered his hand to Vince, but Vince pulled him in for a hug. The kind men don't usually do unless it's goodbye or someone's just died. Biting back tears, Vince climbed behind the wheel of the Chevy. The truck's door creaked shut, heavy with more than just weight. Dust rose as Vince gave it a final slam. Morning light spilled over the flat fields behind Judy and Clem's house, turning everything gold, like it wanted to slow the moment down.

Erma stood off to the side, arms wrapped around Barbara Jean, who clung to her with sleepy eyes and jelly-stained fingers. The child had tucked her favorite stuffed bear under one arm, already missing the porch swing and the smell of cookies from Gammy's kitchen.

"You drive safe now," Clem said, voice gravel-thick. "Ain't nothing in L.A. worth more than your lives."

"We'll be alright," Vince said quietly.

"You're very good people," Judy said, her voice trembling. She reached for Erma, arms open wide, and they embraced like sisters at a train station during war. "You write. I mean it, Erma. Don't leave me wondering."

"I will," Erma whispered. "I'll send pictures of Barbara Jean when we get settled."

The little girl turned to Judy, eyes big and uncertain. "Will you tell the chickens I said bye, Gammy?"

Judy laughed through her tears and bent down to kiss the child's forehead. "Of course, sweetheart. They'll miss you something fierce!"

Erma looked up at the sky - blue and cloudless, like it was mocking her - and then to Vince, who gave a small nod. It was time. She scooped Barbara Jean into her arms, held her tight, "Durn," she said, "she's getting so heavy. I won't be able to do that much longer!" Judy laughed as Erma awkwardly climbed into the cab beside Vince.

The engine groaned, coughed, and then turned over. Judy and Clem stood in the gravel, waving, their hands small in the rearview mirror as the truck rattled away.

No one spoke for a while. The road stretched long and open ahead, lined with sun-bleached grass and the occasional lone tree. Vince reached over and found Erma's hand, squeezing it just once.

"Los Angeles," he said, mostly to himself.

"Los Angeles," she echoed, her voice soft and unsure.

And behind them, the dust settled on the gravel drive, covering the footprints they'd left behind.

CHAPTER 35

Vince sat on the couch, his sleeves rolled up, a cigarette lazily dangling from his fingers, as he read the newspaper. The muffled sounds of honking cars and bustling streets could be heard just beyond their window, a reminder of the lively pulse of Los Angeles. Despite the noise, the apartment felt like a sanctuary, with the three of them nestled in their own little world.

Erma, humming a tune under her breath, was bustling in the kitchen. The scent of a roast cooking in the oven filled the air, rich and comforting. Barbara Jean was playing in the next room, her giggles occasionally rising above the clink of dishes, as Erma prepared dinner. They'd settled into a rhythm in their new life here. The tension that had once gripped them, during the early months of their move to Los Angeles, had faded. It was replaced by something that felt like peace - something they had always longed for, but never quite found until now.

They had moved to Los Angeles about eight months before. Vince's job as a mechanic working on cars and trucks paid well and was a good job. Erma had missed the Burkeys, but she made good on her promise and wrote Judy faithfully - a letter per week. Judy had done the same. The letters helped fill the void of missing them.

"Vince," Erma called over her shoulder, her voice soft but clear. "Do you think we could go out tomorrow night? It's Friday? Maybe we can do something fun? Barbara Jean will be fine with Mrs. Keller next door."

Vince didn't answer right away, his gaze fixed on the newspaper, and his face deep in thought. The world outside their apartment had changed rapidly over the past few years. Years that they had not been there to see, but felt all the same. The economic strains of the Great Depression still lingered, though Los Angeles was finding its own rhythm again, a city of possibility and dreams. Vince had his work as a mechanic, and Erma kept busy with sewing and small jobs around the neighborhood. Still, with all the work and obligations, they had learned to carve out small moments of joy - like evenings out together, just the two of them.

He glanced up, meeting her gaze, and smiled. "Yeah, I think that sounds good. A night out wouldn't hurt. We deserve it. Maybe the movies? I think *Suspicion* is playing."

Erma grinned. She loved the movies, and she liked Alfred Hitchcock the best. And that Cary Grant was a dreamboat. She had been looking forward to seeing *Suspicion* ever since she saw it in the coming attractions. She wiped her hands on a dish towel before placing it on the counter. "I'll go over and talk to Mrs. Keller later to make sure she's okay with it. Barbara Jean seems to enjoy the time with her."

Vince nodded, then exhaled slowly, taking a drag from his cigarette.

Erma continued, "I still can't believe we're here sometimes," she said, almost to herself. "Feels like just yesterday we were scraping by with the Burkeys in San Bernardino, wondering if we'd ever find something better."

"I know," Vince replied, his voice warm with affection, as Erma joined him on the couch.

"But we have found something better. I still miss Judy and Clem, but we've got each other, and now we have a little girl who makes everything brighter." Erma glanced toward the sound of Barbara Jean's laughter and smiled softly.

Vince watched her for a moment, feeling a rush of gratitude. It wasn't always easy, the hustle of city life, but in these little moments, these quiet evenings at home, everything seemed to fall into place. His thoughts turned to the future - the life they were building here in Los Angeles. There was still uncertainty, still plenty of work to be done, but there was also hope. And for once, he could see the possibilities stretching out in front of him.

"I'm glad we did this," he said, his voice low, sincere. "Moving here. You, me, Barbara. It feels like… like we can breathe here."

Erma rested her head on his shoulder, her fingers lightly tracing the back of his hand. "We've got something good, Vince. We just have to hold on to it."

A few moments passed in comfortable silence, the only sound was the soft murmur of Barbara Jean's play. The city outside was full of noise, full of movement, but inside their apartment, there was a different kind of rhythm—one that felt like the beat of their own hearts, a steady, quiet pulse, in the midst of it all.

The evening would be theirs soon - just the two of them. But for now, they were content to sit together, side by side, surrounded by the life they'd built.

"Mama?"

Erma looked over at her daughter. It was hard to believe she had just turned seven a few months ago.

"Yes, honey," Erma replied absent-mindedly.

"What's the wedding gonna be like?"

Erma let out a long, exasperated sigh. "Oh, child, we've gone over that." She looked over at Vince, and the two just grinned,

Barbara Jean's blue eyes sparkled, her look eager to take in the answer.

"Now, I tole ya. The wedding ain't for another ten months, and it ain't gonna be much of one anyways. You and Vince and me are just gonna go down to the courthouse and get the justice of the peace to marry us."

"But why is it gonna be so long from now?"

"We're trying to save up some money and besides…it ain't that long," said Erma, reaching for a worn paper calendar sitting on the end table. "Well, we're planning on getting married next year on May 10th, 1942 - Mother's Day." She pointed to that Sunday and then turned the pages backward and counted the months. "One, two, three, four…see, only five months and that's not so long from today," she pointed to the date. "See here, this is today…"

"December 6th. 1941."

PART III
STORM'S ACOMIN'

"I speak in the name of the entire German people when I assure the world that we all share the honest wish to eliminate the enmity that brings far more costs than any possible benefits... It would be a wonderful thing for all of humanity if both peoples would renounce force against each other forever. The German people are ready to make such a pledge."
Adolf Hitler - 14th October 1933

"We shall not flag or fail. We shall go on to the end. We shall fight in France, we shall fight on the seas and oceans, we shall fight with growing confidence and growing strength in the air. We shall defend our island, whatever the cost may be. We shall fight on the beaches, we shall fight on the landing grounds, we shall fight in the fields and in the streets, we shall fight in the hills. We shall never surrender!"
Winston Churchill - 4th June 1940

Yesterday, December 7, 1941, a date which will live in infamy. The United States of America was suddenly and deliberately attacked by naval and air forces of the Empire of Japan."
Franklin D. Roosevelt – 8 December, 1941

Chapter 36

It had begun like a slow, creeping fog over a valley - hardly noticed at first, but unmistakable once it settled in. And like all things that grow, it bloomed quietly at the edges, soft and imperceptible, until it smothered the land in a grip too tight to slip away from. The world had heard the murmurs of a man, one whose name carried the scent of blood and fire, but they hadn't yet felt the full weight of what that name meant.

Across the fields and roads of Europe, where the soil had tasted war too many times before, the streets started to change. The people began to talk of a man who had sewn his words like thread into the minds of the desperate. This man, Adolph Hitler, did not come as a thunderstorm. No, he came as the slow, insidious whisper of a wind that promised the world would be better if only the broken pieces could be made whole again.

Battered and bruised by the war to end all wars, the war that had nearly torn it apart, Germany was ripe for such talk. The old scars had yet to heal, and the hunger, the poverty, the endless search for meaning, for power, for a way out - these things gnawed at the people, even as they stumbled into the present. They had lost their way, and in their haze, they reached for any hand, any voice, that would promise them something to believe in.

And Hitler's voice was like the sound of a bell in the distance - clear, ringing, and steady. It started in the shadow of Bavaria, with its bruised cities and fields of dust, where men and women, with empty eyes, turned to the man who would lead them. It was there that the march began - at first, only a trickle, but soon swelling like a tide. It wasn't the thunder of armies, but the stirring of thoughts and beliefs, that spread across the land.

Neighbors began to look at each other with new eyes. The air became thick with suspicion, with fear, and with the heady promise of something better. The Nazi banners - first a ripple, then a tide - rose up like an iron fist against the wind, sharp and unyielding. And while the rest of Europe watched from their windows, unsure of what to make of this new figure, the ground beneath their feet began to shift.

And in Japan, the men came down from the hills with calloused hands and sun-browned skin, their eyes shaded by the brims of their straw hats. They spoke little because the words had already been said too many times, and silence was easier to carry. In the village, the air smelled of miso and salt, and the rice was scant. It always was, lately.

But beyond the paddies and the fishing boats, in cities lit by electric wire and ambition, the drums had started. Not the kind made of skin and wood, but drums in the form of speeches, and steel, and rising smoke from factory chimneys. The government men wore fine uniforms with stiff collars, and they used words like destiny and empire. The farmers didn't understand those words, not really, but they knew how to bow low and say yes. You had to, if you wanted to keep your plot of land and your teeth.

Ships were built, and planes were tested, and in Tokyo, the papers told of glory and honor and the strength of the Yamato soul. But in the fishing villages, young boys disappeared into trains bound for the mainland, where they would learn how to shoot and how not to cry. Mothers wept into their sleeves, not loudly, because there was no use in noise.

The land had always asked much of its people, and now it asked for their sons.

Unbroken Hope

The shadows grew longer, and no one could be sure what would happen next. But all of them, in some quiet corner of their minds, knew that the march of the men was only the beginning of something much darker. The rumbling was out there, in the distance - something was coming. They could feel it, like the promise of a storm that would blot out the sun and drown them all in a flood they hadn't yet understood.

Chapter 37

Vince had always been the quiet, determined type, and now, as he stood in the Los Angeles County Courthouse, he felt a deep urgency that seemed to echo through the bustling halls. The air smelled of stale cigarette smoke and the faint scent of perfume worn by harried brides. Grooms looked like scared rabbits, all caught in hurried preparations, surprised by the whirlwind of war. Outside, the streets were alive with the noise of the city, but inside, there was only a sense of quiet anticipation - a moment suspended in time as the world outside shifted.

Erma, as always, was by his side. She had been a whirlwind herself in the last few weeks. Her mind constantly jumping from one thing to the next. Now, as she stood before him in the worn dress that had seen better days, she had the look of someone who had already been through too much. She wasn't worried about the wedding itself. She had long ago accepted the practicalities of life, of love, and survival. But even so, there was a kind of softness in her gaze as she glanced up at Vince, like she was holding her breath, not knowing exactly what was coming next.

Barbara Jean tugged at her mother's hand, her small face full of curiosity. The child was the one who had insisted they get married, after all. A notion sparked by a fleeting conversation, a fleeting hope of stability, before things inevitably changed. "We have to be a family, like other families," the child had said. And that was enough to push Vince and Erma into action. The war had come - something none of them could escape - and they both understood that there was no time for waiting. Their lives, and their daughter's, had already been touched by uncertainty. But this, at least, they could control.

Michael Wells

The judge, a weary man with a permanent frown, glanced at his watch, clearly impatient. He'd seen so many couples come in over the past three months, some of them with dreams, some with only desperation. This one, he thought, was one of the latter, but he couldn't be concerned with that.

"Do you take this woman…?" The judge's voice sounded distant, like it belonged to someone else entirely, not in the moment, but far away, in the future that none of them could predict. Vince said his "I do" quietly, and Erma followed suit.

Vince and Erma exchanged rings - Vince had barely enough money for them, and Erma had insisted on something simple, practical. The metal felt cold against her skin as she slipped it on.

Barbara Jean was too young to fully understand the weight of the moment, but she felt the change. She smiled up at them while clutching her bear, its little paw resting against her cheek. She was eager to be part of the ceremony, eager to have the family she always wanted…to be complete.

With a short, scribbling of a signature and a stamp on the marriage certificate, it was done.

They were married.

Vince kissed Erma lightly on the lips, his hand brushing against the back of her neck as if to reassure her that, despite the strange rush and tension of the day, they would be alright.

"Ready to go home?" he asked, his voice thick with the promise of something more than just survival.

Erma nodded, squeezing his hand tightly as she turned to Barbara Jean , the girl now clutching her side in excitement.

The courthouse doors opened, and they stepped into the warm Los Angeles sunlight, a brief moment of calm before the storm.

Unbroken Hope

What came next would be a challenge, no doubt - preparing for a world that was changing faster than they could understand. But they had each other as they walked into the unknown.

The front door creaked open, and Vince swept Erma up in his arms.

"Whoa, whatya doing!!" Erma squealed with delight as Barbara Jean put her little bear under her arm and began to jump up and down, laughing and clapping her hands.

"I'm carrying my bride across the threshold," Vince said proudly. Then to Barbara Jean, "It's a tradition, Barbara Jean." The girl continued to clap.

Vince stepped into the house and gently set Erma on her feet. She was smiling and stood on her toes and kissed him gently.

The house smelled faintly of baked goods and old wood - a modest, two-room flat tucked in an apartment building. It wasn't much, but for the first time, it was theirs as a family.

Erma set her purse on the sideboard and took a breath, her smile lingering as she looked around. A cake sat waiting on the kitchen table, squat and uneven, frosted with more hope than skill. "Mrs. Keller must've made it," Erma said. "How sweet! She musta got up early to beat the grocers' lines afore they sold out of sugar."

Barbara Jean padded to the table, her shoes tapping softly on the linoleum. "Is it really for us?" she asked, her voice a little awed.

Vince chuckled, dropping his coat on the chair. "All yours, little bird, but only if you promise to save us a slice."

Erma knelt beside her daughter, smoothing a strand of fine, blonde hair behind her ear. "We should light the candle. One candle's enough, isn't it, love?"

"One's plenty," Vince said, striking a match.

The flame flickered to life, casting a gentle glow over the room. The three of them stood in a quiet triangle around the cake, hands loosely clasped, the hush between them full of unsaid things.

"You should make a wish, Barbara Jean," Erma said softly.

The girl squinted at the candle. "Can I wish for something real?"

Erma nodded. "Always."

The girl closed her eyes tightly, lips moving in a whisper too faint to hear. When she opened them, she looked older somehow, as though the weight of the times had brushed her young face.

The candle went out in a soft puff.

They clapped, gently, the way people do when joy needs to be measured, when too much happiness feels like tempting fate.

After cake, came Vince's record player, and he fished out a Glenn Miller tune, the crackling static announcing its age. They danced - first Erma and Barbara Jean, twirling slowly around the table, then Vince lifted his daughter into his arms and swayed with her, her small fingers clasped around his neck like a locket. And then finally with his bride. They moved slowly to the romantic tune.

Outside, the streetlamps hummed, and somewhere a train sounded far off, its whistle carrying across the rooftops. A blackout curtain fluttered at the window, tugged by the January wind.

Erma danced, joy filling her heart.

She didn't say it, but she was thinking what they all were. War was coming. The world beyond their walls was tilting toward something vast and unkind. But tonight, they had a candle, a cake, a record on the player, and each other.

Unbroken Hope

And in the hush between songs, it was all she could hope for right now.

Weeks later, Erma sat at the kitchen table, her hands clasped around a cup of coffee that had long since gone cold. Outside, the wind was picking up, and the sky had that dull gray hue that seemed to hang over everything in times like this. Vince was at the table too but the air between them was thick with unspoken words. He had received his orders to report to the Induction station, but the sense of inevitability was already hanging over them. The letters, the whispered conversations with neighbors, the newsreels - all of it pointed to the same thing: Vince was on his way to war.

They hadn't spoken much about it. What was there to say? Vince had always been ready for this moment. He'd grown up hearing stories of the Great War, watching older men in their uniforms with a sense of reverence. But for Erma, it was different. It was all very real now, and the finality of it stung more than she had imagined.

Barbara Jean was playing with her toys in the living room, blissfully unaware of the gravity between the couple. Erma had tried to keep things normal for her, to keep the routines of their days intact, but inside, everything was churning, changing. She could barely look at Barbara Jean without thinking of the uncertainty ahead. What if Vince didn't come back? The thought, though unspoken, was an ever-present shadow that loomed over them.

Vince glanced over at Erma, his expression soft but distant. He was trying to stay strong for both of them, but Erma could see the weariness in his eyes. She knew he didn't want to leave. He'd never asked for this - none of them had. But it was the way of the world now. It was what they had to do.

"I'll be back, Erma," he said quietly, his voice low but firm. "I promise."

Erma knew he wasn't talking about coming back from the Induction Station. They had already been told he would be sent home for at least 21 days to clear up personal and business affairs. Then off he would go to a Reception Center and then after a few days be sent off to basic training.

Erma nodded, though doubt gnawed at her. Promises like that were hard to hold onto in times like these. But she didn't have the strength to argue or cry. She just nodded and tried to smile, the way she always did when she didn't know what else to do.

Barbara Jean came walking in, her little hands grasping at Vince's trousers. "Daddy, where you going?" she asked, looking up at him with wide, trusting eyes.

Vince leaned down to her level, brushing a lock of hair from her face. "I'm going to help with something very important, punkin. It's for everyone, so we can all be safe." He swept her up into a hug.

Erma's throat tightened at the innocence of her daughter's question. She couldn't bring herself to tell her the whole truth - not now. Maybe later, when the world had changed even more, when Barbara Jean was old enough to understand. But right now, all she could do was watch as Vince held his daughter close, his hand on her back as if he never wanted to let go.

That night, after their daughter had been tucked into bed, Erma and Vince sat together in the quiet of their home. The apartment, once filled with the sounds of daily life, now seemed too still, too empty. The ticking of the clock on the wall was the loudest sound in the room.

Unbroken Hope

"I don't want to leave you," Vince whispered, his voice breaking just a little. "I don't know what's coming, Erma. But I know I don't want to go."

"I know," Erma replied, her voice soft with its thick Oklahoma accent, full of the weight of her own fears. "I don't want ya to either."

The silence between them stretched, filled with the unspoken knowledge that this was the beginning of something neither of them could control. It was the beginning of a chapter they couldn't close, no matter how much they wished to. Erma thought of the days ahead, of the letters she might have to write, of the lonely nights without him. And the possibility - though she didn't dare speak it - that she might have to carry on without him.

But for now, all they had was this night. She reached out to take his hand, squeezing it tightly. She didn't know what the future held, but she would hold on to him for as long as she could.

Vince stood in the long line of men that snaked out the door of the dark grey building in downtown Los Angeles. The cool morning air carried the sharp scent of fresh rain, mixing with the smell of hot asphalt and exhaust fumes from the streetcars passing by. It was 1942, and the world was changing, rippling with the tremors of war. Vince adjusted the stiff collar of his brown jacket, feeling the weight of the moment settle on his shoulders.

He looked around at the men surrounding him, many of them much younger than he. The signs were everywhere: the posters plastered to lamp posts, the radio broadcasts, the headlines in every newspaper shouting about Pearl Harbor, about the Axis powers. And now, Vince was here, waiting with dozens of others, his name drawn from a long list of nervous and reluctant volunteers.

The Induction Station was a nondescript structure, with narrow windows that gave it a clinical feel. Inside, the air smelled of anxiety. There was a buzz of tense energy, the sounds of footsteps echoing off the tile floor, mingled with the murmurs of men trying to talk themselves into or out of what was about to happen. The walls were lined with posters urging them to *Do Your Duty* and *Help Defend Freedom*. In truth, Vince wasn't sure what he was defending yet, but his chest tightened every time he read those words.

"Name?" A sharp voice cut through the low hum of conversation.

Vince turned and saw a young man in his early thirties, wearing the crisp, dark green uniform of a military officer. His face was grim, eyes steady, scanning through the line of men standing before him. The officer's presence was authoritative, like a man who had seen a lot of things and was no longer fazed by the spectacle of young men being pulled from their civilian lives. He checked the list on his clipboard.

"Vincent Rose," Vince replied, trying to keep his voice from shaking. The officer glanced up, nodded once, and motioned for him to step forward.

"Go sit over there," the officer ordered, pointing toward a wooden bench lined up with rows others. The benches were in front of a thick wooden door at the back of the room. Vince moved obediently and sat, his heart hammering in his chest. Around him, the other men shuffled into place - some older, some younger, all of them looking just as unsure as he felt.

The room was filled with an odd mixture of people - blue-collar men in worn suits, teenagers still holding onto the remnants of boyhood, and older men with graying hair and calloused hands. Each had his own reason for being there, but all shared the same fate: they would soon be soldiers. The sharp clinking of boots against the floor added to the rhythm of the anxious silence that filled the space.

Vince glanced around at the facility. It was functional - nothing ornate or impressive, just a series of utilitarian spaces designed for speed and efficiency. The walls were painted a dull, institutional green, and the wooden benches creaked under the weight of the men sitting on them. The air felt heavy, as though even the building itself was aware of the monumental shift taking place within its walls.

He caught sight of the officers and sergeants moving through the crowd, barking orders, checking off names on clipboards, and directing the men to different areas. In the back, a group of nurses could be seen through an open door busily working, their white uniforms a stark contrast to the dusty green of the building's interior. The noise of their conversations, punctuated by the occasional cough or sneeze, filled the space.

"All right, step forward when your name's called," the officer at the front of the room said, holding a clipboard in his hands like a weapon. He looked over the gathered men with the practiced gaze of someone used to handling this kind of chaos.

His name was called.

Vince stood up and stepped toward the officer, his legs feeling unsteady as though he were walking through wet sand. The officer barely looked up from the clipboard as he motioned for Vince to follow him into a small, windowless room off to the side. The door clicked shut behind them.

Inside, the room lacked any warmth with its fluorescent lighting and metal desks. There were two other men already seated at desks, busy filling out forms. A tall, heavy-set man in glasses sat at a desk at the far end, motioning for Vince to sit in the chair across from him.

"Vincent Rose, huh?" The man's voice was calm, almost monotone, but there was a hardness behind it. "Age 36. Healthy?" He glanced down at the paperwork in front of him.

"Yes, sir." Vince nodded, swallowing dryly.

The man didn't look up, scribbling something on the paper. "Married?" he asked, his pen still moving rapidly across the sheet.

"Yes, sir."

"Any children?"

"One, sir."

"Religious preference?"

"Uh…Christian I guess?"

The man's eyes flicked to Vince's face for the first time. "You know you're going to be in the Army now. When we're done here, you will go home for no less than 21 days. You will receive your next orders there to report to a Reception Center. Then, Basic training. Then, Advanced Training . Then, Combat. You will be leaving your life here behind. You ready for that?"

Vince hesitated, his throat dry. "I guess I don't have much of a choice."

The man didn't respond immediately. Instead, he jotted down some notes, before looking up again. "It's not about choice, son. It's about duty. If you're here, you've already been enlisted. It's just a matter of paperwork now. But I'll tell you one thing: life as you know it is over. So don't waste time wondering about *what* could've been. What matters now is what you *do* next."

Vince nodded, though the words didn't quite settle in his mind yet. There were still so many questions he had, but he could feel them slipping away, drowned out by the overwhelming reality of what was happening.

Unbroken Hope

The man stood, signaling that the interview was over. "Head to the next room. They'll do your physical. We'll see if you make the cut."

Vince rose, his knees suddenly weak, but there was no turning back now. As he walked toward the door, he saw the faces of the other men - some nervous, some stoic, but all of them ready in their own way for whatever was coming next. The door to the physical examination room loomed ahead, and as Vince stepped through it, he knew he was no longer just a civilian from Los Angeles. He was something else now - something that belonged to a world in the process of being torn apart.

He was declared fit for service and sent on his way. Now it was time to wait.

Chapter 38

The days seemed to drag on, each one stretching into the next with the same heavy air of uncertainty. Vince stood by the window of their modest apartment, the curtains slightly pulled back, staring out at the barren streets. A faint rumble of distant trucks could be heard, the unmistakable hum of wartime machinery that had become a constant in their lives. But for all the noise outside, the silence within the walls of the house felt oppressive.

Three weeks had passed.

Three weeks of waiting, of not knowing, of constant tension that seemed to rise and fall like the tide. Erma and Vince had argued more in that time than they had in the years before. It wasn't because they didn't love each other - no, it was the stress, the unbearable pressure of the unknown, that pulled them apart.

"Vince," Erma's voice cracked the tension in the air, her hands wringing together as she stood at the kitchen table, glancing over the letter that had arrived that day. Vince had tried to ignore it, and then he stood looking down at it "Are you going to stand there all durned day, you ain't gonna at least purtend to look at this?" she continued.

He didn't respond right away, his mind too caught in the whirlpool of thoughts that never seemed to settle. Instead, he focused on the slivers of daylight that filtered through the window, each beam feeling like a reminder of the time they were wasting while waiting for the orders that could change everything.

"You cain't ignore this forever," Erma continued, the tension in her voice rising. "We need to know what's comin next. This... this being betwixt and between is drivin me crazy." Her accent grew thicker the more agitated she became.

Vince finally turned around, his face drawn and tired. "I'm not ignoring it, Erma," he said, his voice rough with exhaustion. "I'm just... I'm just waiting. What else can I do? I'm afraid of what's inside it."

Erma threw her hands up in frustration. "You ask what else you can do? What else?" She took a deep breath, trying to steady herself. "You cain stop actin like you're the only one who has to bear this. We're all waitin! We're all stuck in this damn purgatory together!"

A long silence fell between them. The kind of silence that had become all too familiar in the past few weeks. Vince clenched his fists at his sides. He knew Erma wasn't wrong. The pressure of not knowing, of waiting for the government's orders, had seeped into every corner of their lives. But it was easier for him to retreat into the quiet, to escape into his own thoughts, than to face the reality of their situation.

Erma sighed and turned her back to him. "I jus... I jus want this to be over. I want to know what's gonna to happen to us."

"Me too," Vince muttered under his breath.

Barbara Jean's voice, sweet and cheerful as always, broke the tension. "Mama? Daddy? Are you two fighting again?"

Erma turned, forcing a smile. "No, sweetie, just a little disagreement. Nothing to worry about."

Barbara Jean, with a curious mind and maturity beyond her years, looked between them with the careful observance of someone who had seen too much of this tension. She had learned early on to recognize the signs of when her parents were on the edge, but she also knew how to diffuse it, how to bring a moment of lightness to a dark situation.

She was thriving in school, as always. Her grades were excellent, and she had made several friends, though some of the kids taunted her. She did seem to understand that war was not just something happening far away, but something that seeped into the lives of everyone. She often wished she could go back to the days before the war, when life felt simpler, when their family was whole in a way that didn't feel so fragile.

"Maybe we can all take a walk," she suggested, trying to break through the tension. "It might help."

Vince's forehead wrinkled with concern, and Erma looked down at the letter on the table, a small, defeated sigh escaping her lips. "You're right," she said finally, her voice softening. "Maybe some air'll do us all some good."

"No, I've got a better idea," he said with a smile. "Let's go to the beach."

The sun was already rising warm over the edge of the city when Vince had said it - too casually, like he hadn't spent the morning pacing the kitchen tile in his socks.

"What?" Erma asked, surprised.

"Yeah, let's go to the beach," he said, flipping his keys into the air. "Huntington. Just for the day. What do you say?"

Erma raised an eyebrow. "The beach?"

"Yeah." He smiled too wide. "Why not?"

Barbara Jean squealed and clapped, already running to grab her sandals. Erma lingered for a beat, studying Vince like she could read the nerves underneath his grin, but she nodded. "Alright. Let's go."

The drive out felt like shedding something - city noise, shadows of phone calls that hadn't come, and the echo of things left unsaid. By the time they reached Huntington, the Pacific was gleaming like polished glass, and Vince felt something unclench inside him.

They set up near a rocky curve of the beach, where the sand was warm but not crowded. Barbara Jean darted between the surf and shore, chasing foam with her bare feet. Vince waded in after her, cold water shocking him awake, and let himself laugh - really laugh - for the first time in days. Erma laid out a blanket and read in the sun, glancing up now and then, smiling when she caught him watching.

They bought ice cream from a truck that rattled down the beach road and ate it with sticky fingers. Barbara's cheeks were pink from sun and laughter. Vince let the rhythm of waves and wind smooth him out, just for a while.

But as the sun dipped lower, casting long shadows over the shore, a familiar tightness returned to Vince's chest. The light changed - so did the air. Then he remembered. Orders. Instructions. A reason for all this waiting.

On the drive home, Barbara Jean fell asleep in the backseat, her hair crusted with salt and sand. Erma reached across and touched Vince's arm.

"You alright?"

He nodded, eyes on the road. "Just thinking."

But he wasn't. He was bracing.

When they got home, Vince went straight for the letter and opened it.

He read it silently, his lips moving but no words coming out.

"What does it say?" Erma asked urgently.

"I report to the Los Angeles Reception Center on Monday."

"Monday! That's only three days from now," Erma said in anguish.

Barbara Jean, eager to change the subject, began telling them about her day at school the day before. "We're studying history," she said, her eyes bright with enthusiasm. "Mr. Reed says that after the war, we'll all need to rebuild. He says that the next generation is going to have to do it. Does that mean me?"

Erma chuckled and nodded, though her mind wasn't fully on the conversation. "Well, not you by yourself. You're doin good in school, though, honey. You're strong. You'll be able to handle whatever comes next."

Vince gave her a quick, tight smile, grateful for her words. He looked down at the girl, the weight of his own thoughts lifting just a little. "We're all strong, kiddo. Stronger than we think."

As the conversation slowed, a rare moment of peace settled over them. It wouldn't last, of course. Nothing did these days. But for now, they could pretend. They could feel the warmth of each other's company.

And their daughter, though only a child, could feel it too. She knew that her parents would always find their way back to each other, even in the darkest moments. And in the meantime, she focused on what she could control: school, her few friends, and keeping herself together for her parents.

The waiting would continue, but at least, they had each other. And that was all she could ask for.

Chapter 39

Vince had spent most of the night staring at the ceiling, the hum of the city outside fading into a distant murmur as the weight of the day settled in. It wasn't just the fact that he was about to become a soldier; it was the uncertainty of it all.

He had read the letters from his friends who had gone before him, heard their half-laughing, half-grim stories of boot camp, of the testing of physical and mental strength, of the endless waiting. But that was all distant, other people's stories. Now, Vince was living it. Tomorrow, he would board a bus with other men like him - strangers now, but comrades soon enough - heading for the Reception Center in Los Angeles.

He checked his watch. 3:00 AM. The last thing his recruiter had told him still echoed in his ears. "Don't celebrate on the night before you leave. You'll want to be on your toes at the Reception Center. Tests, interviews. Get some sleep while you still can."

Vince's bag, which was simple and small, sat by the door. His razor, toothbrush, a change of underwear, and a few extra handkerchiefs were neatly tucked inside. No need for a trunk! The Army had its own way of doing things - no room for extra baggage. He'd taken that to heart.

With a long, slow breath, he finally closed his eyes, wishing he could shake the sense of unease that seemed to cling to him. But sleep didn't come easily, not when the world was about to change in such a big way. He reached over and touched Erma on the hip. She was sleeping soundly.

As the first light of dawn crept through the curtains, Vince got up from bed and dressed. Erma, who had been awake, sat up in bed and watched silently as he got ready. The small apartment felt heavier than it ever had before.

'You want some breakfast?" Erma asked softly.

"Nah," Vince replied. "Ain't hungry."

"Well, you're taking a sandwich," Erma said flatly and rose to fix it.

Vince stood by the door in the freshly pressed clothes he was wearing. The soft hum of the early morning air seemed to pause, as though it too recognized the gravity of the moment.

Erma stood beside Barbara Jean, her hand gently resting on her daughter's shoulder. The girl clutched her small stuffed bear to her chest, her wide eyes brimming with confusion and sorrow.

Vince kneeled down to her level, the corners of his mouth lifting in a bittersweet attempt at a smile. "I'll be back before you know it, punkin. You'll see," he said, his voice thick with emotion. His calloused hands gently smoothed her hair, but he couldn't stop the tremble in his fingertips.

Barbara Jean shook her head with a quiet sob. "Don't go, Daddy," she whispered, her voice barely audible. "Don't leave."

Erma's own tears threatened to fall, but she forced herself to stay composed for her daughter's sake, squeezing her little hand tightly. "He'll come back to us, sweetie," Erma said softly, her voice breaking despite her best efforts. "Yor daddy's strong, and he'll come back to us." She turned to Vince, her eyes pleading with him to reassure their daughter one last time.

Vince could only nod, unable to form words, his throat too tight. He pulled Barbara Jean into a hug, holding her close as if the weight of her tiny body was the only thing grounding him. His heart pounded in his chest, and for a brief moment, he wished he could stay. But he knew he wouldn't, he couldn't. It felt like nothing would ever feel normal or right again.

Duty called. And as much as it tore him apart, he knew he had to go.

"I love you," he whispered to both of them, the words carrying a weight he couldn't possibly describe. "Take care of each other. I'll be back before you know it."

Erma stepped forward, her arms wrapping around him for one final embrace. She buried her face in his shoulder, her tears soaking into his shirt. "Please, Vince... come back to us."

With shaky breath, Vince stepped back, his eyes meeting hers, full of unsaid promises. The door creaked open, and as he stepped into the cool morning air, the weight of leaving behind everything he loved settled heavily on his shoulders.

Barbara Jean watched as her father walked away, her little hand pressed to the glass of the window. Erma pulled her close, both of them standing in silence, the tears falling freely now as the man they loved disappeared into the dawn.

For a long moment, all they could hear was the sound of their own breathing, mingling with the distant echo of footsteps fading into the morning mist.

By mid-morning, Vince stood in a long line, the dull hum of the city now replaced by the buzz of a different kind of anticipation. His heart was pounding in his chest, not from fear but from the adrenaline of what was coming. The men around him looked equally tense, their expressions a mixture of excitement and dread.

"You packed light?" the man next to him asked, his voice cracking slightly as he adjusted his hat.

"Yeah," Vince replied, glancing down at the small duffel in his hand. "Just the essentials. Razor, toothbrush. Nothing extra."

"Good idea. They warned us about that," the man said, his hand twitching as he rubbed the back of his neck. "You don't want to be that guy with too much stuff, you know?"

Vince nodded. No one had told him exactly why, but the message was clear enough: the Army wasn't about personal preferences, about keeping the things that made you comfortable. It was about utility. Efficiency. Control. Somewhere deep down, Vince knew that the Army's job was to break you down and rebuild you into something else, something better, something tougher.

The line inched forward, and before long, they were at the double doors of the Reception Center. And a few moments later, they were inside. The sound of voices, orders being barked, and the shuffle of shoes on linoleum filled the air. A long row of bunks stretched out before them. For a brief moment, Vince couldn't help but think about how different this place looked from the photos he'd seen in the recruiting pamphlets. The photos were always clean, polished, full of pride and promise. The reality, though, was something else entirely different.

He stepped inside, the door slamming shut behind him with a finality that made his stomach tighten. The walls were stark, bare, and functional. There were no comforts here, no room for sentiment. A man next to him coughed, and Vince flinched, surprised at how quiet it seemed despite the bustle around them.

"Listen up, men!" a gruff voice called out from the front of the room. A short, stocky man in an olive drab uniform with sergeant stripes on his sleeve and a jaw like granite stood there, hands on his hips. "No privacy here. Not for you!. You'll eat, sleep, shit, and do everything else with all these men." He motioned to the crowded room.

The starkness of it hit Vince like a slap in the face. He'd been warned, sure, but nothing could have prepared him for the sheer lack of space, the absence of anything that resembled comfort or privacy.

"You'll get one uniform and boots here, they'll give you everything else you need when you get to Basic," the sergeant continued, "Just remember, you lose anything? You pay for it. Don't make me tell you twice."

"Remember, you're not in the civilian world anymore," the sergeant added, his tone almost pitying. "There's no room for personal stuff. Not until you prove you can handle it."

Vince was given a set of fatigues that didn't fit quite right, the seams loose around his chest, the trousers a little too short. He'd always been lanky, and no amount of tailoring could change that. They gave him boots too, scuffed but sturdy, and an old-fashioned razor kit that looked like it belonged in his grandfather's closet. Finally, they gave seven t-shirts, seven pairs of dark green socks, and seven pairs of boxer underwear.

It was a sobering reminder that this wasn't a choice anymore. It was the Army. The life he had left behind, the civilian life he thought he knew so well, had been replaced by something unfamiliar, cold, and regimented.

He was assigned a bunk and a footlocker. He was ordered to change his clothes and put the remainder of his belongings in the footlocker.

After a quick lunch of gray, lifeless meat and limp and overcooked vegetables, Vince sat with the other new recruits in the Reception Center. The conversation was sparse at first, each of them looking around at the strangers who would be their comrades in the weeks to come. As the hours stretched on, they were called in for aptitude and classification tests.

Vince had no idea what kind of soldier he'd be. He wasn't a genius, but he wasn't a fool either. His hands weren't made for delicate work, and he could handle a rifle if need be. In his heart, he knew he'd take whatever they gave him. He didn't have much of a choice, not anymore.

The interviews were a blur. Staff members asked questions about his family, his skills, and whether he had any preferences for assignments. Vince was blunt - he didn't care about the specifics. Just put him somewhere. Anywhere, he could be useful. He was ready.

As the day wore on and the reality of the place settled over him, Vince couldn't shake the feeling that this was just the beginning. There would be no promises. No guarantees. Just tests, evaluations, and assignments. All that mattered now was that he was here. And soon, he would be far from home, facing whatever came next.

It didn't take longer than a few days before he knew where he was headed next. His orders had assigned him to the Army's 1st Infantry Division. He would be headed to Camp Blanding, Florida, to begin his training in earnest.

Chapter 40

Vince arrived at Camp Blanding on a bus. He had ridden from the train station with other men. They had been ordered off the bus and marched into a wooden barrack building. The air was thick and humid. Located near Starke, Florida, Blanding had the reputation of being hell on earth.

The first thing that happened was Vince was assigned to a squad. He was told they would train and fight together, once they shipped out. The first night after they had been assigned, the men got together and introduced themselves to each other. Sitting or standing around a set of bunks, each man took a turn. Vince was given only a moment to try and weigh the mettle of each man. Their squad leader, buck sergeant Matt Miller, was a veteran, and he led off.

"Matt Miller. I am your squad leader. I'm from Seattle, Washington. Been in the Army since '39. I am here even though I have been through basic before. We will be serving together for the duration, so we have a chance to get to know each other before the shit hits the fan," Miller said in a soft but gruff voice. Miller looked to be early thirties and was well built with sandy hair and startling blue eyes. He wore the uniform well, his freshly sewn sergeant stripes on both sleeves. 'You will meet our platoon leader, Lieutenant Bellows, tomorrow." He looked around for questions. There were none. "Tim?" he added, looking over at a corporal.

"Tim Kaine, I am the assistant squad leader," the corporal chimed in. He looked like he was in his mid-twenties with a smile that featured small picket fence teeth. "I'm from Jackson, Mississippi. I was in before, too. Glad to know you guys. Oh, and I love to fish!" The men laughed at the last addition.

"What about you?" Miller pointed at Vince.

"Vince Rose, Los Angeles," was all he said.

"Name is Walter Schmidt," the next man said with a smile. "Yeah, yeah, I know, it's German. So just call me Smitty and forget about the German part." The men laughed. "Oh, I almost forgot. I'm from a little town in western Pennsylvania, Meadville."

A young man who couldn't be older than 18 was looking at each of the men as they spoke. He was by far the youngest among them. "What about you?" Miller asked, motioning toward him.

"R..R…Ray Barnes," he said haltingly. "I'm from Orlando, Florida."

"How old are you, son?" Miller asked.

"Just turned 19, sir."

"No sir, required, Barnes. Just sergeant."

"Yes, sir…er…sergeant." The men laughed good-naturedly

"Mike Stallings, Rockford, Illinois."

"Mike Carson, Richmond, Virginia.

"Wow, wait a minute, two Mikes?" Miller interrupted. "How about we call you, Big Mike," pointing at Stallings, due to the fact that he towered over the much smaller Carson. "You're Little Mike." The men laughed again.

"Homer Hall, Mobile, Alabama," a man with thick, black hair whose ears stuck out from each side of his head said, with a thick southern accent.

"Stan Lowery. I'm from Omaha, Nebraska," then looking at Kaine said 'I like to fish too and hunt! Nice to meet you all!" Kaine nodded in appreciation.

Unbroken Hope

"I'm Jerry Timmons and I'm from, Fresno, California," he said with a smile. "Not far from you, Rose!" Vince smiled back.

"Steve Dolen, Las Vegas, Nevada. Yep, and I love to gamble!"

"I guess last but not least, eh," said a giant of a man. "Name is Charlie Zimmer. Yeh, it's German too, but don't hold that against me." He smiled at Vince, and Vince took an immediate liking to him.

Once the introductions were done, the men talked among themselves for a while and then split off to get their bunks ready.

Seven weeks. That's what it was supposed to be. Seven weeks of being pushed to the edge and then pushed beyond, and then you would be a soldier.

Week One felt like a lifetime, and Week Two only deepened the nightmare.

It was 0430 hours, and Vince was already on his feet and dressed, wiping sleep from his eyes, his uniform stiff with sweat and dust. The barracks was already alive with bodies shifting and shuffling, the air thick with the stink of men too tired to care about anything but surviving the next challenge.

"MOVE! Maggots!" The voice of Staff Sergeant Malone was like a slap to the face, sharp and immediate. Vince had learned in the first three days that the sergeant had no tolerance for delay. "Move, move, move!"

Vince sprang into action, instinctively falling into line with the other men, his boots heavy on the wooden floor of the barracks. The lights flickered on, and with them came the hum of anxiety, the realization that today - just like every other day here - would break something in him.

The training at Camp Blanding wasn't just physical. It was mental, and it was meant to strip you down, force you to face the ugliest parts of yourself, and rebuild you into something new - something tougher. But that didn't make it any less hellish. Having gone through it before, Sergeant Miller was helpful guiding them through the rough stuff.

They had run more miles than Vince could count. They'd climbed more walls, crawled under more barbed wire, and pushed through more muck and mud than any civilian could ever comprehend. And Sergeant Malone made sure to remind them every step of the way that none of it was meant to be easy.

"You think you're tough?" Malone had barked at them the day before, his eyes scanning the line of men. "You ain't tough yet. Not by a long shot. Tough doesn't quit. Tough doesn't flinch. Tough doesn't cry. Understand?"

"Yes, Sergeant!" they had replied in unison, but it was hollow. The words didn't match the fear in their chests.

"What'd you say!" Malone bellowed.

"YES! SERGEANT!!" This time, much louder.

Vince remembered the night he first wanted to quit. It had been the fourth day, and they had run for hours. They'd run with full packs, through the kind of heat that left your mouth dry and your body drenched in sweat. They had carried rifles - M1 Garands - that felt like they weighed a ton. And yet, when they thought they couldn't go on, they were ordered to run faster. And they did.

He remembered the stinging in his legs as the sergeant's voice tore through the stillness of the night: "Pick it up, Rose! You're not dead! Yet!"

His knees buckled, but somehow, he kept moving, one foot in front of the other. Every part of him screamed to stop, to just lie down and rest, but he didn't. He couldn't. If he stopped, if he showed weakness, it would be over.

By Week Three, Vince had grown calloused - his feet, his hands, his mind. He no longer flinched at the thought of running five miles or the sting of the hot Florida sun on his back. But the worst part wasn't the physical pain. It was the constant mental battle, the ever-present voice in his head that whispered to him: You don't belong here. You can't do this. Just quit.

But every time that voice spoke, he fought it down. Every time it whispered, he drowned it with the sound of his own breath, each exhalation a vow to survive.

Sergeant Malone was the embodiment of cruelty and discipline. He would stand over them, watching them suffer, a twisted smile curling on his face whenever a man faltered. His eyes were cold, always scanning for weakness, always hungry for failure. And when it came, when someone couldn't keep up or couldn't carry their weight, Malone would be there.

"Get up, Rose! You ain't dead!" He'd shout, using his pet phrase, his breath hot with rage. "You get back in line, or I'll make you wish you were. You hear me?"

But even as the sergeant's words echoed in his ears, Vince knew one thing for certain - if he could survive this, if he could endure the punishment, the ridicule, and the terror, there would be no turning back. He would be something else entirely. Something forged in the fire of this hell.

By the end of Week Four, Vince had stopped looking for the end of training. There was no end, he realized. There was only now. Only the next task. The next minute. The next drill. The next punishment.

And then came the *Confidence Course*.

It started with climbing a twenty-foot wall. Then you stood on a twelve-inch-wide board and walked thirty feet suspended over hard ground, all with nothing to hold on to. Next came the rope swing over a pit of mud. Finally, you were forced to low-crawl fifty feet under barbed wire that scraped and shredded. All the while, live rounds were being fired over your head. It all added up to one thing - fear. Fear that gripped your heart and tried to tear you down.

He watched as men faltered on the wall. Some hesitated. Others froze, their palms slick with sweat. The rope swing over the pit was a nightmare, and then came the barbed wire.

Vince had never been afraid of heights before - but here, in the cold, wet morning, suspended between the ground and the sky, walking a thin plank that looked narrower the further he went, he felt his heart pound like a drum. His fingers shook, his teeth clenched, and his breath was ragged.

Just keep going, just keep going, he told himself.

There was no turning back.

Week Five blurred into Week Six. The drills became harsher. The Sergeant's insults became sharper. The nights grew colder, the days hotter, and the camaraderie between the men began to feel like the only thing that kept them from going mad. They became brothers who shared in the same pain, the same exhaustion, the same frustration.

And then, finally, it was the last day of Week Seven. Vince stood at attention as the sergeant paced in front of them, inspecting their fatigues, their boots, and their rifles.

"You boys think you're soldiers now?" Malone asked, his eyes narrowing as he stared them down.

"Yes! Sergeant!" came the unified response.

Unbroken Hope

"Well, you ain't. Not yet. But you might be someday. If you survive the rest of this war." He grinned, a cruel twist of his lips. "Now get moving, before I make you regret it. Dismissed"

Vince didn't know if he was a soldier yet, but in that moment, as he stood with his squad, the weight of the last seven weeks pressing down on him, he realized something. He'd made it. Despite everything - despite the heat, the mud, the blood, the fear - he'd survived. And that, in itself, was victory.

As Vince moved away, he turned to look one last time at Sergeant Malone. Malone saw him looking and broke into a big smile. Vince could see the man behind the facade.

That smile told Vince it wasn't just about being tough. It was about enduring. And Vince Rose, against all odds, had learned how to endure.

But his next test was coming with Advanced Infantry Training. His orders were sending him to Camp Edwards, Massachusetts.

Vince arrived at Camp Edwards, eager but anxious about what lay ahead. The base, a strategic location for amphibious warfare training, had been buzzing with activity ever since it had been designated as the U.S. Amphibious Training Base. Located on Cape Cod, it offered an ideal environment for preparing troops for the grueling conditions of amphibious assaults. The harsh reality of the training quickly set in. Vince and his squad endured rigorous drills focused on landing operations - repeatedly storming mock beaches, navigating obstacles, and learning to work together as a unit in challenging conditions.

The men had been told they would be deployed to North Africa, and the weeks spent at Camp Edwards were grueling but necessary for that deployment. Vince often found himself covered in sand, drenched from the water, and exhausted, but the constant pressure forged a sense of camaraderie among the men. Vince learned the personalities of each man in his squad. Smitty was the cut-up, always ready to make them laugh. Dolen liked to talk about food a lot, he was always hungry. Hall, with his thick down-home accent, was quiet and reserved, but he proved to be a talented marksman with the rifle. But it was Charlie that Vince grew the closest to. He wasn't really sure why. They had just sort of drifted toward each other, and the friendship stuck.

The squad had to learn to fight in the surf and sand, under fire, and in the chaotic confusion of beach landings. But more importantly, they were taught how to fight as a team. The instructors, many of whom had seen the brutal reality of amphibious operations in the Pacific, didn't mince words. They emphasized the importance of precision, discipline, and the need to stay calm under fire. Vince knew that mastering these skills would be crucial for survival once the real action began. Sergeant Miller had never done an amphibious landing, so he was paying close attention so as not to mess up.

The camp also provided training in the use of landing craft, the intricate coordination needed between ships and troops during landings, and how to fight on the move, as they advanced inland after hitting the shore. Each day was filled with exhausting drills, but Vince's focus remained on the task at hand - ensuring that when the time came to hit the shores of North Africa, he would be ready. His training in the cold waters of the Cape Cod beaches prepared him for the unknown challenges he would soon face across the Atlantic.

By the time Vince's three weeks at Camp Edwards drew to a close, he had grown stronger, more capable, and far more confident in his skills and the skills of his squad. He was very proud of how well they worked together. The constant physical exertion had taken its toll, but it had also sharpened his resolve. He was now better equipped to survive the

Unbroken Hope

hardships of war, but he also carried the weight of the responsibility for his fellow soldiers. He was now part of something far larger than himself. Vince prepared to ship out to North Africa, where the real test would begin. He and his squad would be joining a unit that was already deployed there and had been in the midst of the fighting. Vince wasn't sure what to expect.

Chapter 41

It was Saturday morning. Barbara Jean stood outside of their apartment building watching the orange glow of dawn stretch across the neighborhood, and tried to picture her father in the dry, blistering heat of North Africa. She'd learned about the desert in social studies class, but it was hard to imagine that her dad, Vince, was really there. Harder still was imagining how long it had been since they'd last heard from him.

She had a box under her bed, tucked away with her most treasured belongings - little notes and pictures that came from Vince. They were the only reminders she had of him now, each one a lifeline across the miles. Maybe it was the war, or the long stretch of time between messages, but the once regular flow of letters had started to dry up. She clung to each one that came.

Barbara Jean was excited because today was Saturday, and that meant it was movie day. Barbara had inherited her love of the movies from her mother. The movie serials, the ones that played before the feature films, had become one of her favorites. Vince's letters reminded her of them. A new exciting adventure with every letter…another cliffhanger. Barbara Jean imagined her dad doing something heroic, just like in the films. Every week, Erma would take her daughter to the theater, and the darkened space felt like a cocoon away from the world outside. Today was no different.

They walked the streets of their neighborhood, arms linked as they headed toward the theater. The sun beat down relentlessly, and Barbara

Jean let her mind drift as she always did, imagining her dad's name flashing across the screen - Vince Rose: Hero of the Desert.

"Do you think Daddy could be in one of those movies, Mama?" the girl asked, skipping a little to keep pace with her mother's long strides.

Erma smiled faintly, her lips dry from the heat. She didn't like to talk too much about Vince with her daughter, but she knew it was what kept her going. "Maybe. The good guys always win in those films, don't they?"

Barbara Jean nodded eagerly, the way she always did when this conversation turned up. "But why do you think the good guys have to wait so long sending their letters?"

Erma's smile faded, but she quickly recovered. She didn't want the girl to see how much it hurt. "I'm sure your dad's busy," she said softly. "You know how it is. But I bet a letter will be here soon. He's probably writing it right now."

Barbara Jean didn't quite believe it, but she nodded. She wanted to believe it. No, she had to.

They bought their tickets, found their seats and then the movie began.

The diner was quiet as Erma set down the coffee pot and wiped her hands on her apron. She had had the job for four months now. She glanced toward the window, where the California sun was beginning its slow descent into the horizon, painting the sky with streaks of pink and lavender. The diner was a small, nothing-special place in the heart of downtown Los Angeles, but Erma did like working there as a waitress serving the same regulars, the same cup of coffee day in and day out. She could find comfort in the routine, even if her mind often wandered to the faraway places where her husband fought a war she didn't fully understand.

A bell chimed as the door opened, and a soldier stepped in. He wasn't a regular. The new faces had become more frequent, though. A few soldiers had come in lately - young men who wore the same expressions of uncertainty, bravado, and homesickness she'd felt in Vince's letters. Erma forced a smile and approached him.

"Hi," she said cheerfully, pushing the hair back from her face. "What can I get you?"

The soldier hesitated, a little startled by her welcoming tone. He was in uniform, his jacket worn and dusty, his eyes looked as if they'd seen more than they should have. "I'll have a coffee," he said quietly.

Erma nodded, moving to get the pot. As she filled the cup, she glanced back at him, wondering if he had any news from overseas, or maybe...if he might know Vince.

"You been in North Africa, sir?" she asked, trying to keep her voice casual.

The soldier's eyes met hers, and there was a moment of understanding. "Yeah," he said, the word almost too heavy to say. "I was shot up pretty bad in Tobruk, and they sent me back stateside. You got someone over there?"

Erma's breath caught in her throat. "My husband," she said, voice low. "He's stationed in North Africa. Vince Rose? First Infantry? Maybe you know him?"

The soldier's face softened, but he didn't answer right away. He shook his head, glancing down at the cup of coffee in his hands. "A lot of us are out there," he murmured. "It's hard to keep track. And I ain't with the Big Red One.... the First Infantry."

She forced herself to smile again, even though her stomach twisted. "Of course. But mayhaps if ya heard anything... anything bout him, you'd let me know?"

The soldier nodded absently, taking a sip from his coffee. Erma retreated to the kitchen, feeling a strange mix of hope and dread. The thought of Vince in that desert was like a constant ache that gnawed at her, but she kept working, kept herself busy. What else could she do?

The next Saturday, Barbara Jean hurried through her morning chores. She always liked to feel that she had earned her trip to the theater, even if she didn't quite know why. It wasn't a typical Saturday, though. Her mother was acting a little strange - distracted, her eyes constantly scanning the room, as if waiting for someone. Barbara didn't ask why. She didn't need to. It was just the usual. Worry.

The movie serials weren't running that day. Instead, a newsreel played, set in the African desert. It was filled with action of the war. It was mild, as most of the violent scenes were left out. Barbara Jean leaned forward in her seat, gripping the armrests, trying to find her father amongst the troops being shown. A close-up of a young soldier made her think even more about her father. He felt close, like she could reach out and touch him. She whispered to herself, "Daddy's out there somewhere. I know he is." The newsreel filled a void in her.

When the lights came up after the newsreel, Barbara Jean turned to find her mother watching her with a sad, gentle smile.

"You, OK?" Erma asked softly, brushing some hair from her daughter's face.

The girl nodded vigorously. "It was perfect, Mama."

Erma's smile faltered, but she wrapped her arm around her daughter's shoulder as they watched the double feature.

Unbroken Hope

As they left the theater, Erma's thoughts were far away, somewhere between the letters that didn't come, the soldier at the diner who might have known something but didn't, and the quiet hope that something - anything - would change soon.

And as they walked home, Barbara Jean clutched the single letter they'd received last week, reading it over and over again in her head, silently counting the days until the next one would arrive. She'd waited this long; what was a little longer?

Erma had always felt like a fish out of water in Los Angeles, with its fast pace and all the strangers around her. The people here spoke so differently than she did, with their smooth, round vowels and clipped consonants. In Oklahoma, her accent had never mattered much - it was home, after all, and everyone spoke the same way. But here, in this sprawling city, she sometimes felt like an outsider, as if her voice marked her as someone less refined.

Her co-workers at the diner had taken to calling it the "Oklahoma twang," and often teased Erma about it. "Erma, you sound like you're from another planet," one of them would say, giggling as if it was some kind of joke. It stung more than Erma let on, though. She wanted to fit in, to blend in with the people around her, especially for Barbara Jean's sake. She didn't want her little girl to grow up thinking she came from a place that was inferior. And the teasing at school hadn't helped.

One evening, as Erma sat at the kitchen table after putting Barbara Jean to bed, she made up her mind. It was time to do something about it. If she wanted to be more like the people around her, if she wanted to give her daughter someone to look up to, she needed to work on herself - specifically, her accent. She had heard of night schools in the city, places where people could take courses in everything from art to business to speech. It was time for Erma to enroll in one of those speech classes.

The next day, after her shift at the diner, Erma went straight to the community center. It was a small building near the edge of the neighborhood, a little run-down but always bustling with activity. She found the bulletin board in the back hallway, posted with all sorts of announcements for classes and events. She scanned through them until her eyes landed on one that caught her attention:

Sound Like a Star!
Improve Your Speech and Talk Like a Hollywood Hero or Heroine!
Do you want to be heard, not just spoken over?
It is important to be able to effectively communicate in a world where first impressions and clear speech can make or break opportunities.
Tired of sounding 'not quite right'?
Don't let your accent hold you back from your full potential.
Master the art of clear, confident speech
Talk like the stars of the silver screen.
Learn these Techniques
Diction: Mastering correct pronunciation and articulation.
Intonation: Learning how to use voice inflection to enhance meaning.
Clarity: Achieving smooth and understandable speech patterns.
Benefit From Our Expert Coaching
And it's Free!

Unbroken Hope

It was exactly what she needed. Without wasting any time, she signed up for the class, feeling a sense of excitement bubble up inside her. It felt like the first step toward making a change in her life, a change that could help her be a better version of herself, not just for Barbara Jean, but for Vince, too.

That evening, Erma went next door to see her neighbor, Mrs. Keller, and asked if she could watch Barbara Jean while she attended the class. Mrs. Keller, a retired schoolteacher, had been a steady presence in their lives since they moved into the apartment complex. She was kind and reliable, and she always took an interest in the girl's development. It didn't take long for Mrs. Keller to agree.

"You go on ahead, Erma. I'll keep an eye on that little one. It'll be good for you to get out of the apartment for a while."

Erma thanked her profusely and left with a smile. She couldn't help but feel a sense of gratitude for Mrs. Keller. It seemed like, more and more, people in this city were showing her kindness, even when she didn't expect it.

The first night of class arrived, and Erma felt a flutter of nerves as she walked into the room. It was full of people - men and women, some older, some younger - who all shared one thing in common: they wanted to improve themselves. The instructor, a well-dressed woman named Miss Harper, welcomed everyone with a warm smile and a firm handshake.

"Welcome, everyone," Miss Harper said, her own speech flawless and precise. "Tonight, we'll begin by focusing on the basics of speech: vowel sounds, consonant clarity, and, most importantly, how to make your voice sound less like you're from somewhere else and more like you belong here. Los Angeles is a melting pot, but if you want to be understood and taken seriously, it helps to sound like you fit in."

Erma sat up straighter, her resolve hardening. She was ready for this. She was ready to change. She wanted to be the kind of person Barbara Jean would look up to with pride, someone who wasn't afraid to keep improving, even in the face of everything else that had been going on in their lives.

In the weeks that followed, Erma attended her classes diligently. After every session, she practiced the new sounds in the mirror, stretching her mouth to make unfamiliar shapes, making sure her vowels were crisp and clear. She worked on the way she pronounced her words, consciously eliminating the old drawl that had been such a part of her for so long.

At the diner, she caught herself speaking more carefully to customers, trying to make the words come out more like the locals spoke. It wasn't easy - there were times when her accent would slip back in, or when she'd catch herself stumbling over a word she wasn't sure how to pronounce. But she didn't give up. Every time she got something right, every time she felt her speech becoming just a little bit more polished, she felt a quiet sense of pride.

And as for Barbara Jean, she was a constant source of motivation. Erma loved hearing her little girl's voice, full of curiosity and innocence. She wanted her to know that there was no limit to what she could do, that she could be anything she wanted to be, no matter where she came from.

Mrs. Keller continued to watch Barbara during Erma's classes, and often the two of them would sit together in the evenings, chatting over tea or pie while Barbara Jean played with her dolls.

Erma thought about Vince every day - his letters, though few and far between, were her lifeline, and she clung to them as if they were the only thing keeping her grounded. But in those moments when she was practicing her speech or spending time with Barbara Jean, she found herself a little bit less consumed by worry. It wasn't that she had forgotten about Vince, or that she was in any way unfaithful to his memory. But she had come to realize that in order to survive this war, in order to keep going, she had to give herself something to focus on beyond fear.

Every night, as she tucked Barbara Jean into bed and kissed her goodnight, Erma felt a quiet sense of accomplishment. She was doing what she could, learning and growing, and trying to be the best mother she could be.

And when she sat in those classes, surrounded by strangers who were all working toward the same goal, Erma knew she wasn't just changing the way she spoke - she was changing the way she saw herself. And that, more than anything, was what she wanted for her daughter. To show her that no matter what life threw their way, they could always keep moving forward.

Chapter 42

The sun beat down on the desert, a relentless heat that burned through the fabric of their uniforms and sizzled the air. Vince felt the sweat pouring down his face, stinging his eyes, but there was no time to wipe it away. His rifle was locked tight against his shoulder, his finger on the trigger, as his squad moved cautiously forward through the craggy, sunbaked hills of North Africa. Their boots kicked up dust with every step, but the noise was drowned out by the thunderous takka takka takka takka of machine gun fire up ahead. Vince was proud to be a member of the second squad of the first platoon of Alpha Company of the 16th Infantry Regiment, part of the 1st Infantry Division, known as the Big Red One because of the Big 1 on their Division patch on their shoulder. It was mouthful to be sure, but it was still something to be proud of.

Both German and Italian troops were stationed in North Africa, but Vince's squad was battling just the Italians now. This would change, but for now, the wops were giving them a hard run for their money.

"Stay low, stay tight!" Sergeant Matt Miller's voice broke through the machine gun fire, his command sharp and seasoned. Vince was impressed. Miller was so calm, even under pressure.

Vince gave a quick glance to his left, seeing Corporal Kaine crouching behind a boulder. The assistant squad leader's face was set in that familiar, determined scowl. Kaine had a way of making the impossible look like just another problem to solve.

"We push through this, we clear 'em out," Vince murmured under his breath.

It had been a week since their squad had come into contact with the Italian forces in this godforsaken stretch of desert, and each day had brought something worse. Ambushes, mortar strikes, and sniper fire. But today felt different. This time, they were the ones pushing into enemy territory.

The squad had been tasked with clearing an enemy stronghold - a heavily fortified position that overlooked a vital supply line. Every step felt like it could be their last.

"Move up, Stallings! Lowery, take point," Miller ordered, his voice controlled and steady, a leader in the chaos.

Mike Stallings, or Big Mike, the first scout, slid forward on his stomach, using every bit of cover as he advanced. Stan Lowery, the second scout, followed him closely, the two of them practically a shadow of each other, moving like water over rocks. Their eyes were constantly scanning, alert to every sound, every movement.

Vince's heart thumped in his chest as he kept an eye on them, his own rifle ready. The adrenaline coursed through his veins, a constant hum of awareness.

"Sniper!" Charlie Zimmer's voice cut through the noise, and just as Vince turned, a sharp crack echoed over the ridge. A bullet whizzed by, close enough that he felt the wind it left in its wake. Even with the sniper, the incessant grinding of the machine gun could be heard in the background.

"Take cover!" Vince shouted, diving behind a low stone wall. Charlie hit the dirt beside him, his face pale, but his grip on his rifle unshaken.

"We need suppressing fire! Dolen!" Miller barked at him. Dolen was crouched behind another piece of cover nearby, his eyes locked onto the machine gun that had been set up on the far side of the ridge.

Unbroken Hope

"Got it, Boss," Dolen said. The gun's barrel began to bark as he let loose, a steady barrage of gunfire that drowned out the sound of the enemy's machine gun fire. His ammo bearer, Smitty, was right beside him, feeding him additional rounds.

As Dolen laid down the fire, Miller signaled to Jerry Timmons. "Move up, Timmons! Now!"

Timmons, always quick on his feet, darted from cover to cover, making his way closer to the enemy position, rifle held low, eyes constantly moving, checking for targets.

"Cover him!" Miller ordered, turning to his left to see Kaine already setting up his own positions, ready to give Timmons the cover he needed. Kaine's M1 growled with each shot from behind cover, each shot adding pressure to the enemy's position. Vince joined in with cover fire.

Vince's heart pounded in his chest, but he could feel the rhythm now, the flow of the battle, as the men moved in perfect synchrony. He was proud of them all - these men who had become more than just soldiers. They were family. The bonds they had forged through fire, through the hell of North Africa, were unbreakable. He was barely conscious of these feelings as they battled, but they were there all the same.

"Keep pushing! Stallings, Lowery, you're up!" Miller shouted, his voice carrying over the din as the two scouts began advancing again, crawling low toward the enemy's flank.

Vince stared at the dust rising from the ridge. The Italians were holed up tight, but they were starting to crack under his entire company's pressure. Dolen's machine gun fire was relentless, and with Timmons moving up and the scouts closing in, the enemy was beginning to lose ground. In the background, he could hear the other squads in his company closing the gap as well.

Then there was a sudden lull in the gunfire. But Vince knew it wasn't over, not yet. Then, a sharp crack from a large gun on the ridge, followed by a scream - Vince didn't have to look to know who it was.

"Stallings!" Lowery's voice was raw with panic.

"Damn it!" Miller's voice cut through the crackle of gunfire. "Carson, Hall, Barnes...More cover fire, NOW!"

Vince didn't wait for an order. He snapped his rifle up, sighting quickly on the ridge where he'd seen the flash of an Italian rifle. His finger squeezed the trigger, one shot, two shots, three. The target dropped, but Vince didn't slow. He needed to move, needed to push forward.

"We don't leave our own behind!" he said through clenched teeth, scrambling forward on his belly, the dry, desert heat suffocating him as he crawled toward the ridge.

Charlie Zimmer crawled beside him.

Vince reached Stallings first - he was down, but not out. A bullet had grazed his side. He was sitting up, with a grin on his face, leaning against a rock.

"I didn't know you guys cared so much!" he said with a smile.

"Big Mike!" Vince said, grabbing his buddy's arm.

"I'm good," Stallings gasped, wincing when he moved. "Just a scratch. Let's get some cover."

"Rose...Zimmer! Report!" It was Miller.

Vince and Charlie didn't hesitate. They moved back to a nearby boulder as the rest of the squad continued their fire. They gave Miller a thumbs-up.

Kaine moved forward next, his rifle sweeping across the ridge, his eyes looking for the next target. "Keep your heads down! We're almost through this!"

They kept moving forward, inch by inch, clearing the way. It felt like they were taking on the entire Italian army. The constant drone of machine gun fire, the crack of rifles, the thud of mortar shells - everything was a blur of sound and fury. But through it all, Vince could hear one thing clearly: the voices of his squad.

"Move up, Rose!" Kaine yelled.

"Got your back, Vince!" Charlie called.

"Need more ammo," it was Dolen calling to Smitty.

And finally, when they broke through the last line of enemy fire, and the ridge lay in ruins behind them, Vince Rose stood still for a moment. His chest heaved, his heart raced, but he let out a quiet sigh of relief. He looked over and gave members of the other squads in his company a thumbs-up. Job well done.

They'd made it. They were still standing!

His squad - his family - was still intact.

But the heat of battle was far from done.

The heat of battle wasn't the only thing hot. The broiling sun of the North African desert pressed in on Vince and his squad as they huddled under the shadow of a crumbling boulder. The sound of distant gunfire and the occasional rumble of artillery filled the air, but for now, they had a brief respite. The Italians were on the run, their lines broken, and Vince's squad had played their part in pushing them back. Now, in the brief lull, it was time to refuel and catch their breath.

Vince sat cross-legged on the dusty ground and tore open his K-rations. Using the P-38 can opener that came with each ration, he quickly opened a can of potted meat. Soon, the familiar smell of canned meat and crackers filled the air. He popped a chunk of meat into his mouth and glanced around at the others. Sergeant Miller was leaning against a nearby rock, picking at his rations with a half-smile on his face. Smitty and Dolen were on the other side, quietly laughing over something Smitty had said, their voices low but hearty in the dry heat.

Carson and Hall had already eaten. Little Mike was helping Big Mike clean up the minor wound he had received.

Vince took another bite of his cracker and wiped his face with his sleeve, leaving behind streaks of mud formed from the combination of sweat and dust. As he chewed, his eyes drifted over to Miller, his gaze lingering. There was something off.

Blood!

A trickle of red was dripping down Miller's right cheek, slowly making its way to his chin, where it pooled before dripping onto the desert floor.

Vince squinted. "Hey, Sarge," he called out, a frown knitting his brows. "You've got a bit of a leak there." Motioning to Miller's cheek.

Miller didn't seem overly concerned, still chewing the last bite of his food as he wiped his mouth with his sleeve. He looked over at Vince, his expression cool but tired. "It's nothing," Miller said with a small shrug, his voice raspy from the dry air. "Just a scratch. Must've caught something when we were pushing through that last trench. It'll stop soon." He wiped the blood away with his sleeve.

"Let me look at it," Vince said as he stood up and looked down at Miller. "Give me your canteen. We need to clean it up." He removed a bandage from Miller's first aid pouch, then poured water onto a strip of bandage.

"You're right, Sarge, it isn't going to kill you, but it is more than a scratch. Gonna leave a scar." Vince spotted a medic and waved him over. The medic took over. Vince watched as he cleaned the wound and poured sulfa powder on it to fight infection.

"Ain't you gonna sew him up, Doc?" Vince asked.

Unbroken Hope

"Nah, better to keep it like it is. Just keep it clean." The Medic dryly responded.

"Well, that will be a trick!" Miller said with a laugh.

"Well, try to keep it clean. Ain't even worth a bandage. See you boys, later." The medic went hopping off to find his next patient.

"We certainly hope not!" Vince yelled after him with a laugh.

The medic just waved over his shoulder at the comment.

Yes, Miller had been hit, but Vince had seen worse. Hell, they had all seen worse, much worse. They had all taken hits before, and there was no time to dwell on every scrape or nick. The war didn't stop for cuts. Still, something about seeing blood so casually dripping from his sergeant's face made Vince uneasy. He felt the pull of his own memories - the faces of men other squads had lost, the way wounds never really went away. But the good news for his squad was, it seemed that Miller was tough as nails, as usual.

Charlie caught Vince's glance and shook his head, rolling his eyes in exaggerated mockery. "You worrying about the Sarge? The man's got a face like a brick wall."

"And as ugly as one, too," Smitty chimes in.

Then Little Mike looked over his shoulder and cracked, "The Sarge, he could bleed out and still march on."

Miller chuckled, the sound rough but genuine. "That's right, Little Mike. Ain't nothing but a little blood, right?"

The squad laughed softly at the banter, the tension of the battle fading, replaced by a camaraderie born of survival and shared experiences. There was something comforting about this moment - their usual routine, the jokes that always seemed to find a way to cut through the worst of times.

Vince cracked a smile, his earlier concerns melting away for the moment. The men around him were alive, they were together, and they were sharing what little they could in this desolate place. They were soldiers in the worst kind of war, but in that moment, they were something more.

"Alright, alright," Smitty, the squad's clown, made another quip. "Let's just hope we don't have to run into any more Italians anytime soon, yeah?" then paused with a thought. "Come to think of it, I could use some real Italian *food*, though. Think if we could capture a couple of em, they could whip us up some good spaghetti and meatballs? I'm starting to lose my taste for K-rations."

There was a chorus of laughs as the men settled into a more comfortable silence. The jokes slowed, but the mood didn't shift. They weren't naïve. They all knew they'd be back on the move soon enough, that the war wasn't done with them yet. They were just soldiers, resting under the sun, sharing a small bit of peace that came with the lull in the fighting.

Vince glanced at Miller once more, noticing that the blood had stopped dripping, the cut no longer fresh. The sergeant was right. It wasn't much. It wasn't anything that would slow them down.

"To tomorrow," Vince said quietly, raising his canteen.

Miller raised his own, his eyes catching Vince's. "To tomorrow," he echoed.

And with that, the squad continued their rest, finding solace in the quiet moments amidst the storm of war.

Chapter 43

The sound of Barbara Jean's pencil moving across the paper was the only noise in the small kitchen, as Erma stood by the stove, frying bologna. It was late afternoon, the kind of quiet that settled in just before the evening dark. The days were really warm now, the air arid at the height of summer. Summers in Los Angeles could be brutal, and the warmth of the stove couldn't help but add to the overbearing heat in the kitchen.

Barbara Jean sat at the kitchen table, bent over her homework. Her small frame hunched slightly, her light hair tied back with a ribbon that was a little too bright for the drabness of the season. She had grown taller in the past few months, though not much - still slender, still seeming a little too thin. Erma didn't mind the way she looked, but it did worry her that she'd stopped growing in the way the other girls did. Her shoes, scuffed and worn, didn't fit as well as they used to.

"They're still calling me that," Barbara muttered under her breath, eyes on her math problems.

Erma paused for a moment, her hand froze, fork still in it. It was a small comment, but it stung. She knew what "that" meant.

"Who?" Erma asked softly, without turning to look.

Barbara Jean chewed the inside of her cheek, the pencil tapping against the edge of the paper. "The kids at school. They keep calling me 'Oakie.' And 'Dummy.' And some new one - Squinty.'"

"Squinty?" Erma asked, her voice tight, trying to conceal a laugh. "Well, that's a new one. Why Squinty?"

"Oh, who knows?" Barbara Jean said, exasperated. She looked over at her mom with an exaggerated scrunched up squint and then laughed.

Erma laughed. She enjoyed her daughter's sense of humor. It was good to see.

Erma finished cooking the bologna and put the slices on a plate. She stirred the cut potatoes in their pan of water, then set the spoon down with a deliberate clink. She turned to her daughter, brushing a stray lock of hair from Barbara Jean's forehead. "Ignore them, Barb. They're just trying to get to you. You're smarter than they are. They can't touch that."

Barbara Jean gave her a small smile, but it was weary. She wasn't convinced. "I don't know, Mama. Maybe I'm not so smart if I can't even make friends."

Erma said, "Well, those kids aren't your real friends. You have other friends who are your real friends. They are the ones that count."

Erma's heart ached, but she didn't show it. Instead, she put a hand on her daughter's shoulder. "People aren't your friends just because they call you by the right name. Friends are the ones who see you really are, even when the world's trying to make you something else…something you're not, Barbara."

The girl didn't answer immediately. She just stared down at her homework, chewing on her bottom lip. Erma hated to see her like this, but there wasn't much she could do. It was the war, the time they were living in. And sometimes it felt like it was wearing thin for both of them.

Then Erma thought about something. She hadn't called her baby girl Barbara Jean in a long time…just Barbara or sometimes Barb. Her little girl was growing up

The doorbell rang. A sharp, unexpected sound that broke the silence. Erma jerked in surprise as she turned toward the door.

Unbroken Hope

When she opened the door, she saw the familiar figure of Mr. Stokes, the neighbor, standing with a letter in his hand. He held it out to her with a smile. He was an older man, in his late sixties, with a slow gait and graying hair, always trying to be helpful but often unsure of how to be.

"Mail for you, Erma," he said, his voice kind. "Thought you might want to know. It came just as I was heading out for the evening."

"Ah, thanks, Mr. Stokes," Erma said, taking the envelopes from him, her heart skipping in her chest. "You doing alright?"

"Yeah, good as can be expected," the old man replied. "Any news from Vince?"

She looked down at the envelopes. She didn't even need to look at the return address to know who they were from. Vince and Mamie. She held it up. Vince's. "Yeah, right here."

"Well, hopefully it's good news." He waited to see if Erma responded, but she was focused on the envelope. "Well, see ya!" he said abruptly, and he was off. Erma murmured a goodbye and then quietly shut the door behind him.

Her eyes immediately went to Barbara, who had sensed the shift in her mother's expression. Erma didn't say anything. She just opened the letter carefully, the paper crackling as she pulled out the pages.

"Mom?" Barbara asked, voice quiet but hopeful.

Erma scanned the letter quickly. There was no date, but it was clear this was Vince's handwriting, his careful script, with his signature at the bottom.

Michael Wells

Dearest Erma and Barbara,

I hope you're both doing good, at least as good as possible these days. I'm sorry I haven't written sooner - days seem to slip by here faster than I can keep track of them. But I think of you both often. I have to. There's no way not to.

The company has moved again. We're heading to Italy now. I don't know how long we'll be stationed there, but I'm hoping it's not too long. I just know I'm glad to have Africa behind me. I can't promise when I'll write next, but I will when I can.

I'll tell you this much: I've seen things that will haunt me forever. I wish I could protect you from it, but I can't. Just know that I'm doing everything I can to get back to you, both of you. I miss you more than you can possibly imagine. Please take care of each other. I love you both.

Yours, Vince, Daddy.

Erma's hand trembled as she finished reading. Her eyes were blurred, the weight of the letter sinking into her chest like a stone.

Italy.

She couldn't remember the last time she'd felt this cold - this empty. The letter felt far too distant, far too impersonal, even though she knew it wasn't. He couldn't help where he was, couldn't help how far away he was.

Barbara stepped closer, peering over Erma's shoulder at the letter. "He's in Italy now?" she asked quietly, her voice small.

Unbroken Hope

Erma nodded, folding the letter carefully and tucking it into her pocket. She swallowed hard, fighting the lump in her throat. "Not yet, but he's heading there."

Barbara bit her lip. "When will he come home, Mama?"

Erma pressed her lips together, not knowing how to answer. The truth was, she didn't know. Nobody did. There was no guarantee. There was just the waiting - the waiting that felt like a lifetime, the waiting that made everything feel suspended in time.

"Soon," Erma said, trying to sound more confident than she felt. "I don't know when, but soon. He'll come back. I know he will."

Barbara seemed to accept this answer, even though it wasn't one that satisfied her. She turned back to her homework, but the silence between them now was thick and heavy.

Erma then turned her attention to Mamie's letter. It held the same old news from back home. Although it did say that they had been able to save a little bit of money. That news was quickly forgotten, and Erma's mind went back to Vince.

Erma walked to the stove and stirred the potatoes again, her fingers shaking. She didn't know if it was from nerves or the emptiness that came with Vince's letter. Either way, it hurt.

It had been so long since Vince had sent anything. So long since they had heard from him. And now, knowing he was on his way to Italy, so far away, it only felt further and harder.

But for Barbara's sake, Erma would keep going. She would find a way to make things feel normal, even when nothing felt normal anymore. She would keep up the pretense of routine, because what else could she do?

Barbara would get through this. And so would she. They would both keep waiting.

And one day, Vince would come home.

Chapter 44

Vince felt the ship lurch beneath his feet as the convoy of vessels slipped into the dark Mediterranean Sea. The low hum of the engines beneath the deck matched the tremor in his stomach. He wasn't sure what was worse - the unease that came with the vastness of the sea or the growing anticipation of what lay ahead. The heavy, humid air of the Tunisian coast of North Africa still clung to his skin, a reminder that only days ago they had been marching through North Africa's dust, but now, it was as though the very air had changed.

It was July 1943, and Vince's squad was heading to Italy. He had served in North Africa for a little over a year. The victory at El Alamein had shifted the tide there, and after that, the Axis troops had been forced from the continent. The Allies were now advancing through Sicily as part of Operation Husky. Vince's unit was moving quickly to meet up with them. Vince had seen too much to be fooled into thinking the fighting was done; victory in Africa had just been the prelude to the real battle - the one that would be fought across the hills and cities of Italy.

The big Landing Ship Tank, known as the LST, carrying Vince and his Company rolled on the waves. He could hear the noise from the men on deck, the chatter, the clatter of rifles being inspected, and the low murmur of someone singing. It wasn't exactly the scene of high spirits, but there was a sense of determination in the air. Soldiers had grown accustomed to the grind of war, and though the men of the 1st Division had made their mark in North Africa, they knew this next stretch wouldn't be any easier. They were prepared to bring the fight to Italy.

But the brass had pointed out they would be facing three enemies. First, the Germans, who initially augmented the Italians, but then ultimately took over much of the fighting for them. The second enemy was the remaining Italian forces, who chipped in where they could. And the landscape formed a third enemy. The Germans and Italians were entrenched in the mountains. A rough, rocky landscape that would fight Vince and his companions every step of the way.

Vince shifted his weight and leaned against the steel wall of the ship's interior, eyes fixed on the distant horizon. The soft light of the morning sun cut through the haze, and for a moment, his thoughts drifted back to the days before they had sailed from Africa. He could still hear the voice of Lieutenant Bellows, his platoon leader, echoing in his head, the briefings, the orders, and the promises of reinforcements as they prepared to storm Sicily's shores. In Africa, they had been part of something big - a turning point in the war. But Italy? This felt like the real test.

"Hey, Vince!" a voice called out.

Vince turned to see Charlie, making his way down the narrow corridor. Charlie was a big guy, built like a brick house with arms as thick as a mule's legs. He slapped Vince on the back as he came closer, a half-grin on his face despite the evident fatigue in his eyes.

"You ready for this?" Charlie asked, glancing over his shoulder at the men still milling around the deck above.

"As I'll," Vince started, then the two finished their pat response, "ever be." They both laughed.

"I don't think anyone's ever really ready for it," Vince then said. "But we do what we gotta do."

Charlie chuckled. "That's the spirit. I just hope those krauts and wops don't give us too much trouble. Can't be worse than the desert though, right?"

Unbroken Hope

Vince didn't answer immediately. He had learned a long time ago that soldiers didn't always need words to understand each other. Both of them knew that the Italian campaign wasn't going to be like North Africa. The mountains, the narrow roads, and the entrenched positions the Italians and the Germans would no doubt defend - they would make the fight even harder. But Vince had survived North Africa, and he had a feeling that grit, luck, and sheer willpower would see them through once again.

Before he could say anything more, the ship's loudspeaker crackled to life, a voice shouting orders in clipped tones. The 1st Infantry was about to land. Vince glanced at Charlie, and they both stood straighter, an instinctive shift as the weight of what was to come pressed in on them. They moved toward the back of the ship, where the landing craft would soon be deployed.

It wasn't long before they were ordered into the boats. Vince settled into the cramped space, his rifle ready, the familiar cold steel feeling solid in his hands. The tension was palpable. Every man in the boat seemed to be holding his breath, eyes scanning the shore ahead. A few muttered prayers slipped through the air, but for the most part, it was dead quiet.

And then all hell broke loose as Navy ships pounded the coastline with heavy artillery, the guns firing multiple rounds of fire, one after another. The barrage kept up for what seemed like an eternity but in reality, it was no longer than thirty minutes.

And then the landing craft came to an abrupt stop as it hit the sand of the beach on Sicily.

As the ramp of the boat hit the sand, the world seemed to explode in a haze of gunfire, smoke, and shouting. Vince's heart raced as the beach turned to chaos around him. Bullets zipped through the air like angry bees, and men hit the sand with the sickening thud of bodies hitting the ground. He didn't have time to think - just move. Move forward. Get to cover.

"Get down!" Charlie shouted, shoving Vince into a small trench along the beach as the first salvo of artillery thundered overhead.

Vince's chest was tight with adrenaline, his brain working faster than his body could keep up. He could hear the orders shouted, the constant rattle of machine guns hiding in their well-fortified positions up the cliffs.

The ground beneath Vince's boots was littered with debris - broken equipment, abandoned packs, and the hollow-eyed stares of fallen men. But there was no time to mourn. The next wave was coming. With his rifle steady in his hands, he pushed forward, his legs burning with the effort. The roar of artillery was deafening, but the orders were clear. Move. Advance.

By the end of the day, the beachhead was secured, though at a heavy cost. It had taken a hundred men scampering up the side of the cliff to take out the machine guns. Once that happened, it all fell quiet.

Vince's hands were slick with sweat and the blood of his comrades as he crouched in a temporary foxhole, waiting for the next assault. The sounds of battle had been all-consuming - the crackle of gunfire, the staccato of explosions, and the distant wail of wounded men. But beneath it all, Vince had kept moving, had kept fighting.

They were in Italy now. There was no turning back.

Vince glanced at Charlie, who was still alive, still beside him. They had made it through the day, but the road ahead was long, and the real fight had only just begun. Now they had to get up that cliff.

Unbroken Hope

Vince leaned against the cold, rough stone of the farmhouse wall, watching the last light of the day fade from the sky. It had taken the better part of the day to scale the walls of the cliff and overpower the Germans at the top. But it had been done. Now, the fields of Italy stretched out before him, still and peaceful, but he knew that peace wouldn't last. Not here, not now.

"Hey, you okay, Vince?" a voice called softly, and Vince turned to see Charlie leaning on the edge of the wall.

"Just thinkin', Charlie," Vince muttered, rubbing his thumb along the stock of his rifle. "About my family back home. About what we're doing here. We're too far from our families now, you know? Feels like we're a lifetime away."

Charlie didn't reply at first, just looked over at the line of men preparing their gear for the next push forward. The rumble of distant artillery echoed through the hills, a reminder of what was to come.

"We're all thinking about home," Charlie said finally. "But we can't afford to get lost in it. We've got a job to do, Vince. For them. For everyone." In a way it was easy for Charlie to say this, a bachelor, he only had his parents waiting for him.

Vince nodded, though the weight in his chest didn't ease. He'd known Charlie for a little over a year, but it seemed like a lifetime.

The 1st Infantry had advanced from the beaches of Sicily into the heart of the island, but it hadn't been easy. The enemy was dug in, entrenched in the mountains that rose up like jagged teeth against the sky. And the terrain - rough, unforgiving - made every step a struggle. The night sky was no longer a comfort, and the days had become a blur of marching, fighting, and moving deeper into enemy territory. They were pushing toward Troina now, aiming to break through, but each village they came to was another obstacle to overcome until they achieved their objective. Every corner could hide a sniper, and every patch of land could be laced with mines.

Vince checked his watch. It was nearly 1900 hours. The whole company was getting ready to move at dusk, slipping through the valley and up into the foothills where the next objective waited.

"We're moving out tonight?" Vince asked, glancing at Carson.

"Yeah, Sarge says we've got to clear out this next sector by morning," Carson replied, eyes narrowing. "Expecting a hell of a fight. We've got word the dagos and the krauts are dug in up there pretty deep."

"Well, when have they *not* been dug in deep!" Vince cracked.

Carson nodded with a smile.

Vince's stomach churned, but he didn't show it. He'd fought enough to know what it was like to be on the receiving end of enemy fire, but it never got any easier. He could already hear the roar of artillery as the Germans prepared for their own assault. It was always a dance between the frontlines, with the silence before each engagement only fueling the dread of what was to come.

"Better make sure your ammo's ready," Lowery added. "And your bayonet's on tight. You ever used one of those?"

Vince grinned despite himself. He had been trained on how to use it, but that was now years ago. "Can't say I have, but I reckon tonight's a good night to find out."

"That's the spirit. Just don't forget, Rose. You can't hesitate in this goddamn war," Lowery replied dryly

"I won't," Vince said, his voice low, determined. He hadn't hesitated yet, and he wasn't about to start. Not with everything on the line.

Unbroken Hope

The orders came soon after, and they moved quickly, slipping through the shadows of the Italian countryside. The hills rose steeply in front of them, craggy outcrops where the Germans had set up positions. Vince's boots crunched over the gravel road, every sound amplified in the stillness. He could hear the murmurs of the men around him, the occasional cough, the low, muffled prayers. Leonforte lay straight ahead, and beyond that Troina.

As they moved forward, the air turned colder. Vince moved steadily, the weight of his gear making every step feel heavier. The fog of war seemed to settle around him, the uncertainty of the mission pressing in. But there was no turning back now. Vince had noticed that he had seen a lot more German soldiers than Italian. He now knew for certain the Germans had taken over in Italy. The battle lines were close, and their objective - taking Leonforte and securing the way to Triona - was more vital than ever.

They reached the top of a rise as darkness swallowed the landscape. Vince's breath came out in visible puffs as they huddled behind rocks, waiting for the signal to advance. The faint smell of smoke drifted down from the cliff above. Vince wasn't sure exactly what it was, could be cigarettes, rifle smoke, even a campfire, but it made him realize how close they were to the enemy. He heard the crackle of a radio, followed by a whisper from Sergeant Miller.

"Alright, boys. We move on three. Stay low, stay sharp. And remember - no one gets left behind. Let's make this clean."

Vince's grip tightened on his rifle. This was it. He looked to Smitty, who gave him a quick nod. Then the signal came. A flare shot up into the air, illuminating the landscape in a brief flash of white. In that split second, Vince's heart raced. His feet moved before he even thought about it, charging up the ridge alongside his brothers-in-arms.

The sound of gunfire erupted almost immediately, bullets whizzing past him, bouncing off rocks. Vince ducked low, heart hammering in his chest as they rushed up, adrenaline fueling every step.

"Keep moving!" shouted Sergeant Miller from the front. "Hall, Barnes, Carson on the left, Dolen, Smitty set up over by that boulder. Once you're set, lay down some suppressing fire. We've got to push them back!"

"You got it, boss," Dolen said and grabbed his Browning machine gun. with Smitty right behind him.

The first German machine gun opened up, the rattle of bullets slicing through the air. Vince could see the gunner in the second story of a building on the outskirts of town. Dolen returned fire. His tracer rounds painting a picture of the bullets' flight.

Vince dove to the ground, feeling the earth tremble as the rounds impacted nearby. He squeezed the trigger of his rifle, but the sight of the enemy position had become obscured by the smoke and the haze of the battle. His world shrank down to the sharp, harsh sounds of war - explosions, screams, gunfire.

Vince edged toward his left and reached the outside wall of a small stone building off the side of the road. He rested his back against the wall taking a breather.

Then, a shout rang out.

"Grenade!"

Vince didn't have time to think. He hit the ground again, covering his head as the explosion erupted 50 yards to his left, sending dirt and shrapnel flying. He rolled instinctively, rising to his knees, he could feel the pounding of his heart. He quickly checked to see if he was hit. Thankfully, no!

The enemy was not giving up easily, but his squad continued to work their way into town along with his company. The road into town didn't offer much in the way of cover, so Vince and the rest of the men with him were spread out, hiding in dense bushes and trees a short distance from the road. Their attackers, on the other hand, were well-positioned and holed up in buildings in Leonforte. Vince kept moving, firing at the flashes of enemy positions in the dark, relying on muscle memory to guide him.

Through the haze of chaos, a figure appeared - a German soldier, sprinting down the edge of the road toward him. Vince could barely make him out in the dark. He didn't hesitate. He raised his rifle and fired.

The soldier crumpled, falling silently to the ground.

Vince didn't feel a surge of victory. There was only the cold, unyielding reality of war. Vince was puzzled as to why he was running at them when his fellow soldiers were so well concealed. It would remain another mystery of war.

"Let's go, Rose! Move!" Charlie's voice broke through the fog of battle, and Vince snapped back into focus. Vince knew Charlie meant business because he called him by his last name. Vince stood and met Charlie's eyes. Then they began advancing, staying low, pushing toward a short hill, with Leonforte slowly rising up before them.

The battle raged through the night. By morning, the town was theirs - but not without heavy losses. The smell of blood and gunpowder lingered in the air as the men regrouped, their faces drawn and tired. The objective had been reached, but it felt hollow. The men who hadn't made it were already being carried back down behind the lines. Some of them would never walk again. But miraculously, Vince's squad was still intact. They had rounded up a number of straggling German soldiers and had sent them back down the line as prisoners of war. "Well, they should be happy," Vince muttered to himself. "At least they're still alive."

A few minutes later, Vince stood at the crest on the edge of Leonforte, overlooking the valley, his rifle hanging limply by his side. The landscape was beautiful - rolling hills, green fields, and the distant outline of Troina - unspoiled and serene, at least for now.

But the road ahead would be long and bloody. And no matter how many hills they conquered, no matter how many villages they liberated, they, the soldiers - the brothers - would carry the weight of it all.

He closed his eyes for a moment, letting the wind pass over him. Then he turned, ready to face the next battle.

Simply because…that's what they did.

The battle for Troina was brutal, a true test of endurance and courage. Vince and his squad found themselves on the frontlines of a vicious struggle. The Germans, entrenched on the high ground, had a commanding view of the entire area, and they used it to devastating effect. Every move the Americans made was under constant observation, and the German defenders unleashed a relentless barrage of artillery and machine gun fire.

The terrain was a nightmare. The rocky, uneven hillsides were difficult to navigate, and the light brush offered little cover from the enemy's sights. Vince's squad had to move cautiously, always aware of the danger lurking above them. Their orders were simple: take Troina. But the reality of doing so was anything but straightforward. The Germans had fortified the town and the surrounding high ground with well-prepared defenses, making each step forward costly.

Hall was crouching next to Vince. "I always did want to see Italy," he quipped in his southern drawl. "But not like this!"

Vince chuckled. He, like the rest of his squad, felt the weight of the situation. Each man had been through hell before, but this battle felt different. It was as though the very earth beneath their feet was fighting

Unbroken Hope

against them. They pushed on, inch by inch, with determination that came from the knowledge that failure meant death, and victory meant one more step toward pushing the Nazis out of Italy.

As the days wore on, the heat and exhaustion took their toll. Men were injured, some quite seriously, while others died. The toll on the men was staggering. Vince, despite his grueling fatigue, stayed focused on the mission, driven by the thought of his fellow soldiers and the need to honor those who had already fallen. The squad kept moving forward, using the cover of night to advance when possible, launching small but fierce attacks on the German positions during the day. Every attack was met with fierce resistance, but the Americans knew they had no choice but to keep pushing.

By the end of the last week of July, after days of intense combat and heavy casualties, the Americans had made significant inroads into the town's outskirts. The Germans, however, weren't ready to give up. They continued to launch counterattacks, hoping to throw the Americans off balance. But the First Infantry was determined. Its leadership inspired the soldiers, giving them the strength to hold their ground and advance when others might have faltered.

One day, as Vince and his squad made their way up a narrow path, a sudden burst of German gun fire rang out from a distant position. Vince hit the ground instinctively, his heart pounding. Sergeant Miller motioned for them to move forward, closer to a small outcropping of rocks that would offer better cover. They scrambled, navigating the rocky terrain, with the constant sound of bullets slicing through the air around them.

It was during all of this that Charlie was hit. The round grazed off of his helmet. Vince's friend, who had always kept the morale high with his jokes and good-natured spirit, fell to the ground. Vince, desperate, wanted to crawl toward him, but the enemy fire was too intense. Charlie looked over at Vince and gave him the thumbs up.

When the shooting slowed, Vince made his way and then sat next to Charlie, not knowing what to say. The weight of war felt heavier than ever before. They had all known the risks, but it didn't make the pain any easier when it hit so close to home. But this was a brutally close call.

Despite the loss of life and the staggering number of casualties, the Americans continued their push, inching ever closer to Troina. Every day, they faced the Germans' entrenched positions, determined to make progress despite the overwhelming odds.

After nearly a week of punishing combat, the Big Red One had secured a foothold in the town. It wasn't the victory they had hoped for, but it was a victory nonetheless. The Germans, realizing they were losing ground, withdrew, leaving behind a town battered and broken, but free from occupation.

As Vince and his squad surveyed the ruined town, they felt a mix of exhaustion and relief. They had fought with everything they had, and though their company had lost men along the way, they had succeeded in their mission, and Vince's squad was still intact. A major miracle, really. But Vince knew, as did all the men around him, that there would be more towns to liberate, more lives to risk, and more sacrifices to make.

They could breathe finally, if only for a moment. The road ahead would be long and fraught with danger, but the men were ready. The battle for Troina was over, but the fight for Italy was just beginning

As Vince and his squad took a much-needed breather, the weight of the battle seemed to lift from their shoulders, if only for a moment. The sound of distant gunfire faded into memory, replaced by the

peaceful ambiance of the Italian countryside. The men leaned against stone walls, checking themselves for scrapes and cuts, and caught their breath after the intense struggle to capture Troina. The hills around them, once echoing with the chaos of war, now seemed eerily quiet.

Then, a smell reached Vince's nose - something rich, savory, and distinctly homemade. He frowned, sniffing the air again. The scent of garlic, herbs, and roasting meat wafted through the village, and it was clear that someone was cooking a meal. His stomach, sick of nothing but field rations, rumbled in response.

"Do you smell that?" Vince asked Charlie, who stood beside him.

Timmons sniffed the air and grinned. "That's not our usual K rations. Smells like someone's having a feast!"

"Let's see if we can get in on that," Vince suggested with a smile.

The squad, curious and desperate for a break from the unending grind of combat, followed Vince as he led them toward the source of the delicious aroma. They crept carefully through the narrow, winding streets of the village, alert to any signs of danger. But as they approached the house, there was no sign of enemy movement - just the low sound of lively, peaceful conversation from within, and the escaping, delicious smells of Italian cooking filling the air.

They knocked on the wooden door, its paint chipped and faded from years of exposure to the elements. After a brief moment, the door cracked open, and an elderly woman peaked outside.

"Americani?" the woman asked in a soft, cautious voice.

Vince nodded, his accent heavy but sincere. "Sì, signora. We mean no harm. We're just hungry."

The woman studied Vince for a moment, her eyes searching for any sign of danger or deceit. But when she saw the weariness in his eyes and the exhaustion on his face, her suspicion faded. Instead, a gentle smile spread across her face.

"Americani!" she said as she flung the door open. A middle-aged man stood behind her, both with faces that had seen hardship, but were softened with the warmth of kindness.

"Americani!" she said to the man, certainly her husband.

"Americani" was all she could muster as she threw her arms around Vince hugging him tightly. "Grazie, grazie!" she said repeatedly.

She then saw the rest of Vince's squad standing behind him, and she motioned all of them to enter.

"Come in," ushering them inside. "Benvenuto! Welcome! We have...abbondanza." Then she added in heavily accented English. "To share."

The squad filed into the small, humble kitchen, where a fire crackled in the fireplace, and a pot of stew simmered over the flames. The aroma was wonderful - rich, hearty, and welcoming. The rough stuccoed walls were adorned with family photographs and a small crucifix, all symbols of resilience and faith amidst the turmoil of war.

The woman introduced herself as Maria, and her husband, Giovanni.

A young girl, no more than 12 or 13, peeked from behind a door, curious about the visitors but too shy to approach. Maria motioned her to come out. The girl slowly entered. "Questa è mia nipote," Maria said with a smile, "Our granddaughter. Elena." The squad all nodded toward her, acknowledging her. The set of her mouth changed into a bright smile, revealing perfectly straight white teeth. Her shoulder-length brown hair looked like it had just been washed.

Each of the soldiers introduced themselves with a short, informal bow of the head.

After the formalities, Giovanni offered them seats at the worn wooden table, on the hearth, and several dilapidated chairs from the living area. The twelve men filled the room. It was cramped, but it felt wonderful. Without a second thought, Maria began dishing out bowls of the stew, adding slices of fresh bread with a drizzle of olive oil delicately poured on each slice.

Vince and his squad hesitated for only a moment before accepting their meal with "Thanks" or "Grazie" and then sitting down. It had been days since any of them had tasted a meal that wasn't bland or pre-packaged. The stew was filled with tender meat, root vegetables, and herbs - flavors that felt like a distant memory from a world before the war.

"This is incredible," Sergeant Miller said between mouthfuls, his voice thick with appreciation. "I haven't had a meal like this since... well, since I was home."

Giovanni and Maria watched with silent joy as the soldiers ate. They didn't speak much, but the gratitude in their eyes was enough to convey their feelings. It was clear that they were offering not just food but a piece of humanity in the midst of such brutality.

Elena was still watching from the doorway. "Elena offre ai nostri ospiti dei pasticcini?" her grandmother asked. Elena nodded and picked up a small tray from the counter, and then carried it to each soldier. On it were small, round pastries, warm from the oven. "Per favore," she said shyly, offering them to each of the men.

Vince smiled warmly and took one, savoring its sweetness. "Grazie, Elena," he said. "These are amazing. Molto bene!"

The soldiers, full for the first time in days, exchanged looks of surprise and satisfaction. For a brief moment, it was as if the war had stopped, and they were simply men sitting down to enjoy a meal with people who cared for them, people who, despite the hardships they faced, still had something to offer.

Giovanni finally spoke, his voice hesitant, emotional, in broken English. "We lose much," he said softly, his eyes meeting Vince's. "But today, you bring us, eh…how you say…qualcosa? Uh…something… we thought we have lost - hope. Capisci? Eh…understand?"

Vince felt a lump form in his throat. There was no denying the pain in Giovanni's voice, but there was also a glimmer of something else - a quiet determination. A resilience that mirrored the men sitting at his table.

"We're just doing our job, sir," Miller replied. "But we won't forget this. Not for a second."

The soldiers stayed for a few hours, talking quietly, resting, and laughing. It wasn't much, but it was enough to remind them of the world they were fighting for - a world where families could still share a meal, even in the shadow of war. When they finally stood to leave, Giovanni and Maria insisted that they take what was left of the bread and pastries, along with a small jar of olive oil. All three in the family made sure to hug and give thanks to each of the men.

As Vince and his squad walked back to their post, they felt a renewed sense of purpose. The battle for Troina had been fierce, and there were many more ahead. But in that small house, around that simple table, they had been reminded that even in the darkest times, kindness could still shine through.

And that was worth fighting for.

Chapter 45

Erma sat in the small, dimly lit corner of the diner. The smell of grease and old wood clung to the air, but it was familiar, a part of her now. The diner's bell jingled above the door as it opened, and a brief gust of cold air swept in, making her shiver. She didn't have time to notice, though. Her eyes were fixed on the letter sitting in front of her, the edges creased from the countless times she'd picked it up and set it back down over the past few days.

It had been nearly a month since she'd last heard from Vince. A month since the last letter, that one full of promises and half-sentences, all smudged with sweat and dust. His handwriting had been hurried, as if he didn't want to take too much time writing. She'd clung to every word.

But this letter, the one that had come yesterday, this letter was different.

She picked it up again and turned it over, running her thumb along the edges of the rough paper. The military stamp, so official, was printed in bold black ink. Vince's handwriting appeared in sharp, slanted letters beneath it: For Erma. Private. She had read it last night and had brought it this morning from home.

Erma swallowed and opened the envelope, her hands shaking slightly despite herself. The paper inside was stiff and formal. She unfolded it slowly, as though she was afraid the words would vanish the moment she let them go. She read the letter for the second time.

Michael Wells

January 5th, 1944

My Dearest Erma,

I hope this letter finds you and Barbara in good health. It seems like the days go by slower here than the clocks at home. Every morning, I wake up to the same faces, the same crazy world. I've lost track of time, really - I'm not sure if it's been weeks or months since I last wrote you. But please know that you're always in my thoughts.

The unit is being moved soon, though I can't say where. I've been told it's top secret. Don't worry, though. Wherever they send me, I'll be there doing my part, thinking of you and Barbara, and counting the days until I can come home.

I miss you more than I can put into words. It's hard being away from you, harder than I thought it would be. But I know you're strong, and I know you're doing well in Los Angeles. I hope you're still taking those speech classes you mentioned. I can't wait to hear how you sound when I get back.

Give my love to Barbara and know that I love you with all my heart.

Your Vince.

    Erma felt a tightness in her chest as she folded the letter back up and set it on the table. It wasn't the words themselves that made her heart ache - it was the silence between them, the distance, the unspoken weight of the war pulling them all in different directions.

    Erma took a deep breath, hoping to relieve the ache of longing tightening around her ribs. She was used to the loneliness now. Every night, after the diner closed and the last straggling customers had left, she'd return to their small apartment, empty except for the two of them. Except for the nights she went to her class.

On those nights, Barbara would already be asleep, her small body curled up in her bed. Mrs. Keller would rise and then, after some brief conversation, would quietly leave. Erma would then sit at the kitchen table, the cold light of the lamp the only company, as she practiced her speech.

Her instructor had said she was almost there, that she was speaking like an L.A. native now. Almost. Erma had come a long way since her first lessons, the clumsy sounds and awkward vowels that had once slipped from her tongue replaced by a smoother, more deliberate sound. She had learned the rhythm, the lilting tone of it. It was a small thing, but it made her feel closer to the world she was striving to be a part of. The world where Vince would be with her, where she worked every day in the diner, where her daughter went to school, where the future lay just beyond the edge of her reach.

She couldn't afford to let it slip away.

But at night, after the practice and the lonely hours, she'd take the letters from Vince out again, running her fingers over them, reading his words, hearing his voice in the spaces between the ink. She would let herself remember him, let herself be that girl who had fallen in love with him before the war had taken him away.

Erma closed her eyes for a moment, holding the letter tightly to her chest. She had no idea where Vince was going or when he would return. But as long as there were letters, there was hope.

And that was all she had left.

Chapter 46

Vince stood outside his tent in the British countryside, a pounding, unrelenting rain drenched the ground. Puddles dotted the sparse grass field. Rain cascaded off the steel pot Vince wore on his head, a helmet that was meant to protect him in battle. It was June 5th, 1944, and everyone in camp was tightly wound. What was known as D Day had been cancelled that day due to the poor weather. It was hoped tomorrow would be better. As he looked around at the faces of the men, there was a sense of urgency, of destiny, as if the world was holding its breath for something monumental to occur.

He recalled the day he left home in Los Angeles, kissing his wife, Erma, goodbye, her eyes filled with worry and unspoken fears. He had picked Barbara up and hugged her close to him. Erma and he hadn't talked much about the possibility of him not returning, but he saw the look of fear in her eyes. He had tried to reassure her, but that look had haunted him every time he boarded a train to a new base, every time he sent her letters from the battlefield.

Now, two years later, the battles of North Africa and Italy were behind him, Vince was standing at the edge of something even more uncertain. But he was now a battle-proven veteran. It didn't relieve the anxiety gnawing in the pit of his stomach though.

After leaving Italy, he had arrived in Liverpool and had been training in Bryanston, England. In England, the division prepared mentally and physically for the invasion. Housed in a gigantic tent city, the conditions were rough but suitable. Command deemed them ready.

Now, the invasion of Normandy was looming, and with it, the promise, once again, of an uncertain future. On the trip from Italy to England, he had been able to catch up on some much-needed rest. He had also been able to reach out to Erma and Barbara via letters. He had spent the last few months learning everything from field tactics to how to storm a beachhead under heavy fire. The landing at Sicily had been a breeze with the calm waters of the Med. This was going to be different. He had never been much of a swimmer, and the thought of wading into the frigid waters of the English Channel, with German guns trained on him, made his stomach twist into knots.

But the Army had prepared him for this. He had grown accustomed to the routine of military life, and despite the fear and anxiety that bubbled beneath the surface, he had learned to push it aside. It wasn't about fear; it was about duty. As a rifleman Vince had learned early on that the best way to face fear was to confront it head-on.

The night before D-Day, Vince sat in a dimly lit tent with his fellow soldiers, the sound of nervous chatter filling the room. The smell in the tent was astounding. A mix of body odors and tobacco smoke. It almost made his eyes water.

He was playing poker with three other riflemen, Barnes, Carson, and Hall.

As he waited for the next deal, he looked around. He was surrounded in total by the twelve men in his squad. His squad leader, Sergeant Miller, had a large scar on his right cheek that he had earned in the Africa campaign. He had proven to be a good leader. His squad had come through Sicily fully intact. Which was saying a lot. In the corner was Dolen, the machine gunner, field cleaning his weapon for the hundredth time, his brown hair falling over his forehead as he focused on the cleaning. Smitty, his ammunition bearer, was reading an Archie comic book. Periodically, he laughed at the antics of Jughead, Veronica, Reggie, Betty, and of course, Archie. Smitty's red hair was just like his hero, Archie's. Timmons was reading a letter from home, again, out loud to one of the unit's seven riflemen, Ross, and the assistant squad leader, Corporal Kaine. Although appearing busy, they were all going through the same thoughts, the same silent dread. The two Scouts, Stallings and Lowery, were trying to sleep, but sleep wasn't coming easily. Vince could hear the sounds of prayers mixed with the soft sound of cards shuffling.

"Tomorrow's the big day, huh?" Ray Barnes said softly, looking up from his hand of cards.

Vince nodded. "Yeah, if the weather holds."

Ray was only 20, but today he looked like he was barely out of grammar school. His face was pale, and his eyes were wide set apart, a kid who had been thrust into a situation far beyond his comprehension. But he had shown his worth...a battle veteran. But, Vince could see the fear there, the way the kid kept glancing at the door, as though he was waiting for someone to burst in and tell him that it was all a mistake - that they were all going home. A battle veteran has fears, too.

But no one was going to burst in to stop it. These men were soldiers and knew what they had to do.

"Yeah," Vince repeated, his voice low. "It's gonna be a hell of a day."

Ray didn't respond. He just shuffled the deck again, the cards flicking against each other as the soft murmur of men's voices continued. Vince wasn't sure if the kid was trying to block out his own fear or if he was simply too scared to speak. Either way, the silence spoke volumes. They all thought they knew what was coming. But they also knew that they didn't.

Finally, Vince looked over at his best friend, Charlie. Charlie was from Brooklyn and had shown he had an easy, wisecracking way about him. He was staring off into space, a smoldering cigarette in his right hand. He absent-mindedly would take a drag every few moments. Charlie and Vince had been through a lot. Hopefully, their luck would stick.

The morning of June 6 came too quickly. The men were loaded onto landing craft in the early hours before dawn, their faces grim as they waited for the signal. Vince could feel the weight of his pack pressing down on his shoulders, the rifle cold against his body, and the weight of history hanging heavy in the air. As the boat began to move, the hum of the engines beneath them vibrated through his bones, a constant reminder of the momentous task ahead. The men of his squad looked at each other's grim, determined faces. All sharing the same expression.

The Channel was rough that day, the sea churning beneath them like a living thing. Vince clutched the sides of the boat as it bobbed and dipped in the waves. He tried to calm his racing thoughts, but they wouldn't stop. What if I don't make it? What if I don't survive this? Cut it out, he would then think…that ain't helping any!

But the voices of his squad, tense but steady, anchored him, though they could barely be heard above the roaring waters of the channel and the boat's motor straining to propel it through the water. He could hear one by one, the men yelling small things to each other - phrases to steady their nerves, to remind themselves that they were all in this together. Vince caught Charlie's eye. Vince gave him a solemn nod, as if to say, we'll get through this together, or not at all. Charlie just smiled and winked. That said it all.

Unbroken Hope

As the boat neared the beach, the distant rumble of artillery fire began to rise above the waves. Hundreds of ships, battleships, cruisers, destroyers, had been called to duty and were firing artillery. It was a sound that both terrified and galvanized them. The landing craft his crew was on, an LCVP commonly referred to as a Higgins boat, had a relatively low profile, so Vince and his fellow soldiers could look over the top, allowing them to see the beach and the surrounding area before reaching the shore. He could make out some of the Navy ships, the USS Texas and USS Arkansas, two battleships. He could see others but didn't know what they were.

The Germans were waiting, no doubt, ready to rain down hell on the incoming invasion force. Vince's heart hammered in his chest as he thought of Erma back home. Would she ever know if he fell here today? Would she ever hear his name spoken in the same breath as the heroes of this day?

A voice snapped him back to the present. "Ready, Rose?" It was Sergeant Miller. Vince nodded, tightening his grip on his rifle. "Ready as I'll ever be."

The closer they got to the shore, the more real the fear became. Vince could hear the screams and cries coming from the beach, over the roar of the motors. The constant barrage of enemy fire from the Germans entrenched on the cliffs above, and the sound of explosions from bombs and shells that shook the ground were overwhelming.

Then BAMMMM!! The ramp of the landing craft dropped with a harsh clang, and in an instant, the squad surged forward, charging through the icy water toward the beach. Staring enemy fire in the eye. The beach was littered with obstacles - barbed wire, land mines, and "Hedgehogs" - iron structures designed to slow down the landing. The mud and debris made it hard to move, and it was difficult to know where to go or what to do.

The landing was a hellish blur. Some men didn't make it out of the craft, while others fell almost immediately as they tried to move forward. The survivors sprinted, crawled, or huddled behind whatever cover they could find. The beach was under constant bombardment, the sound of explosions deafening. But in those moments, survival was the only thought. The world seemed to slow down in the chaos, every movement feeling like an eternity.

The sound of gunfire was deafening - pounding, like the roar of a storm - coming from every direction. Men were falling around him, some of them silent as they were hit by the enemy's barrage, others screaming in agony as they collapsed onto the sand. Stallings, Big Mike, who was next to him, had his head nearly blown off and dropped in his tracks. Blood sprayed all over Vince's face, almost blinding him.

Vince had no time to mourn. His legs burned from the effort of wading through the surf, but there was no time to stop. His heart was pounding in his ears, and adrenaline pushed him forward. The beach seemed to stretch out in front of him, a chaotic hellscape where men fought and died in the sand and the blood. Machine gun rounds repeatedly hit one man forcing him into a spasmodic dance of death. He finally, thankfully, hit the ground. In the distance, he could see the smoke rising from the shoreline as artillery shells exploded around the landing troops. Bullets were zinging overhead, and down the beach, he could see nothing but chaos.

He kept moving, trying to find cover, trying to stay low. But cover was sparse. He was a sitting duck. The world had narrowed down to the single goal of survival, and every step felt like an eternity. His training kicked in, instincts taking over as he moved with his fellow squad members through the carnage, returning fire when he could, using the remnants of beach fortifications to shield himself. He came to a body writhing in the sand. The soldier was screaming. His legs were blown completely off. He looked down, it was the kid, Ray Barnes. He knelt down, grabbing for his hand, stared into his eyes, speechless, and watched the young kid die. He had little time to consider this, so he moved on, bullets racing over his head.

Somewhere amidst the battle, Vince lost track of time. His body was on autopilot, each movement dictated by instinct. He could hardly remember if it was morning or afternoon, or how long they had been fighting. His mind was numb with the weight of it all.

Hours later, as the sun began to sink lower in the sky, the tide of battle began to turn in the Allies' favor. Vince, covered in dirt, sweat, and the stench of blood, looked around him. The beach was littered with bodies - some familiar, some not. But the first wave had made it ashore, and the beachhead was secured. And he was alive.

Vince collapsed behind a sand dune, his body shaking with exhaustion. His face was streaked with grime, his uniform torn and bloody, but he was alive. He had made it through D-Day. He caught Charlie's eye and gave him a thumbs up. Charlie returned the gesture.

He closed his eyes for a moment, the weight of the day finally crashing down on him. As the sound of battle continued in the distance, Vince thought of Erma again, of the life they had dreamed of before the war had taken it all.

Of the twelve men in his squad, five of them had been cut down and left for dead on the beach. Two more were gravely wounded and being attended to by medics. That left just five men in his squad. Sergeant Miller had been one of the lucky ones.

Vince hadn't known if he would survive this day, but now, as he lay in the dirt, he realized that he wasn't just fighting for his own survival. He was fighting for a future - a future where men like him could return home to the lives they had once taken for granted.

CHAPTER 47

Los Angeles stretched out in every direction, a vast sea of cement, and metal that seemed indifferent to the people who lived within it. The air settled over the city like a heavy, dirty blanket. On the surface, life seemed to keep moving forward, but beneath it all, Erma knew better. The world had changed and so had she.

For the past two years, with Vince away, every letter she received was a lifeline, a small thread of hope that kept her going. But with each passing day, it became harder to hold on to that hope. The war had a way of hollowing out those who were left behind and leaving them with the endless ache of waiting. Waiting for a letter. Waiting for a sign. Waiting for him to come home.

Barbara, now almost 9, had begun to notice. She missed her father, the empty chair at the dinner table, the way her mother's hands trembled when she opened a letter. Erma tried to shield her from the harshness of it all, but there was only so much she could do. Barbara was too perceptive, too aware.

"Is Daddy coming home soon, Mom?" Barbara asked, for the hundredth time, one evening as they sat at the kitchen table, the faint hum of the radio playing in the background. Even though he was her stepfather, he was really the only father she had ever known.

Erma paused, her fingers still on the edges of the letter she had just opened. The words blurred before her eyes as she tried to find the strength to answer. Vince's letter was filled with the same hope and reassurance he always gave her, but it didn't make the wait any easier.

"I don't know, sweetheart," she said softly, folding the letter and tucking it into her pocket. "He's doing important work over there, and it's going to take time. But he loves you very much, and he's thinking of you every day."

Barbara didn't look convinced. She stared out the small window that overlooked the street, watching the shadows lengthen as the evening settled in. The street outside was quiet, the bustle of the day having stopped for supper. It was one of those moments when the silence between them felt heavier than words.

They didn't talk much after that. Erma had learned that sometimes, silence was the best way to protect her daughter from the truth. They made do with what they had - a roof over their heads, a meager but steady income, a Saturday at the movies, and the few moments of joy that managed to seep through the cracks of their hard reality.

Still, it wasn't enough. Erma's mind raced, constantly planning, constantly trying to stay one step ahead. There were bills to pay, groceries to buy, and a future to plan, one where she could keep Barbara safe and whole, despite the chaos around them. Every day was a balancing act, a careful dance between survival and despair.

One evening, after Barbara had gone to bed, Erma sat in her easy chair in the living room, her hands wrapped around a cup of coffee that had long since gone cold. The radio crackled, a lone announcer's voice cutting through the stillness, giving updates on the war. The words sounded distant, almost meaningless. The real war was here, in her home, in the struggles that no one spoke of.

She thought of Vince, thousands of miles away, fighting in a foreign land. She thought of the soldiers he fought alongside, the ones who wouldn't make it back. She wondered if he was safe, if he was cold, if he was hungry. And she wondered if he would ever come home.

Unbroken Hope

The door creaked open, and Barbara appeared in the doorway, rubbing her eyes sleepily.

"Mama? Are you okay?"

Erma smiled softly, wiping away the tears she hadn't even realized had started to fall.

"I'm okay, sweetie. Just thinking."

Barbara hesitated for a moment before walking over to her mother. She climbed onto the chair next to her, curling up against Erma's side.

"I miss Daddy," she said, her voice small and fragile.

"I know, honey. I miss him too." Erma wrapped her arms around her daughter, pulling her close. "But we're going to be okay. We've been through a lot already, and we'll get through this too."

Barbara nodded, though the uncertainty in her eyes didn't fade.

"Do you think Daddy's thinking about us?" she asked softly.

Erma kissed her daughter's forehead, her heart aching at the thought.

"I know he is," she said, her voice steady. "Every day."

The days rolled on, and the weight of the world never seemed to lift. Erma's routine remained the same: work at the diner, cook, clean, write letters, and wait. There were moments of joy, brief flashes of light that pierced through the gloom. Barbara had taken up painting, filling the small apartment with colorful pictures of flowers, birds, and happy faces. Erma couldn't help but smile whenever she saw one of Barbara's crude paintings - it was like a piece of sunshine in the dark.

But even the small victories weren't enough to quiet the constant fear that gnawed at her insides. The worry over Vince's safety and the uncertainty about the future were all-consuming. She hadn't allowed herself to truly consider the worst-case scenario, but the thought was always there, lurking just beneath the surface.

One afternoon, while Erma was walking to the grocery store, she saw a man in uniform standing near the corner of the street. His face was slack, his eyes distant, unfocused. He wore the same uniform Vince had worn, the same dark olive green that seemed to belong to another world. A garrison cap was placed smartly on his head. The man was smoking a cigarette, and his hands shook slightly as he held it.

Erma stopped in her tracks. The sight of him, the uniform, the cigarette felt like a punch to the stomach.

She didn't know what it was, but something in her gut told her that this was the moment. She needed to be strong for Barbara. She needed to be the one who held it together, and who found a way to keep their lives moving forward.

With a deep breath, Erma continued on her way.

At night, when the stars were just beginning to peek through the veil of city lights, Erma and Barbara would sit together, with the radio playing softly in the background. Sometimes they would talk, other times they would sit in silence, each lost in their own thoughts. But they were together, and that was all that mattered.

Erma had learned to live with the uncertainty, the fear, and the loneliness. She had learned that strength wasn't about never breaking, it was about getting back up, no matter how many times the world tried to knock her down.

And as long as she had Barbara, she would keep fighting. They would survive. They had to. Because there was no other choice.

Chapter 48

Vince felt the sweat dripping down his face, the stickiness of it mixing with the grime of the battlefield. The Allies had secured Omaha Beach on D-Day, after a bloody battle, that lasted throughout the day. But it was a long week of brutal fighting that forced the Germans into a retreat.

Vince looked down at his boots. The Normandy soil had a peculiar texture to it, a mud that clung to his boots, weighing him down with every step. The air smelled of smoke, metal, and something almost sweet from the flowers growing in the hedgerows that bordered the fields. It was the kind of sweetness that belonged to something forgotten, that had somehow been tainted by war.

The company's primary objective as part of the Allied forces was to capture the town of Caen, a strategically important road junction that would allow them to break out of Normandy and advance further into France, eventually pushing towards Germany.

The squad had been reinforced with straggling members from two other squads. Alpha platoon was now down to two squads at a full strength of twelve. They were hoping for reinforcements as soon as the brass could make it happen. Sergeant Miller had accepted the new members but seemed to rely mostly on those men who had served under him the longest.

Charlie was just ahead, his back to Vince as the two of them moved along the dirt path between the rows of thick, overgrown hedges and a stone wall. The squad had split up, moving along different positions on the path. The chatter of distant gunfire - both American and German -

had become a constant presence, a soundtrack to the madness of the days since the invasion. They had pushed past the beachheads, past the initial wave of chaos, but the real battle was only just beginning.

"Vince, you good?" Charlie's voice came over his shoulder, low and steady, but carrying the wear of days without sleep.

"I'm good," Vince muttered, adjusting the strap on his M1 rifle.

"Just keep moving. We don't want to get stuck out here when the sun sets."

Vince grunted a response.

They had been moving eastward through the fields for hours, now nearing a diminutive French village on the outskirts of Caen. The plan was to push forward, consolidate positions, and secure key locations. Intel had told them there was a German stronghold near the village. The men of Alpha Company were getting their orders piecemeal, and those were then spread down to the squads. The men were left trying to fill in the gaps as they advanced.

A faint rustling came from the hedge to Vince's left, followed by a sharp crack. Vince's heart skipped a beat, but Charlie was already on it, pulling him to the ground behind the nearest stone wall. The sound of a bullet slicing through the air above them was unmistakable.

"Sniper," Charlie hissed, his voice tight. "Don't move."

Vince held his breath, trying to quiet the beat of his own heart. He couldn't see the shooter, but the sound of the bullet - sharp and fast - made it clear that they were in someone's sights.

The two of them lay still, pressed against the cold stone of the wall, eyes scanning the surrounding fields. The distant echoes of artillery and the bursts of machine gun fire made it hard to focus, but in the moments before. Everything became a blur of motion and noise. Vince saw something - movement in a distant building. A flicker of light reflecting off a German soldier's helmet, belt buckle or other piece of metal. A dilapidated barn also stood in the distance.

"That's our guy," Charlie whispered.

Without another word, the two of them scrambled back, moving fast and low through the underbrush. The hedgerow was thick here, and it provided them with some cover, but there was no telling how much time they had before the sniper got another shot.

Vince looked over at Sergeant Miller, who signaled them toward the barn. His message was clear. Take out that sniper.

"Vince," Charlie said, glancing over his shoulder. "We make a break for the barn. Keep low. We'll have some cover, and maybe we can get a better shot at him from there."

Vince simply nodded.

"On three," Charlie said.

Vince's hand clenched tighter around his rifle. They both knew that every second mattered. The sniper was good. The crack of a rifle shot followed them as they sprinted, zig-zagging for the barn, each step a gamble. Charlie took point, ducking low into a crawl as they reached the barn doors. Vince followed close behind.

"Clear," Charlie hissed, poking his head around the corner of the barn. Vince followed, rifle raised.

The barn had seen better days, but for now, it would have to serve as shelter. They both ducked inside, crouching behind a stack of hay bales that offered decent cover.

Charlie poked his head around the corner again, squinting as he tried to spot the German sniper.

"Vince, you see him anywhere?"

Vince scanned the surroundings through the gap between the bales, his heart hammering. The sniper was somewhere out there, but whether he was still in position or had moved was anyone's guess.

"I don't see him," Vince muttered. "But if he's smart, he's waiting for us to make the next move."

Charlie grunted, frustrated. "We can't just sit here."

Before Vince could respond, there was a soft click - a trigger pulled. But it wasn't the crack of a rifle. It was closer, a metal sound echoing from a side door of the barn. The hairs on the back of Vince's neck stood up.

"Stay down," Charlie whispered, his voice low but commanding.

Vince felt his pulse quicken. It wasn't German soldiers coming. They'd have made more noise. No, this was something else.

A muffled voice reached their ears - French. Desperate. The side door creaked open wider.

Charlie moved first. Quick and fluid, he dropped to his belly and scrambled forward further into the barn, behind more bales of hay. Vince followed, pulling himself into the shadows, his boots barely making a sound on the dirt floor.

It wasn't until the Frenchman stepped fully inside, a young man, barely more than a boy, covered in the dust of battle and the smell of fear, an old antique rifle in his hand. Charlie stood up from behind the hay bales.

The boy froze, his eyes wide as he raised the rifle, but Charlie was faster, pushing the rifle barrel against his chest.

"Easy, kid," Charlie muttered. "We're not here to hurt you."

The young man gulped, his hands trembling as he dropped the rifle. The confusion was clear on his face. He wasn't sure whether to trust these men - American soldiers who had just landed in the chaos of his home country. But the fear in his eyes was undeniable.

"Je ne suis pas un soldat" the boy stammered in French and then in broken English, "I...I not soldier," "I... I just trying take my Sœur?...my sister to be safe. They - " he broke off, his breath coming in ragged gasps. "Ils viennent la nuit. Zee Germans. At night. They are in my Bourgade...how you say...village?"

Charlie lowered his rifle, sensing the truth in the boy's voice.

"You're with us now, kid," Charlie said slowly, looking over at Vince. "We'll help you. But you stick close, alright? Is there someone up in the loft?" Charlie motioned toward the roof.

The boy shrugged. He didn't know or didn't understand.

Charlie motioned for Vince to go up the ladder. Carefully, Vince made his way up the ladder to the loft. As he climbed, Charlie kept aim on the loft. Suddenly, a German soldier leaned over the edge, a rifle aimed downward. Charlie shot him, and the soldier tumbled to the ground, almost taking Vince with him.

Vince looked over at Charlie. "That's not our sniper, Charlie. He's still out there." Vince mumbled. Charlie motioned him to climb up the ladder to make sure no one else was up there. When he got to the top, a young teenage girl was sitting trembling in the straw. Her blouse had been torn. Tears streamed down her face.

Vince looked down from the loft and whistled softly to the boy. He then pointed at him and motioned with two fingers for him to come up.

After some simple coaxing from her brother, the girl climbed down the ladder, followed by the boy and Vince. On the ground floor, Vince offered the boy a tight smile, then said slowly, "You're not alone anymore. You and your sister are OK. But we need to get you somewhere safe. We have a sniper we need to take care of first." He pointed in the direction of the sniper, then pantomimed shooting a rifle. The boy nodded in understanding.

Charlie and Vince moved over to the wall facing the sniper, hearts thudding in their chests as they scanned the countryside through the cracked wooden slats. The sun had just dipped below the horizon, and a muted orange glow barely illuminated the shadows that cloaked the surrounding fields. Off in the distance, hidden in a second-story window of a farmhouse, the Nazi sniper had set up camp. Now, Charlie and Vince had to deal with him.

Charlie adjusted his rifle, working the bolt-action that had seen its share of combat. He glanced over at Vince, who was scanning the area through binoculars.

"Think you can spot him again?" Charlie asked, keeping his voice to a whisper.

Vince nodded, still staring through the lenses. "I've got a bead on the window. He's up there."

Charlie's fingers tightened on the rifle, but he held off from taking a shot. "We can't rush this. One mistake, and he's got us both. He's dug in, and we don't know if he has a backup or where he is."

Vince nodded, looking over at the two French siblings. "Yeah, but we also can't wait forever. We've got those two to worry about, and if we don't take him out soon, he's going to keep tearing our unit apart."

That being said, the sniper pointed the rifle out the window and let a shot fly down at Vince's squad. Then he ducked back in the window.

"I got him!" Vince said excitedly.

Charlie understood the urgency. They were a hundred yards away, and even with the steady hands that both he and Vince had, that was still a decent distance for a long shot. But there was no choice - they had to make it work.

"Alright," Charlie said after a pause, a plan forming in his mind. "I'll take the shot, but you need to cover me. If I miss, we'll only have one chance before he knows exactly where we are. But you need to get him to fire on you so he'll be in the window again."

Vince exhaled slowly and nodded. "Got it."

They moved quickly into position, Charlie crawling on his stomach across the barn's floor to an open window where he could get a better view of the farmhouse. He kept low, keeping his head down, but just high enough to steady his rifle. The wind was light, the air crisp, and his hands were steady despite the pressure building in his chest. He took a breath, exhaled slowly, and zeroed in on the window.

Vince had taken up a position on the opposite end of the barn below another window, peeking out just enough to make sure no one would surprise them from behind. He kept his eyes trained on the horizon, knowing the sniper wouldn't hesitate to take a shot at them once he saw their position.

Charlie adjusted his hold, compensating for the wind. The seconds seemed to stretch, the tension mounting. He looked over at Vince and nodded.

Vince jumped up in the window, screaming and waving his arms, then dropped back down.

Charlie caught a glimpse of movement. A flash of uniform. There. The sniper's head - just enough to see the outline.

Charlie didn't wait. His finger pressed the trigger, the sound of the shot ringing through the barn like thunder.

For a heartbeat, everything was still. Then, the sniper's silhouette crumpled in the window, disappearing from sight.

Vince's voice came through, tight with urgency. "Did you get him?"

Charlie kept his rifle raised, his eyes on the spot where the sniper had fallen. "I think so. But we better move fast. If he had anyone else up there, they'll be coming after us."

Vince didn't need to be told twice. They quickly gathered their gear, ducking low as they exited the barn. Pushing the two French kids as they sprinted toward the tree line, the sound of distant gunfire echoed across the fields, but neither of them looked back. They had taken out the sniper, but they both knew there would be more to come.

When they gathered back with their unit, they found someone to take their two companions to safety behind the lines.

As they watched the two young people move away…in that moment, the war seemed distant - the cries, the gunfire, the endless march. It wasn't just about survival anymore. It was about something more. In the midst of it all, there were still people trying to live, trying to rebuild what had been shattered. People that were dependent on them. It was a big responsibility.

Vince and Charlie were reminded that the fight they were fighting wasn't just for land or for victory. It was for people like the boy and his sister, people whose lives had been torn apart by a war they never asked for.

As they made their way back into the hedge rows, the distant rumble of artillery was still echoing, Vince knew they had become more than just soldiers and the realization shifted something inside him. He felt proud.

And as the sun dipped lower, the shadows of war grew longer. But Vince knew, if they stuck together, they had a fighting chance.

Chapter 49

The bus rumbled through the foothills east of Los Angeles, its windows clouded by the heat of early afternoon. Erma shifted in her seat, smoothing her skirt with one hand, while the other rested protectively on Barbara's tiny shoulder. The child had long since dozed off, her head tilted at an awkward angle against the window, hair stuck to her forehead from the sweltering ride.

It had been almost three years. Three long years since she and Judy had embraced in the gravel driveway of Burkey Farms, the scent of orange blossoms in the air and the sound of cicadas humming in the heat. Letters had flown faithfully between them since - pages worn at the creases, corners smudged by tears and dirt, always signed with love. But no letter, however lovingly written, could replace a hug.

Erma leaned her head against the cool metal frame of the bus and let her thoughts drift to Vince. France, the last she'd heard. Still alive, thank God. Still writing. But even the steadiest handwriting couldn't disguise the weariness between the lines. She held on to those letters like lifelines, rereading them in quiet moments, often after Barbara had gone to sleep.

The bus jolted as it turned off the highway and onto the familiar country road. Erma sat up straighter, blinking as the land opened before her - rows of citrus trees stretching into the distance with the mountains hazy blue in the background. She recognized the bent eucalyptus tree at the crossroads, the one Judy once joked was older than the farm itself.

"Barbara," she whispered, gently shaking her daughter's arm. "We're almost there."

The little girl stirred, rubbed her eyes, and smiled sleepily. "Are we gonna see the chickens?"

"Maybe, if they haven't wandered off," Erma said with a chuckle.

The bus hissed to a stop just past the split-rail fence, and Erma stood, heart thumping faster than it had in weeks. She stepped down onto the warm dust of the road, Barbara's small hand in hers, and there - on the porch - stood Judy, her arm wrapped around Clem's waist, their faces lighting up like morning sun. They both made a dash for the bus.

"Here, let me help with those," Clem said after giving them both ample hugs. He took off with the two worn suitcases, heading inside.

"Let me look at you,' Judy said, holding Barbara at arm's length after giving her a tremendous hug. "You have gotten so tall!"

"Aw, Gammy," Barbara said in an aw-shucks manner.

Judy then turned her attention to Erma, grabbing her and pulling her in tight. "It's been way too long!"

"It has," Erma replied simply.

"OK, let's get you two in the house. Got your old room all set up!"

Inside the farmhouse, time had hardly moved. The wallpaper, once cream with little green ivy leaves, had yellowed some at the corners, but the scent of cinnamon and dried herbs still clung to the air like a memory. Judy had baked a pie - Erma could smell it before she even stepped through the screen door. Apple, most likely. She remembered how Judy always added a dash of nutmeg, even when the recipe didn't call for it.

Barbara trotted ahead into the kitchen, already at ease, her shoes clicking across the worn floorboards. She turned to Judy. "Gammy, that smells sooo good," she said as she turned to investigate what was cooking.

Unbroken Hope

Judy watched her go with a soft smile, then turned to Erma and placed a gentle hand on her shoulder. "You're thinner," she said simply.

Erma let out a breath and managed a crooked smile. "Aren't we all, these days?"

They moved to the old pine table, still ringed with the faded scars of canning jars and sewing projects. Erma sat heavily, as if her body had finally admitted to the weight her heart had been carrying. Judy poured two cups of coffee, strong and dark, the way they used to drink it.

For a while, they didn't say much. Barbara chattered in the other room, playing with a faded rag doll Judy had pulled from a trunk upstairs.

Then Judy said, "Is he alright?"

Erma nodded, then shook her head, unsure. "He writes when he can. His last letter… they'd taken a small town in France. He didn't say much about it. Just that it had been hard." Her voice caught, and she looked down at her coffee. "He signed it with a little drawing of a little package of spinach seeds. Said it reminded him of the day we met." Erma paused to take a deep breath.

Judy reached across the table, covering Erma's hand with her own. Her touch was firm, grounded. "You're doing better than you think," she said.

Clem came down from upstairs and stood for a moment watching the women. Then, realizing he had nothing to add, he exclaimed, "Well, I guess I'll let you girls have at it. Think I'll go to the barn. Couple of things I need to look after." He moved toward the back door and then, as an afterthought, "Erma, I am so glad you are here. We've missed you."

Clem left as he eased the back door screen behind him so it wouldn't slam. The clock ticked softly from the mantle. Outside, a crow called from the windbreak, and somewhere in the distance a tractor rumbled to life. The farm was still running, if slower now. Judy and Clem did what they could.

"I kept meaning to ask," Erma said, glancing toward the window, "how have you managed it all, Judy? The crops, the house, the worry…"

Judy smiled, but her eyes were tired. "I just keep waking up and doing the next thing. All our men were called away, but you know that from my letters. We're just trying to keep things upright."

They both laughed - softly, but it was real. The kind of laugh that reminded them they were still women beneath the grief and ration stamps. Still friends. Still holding the line, in their own quiet way.

"Hey, Miss Erma," a familiar voice asked.

Erma turned to see Archie, now a strapping young man. "Archie!" Erma shouted as she jumped to her feet. "Let me look at you." She exclaimed. "You're almost grown!"

"I know," Archie replied. "I'll be eighteen in a few months, and then I'll have to go serve." Archie bowed his head as if realizing what the word serve meant.

Erma was saddened by the news, but could think of nothing to say but a halting, "oh."

"Well, I just wanted to say hi. I know you're staying for a few days, so we can catch up."

He grabbed her in a hug. "It is so good to see you," he added.

"Say, Archie?" Judy asked. "Can you do me a favor?"

"Sure."

"Take Barbara and show her around. I'm sure she's interested in how things have changed around here."

"Happy to, Miss Judy."

Archie moved into the living room, where the women could hear him talking to Barbara, but they couldn't make out everything he was saying. Then they heard Barbara say, "Can we go see the chickens?" Then the screen door slammed.

Unbroken Hope

"And off they go!" Judy said with a laugh. "I am so glad to see you."

"Goes double for me," Erma replied with a smile.

The next morning broke with a thin ribbon of gold rising over the San Bernardino hills. The air was cool and still, heavy with the scent of earth and the faint sweetness of citrus. A rooster crowed from somewhere near the barn. Erma was already awake, watching the soft light slip through the lace curtain of the guest room.

Barbara stirred beside her, curled like a kitten under the patchwork quilt, one arm flung over the doll Judy had given her. Erma smiled, touched her daughter's cheek, and slipped quietly from the bed.

She found Judy in the kitchen, already dressed in her work pants and flannel shirt, hair pinned up haphazardly. A kettle whistled softly on the stove.

"I was going to let you sleep," Judy said, pouring the hot water into a chipped teapot. "You must be tired after yesterday. Thought we might have tea this morning. That OK?"

"I've been tired for three years," Erma said, pulling on a borrowed sweater from the peg by the door. "Besides, it feels good to be up before the day starts."

They walked out together, carrying their large mugs of tea, shoes crunching on gravel as the early light cast long shadows over the orchard. The trees stretched in tidy rows, still heavy with late-season fruit, the oranges glowing like little suns. The leaves whispered gently overhead.

"I forgot how quiet it is out here," Erma said, her breath visible in the crisp morning air. "Los Angeles is just - noise, even when it's asleep."

Judy handed her a canvas sack. "You remember how to pick? Just put your mug down there."

Erma slipped the loop over her shoulder and reached up, twisting a ripe orange from the branch with practiced hands. "Like riding a bike," she said. "Except stickier."

They moved slowly down the row, working side by side as they had in summers past, back when the men were still home, and laughter came easier. For a while, neither spoke. The work was its own kind of prayer.

At the end of the row, Judy paused and looked out over the trees. "I think about him sometimes," she said. "Your Vince. How he used to tease me about putting too much lemon in my pie."

Erma laughed softly. "He was always a know-it-all about dessert."

"I miss him too," Judy said, almost in a whisper.

Erma blinked against the sunlight. "He's still out there. Still coming back to us."

Judy nodded. "Yes, he is."

Just then, among the trees, with the sun rising and the baskets slowly filling, they weren't two women waiting - they were two women living.

They didn't speak for a long while. They just walked on picking oranges.

By the third day, the wind had shifted. It carried with it the dry rustle of autumn, and a thin veil of dust swept across the fields, as if even the land knew it was time to let go.

Erma packed their things slowly that morning, folding Barbara's small dresses with care and tucking a jar of Judy's homemade peach preserves between socks and a worn storybook. Outside, the bus would be by before noon, winding its way along the familiar road past the orange groves and eucalyptus trees.

Barbara sat on the steps of the porch, her legs swinging over the edge, clutching the doll her Gammy had given her, as she watched the

Unbroken Hope

wind play in the tall grass. Judy knelt beside her, tying the child's shoelace tighter and brushing dirt from her knee.

"You be good for your mama," she said, smoothing Barbara's hair. "And when the mailman comes, you tell her to let you open my letters first, alright?"

Barbara grinned. "I will Gammy!"

Inside, Erma ran her hand over the kitchen counter one last time, as if trying to memorize the grain of the wood, the feel of this place that had held her so gently these past days. When she turned, Judy was already at the door.

"You'll write when you get home?" Judy asked, her voice steady but thick at the edges.

"Of course," Erma said. "Soon as I get the kettle on."

They embraced again - not the desperate kind of hug they'd shared when she first stepped off the bus, but something quieter. Something fuller. A knowing kind of embrace. The kind you give someone who has held your sorrow without judgment and shared your silence without fear.

Clem and Archie appeared as if by magic, sensing the visit had drawn to a close.

As the bus came into view, rumbling in the distance, Barbara ran to Clem, and he picked her up, and she gave him a big hug and kiss.

"You take care of your mom now, you hear?" he said with a smile

"I will. I promise."

He put her down, and Archie knelt down so that he could look her directly in the eye. "It was great seeing you again, squirt."

Barbara didn't say anything, just squeezed his neck.

Erma gave Archie a big hug and said, "You take care of yourself, you hear?" As she touched his cheek gently.

"Yes, ma'am." Tears were welling up in his eyes.

"Bye, Clem. Thank you for everything."

"Erma, you are welcome here anytime. We miss you." Clem turned to hide his tears.

Erma lingered one more moment at the edge of the porch, eyes locked with Judy's.

"Take care of yourself, Erma," Judy said. "And when this war ends, we'll have a big dinner here. Vince at the head of the table. We'll toast that we all made it through it."

Erma smiled through the tightness in her throat. "I'll hold you to that." The two women clung to one another, not knowing when they would see each other again. Then they held each other at arm's length and, between moist eyes, they nodded their goodbyes. Nothing more needed to be said.

The bus door opened with a hiss, and Erma helped Barbara up the steps before turning for one last wave. Judy stood tall in the dusty yard, one hand raised, the other resting on her hip - like always.

And as the bus pulled away, San Bernardino faded behind them, but the feeling of Burkey Farms stayed with her. The warmth. The friendship. The stillness inside the noise.

On the return trip, Erma sat on the bus, staring out the window as Los Angeles unfolded around her. The city was bustling, with its bright lights, towering buildings, and the hum of thousands of lives. She had never been here before marrying Vince. Now, though, she was part of it.

It wasn't the grand life she had often dreamed of, but it was something. Something to start with. She had the job at the diner. Though menial, it felt like a lifeline. She had no formal education, no previous job skills to speak of, but she had learned early in life to work with what she had. The kitchen at the diner was grimy and noisy, but it was a job. The pay was almost nothing, but it was a chance. She took orders, washed dishes, and mopped floors with a determination she didn't know she had left in her. Her pay helped augment what the government paid Vince.

Barbara was adjusting too. It seemed she had finally found her rhythm in school. When they first moved here, Erma had been nervous about Barbara going to school, but Barbara was resilient. The city felt big and foreign to her at first, but her daughter adapted quicker than expected. There were moments when Erma caught Barbara staring at the skyline, her eyes wide with wonder.

Still, the new life wasn't without its struggles. Barbara came home every other day with a heaviness in her heart, a silence Erma couldn't ignore.

"Mom," Barbara began one afternoon as they sat at their tiny kitchen table in the apartment. "Some of the kids... they still call me 'Oakie.'" Barbara thought that word was going to follow her for her entire life

Erma's heart twisted at the word. She knew what it meant. The term, often used as a slur in California, was a painful reminder of their past. A label that stuck to people like them - the ones who had left the dust and hardship of the plains for the promise of something better. It hurt to hear her daughter bear that burden.

"What do you tell them?" Erma asked quietly, her fingers wrapping around the chipped mug in front of her.

Barbara shrugged, staring down at her hands. "I don't know. I don't want to fight them. But it's... it's not nice, Mom."

Erma's fingers tightened around the mug, her heart breaking. "You don't have to fight, sweetie. Just know that you're not what they say. You're better than that. The fact is you are an Oakie...someone from Oklahoma. You should wear that proudly."

Barbara gave a small nod. Not sure she believed it.

Erma wished she could do more. She wished she could shield Barbara from the harshness of the world, from the sting of every insult that came her way, but she couldn't. All she could do was try to make their life here as stable as possible.

The next morning, Erma walked Barbara to the school gates, holding her daughter's hand tightly in hers. She watched as the other kids streamed in, their laughter ringing in the air. Some of them looked at Barbara with curiosity, some with judgment. But there was one thing Erma knew for sure. Her daughter would rise above it. The taunts were nothing more than noise, and eventually, they would lose their power.

As Barbara turned to enter the schoolyard, Erma bent down and kissed the top of her head. "You're stronger than you know, Barbara. You're going to do great things."

Barbara smiled up at her, her face a little brighter than it had been the day before. "I hope so, Mom."

Mom, Erma thought. It wasn't that long ago she called me Mama, and she noticed that she had stopped using Barbara's middle name when she referred to her. Maybe they were both evolving into something that Erma had no name for. But it seemed her little girl was growing up.

Erma watched her daughter walk away, her heart heavy but full of hope. Wearing a faded blue dress that was beginning to be too small, Erma's heart winced. Barbara was growing up and learning more about the hard world than she had any right to. It was a strange thing, this city. It could be cruel, and it could be kind. But in the midst of it all, there was still a spark, the gold ring, always a chance for something new right around the corner.

Unbroken Hope

Barbara sat at her desk, the sound of laughter echoing around the classroom. It wasn't directed at her, but it always felt like it might be. The teasing had started years ago when the other students noticed her worn shoes, the way she tucked her sleeves too tightly, around her wrists, and the way her hair, always in the same neat ponytail, seemed just a little too flat compared to everyone else's. They would giggle behind her back, making jokes about how she looked like she belonged on a farm instead of a city. She had thought they would eventually grow tired of teasing, but they never did.

In 1944, being a fourth grader in Los Angeles wasn't easy for Barbara. The war was still fresh in everyone's minds, rationing was a regular topic of conversation, and the world seemed to be spinning in ways that she didn't understand. Her mother worked long hours at the local diner. But they didn't have extra money to spend on frivolous clothes for Barbara so that she would fit in better at school. They did their best, but there was only so much they could afford, especially with so many things being saved for the war effort.

Every day, Barbara tried to ignore the teasing. She focused on her lessons, her pencil gripped tightly in her small hand, and hoped the day would pass without incident. But the whispers, the giggles, and the looks always seemed to follow her. It wasn't that the other students were bad kids - just that they didn't understand her.

One afternoon, after an especially tough day, Barbara walked home slowly, dragging her feet in the dirt. She passed by the little shops along her street, hearing the chatter of people talking about the war and wondering exactly where her father was.

That evening, as her mother prepared a simple dinner in the kitchen, Barbara sat quietly at the table. She had told her mom before about the teasing and about how it hurt. Her mother, always so busy with work, seemed to have her own worries, so Barbara kept her feelings to herself this time, thinking that if she didn't talk about it, maybe it would go away on its own.

But it didn't. Instead, it only grew worse. The taunts became more personal, focusing not just on her clothes or her appearance, but on things she couldn't control - like her family's situation. Her classmates would call her "poor girl" in a sing-song voice, or mock her accent, which was influenced by her mother's Oklahoma accent.

Then, one day, something happened. Barbara's teacher, Miss Henderson, called her to the front of the class to read aloud. It was a weekly tradition, and though Barbara was shy about speaking in front of the class, she loved reading. She stood up, holding the book a little too tightly, and began to read from the page. The words felt like old friends in her mouth, and for the first time in a long while, she forgot about the teasing.

But as she read, she noticed something. The laughter that had once filled the room was quiet. The whispers had stopped. Slowly, her classmates began to listen. Even those who had been the hardest on her were watching with a new kind of respect. Barbara, without realizing it, had found a way to stand out, not because of her clothes or the things they teased her about, but because of something she loved - reading.

When she finished, Miss Henderson smiled at her. "Well done, Barbara. You're a natural," she said, her voice warm and encouraging. Barbara's face flushed with pride, and for a moment, it felt like she belonged.

That night, Barbara finally told her mother about what had happened. Her mother listened carefully, giving her a hug and assuring her that being different wasn't a bad thing. She told Barbara that what mattered most was her heart and the things she loved - like reading - and no one could take that away from her.

Unbroken Hope

The teasing didn't stop overnight. It would take time, but for the first time, Barbara felt a spark of confidence. She realized that maybe the world wasn't as focused on her as she thought. And if she could just keep doing what she loved, maybe the teasing would eventually stop altogether.

Chapter 50

The First Infantry was on the move again. The hedgerows of Normandy with its dense fog had given way to the lush farmlands and vineyards of France.

It was early morning and Vince adjusted his helmet, feeling the weight of the gear on his shoulders. His fatigues were now slick and dark with the morning mist. His rifle, once so clean and cared for, was dirty and scratched. The wind had a bite to it, cutting through the fabric of his jacket, but the cold was the least of his worries. The war had settled into a brutal routine, every day spent in survival mode, each step forward an inch closer to routing the enemy, each night colder than the last.

"Vince!" Charlie's whispering shout broke through the fog. Vince turned, spotting his buddy just a few paces behind, slinging his own rifle over his shoulder. His face was pale, but his eyes, though tired, still had the familiar resolve.

Charlie wiped his face with the back of his hand, a move that had become automatic, like everything else since the invasion. "Six weeks, huh? Feels like it's been six years."

Vince grunted in agreement. "Time's all mixed up now. All the days are running together. Only thing that's clear is that we're still here!"

"Not all of us," Charlie muttered. His gaze shifted, and Vince followed his friend's line of sight. A few yards away, a litter-bearer team moved toward the rear, a stretcher between them. The man on it, Timmons, was covered with a blanket, but the way his arm hung off the side told its own grim story.

"We've got to keep moving," Vince said, his voice low but firm.

Charlie didn't respond immediately. Instead, he adjusted his pack and peered down the narrow lane between rows of grape plants in the vineyard. The grape plants bulged with large green leaves and bunches of red fruit that had somehow survived. The grapes shone brightly from the slick dew on their skins. Vince and Charlie had eaten their fill of the grapes, as had the others. Harvesting had been a challenge, what with the German occupation. So, the grapes had waited to be liberated by the American soldiers.

The sounds of distant gunfire punctuated the air, but it was hard to tell where it was coming from anymore. German stragglers were still putting up a fight. The skirmishes had spread out across the countryside, a chaotic web of firefights that spanned miles.

"You think the Germans are still dug in ahead of us?" Vince asked, finally breaking the silence.

Charlie thought for a moment, rubbing dirt from his nose. "Don't know, but there can't be many of them left."

"I'm sure they don't like getting their asses kicked," Charlie grunted.

"We'll get the rest of them," Vince said, though it was more for his own reassurance than anything else. "They can't last forever. They didn't count on us being this tough." And then repeated, "They can't last forever", then added, "Can they?" Hoping for confirmation.

"No, they can't last forever," Charlie replied with a smirk, his mouth still had a firm set to it. "Still, it's hard not to wonder… how many more days of this do we got left?"

Vince didn't have an answer for that. Instead, he scanned the line ahead, where other members of Alpha Company were moving cautiously from one alley of vine plants to another. Every movement, every sound, felt magnified in the stillness. They had learned to be quiet, to avoid the kind of careless noise that might draw the attention of snipers or patrols, though he could hear the rustle of leaves as the men moved along.

A whistle from up ahead broke the silence. A signal. Vince and Charlie immediately dropped to the ground, instinctively reaching for their weapons. Moments later, the rest of the squad followed suit, lying in the wet dirt, listening.

"Looks like we've got a push ahead," Charlie said under his breath. He was already checking his rifle.

"Looks like," Vince replied. "Ready?"

"As I'll ever be," Charlie answered, their standard reply.

The signal came again, a sharp, short blast of the whistle followed by a yell. "Move out!"

Vince's heart skipped a beat. It was time. The entire company shifted at once, the low murmur of orders passing between the men. They knew the drill. The line moved slowly, carefully, until they were within a few yards of the enemy's position. The first burst of machine-gun fire shattered the silence, and Vince dropped into a low crawl, the earth around him flying from the force of the rounds. Beside him, Charlie swore under his breath, but kept moving.

"Well, shit!" Vince heard someone curse.

"Stay low!" Vince shouted, though he wasn't sure Charlie could hear him over the roar of gunfire.

They kept pushing forward, the vine plants providing some cover but also limiting their movement. Every few seconds, rounds would fly overhead, or a tracer would streak through the air, a brief flash of green or red against the dull sky. Vince's hands were slick with sweat as he gripped his rifle, his breath coming in short bursts. He could feel his heart pounding in his chest, and though he wanted to focus on the enemy ahead, he kept thinking about the men who had fallen in the past few days, the ones who wouldn't make it through the next fight.

Then, as if to add to the chaos, the sound of artillery rang out in the distance. But he couldn't tell if it was the enemy or friendly fire.

"Get ready to move!" Sergeant Miller's shout broke through the din, and Vince glanced over at Charlie, who gave him a grim nod. They were as ready as they'd ever be.

The next moments were a blur. The fire from the Germans increased in intensity, but the squad pressed forward, inch by inch. Other squads to the left and right of them were doing the same. Vince and Charlie kept their heads down, moving between the rows of the vineyard like ghosts, each step taking them closer to the enemy.

As they neared the crest of a hill, Vince could hear the crackle of radio static, but he couldn't make out what was being said.

When they finally reached the top of the rise, Vince paused, his breath ragged. The view stretched out before him - an open field littered with the remnants of battles past. The German positions were up ahead, but now, they were within striking distance. They were still firing, and then firing abruptly stopped. Vince could see the Germans breaking camp and retreating!

"What the?" he mumbled.

Vince looked over at Charlie, who was scanning the field, his face set in a determined mask. For a moment, they shrugged at each other.

Sergeant Miller came walking over. "Just got word over the radio, the Germans have surrendered to the 4th Infantry in Paris. Those fellas are retreating. We're on our way now. Going to Paris, Boys!"

Chapter 51

The sun was shrouded by clouds over Los Angeles, casting a haze across the city. Barbara stared out the window of their small apartment, the familiar sights of the city blurring in front of her.

Erma was sitting in the kitchen, humming softly to herself as she moved about. Her hands were shaking slightly as she stirred a pot of soup on the stove. Erma had kept a small garden behind the apartment building. This is where she carefully raised vegetables to make soup.

Erma's movements were slower than they used to be, the rhythm of life in the kitchen, something Barbara had grown up with, but now found unsettling. Erma had always been a whirlwind, a constant presence in the house, but now, there was something different in the air - a subtle shift that Barbara couldn't ignore.

Barbara closed her eyes and listened to the soft hum of her mother's song, the words lost in the swirls of the melody. Barbara could make the words out, though. It was one of her mother's favorite songs.

Pack up all my cares and woe, here I go, singing low
Bye, bye, blackbird

For a moment, the noise of the world outside faded away, leaving only the hum and the heavy silence that settled between them. It wasn't that her mother was unwell - at least not physically - but the change in her was undeniable. Erma had always been the rock of their family, the one who made sure everything held together, no matter the storm. But now, she was starting to crack at the edges.

Barbara couldn't pinpoint exactly when it had begun, but she felt it every day. It was the small things - the way Erma would forget where she put things, or the way she seemed to lose track of time when she was alone. And the letters. The letters from Vince had become fewer and fewer, and each time one arrived, it was like a brief moment of hope that quickly vanished as she read the short, sometimes detached, notes he sent from the front lines. Vince had always been a man of few words, but now, it felt as though the war was draining even the little he had left to offer.

Erma's heart ached as she thought of her husband, fighting across an ocean, while she tried to hold onto the remnants of their life in Los Angeles. There were days when the weight of everything - the bills, the war, the constant strain of keeping the apartment, and her job - felt like it was too much to bear. She tried to keep her daughter from noticing, tried to keep up appearances, but it was getting harder to hide the exhaustion that clung to her.

One evening, as the sun set behind the city, Barbara sat at the small kitchen table, the dim light of a single lamp casting long shadows across the room. Erma was still humming, though it lacked the cheer it once had. It was almost as if she was drifting away with each note, lost in a melody only she could hear. Barbara watched her mother, and her heart grew heavy with worry.

"Mom," Barbara said softly, her voice barely breaking the silence.

Erma paused, the spoon hovering over the pot. She turned to Barbara, her eyes wide, as if she had been snapped from a dream. "Yes, baby?"

Barbara hesitated, unsure of how to ask the question that had been nagging at her for days. "How're you feelin? OK?"

Erma's face softened, and she smiled, but it was a smile that wasn't quite convincing. "Oh, you know me. I'm fine. Just tired, I suppose."

Unbroken Hope

Barbara nodded, but the lie hung between them, unspoken. She knew her mother wasn't fine. Erma's hands were trembling now, the soup threatening to burn on the stove as her attention drifted.

Barbara stood up and walked over to her, placing a gentle hand on her shoulder. "Maybe you should take a rest. I can finish up here."

Erma looked at her, and for a brief moment, something flickered in her eyes. A shadow of confusion, or perhaps recognition - Barbara couldn't tell. "I'm fine, sweetheart," Erma said again, though her voice lacked conviction. But she turned back to the soup, stirring.

Barbara bit her lip, but didn't argue. She knew that trying to confront her mother directly wouldn't help. Instead, she watched her as Erma slowly moved away from the stove, mumbling to herself as she shuffled toward the living room. The quiet creak of the floorboards seemed to echo in the stillness, and Barbara couldn't shake the feeling that the weight of the war was starting to crush both of them in different ways.

As the days passed, Barbara began to notice other things. Erma would leave the door slightly ajar when she went out to the market, forgetting that the heat of the day would soon creep in. Or she would misplace Vince's letters, hiding them under piles of old newspapers, and forgetting she had even seen them. The smallest details, the ones that never mattered before, now seemed so significant - each one a quiet sign of the unraveling she couldn't ignore any longer.

Barbara sat down at her desk one evening, staring at the letter from Vince. It had come in a week ago, a few short sentences that barely conveyed anything. "I'm well. The front is quiet. I'll write again soon. Love, Vince." It wasn't the letter she had hoped for, but it was all she had. She wondered if it would be the last one. Would she ever hear from him again?

The weight of everything was pressing down on Barbara. The war had taken Vince from her, and now it was taking her mother too. The loneliness she felt had begun to settle deep in her bones, a permanent companion. But she couldn't let go - not yet. She couldn't abandon her mother, no matter how much it felt like her mother was slipping away from her.

The sound of Erma's humming drifted in from the living room again, a soft, off-key melody that made Barbara's chest tighten.

"Pack up all my cares and woe, here I go, singing low; Bye, bye, blackbird."

She could hear the tremor in her mother's voice now, as if she were reaching for something she couldn't quite grasp.

Barbara stood up from the desk, her heart heavy with an emotion she couldn't name. She needed to hold on, to keep going, but the truth was that she was scared. Scared of losing her dad, scared of losing her mother, and scared of the future that seemed to stretch out before her like an endless road.

Turning off the soup, she walked into the living room, finding Erma sitting in the old chair by the window, her eyes distant as she stared out at the setting sun. Barbara didn't say anything. She simply sat beside her mother, taking her hand in her own, and together, they watched the world outside fade into the evening.

The silence between them felt like it could stretch on forever, Barbara didn't mind. It was enough just to be together.

It was late on a warm Saturday morning when Judy Burkey's dusty, weathered truck rumbled down the narrow, palm-lined street that led to the small Los Angeles apartment building where Vince, Erma, and

Unbroken Hope

Barbara had made their home. Judy had not come to visit since Erma had moved away, but today, the winds had shifted, and she was here, a surprise gift from Barbara who had secretly written Judy out of alarm for her mother's well-being.

The moment Judy stepped out of the truck, a rush of excitement and nerves jolted her. She glanced at the apartment building. The roses were blooming, the paint on the shutters faded from the relentless sun, but everything else looked good to her. Judy wiped her hands on her worn jeans, took a deep breath, and walked up to the apartment door.

Inside, Erma was in her bedroom, dusting. In the kitchen, a half-finished letter to Vince was waiting for her on the table. She hadn't been able to pick the pen up in days, her thoughts scattered, the words failing her. Barbara, on the other hand, was lying on the sofa flipping through a magazine, trying to drown out the silence that had started to feel unbearable.

The doorbell rang. Erma came out of the bedroom and looked quizzically at Barbara, a moment of confusion hanging in the air. Erma went and opened the door.

"Judy!" Erma gasped, her voice shaking with disbelief, as she jumped back in surprise. Barbara was stunned with surprise as well.

"Well, I figured you two could use a little something to brighten the day," Judy grinned, stepping into the house with a swagger that was equal parts confidence and affection. "Thought I'd stop by and shake things up a bit!"

Erma's face softened with emotion, the relief evident as she threw her arms around her friend. "I can't believe you're here, Judy."

Judy hugged her tightly, giving her a quick kiss on the cheek. "I know, Erma. But I thought maybe I could bring a little sunshine into this house. It's been hard, huh?" She glanced at Barbara, who was wiping a tear away from the corner of her eye. The strain of those long months, missing their man, was written all over her.

Barbara nodded as she went to give Judy a huge hug, trying to keep her composure. "Oh, Gammy, it's just been... lonely. Every day feels like the last. I know Daddy is doing his part, but it doesn't make it any easier."

Judy could see it in their eyes, the weight they carried. She always knew how to lighten the mood, how to bring a little laughter into the most somber of moments. She took a step back, hands on her hips, eyes mischievous. "Well, I didn't drive all the way from San Bernardino to let you two sit around all day feeling sorry for yourselves. How about we take a walk? Get a little fresh air. I saw a cafe down the street. Sign there said they had the best pie in town."

The mention of pie was enough to coax a laugh from both Erma and Barbara. A shared moment of understanding passed between them, a reminder of what they still had - each other - and how laughter was still a lifeline, even in the darkest of times.

The two women and the young girl set out for the cafe, their voices filling the street as they walked. Judy's stories of life on the farm, with its ups and downs, had Barbara and Erma laughing, their spirits rising with every word. It was almost as if time had been rewound, and they were back in their carefree days before the war.

But as the day wore on, the sun began to dip low, casting long shadows over the streets. The weight of the inevitable goodbye loomed, though neither Erma nor Barbara wanted to admit it.

As Judy loaded her things into her truck later that evening, the quietness of the moment hung thick between them. Erma stood by the tailgate, arms crossed, and Barbara stood beside her, both of them holding back tears.

"I'll come back as soon as I can," Judy said with a smile, though there was a sadness in her eyes. "You're not rid of me just yet."

Unbroken Hope

"I know," Erma said softly, her voice cracking. "I know. We'll get through this, Judy. We always do."

Barbara reached out and gave Judy a quick hug. "I love you, Gammy. Thank you for coming. I knew I could count on you." She whispered.

Speechless, Judy simply hugged the girl tighter.

Judy climbed into her truck and started the engine. She waved as she drove off, the sound fading into the distance.

Erma and Barbara stood there for a moment longer, watching the truck move into the distance, before turning back toward the house. Goodbye was always the hardest part. But they had each other.

Chapter 52

The night was cool as the streets of Paris flickered with the soft glow of lamplights and the echo of distant celebrations. The city had just been liberated by the 4th Infantry Division, and the streets were filled with the joy of French civilians. Vince and Charlie had spent the day marching through the outskirts with elements from their own Division, but now, they were finally stepping onto the streets of the glorious City of Lights.

The tension, the strain of months spent fighting through the brutal European theater, seemed to melt away the moment they crossed the Seine River into Paris. It was surreal, the thought of walking through a city that had been under Nazi occupation for years, finally free. Vince took a deep breath, inhaling the crisp air.

"Well, Charlie, looks like we made it," Vince said, a wide smile on his face. His voice was deep but laced with an excitement that was hard to contain.

Charlie, adjusting his helmet with a grin, "Didn't think I'd see the day. First thing we need is a drink."

Vince laughed with a sharp nod. "I hear the Parisians know a thing or two about that."

The two of them made their way toward the heart of the city, passing through streets where the cheering crowds seemed to erupt in spontaneous bursts of joy every few minutes. French men and women clapped their hands and waved, some offering bottles of wine in celebration, others holding flowers aloft. The air was thick with the scent of liberation - of freedom - of life.

They passed an old café where a French woman, her eyes sparkling with tears, handed them each a glass of champagne. She kissed each of them on the cheek, and they both blushed, taken off guard by the warmth and gratitude of the moment.

"Vers la liberté," she said, raising her glass.

The men looked at her, puzzled.

"To Freedom," she cried triumphantly.

"To Freedom," Vince and Charlie called out, holding their glasses aloft.

They all clinked glasses and took a long sip. Vince let the bubbly drink roll across his tongue, the sharp tang cutting through the dusty dryness of the day's march.

"I think we're going to get along just fine here," Charlie said, looking around the Parisian streets - in awe.

They walked further into the city, their laughter blended with the jubilant sound of the crowd. The sounds of French songs, some old, some new, rang out from every corner as if the whole city had come alive in celebration.

At one point, they spotted a small group of American soldiers sitting at a table outside a café near Rue des Martyrs, a few bottles of wine already empty. They waved Vince and Charlie over, urging them to join.

"Gentlemen!" one of the soldiers, a wiry guy they would learn later was named Eddie, shouted, "Get over here and have a seat. Paris is a damn sight better than the front lines, don't you think?"

Without hesitation, they slid into the chairs. Vince and Charlie didn't know them, but it hardly mattered. They quickly introduced themselves. And in that instant had made good friends.

Vince raised an eyebrow. "Hell yeah. I'd say we earned this."

Unbroken Hope

Charlie chuckled. "We earned a lot of things. But right now, I think a hot meal sounds better than anything else."

Before they could say much more, the café owner, a stout, middle-aged man, came over with a basket of fresh bread and a tray piled high with pâté, cheeses, and slices of smoked meats. He placed it all down with a proud smile, speaking in rapid French, though Vince and Charlie caught enough of it to know he was thanking them for their service.

"Vince," Charlie whispered, leaning in, "this is more than I ever imagined. I never thought we'd be here, you know?"

Vince glanced around, feeling the weight of Charlie's words. The city that had seemed so distant only weeks ago was now right in front of them - alive, thriving, and grateful. "I know, buddy. I know."

They sat back, enjoying the food, the wine, and the camaraderie of soldiers who had shared the same hardship and finally had the chance to savor a moment of peace. As they talked, they learned that the Germans had formally surrendered, thanks to the 4th Infantry's relentless advance. But Paris wasn't just about military victory - it was about the spirit of a city that refused to be broken.

The night continued to sit quiet over Paris, a smoky hush draped in war's weariness. The air was cool, heavy with soot from the recent battles.

Eddie, sitting cross-legged, started to hum - soft at first, barely audible above the static hush of night. Vince didn't recognize the tune. A lullaby, maybe? Or some old church hymn? Vince looked at Charlie quizzically.

Charlie's head tilted. Another soldier nearby picked up the hum, then another. It caught like a breeze catching wheat, swelling slowly, like breath drawn in before a song. Vince squinted at Eddie, watching his lips move ever so slightly, as if whispering the notes to himself.

Then it hit him.

Michael Wells

The World War 1 classic, Over There...

The melody wrapped around him suddenly, as familiar as the scent of spring grass, as vivid as technicolor dreams.

"Over there, over there, Send the word, send the word over there - " someone sang - off-key but earnest. A ripple of quiet singing spread through the group, voices hushed, reverent.

Vince's throat tightened. He joined in, quietly at first.

"That the Yanks are coming, The Yanks are coming..."

He could see them - Erma clutching her popcorn tub with both hands, eyes wide, and Barbara, nearly falling out of her seat, kicking her shoes against the theater floor. The screen had glowed, casting rainbows over their faces. The film was James Cagney in Yankee Doodle Dandy. The story of George M. Cohan, composer of Over There. Erma had written Vince that they had gone to see the movie. Back when the world had made some sort of sense.

Now, the singing felt like defiance. Like memory. Like home. A small group of locals stopped to listen. The group slowly grew.

A searchlight skimmed the rooftops across the Seine, but no one stopped. The tune drifted out into the Parisian night, winding through alleys and shattered windows.

Vince's voice cracked on the final line.

"We'll be over, we're coming over, and we won't come back till it's over, over there!"

He wiped at his eyes, blaming the smoke. Charlie said nothing - just patted him once on the back, firm and understanding.

Their audience burst into cheers and applause and then started to disperse.

Vince looked at Charlie and grinned, for just one damn minute, the war didn't feel like the only thing in the world.

Unbroken Hope

The sun began to set, casting an orange glow over the rooftops as the streets grew quieter, the celebratory energy turning into a calm contentment. Vince leaned back in his chair, gazing up at the sky. For the first time in a long time, he felt like he could truly relax.

Charlie nudged him with an elbow. "Vince…what do you think the folks back home will say when we tell 'em about this?"

Vince laughed, shaking his head. "I don't know, but I'll tell you this much: no one's going to believe we spent the night in Paris singing Over There!"

Charlie grinned, picking up his glass. "I'll drink to that."

The two of them raised their glasses to the night, to the city, to the memories they'd carry with them, and to their fallen comrades.

As they finished their drinks, a light breeze blew through the café, carrying with it the distant sound of more cheers, more music. It was the kind of moment that made everything - the fighting, the losses, the long marches - worth it. The city was free. And so were they. For just a moment, Vince and Charlie allowed themselves to enjoy it. To be soldiers who were finally on the winning side of history, their boots planted firmly in a place that had been the dream of so many.

As the last light of day faded, they stood up, ready to explore Paris further, side by side. The world was at peace for now, so they bid adieu to their newfound friends and wandered into the unknown night of a liberated Paris, with nothing but the stars and the city's glow lighting their way.

Chapter 53

It was November 23, 1944 – Thanksgiving Day. Erma sat at the kitchen table, the sharp scent of roasting chicken filling the room, mingling with the scent of a freshly baked pie and the spicy aroma of the cranberries she had simmered down. Erma would have liked to able to buy a turkey, but it was far too expensive for her to buy. It should have been a time for gathering, for laughter, for a moment of respite amidst the hardships of the war. But no one was in a festive mood.

The kitchen table stood quiet, save for the rhythmic scratching of Barbara's crayons on the paper at the corner. The girl was drawing another picture - her mother assumed it was a family portrait - but it had been days since Erma had been able to make out much of Barbara's art. The girl's hand then went still, she frowned in concentration, but it was as though her mind had wandered to places far beyond the walls of their home.

Erma's own gaze drifted to the chair at the end of the table. Vince's chair. Empty. There was no comforting weight of his presence to fill the space, no laughter, no booming voice to match the rustling of leaves outside. He had been gone so long, longer than she had ever imagined, and every day she tried to hold onto the memories of his touch, his words, the way he'd made her feel safe in a world that seemed to be falling apart around them.

The war had dragged on, and with it, the unbearable silence of not knowing. For months now, they had received nothing. No letters. No word of where Vince was - or if he was alive or not. The last letter he had sent was from Paris. But that was in August. Her heart twisted at the thought, a daily ache she had grown accustomed to. It was almost as if the war had become a shadow that loomed over her family, growing longer and darker as the days passed.

Barbara looked up from her drawing, her blue eyes meeting her mother's. "Mom?"

Erma forced a smile, wiping her hands on her apron. "Yes, sweetie?"

Barbara hesitated, her fingers still clutching the crayon tightly. "Do you think Dad's okay?"

The question sliced through Erma's heart. She swallowed hard, trying to push down the lump that had formed in her throat. "Of course he is, honey. He's strong. He'll be home soon, I'm sure of it." She was so sick of saying those same exact words every time Barbara asked.

Barbara nodded, though her expression told a different story. "I miss him."

"I know you do," Erma whispered. She walked over to Barbara, crouching down to be eye-level with her daughter. Her hand gently stroked Barbara's hair, the softness of it somehow grounding her in the moment. "I miss him too."

The silence stretched between them, the weight of unspoken fears settling over the house like a heavy blanket. Erma didn't want to tell Barbara the truth. She didn't want to say the words that might shatter the fragile hope her daughter still clung to. That Vince's absence wasn't just a temporary thing. The longer they went without news, the harder it became to believe he was just delayed or caught in the fog of war. But how could she tell her little girl that she, too, was beginning to wonder if the man she had loved for so long was ever coming back?

"I'll set the table," Erma said, pulling herself together, forcing the emotions down where they couldn't rise to the surface. She tried to make her voice light, like it used to be, before the war. Before the letters stopped coming.

As she moved to the cupboard to pull out the plates, Barbara spoke again, her voice quieter this time.

"Mom?"

"Yes, sweetheart?" Erma answered patiently.

"When we say thanks today... can we say thank you for Dad?"

Erma's hands trembled for a moment as she reached for the silverware. "Of course we can. We'll say thank you for him, for all the people fighting, for everyone who's keeping us safe." She bit her lip, the words bitter on her tongue, but she didn't let them slip away. "And we'll thank God that he's coming home soon."

Barbara smiled, her small face lighting up for a moment, before she turned back to her drawing. Erma caught a glimpse of the picture - a sketch of a man in a soldier's uniform, standing tall, holding a letter in his hand. Beside him, a woman with her arms stretched wide, and a little girl by her side.

Erma's heart clenched again as she saw the likeness - Vince was there, in every line of the drawing. And so was she. So was Barbara.

The front door opened with a creak, and Barbara's head snapped up. But it wasn't Vince. It was just the wind, pushing the door slightly ajar. Erma's chest tightened, a flicker of disappointment sparking in her, but she quickly masked it, locking the door before turning back to the task at hand.

The chicken was almost done, and the table was set. Everything was ready for a family celebration. But the absence of one person - the one person who mattered most - lingered in the air like a specter.

Dinner passed quietly. The food was warm, and the conversation forced, like a pale imitation of what they once had. Erma tried to smile, to keep the mood light, but there was no escaping the hole that had formed in their lives. Every time she caught herself laughing, she remembered Vince's absence, and it felt hollow.

After the meal, Erma and Barbara sat on the porch bundled under a heavy blanket, looking out at the darkening sky. It was chilly, the wind biting, but the stars above were clear and bright, as if the heavens themselves had gathered in quiet tribute to the lost and the missing.

Barbara leaned her head against her mother's shoulder, and Erma wrapped an arm around her, holding her close.

"Do you think Dad is looking at the stars right now?" Barbara asked softly.

Erma kissed the top of her daughter's head. "I like to think so. I think he's looking at the same stars we are. And he's thinking of us."

Barbara nodded, though her eyes were distant, lost in the world she had created within her mind.

Erma didn't have the answers. She didn't know when or if Vince would return, but she would continue to believe, if only for Barbara. If only to give them something to hold on to when the darkness seemed endless.

"Happy Thanksgiving, sweetie," Erma whispered, pressing her lips to her daughter's forehead. "We'll get through this. Together."

Barbara didn't answer, but she leaned closer to her mother, the warmth of her small body a balm to the cold ache that gnawed at Erma's heart.

And as the night wore on, Erma held onto that small, fragile hope - the hope that, someday, that empty chair at the table would no longer be empty. That Vince would come back to them.

And until then, she would keep the faith.

Chapter 54

The cold was unbearable in the Hurtgen Forest, each breath they took stung like pieces of ice were being forced into their lungs. The ground was combination of being frozen and slick, a deadly combination that made every step feel like they were one moment away from falling and breaking a bone. A dense fog had settled over the trees, making it seem like the world had shrunk to nothing but the shadows of pines and the faint crunch of boots on brittle twigs. The only sounds were the distant cracks of gunfire and occasional thump of artillery, as if the earth itself was breaking apart under the strain of the war.

Vince clutched his M1 rifle, its cold metal stinging his hands through the woolen gloves, as he moved through the fog alongside his squad. The remnants of the First Infantry Division were spread out across the front line, but the atmosphere was thicker than just the fog. It was as if the very forest itself was suffocating them. He had been in combat for years now, but nothing had prepared him for this place - this grim, endless stretch of freezing, cold woods that seemed to hold more than just trees.

"Keep moving," Charlie whispered hoarsely, just close enough for Vince to hear. His voice was like gravel, his face gaunt. There was a grim determination in his eyes, though it didn't quite reach the edges of his mouth, which was drawn tight in a line. "Don't stop. We're almost there."

Vince nodded, his throat dry. He hadn't heard Charlie speak like that in a long time - he knew what it meant. There was no 'almost there' in the Hurtgen Forest. There was only the next step. And the one after that. Survival. The ground beneath them felt like it had been clawed apart by something unnatural, a reflection of the horrors that had already taken place here.

The squad moved in formation, each man taking care to keep his distance from the others - silent signals traded with nervous glances. Every step felt like they were trespassing, as though the frozen ghosts of soldiers who had come before them still lingered in the shadows. Vince could feel the weight of the loss pressing down on him. He didn't know if he was more afraid of the Germans or the deep, oppressive silence that came with the forest's unnatural stillness.

They'd been part of the push into Aachen, had fought hard to capture it, and for a fleeting moment, there had been a sense of victory. But the elation quickly faded when they were sent into the Hurtgen, ordered to hold ground in a place that felt more like a tomb than a battlefield. The Germans had dug in deep here. They knew this terrain like the back of their hands. It was a perfect place for a slaughter.

Suddenly, the unmistakable blast of an artillery round exploding nearby, followed by a scream ripping through the air. The ground shook, throwing Vince off balance for a second. His heart hammered in his chest, but he didn't hesitate. The squad dropped to the ground instinctively, their bodies pressed into the frozen earth. A few of the men were already shouting as the barrage began.

"Get down!" Charlie shouted, his voice barely audible over the explosions. His command was clear.

The forest erupted into chaos as the first wave of German artillery slammed into the woods. Vince's eyes widened in horror as splinters of bark, chunks of ice, and earth flew through the air, the sheer force of the blasts sending tremors deep into his bones. The men scrambled to take cover, ducking behind trees, large roots, anything that could protect them from the rain of shrapnel.

Unbroken Hope

Vince pressed his back against the trunk of a large pine, his breath shallow, the acrid scent of gunpowder stinging his nose. His mind raced, but he fought to focus. They had trained for this - had been prepared for the constant threats of exploding rounds, sniper fire, and ambushes. But nothing could have prepared him for the crushing weight of fear that gripped his chest every time a shell landed too close.

Charlie had been promoted to corporal and now was the assistant squad leader. He moved quickly, his sharp eyes scanning the battlefield even through the smoke and debris. Vince couldn't hear him over the explosions, but he could see the way Charlie's jaw tightened as he signaled to the squad. Vince looked at the men around him - faces smeared with dirt and frozen blood - before turning his attention back to the forest ahead.

The German forces weren't far. He could feel them. It wasn't just the noise, but the air itself - electric, charged with the tension of an imminent confrontation. The trees in the distance swayed, the darkness beyond them broken only by the occasional flash of gunfire. Vince could hear the hiss of bullets flying past, but none of them were close enough to matter. Not yet.

Suddenly, a shrill whistle pierced the air - too close to be ignored. Vince's heart stopped for a split second, his body reacting before his mind caught up. He dove for cover just as the first wave of rounds landed.

The explosions that followed were deafening. Vince's ears rang and his vision blurred with a sudden rush of panic. His body slammed into the ground, his rifle thrown aside by the force of the blast. Dirt and debris rained down on him, and he struggled to move, to breathe. He wiped the blood from his face, but it wasn't his. The familiar metallic taste filled his mouth. His body felt heavy, and for a second, he thought he had been struck, but then he saw Charlie moving toward him.

Michael Wells

"Get up, Vince!" Charlie's voice cracked through the haze. There was something in his eyes now - a fierceness, a desperate urgency that Vince had seen before in battle, but never with such intensity.

Vince nodded, forcing himself to his knees, fighting against the heavy air that seemed to weigh him down. The sound of approaching soldiers broke through the fog - the Germans were closing in.

The next few minutes were a blur. The squad regrouped quickly, firing back at the Germans who were rushing forward through the woods, their faces barely visible in the smoke and shadows. Vince's rifle felt like an extension of his arm as he fired at anything that moved. His pulse pounded in his ears, and every shot was a prayer - a desperate hope that they would make it through this frozen hell.

The forest became a maze of explosions and gunfire, and the dense fog only amplified the confusion. The squad held its ground, fighting tooth and nail, knowing that they couldn't afford to lose this stretch of ground. They had to keep pushing. For Aachen. For the men who had already fallen.

Charlie's voice broke through again, sharp and commanding. "Rose! Cover me!"

Vince snapped his attention to Charlie, who was moving forward, rifle in hand, toward a small group of German soldiers attempting to flank them. Charlie was always the first to lead, but Vince knew better than anyone that this could be the moment that would change everything.

With grim determination, Vince aimed his rifle, locking his eyes on the shadows ahead. The Germans weren't going to overrun them. Not today.

The Hurtgen Forest had claimed too many lives already, but Vince and his squad weren't ready to be added to that list just yet.

They still had a fight to win. And they did.

Chapter 55

The Christmas season had started off in a bad way. Erma had gotten a letter from Clem Burkey carrying terrible sad news. Judy had taken ill in early December and had never recovered. She had died on the 17th. Erma was devastated. She took to her bed and didn't get up for three days.

Now it was Christmas Eve day and the apartment was quiet, save for the occasional clink of a spoon against a cup, and the faint hiss of the radiator trying its best to keep the chill at bay. Erma sat at the kitchen table, absentmindedly stirring her coffee as the dim December light filtered through the curtains. Outside, Los Angeles was cold in a way that was unfamiliar. It wasn't the biting, wind-chilled cold of the East or the crisp air she had gotten used to in Oklahoma. No, this was a dry, almost brittle cold. The kind that felt like it might crack the earth in two if it tried any harder.

Barbara had gone to the corner store, leaving Erma with her thoughts. Barbara was ten and a half but mature for her age, so Erma depended on her to run errands like this. But even Barbara's quiet, steady company was not enough to lift the weight that had settled on Erma's shoulders over the past few months. Judy was gone and her heart cried at the loss of her friend.

And then there was Vince. His letters, few and far between, which had become her lifeline to the man she had once laughed with in the kitchen of their apartment. She had still not heard from him since that past August from Paris until today.

Michael Wells

She missed him in a way that was difficult to put into words. It wasn't just his presence - though God, how she longed for that more than anything - but his reassurance, his laughter, the way he would hold her when she was on the verge of tears, even if she didn't know why. But it had been almost three years. How had he changed? How had she?

They'd tried to make the best of it, Barbara and Erma. Christmas was still here, even if it felt odd and sad. There wasn't much to celebrate. They had decorated a small tree in the corner of the apartment - nothing fancy, just a few ornaments from the dime store and some tinsel - but it didn't have the same warmth it once would have had. Erma tried to keep the mood light for Barbara's sake, but deep down, the melancholy gnawed at her.

Barbara came back through the door, balancing a bag of groceries bigger than she was. She hung her coat up with a sigh and smiled weakly at Erma.

"Did you get everything?" Erma asked, standing up from the table to help her with the bag.

"Yep." Barbara's voice was tired, but she tried to hide it behind a smile.

She looked at the short stack of letters in front of her mother, "Did we get any news from Daddy?" Barbara asked, her tone betraying the hope she couldn't quite bury

Erma stood there frozen, and then she nodded her head. "We did." She quickly read her daughter the contents of the letter. "I'm sure he's fine. It's just... hard, you know?"

Barbara set the bag down and joined Erma at the table, her eyes tracing the edges of the table as though looking for something to focus on. "I don't know, Mom. Sometimes it feels like... like everything is just moving without us, you know? "

Unbroken Hope

Erma nodded, her hand resting on the cup in front of her. "I know. I keep telling myself it's only temporary. But when he's been gone this long…" She trailed off, unsure how to finish the thought. Every day felt like a year.

They sat in silence for a while, the hum of the radiator filling the space between them. The sounds of the city outside felt muffled, as though the whole world was holding its breath.

Finally, Barbara spoke again, her voice soft. "You think he'll come home soon?" This seemed like the thousandth time she had asked this question

Erma looked at the little tree in the corner of the room. Its lights twinkled faintly, almost in mockery of the solemnity in her heart. "I don't know. I hope so. But I don't think… I don't think it'll be as soon as we hope. The war… it's still going, Barbara."

Barbara looked down at her hands. "I know. I just wish I knew where he was. I just want him to be safe."

Erma reached over, squeezing Barbara's hand. "We'll get through this. We just have to hold on a little longer. We don't have it nearly as bad as he does."

The clock on the wall ticked steadily, each second seeming to stretch into eternity.

The next day, Christmas Day, they sat down to a meager Christmas dinner. Mrs. Keller had brought a turkey earlier that day, and then later she sat with Erma and Barbara to enjoy their meal. The turkey was small, but they made up for it with all the trimmings: dressing, mashed potatoes, green beans, cranberry sauce, and a pie Erma and Barbara had baked together that afternoon. It was a feast, but no one was really hungry.

Afterward, when Mrs. Keller had gone home, Erma and Barbara bundled up in blankets and sat together on the couch, listening to the radio. The familiar voice of a news anchor broke through the airwaves, his tone serious but clipped.

Reports coming out of Europe tonight suggest the Germans are making a push through the Ardennes region. Early estimates suggest a significant attack on the Western Front, though details are scarce. This is being called the Battle of the Bulge, as German front lines appear to bulge inwards toward the Allies. I repeat, the Germans are going on the offensive in the Ardennes region of Belgium. The weather is forecast to be bitterly cold.

Erma froze. Battle of the Bulge, the words seemed ominous, but Erma couldn't figure out just why. And Vince - Vince was out there, somewhere, in the middle of it.

Barbara turned to her, her face pale. "Oh God."

Erma's heart raced in her chest. She grabbed the most recent letter from the pile of mail on the table, fumbling with it in her hands.

"Remember the letter yesterday, your daddy had said something about Belgium," Erma said quietly.

She stared at the letter, hoping against hope for something that would make sense of the fear that had suddenly gripped her.

As she read the letter aloud, the words blurred into a frantic rush:

Unbroken Hope

I can't say much, but we're in the thick of it. Things have been... hard. We've been in Belgium. The fighting has been unlike anything I've ever seen. We are resting up now, but we'll be going back out soon, just not sure when. But, Erma, it is so damned cold. I wish I could hold you, Erma. I wish I could be home. But for now, all I can ask is that you wait for me. I'll be back.

The letter dropped from her hands, her heart sinking as the weight of the situation settled in. He was fighting in that very battle. The one they had just heard about. The one that would come to define the war's final months. But they didn't know *that* at the time.

"I knew it," Barbara whispered. "I knew he was in danger. I just -" She broke off, her breath catching in her throat. "Mom, I - I don't know if I can do this."

Erma gathered her close, holding her tightly as the weight of the world pressed down on them both. "We have to," she whispered. "We have to keep going. For them. For Dad."

Outside, the wind howled against the windows, but inside, the mother and daughter sat together, holding on to each other in the quiet of a war-torn world. And as Christmas night stretched into the cold early morning hours, they waited for the man they loved, praying that somehow, against all odds, he would come home.

Chapter 56

The bitter cold of December gnawed at their bones. The frost creeping into every crack and crevice of their clothing, no matter how tightly they clinched their coats. The land around them was barren, a frozen wasteland of muddy trenches and icy ridgelines that cut across the Belgian countryside like jagged scars on a dead man's face. Tall snow drifts stood everywhere. The snow was soft, but the earth was hard and unforgiving, turning their boots into cement as they trudged through it. The weight of exhaustion pulling at every step.

Christmas Day, 1944, but there was no joy to be found here - only the biting sting of frostbite and the deafening roar of gunfire. Vince could see his breath, his rifle shaking in his hands as the sounds of fighting echoed through the dead landscape. The Germans were relentless. The staccato of machine guns and the whistle of artillery shells overhead were a constant reminder that death could come at any moment.

German troops had been issued specific white camouflage uniforms, while American soldiers had to improvise with whatever white material they could find, mattress covers, parachute silk, and even local civilian bedsheets, to create their own makeshift white camouflage. Vince's uniform was a hodge-podge of white material.

The men of Vince's company, ragged and broken, barely able to hold themselves upright, moved with a desperate kind of will. Ammunition was scarce. Rations were even scarcer. They hadn't eaten in days. Their stomachs growled in the empty void, but their bodies had long given up protesting. They were used to hunger, to the gnawing ache in their bellies, to the hopelessness that seemed to swallow the very air they breathed.

"Charlie!" Vince shouted above the din of explosions. His voice sounded foreign to him, thin and brittle, like wind scraping across the frozen tundra. He couldn't feel his hands anymore. His gloves had worn out weeks ago, and now his fingers were numb, stiff, and clumsy. "Charlie, you still with me?"

Charlie, looking dazed, was sitting next to him. He turned his head, his face a mask of grim determination. "I'm here, Vince. Always. We're not giving up."

They crouched in a shallow, make-shift foxhole in the snow, the frozen mud slipping beneath them as they braced for the next onslaught. The Germans were relentless, sending wave after wave of infantry, their white uniforms blending into the shadows of the winter night like ghosts.

"Keep your heads down!" Sergeant Miller ordered, his voice sharp, as the unmistakable sound of approaching boots rang out in the distance.

Vince tightened his grip on his rifle, scanning the horizon. The world around him seemed to narrow. It was a world of snow, ice, and steel. Nothing else mattered now - only survival. The crack of gunfire pierced the air, followed by the thunderous boom of artillery rounds. The ground heaved beneath him, the cold seeping deeper with each explosion. He didn't know how much longer he could last. None of them did.

"Rose!" Sergeant Miller called in an exaggerated whisper as he scurried over to find Vince hunkered down.

"Yeah, Sarge! Here!" Vince croaked'

Unbroken Hope

Miller slipped in the snow and slid into Vince, hitting him hard with his boots. Vince yelped quietly.

"Sorry," Miller offered, and then said in a low voice, "I want you to take off." He pointed to the right. "Go about 100 yards and take up a position where you might be able to see them. If they're there, report back." With the heavy snow, Vince thought that the order was going to be impossible, but an order was an order.

Vince moved out. The snow was blinding.

Vince's breath came in ragged gasps as he fought the cold, his body battered and bruised from the relentless combat. The fighting had been brutal, each moment a struggle for survival. He had gone about 80 yards when an explosion sent him tumbling into a deep ravine in the harsh wilderness with the Germans nearby. Machine guns from the German side opened up, and he could hear his squad returning fire. His rifle, though still by his side, was nearly useless now. Blood oozed from a deep gash along his side caused by shrapnel, the pain almost unbearable. The ground beneath him was frozen solid, but it felt as though he was sinking into the depths of some icy hell.

He had tried to keep moving, tried to make it back to his squad, but the wounds drained him, and his strength was quickly fading. The uphill climb was too much. The cold, too, was unbearable - seeping into his bones, freezing him from the inside out. His eyes grew heavy, and soon, he couldn't fight the pull of unconsciousness. He collapsed into the snow, his body no longer capable of holding itself upright.

Hours - or was it days? - passed. The world around him seemed to spin, time blurring into an indistinct haze. He could barely feel his fingers, his limbs stiffening in the cold. Every breath felt like it could be his last, and still, a part of him didn't want to let go. He could hear faint sounds - echoes of voices, gunfire in the distance - but they grew quieter and quieter. Vince fought to hold on, but the darkness swallowed him whole.

Charlie stood at the edge of the ravine with snow swirling around him in fierce gusts of wind. His eyes scanned the horizon, the unfamiliar pain of losing his best friend weighing heavily on him. Vince had been with him from the very beginning, like a brother.

He had searched the immediate area after the final shots were fired, but there was no sign of Vince. Desperation had quickly turned into a grim reality: his friend was gone. But Charlie couldn't bring himself to accept it. He knew Vince - Vince wasn't one to go down without a fight. And Charlie wasn't going to leave him behind.

The landscape seemed endless - snow covering the ground like a thick, impenetrable blanket. Then something caught his eye - a slight hump in the white expanse of the slope of the ravine…casting a soft shadow against the snow. A rifle barrel was exposed near the hump. He froze, his heart pounding in his chest, as he took a cautious step forward. His boots crunched in the snow, and as he slid down the hill, the shape grew more distinct.

The wind cut through the trees like knives, but Charlie barely noticed. His fingers, numb and bloodied, clawed at the snowbank, heaving aside icy clumps with a desperation born of hope and fear. And then - he froze.

A sleeve.

Charlie dropped to his knees, heart racing. "Vince?" he whispered hoarsely, brushing the frost away. The face beneath was pale as bone, lips tinged blue, eyes shut. But there - just there - a tremor, a flutter beneath the lids.

Unbroken Hope

He was alive! Charlie dug frantically. The snow was light powder and easily moved.

"Jesus, Vince!" Charlie choked, yanking off his coat and pressing it around Vince's shaking body. He cradled him close, rubbing his arms, slapping his cheeks lightly. "Stay with me, alright? Stay awake. You hear me?"

Vince's eyes fluttered open - barely. A flicker of recognition sparked, and he tried to smile.

"You idiot," Charlie laughed through tears. "Only you would get buried in a blizzard and still look smug about it."

Vince coughed, a wet sound that made Charlie wince. "Was... trying to find you…"

"Well, you found me, dammit." Charlie pressed his forehead to Vince's. "You found me."

Silence fell for a beat, save for the wind. Then Vince's fingers twitched, finding Charlie's hand.

"Erma and Barbara," Vince rasped.

"Don't worry, buddy, you'll see them again."

"Paris," Vince said, his voice strained.

Charlie nodded slowly, a lump rising in his throat. "Yeah," he said. "Paris. In that little café. You remember that?"

"We sang," Vince murmured, voice barely more than a breath. "'Over There.' Loud as hell. People stopped and stared."

Charlie laughed softly, broken. "You said I sounded like a cat getting strangled."

"You did."

They both managed a breath of laughter before Vince's body tensed, and the warmth began to fade from his grip. Charlie held him tighter.

"No, no. Don't do this, not yet," he whispered. "You hold on. You don't get to leave me like this."

Vince looked up at him, calm now, almost peaceful.

"I'll always remember you," Charlie whispered, voice cracking.

Vince's eyes closed, slowly. The long last exhalation signaling the end had come.

"Always," Charlie repeated, his voice lost to the wind now. "I'll always remember you…" Charlie then began to sing softly, "And we won't come back till it's over, over there." His voice cracking with the tears.

Snow drifted down, soft and soundless. Charlie stayed there, rocking him gently, as the world fell still around them.

There was no response, no flicker of life. The world around Charlie seemed to blur, and he pressed his forehead against Vince's, his voice barely above a whisper.

"I'm here, Vince," Charlie's voice quivered. "I'm here…" he repeated as he trailed off. The words felt hollow. Vince, his best friend, his brother in arms, was gone. It was Christmas, but the world had forgotten them.

The bitter wind howled through the barren landscape, but Charlie didn't care. He refused to leave Vince behind, even in death. With a final, painful glance at the face of his fallen comrade, Charlie began to gather what was left of his strength, knowing he would carry his friend back. He wouldn't let Vince's sacrifice go unnoticed. Not like this.

The snow kept falling, but for Charlie, the battle was far from over. With much difficulty, he hoisted his friend over his shoulder, tears streaming down his face, freezing almost as quickly as they fell. Charlie, knee-deep in snow, began the long march back, stumbling every few steps. *You're done with all this, buddy*, Charlie thought.

Vince's tour of duty was finally over…over there.

Chapter 57

The letter arrived on a gray morning, wrapped in an envelope that seemed too official to bear good news. Erma had opened it slowly, with the trembling hands of someone who feared the inevitable yet still clung to hope. The letter was dated February 3, 1945.

Erma read the letter aloud to Barbara when she had gotten home from school.

> Dear Mrs. Rose,
> It is with profound sadness that we must inform you of the passing of your beloved husband, Private Vincent A. Rose, who bravely gave his life in service to our nation during the recent battles in the Ardennes Forest, commonly known as the Battle of the Bulge.
> Private Rose demonstrated exceptional courage and dedication throughout his service, and his actions during this critical engagement exemplify the highest ideals of the United States Army. While we grieve his loss, we are deeply proud of his commitment to duty and the sacrifices he made for our country.
> His remains are being kept safe and will ultimately be interred in an American cemetery in the Ardennes Forest that will be created. In the future, you may request that his remains be returned to you for a burial in the United States.

The words blurred into one another, and she found herself staring at the page, willing herself to understand. But no matter how long she stared, they didn't make sense. It couldn't be true. Her Vince, her solid, dependable Vince, couldn't be dead. How could he? How could he just... be gone?

But the ink was cold and unyielding, a finality that buried her within its letters.

"He ain't ever coming home," Erma cried. It was all she could say. Barbara stood stunned.

Days turned to weeks. The house, once filled with the warmth of laughter and the hum of daily life, grew quieter. The tick of the clock became a constant, an intrusion. The shadow of Vince's death loomed, pressing in on her chest, making it harder to breathe.

Barbara had tried to keep things normal, tried to smile and ask if they could play, if they could go out for a walk. But Erma, staring blankly at the walls, couldn't bring herself to respond. The loss of her husband had cleaved something deep within her, a hollow where joy used to live. She spent her days in the chair by the window, her eyes vacant, her mind unreachable. She could hear Barbara playing in the yard sometimes, her little voice high and hopeful, but it only seemed to make the silence inside Erma's heart grow louder.

Barbara would go off to school, and when she returned in the afternoon, Erma hadn't moved. It was all Barbara could do to get Erma to eat.

Erma's grief pressed down on her like an anchor, holding her in a place where nothing moved, nothing changed. The days began to shift, but Erma remained as still as stone, her body tired, her spirit more so. Barbara grieved losing Vince, too, but her present worry was the motionless shape that used to be her mother.

Unbroken Hope

One day in early March, the weather had warmed enough for Barbara to play outside. Barbara was in the backyard, playing with the old wooden shovel. She was trying to dig a hole, pretending to bury treasure. Erma watched her from the porch for a long moment, her eyes unfocused, her mind elsewhere. Erma got up and made her way down the steps toward Barbara. The soil was rich and damp from a recent rain, but it was solid under Erma's bare feet.

Slowly, Erma crouched down beside the girl, her fingers brushing through the dirt, feeling the cool earth give way to her touch. Barbara looked up, smiling, but there was a flicker of concern in her eyes, as though she could sense that something wasn't right with her mother.

"Mom? Mama?" Barbara said softly. "Are you all right?"

Erma didn't answer right away, her fingers continued to claw through the dirt as if searching for something - anything - that could fill the emptiness inside her. She felt the hard edge of a rock beneath her hand. Without thinking, she pulled it free, holding it up in front of her face. Then her lips formed a smile.

Barbara's eyes widened, expecting her mother to speak, to do something that would bring them back to the world they once knew. But instead, Erma gazed at the rock with a strange, fixed expression. Her breath caught in her throat as her lips parted.

"Look, Barbara," Erma murmured in a voice that was distant, as though someone else had taken control of her mouth. "Look at this nice potato. There are probably more. We can have em for supper."

Barbara froze, her small hands shaking as she dropped the shovel and took a step back. "Mama?" Her voice was small, tentative, unsure.

Erma's gaze never left the rock. It was round and lumpy, the kind of shape that might have resembled a potato if one didn't look too closely. But it wasn't a potato. It was just a rock - cold, hard, and unyielding. Yet to Erma, it had become something else, something that made sense in the madness of her grief.

"It's a nice potato," Erma repeated, almost to herself, as if she had forgotten what she was holding. She smiled, a thin, vacant smile. "Just like the ones we used to grow in the garden... so many potatoes…"

Barbara's heart pounded in her chest. She wanted to call for help, to scream for someone - anyone - to come and take her mother away from this strange, broken place. But all she could do was stare, her mind struggling to comprehend what had happened to the woman who had once been her everything. The woman who had held her close, who had kissed her forehead and whispered that everything would be okay.

"Mama," Barbara said again, her voice trembling. "Please... you're scaring me."

But Erma didn't hear. Or if she did, she didn't understand. She reached out, holding the rock toward Barbara with a strange, childlike eagerness. "See, it's perfect," she whispered, her voice far away. "It's so perfect."

Barbara backed away, fear rising in her throat. Her mother had always been strong, always the one to keep things together. Now, she was someone else - someone unfamiliar and terrifying.

"Mama, please..." Barbara whispered again, her tears running down her cheeks. She didn't know how to fix this. She didn't know how to get her mother back.

The sound of a door opening made Barbara jump, and she turned to see the neighbor, Mrs. Keller, standing in the doorway, her face pale with worry. She must have seen them from her window.

Unbroken Hope

"Is everything alright, dear?" Mrs. Keller called out, her voice tentative.

But Barbara couldn't answer. She couldn't explain what was happening to her mother. And she couldn't bear to look at the vacant, broken smile on Erma's face, the way her mother held the rock like it was the most precious thing in the world. She only knew one thing for sure: she was terrified.

The weight of Erma's grief had shattered something inside of her. And now, there was only silence.

The next day, a woman came and took Erma and Barbara away. They took Barbara to a big, grey, concrete building. She looked up at it with tears in her eyes.

She just knew she would never see her mother again.

PART IV
SURVIVING L.A.

"Come to Los Angeles! The sun shines brightly, the beaches are wide and inviting, and the orange groves stretch as far as the eye can see. There are jobs aplenty, and land is cheap. Every working man can have his own house, and inside every house, a happy, all-American family. You can have all this, and who knows... you could even be discovered, become a movie star... or at least see one. Life is good in Los Angeles... it's paradise on Earth."

    Advertisement promoting Los Angeles - 1946

"I want to live in Los Angeles, but not the one in Los Angeles. The one in the movies."

                   Frank Black

"L.A. is the loneliest and most brutal of American cities."

                      Jack Kerouac

Chapter 58

The sky above Los Angeles was heading toward a brilliant blue in the early morning light. But the city seemed to breathe slowly, as if the long years of conflict had left it tired, stretched thin across the land like a blanket too worn to keep anyone warm. In the streets, the hum of old cars and the shuffle of tired feet filled the spaces between the empty promises of a world at peace. It was a place where dreams were both sold and forgotten, where the past and future seemed to collide with no particular purpose. But there was no peace yet.

Men and women walked side by side, but they were not together. Many had come back from the war, from the dust of foreign lands and the smoke of distant fires, but they had not come back the same. The young men, battle-scarred soldiers, were scattered across the sidewalks and leaning against the buildings like discarded tools - carried in their eyes the faint weight of memory, a quiet thing, like an ache that never quite went away. The women, too, had changed, their soft faces drawn from the hours of labor and sacrifice. They worked at the new factories, sold in the stores, and raised children who would never quite know the sound of war but felt its echo in their bones.

The city stretched out, endlessly, as it always had, but something was shifting. The streets, now paved over with the fevered hopes of a thousand cast-offs, echoed with the sound of things unfinished. The old jazz clubs, where men with instruments of wood and brass had once fought their way through the night, had been replaced with fast cars and faster ambitions. The factories that once roared with the noise of wartime production, now slowed down.

Michael Wells

Los Angeles, you could say, had outlived its innocence, but it hadn't yet figured out what to be without it. The war had left a mark on everyone, even if they didn't know how to see it. And for all the shine and splendor that had drawn men from every corner of the earth, the city of angels was no longer a city of redemption. It was a city of waiting. For what, no one could say. But it was there in the air, thick as the smog that hung low over the hills, a feeling that everything, somehow, had stopped making sense. The war in Europe seemed close to an end after the Battle of the Bulge. But there was still no peace there. And the Japs kept fighting on.

March 1945 was a month that stretched on like an endless winter, gripping the minds and hearts of those at home as much as it did the soldiers on the front lines. In Europe, the Allied forces were advancing into Germany only to discover the horrific tragedy of Jewish Concentration Camps. While in the Pacific, the brutal fight for islands continued, each day a new nightmare. But in Los Angeles, in the warmth of the sun and the noise of its sprawling streets, life moved at a slower pace - a pace that felt like a cruel mockery of those suffering thousands of miles away.

Chapter 59

Barbara had never known a world so quiet, not even at night. The silence was thick, a blanket over everything. There was no sound of cars, no laughter, no hum of distant voices. Only the steady sound of her shoes against the cold floor of the building.

Her small hand was clasped in a stranger's firm grasp. He was tall and wore a gray uniform with a name tag that read "Harris." He didn't look at her, didn't speak to her. They just walked in silence down an endless hallway, lined with doors and flickering lights. Barbara tried to count the doors, but her thoughts kept jumping. She couldn't help herself. Every time she thought of counting, her mind would suddenly return to the car, the sudden rush of men in uniforms, the loud voice of the officer, the way her mother had looked before they pulled her away.

Her mother's face. She kept seeing it. The dull, blank stare, not even seeing her child being led away.

Barbara squeezed her eyes shut, but the image didn't go away. She wished it would. She wished it would stop.

They passed a window, and the dull light outside made her squint. There were no trees, no grass, no birds. Just a cold gray world, stretching out into the distance. She had forgotten how much she hated the color gray. The world outside looked as if it had been painted over with sadness, like nothing had ever been allowed to grow there.

"Here we are," the man said, finally breaking the silence. His voice was low, flat, and it made Barbara's stomach knot. She looked up at him, but his eyes were focused on the door in front of them.

He knocked once, sharply, and then opened the door.

Inside, the room was even more sterile than the hallway. White walls, metal chairs, a single desk with papers scattered across it. It faintly smelled of bleach, a scent Barbara would never forget. At the desk sat a woman in glasses, her hair pulled back into a tight bun. She smiled, but it wasn't a warm smile. It was the kind of smile Barbara had seen on people before when they were about to say something important, something she wouldn't understand. How could this woman stand that smell? Barbara thought.

"Barbara," the woman said, her voice soft but professional. "Please, sit down."

Barbara hesitated, her feet dragging as she crossed the threshold into the room. She had never been in a place like this. It felt wrong, like something that wasn't supposed to be real. She wanted to turn and run, but there was nowhere to go. Her body refused to listen to her.

The woman motioned to the chair across from her. "Please, sit," she repeated firmly.

Barbara's heart beat fast. She wanted to ask where her mother was, but she already knew the answer. She wasn't here. So instead, she climbed onto the chair, sitting stiffly, her hands clasped tightly in her lap. She stared down at the floor, unwilling to meet the woman's eyes.

"You've had a very hard day, I'm sure," the woman continued. "I understand this is a lot to take in. But I'm here to explain what comes next. I'm sure you have many questions."

Barbara didn't respond. What could she say? Nothing made sense anymore.

The woman's smile remained as she folded her hands on the desk. "I know this is scary. But we have a system in place to help children like you. First, we tried to reach out to your mother's sister - your aunt - Mamie Driggers, in Oklahoma. Apparently, they have moved and left no forwarding address. So that leaves us with no other option. You'll be placed with a family, someone who will care for you and keep you safe. They'll be your foster parents."

Barbara's throat tightened. Foster parents. She had heard of them before. People who took children in when their real parents couldn't take care of them. The woman was still talking, her voice a smooth hum in the background, but Barbara didn't hear the words. Her mind had shut them out, like a door slamming shut.

Barbara's world had always been simple. Her mother, she had always been there. The two of them. Then Vince came, but he died. So, it was back to the two of them. They didn't need anyone else. But now…

"Do you understand?" the woman asked.

Barbara blinked, trying to focus on the woman's face. She didn't understand. How could she understand? How could anyone understand what it felt like to have everything you loved ripped away?

"Where's my Mother?" Barbara asked softly.

She felt her lip tremble. She fought the urge to cry, but it came anyway, hot tears rolling down her cheeks. She wiped them away with the back of her hand, trying to be brave, but it didn't help. There was no bravery left inside her. Her heart was a fist of pain, clenched tight and unrelenting.

The woman's eyes softened, but only for a moment. "I know this is difficult, Barbara. But you have to understand, this is the only option right now. Your mother is… well, she can't take care of you. It's for your safety."

Barbara flinched, the words cutting through her like glass. Her mother wasn't the problem. Her mother was the only one who had *ever* cared for her, the only one who had *ever* made her feel safe. She didn't understand how anyone could think otherwise.

"Where's my mother?" Barbara asked again more emphatically.

The woman leaned forward, her voice lowering to a soft, almost soothing tone. "We're doing everything we can. Your mother had to go away. You'll be fine. I promise."

Barbara's chest tightened. She wanted to scream at the woman. To yell that she didn't want to be fine. Not without her mother. Not like this. But she was too small, too weak. So instead, she just nodded, her throat raw with unspoken words.

Another door opened, and a man stepped inside. He was middle-aged, with a kind face, but his eyes were filled with a kind of pity that made Barbara feel small.

"I'll take her from here," the man said gently, looking at the woman. He turned his gaze to Barbara. "Hi, there. I'm Mr. Walker. I'm going to make sure you get settled in. I know this isn't easy, but you're not alone. We'll take good care of you."

Barbara couldn't look at him. She couldn't look at anyone.

"Let's go," Mr. Walker said softly, his hand resting on her shoulder. "You're going to be fine. I promise."

The cold hallway stretched out in front of her, endless and lonely. She had no idea where she was going or what would happen next. But she couldn't stop the tears from falling as she followed Mr. Walker down the hall.

And for the first time since her mother had been taken away, Barbara felt truly, completely, alone.

Chapter 60

Barbara's hands trembled as Mr. Walker knocked on the door of the small suburban house. She stood like a statue, a small blue cardboard suitcase in her left hand. The agency had given it to her to hold her few belongings. The neighborhood was pristine, its streets lined with rows of houses, neatly trimmed lawns, and well-kept hedges. Everything looked perfect, almost too perfect. The scent of fresh grass and freshly baked bread lingered in the air, mingling with the faint chirping of distant birds. It felt like a place out of a storybook.

She had seen so many places like this before - pictures in the Foster care pamphlets that the woman had had on her desk - the bright smile of the caseworker, the hopeful promises. But this was her first placement, and the weight of the moment made her heart race. A thousand thoughts flooded her mind. Would they be nice? Would they understand her? Or would this just be another chapter in a long, endless struggle of feeling like a stranger in a world that didn't quite understand her?

The door slowly opened, revealing the couple. The woman, petite and pale, stood with a wide smile, her dark hair perfectly combed and her eyes bright with intensity. Beside her, a tall man with graying hair and a soft face greeted Barbara with a reserved nod. He was wearing a cardigan, even though the day was warm. The woman's smile never wavered, but there was something about it that didn't quite match the gleam in her eyes.

"Barbara, I assume?" the woman asked, her voice smooth like honey, though it carried an edge of something more - something artificial.

"Yes," Barbara replied, her voice almost a whisper.

Mr. Walker gave Barbara a reassuring pat on the back, though his touch felt oddly distant. "This is Mrs. and Mr. Thompson. They'll take care of you while you stay with them."

"Please come in," Mrs. Thompson said.

"Thank you," Mr. Walker said to the couple.

They stepped inside, Barbara's eyes were immediately drawn to the pristine living room. It was as if no one had ever used the space. The furniture was a light floral print, and the air smelled faintly of lavender. There was no sign of life, no clutter, no indication that anyone truly lived here. The walls were adorned with pretty paintings, landscapes that looked like they belonged in a museum. Everything was perfectly arranged, from the stack of books on the coffee table to the flowers in the vase on the side.

Mr. Walker and Barbara sat on the sofa at Mrs. Thompson's urging.

Mr. Walker began to speak about Barbara as if she wasn't there. The Thompsons listened quietly.

Then Mr. Walker quickly rose. "Well, I must be going. Please let me know if you have any issues."

"Sure thing," Mr. Thompson replied, as he closed the door behind the caseworker.

"Welcome, dear," Mrs. Thompson cooed, focusing on Barbara. "We've been looking forward to meeting you."

"Thank you," Barbara mumbled, her voice almost lost in the tension of the moment.

"Yes we have…been looking forward to this," Mr. Thompson said with a soft, welcoming tone, though there was something unnervingly flat about it.

After that, the conversation screeched to a halt, and then the house fell quiet…Too quiet.

"Let me take you to your room," Mrs. Thompson finally said sweetly.

They walked down a short hallway. The door was open to a small bedroom.

"This is your room, dear."

Barbara stepped in. It was modest but tidy. The walls, pale, cream, had seen better days, with the faintest outline of previous wallpaper left behind, now faded by time. The room was sparsely furnished: a single metal bed with an iron headboard. The bed was covered with a thin, worn quilt that had seen many washes. It was a soft, muted green - almost the color of old moss. The mattress was lumpy, but it was the only softness in the room. A small, wooden nightstand sat beside the bed, its surface scratched and slightly uneven, holding a few stray books, their covers frayed.

"I know it's not much, but we plan on fixing it up. We were just waiting so that you could help us pick things out," Mrs. Thompson said with a smile.

There was a single window, but the curtains were thin, faded, and hung unevenly, letting in only a sliver of daylight. The view outside was blocked by an overgrown hedge, but there was a patch of sky that Barbara could see when she stood on tiptoe. The room smelled of lavender soap, and of something faintly musty, a reminder that things here were old.

A small wooden wardrobe stood against one wall, its door slightly ajar, revealing a few neatly hung dresses, all secondhand, but clean. They looked like Barbara's size. A worn rug lay on the floor, with its edges curling up slightly from years of use.

The look of the room contrasted with the rest of the Thompson's home. Barbara frowned. Mrs. Thomspon smiled again, "Not to worry, we will get it fixed up." A promise that didn't happen.

Though it was quiet and still, there was an uneasy sort of solitude that settled in. The room carried the weight of abandonment, a place that was never quite meant for her. She looked at Mrs. Thompson and shrugged, indicating that it mattered little to her.

"We have a lovely dinner for you." Mrs. Thompson said cheerfully. "Why don't you put your little suitcase on the bed. You can unpack later."

They went out to the living room.

"Please, sit down," Mrs. Thompson insisted, motioning to the armchair closest to the fireplace. "Dinner will be ready in just a moment." She then headed off to the kitchen.

Barbara slowly sank into the chair, feeling the stiff cushion beneath her. Her nerves were on edge. There was a quietness in the house that was unsettling, a stillness that stretched too long. Even the air felt heavy, as if it were holding its own breath.

Mr. Thompson, sitting on the sofa, studied her for a moment.

"So, Barbara," Mr. Thompson began, his voice low and even. "Tell me about yourself. What do you like to do?"

Barbara shifted uncomfortably in her seat, feeling the weight of his gaze on her. She swallowed hard, unsure of what to say. They seemed so interested, almost too interested, as though they were waiting for her to reveal something - something deeper than just the surface.

"I... I like reading," she said, her voice trailing off. "I draw and paint sometimes."

"That's wonderful," Mr. Thompson said, his voice a little too bright, a little too eager. "You'll have all the time you need here. Mrs. Thompson and I don't have any children, you see, so we can give you all our attention."

Barbara nodded, though her skin prickled. There was something off about the way he said it - like it wasn't a choice, but a need. Like they had been waiting for her, as if she were a puzzle piece they'd been trying to fit into their perfect life.

"Dinner is served," Mrs. Thompson said, almost too cheerfully. Mr. Thompson rose and Barbara followed him into the dining room. The table was set for three, the plates gleaming under the soft, warm light of a small chandelier. Everything was meticulously arranged, the silverware polished to a mirror shine. Barbara thought about all of this and compared it to her room. The food - roast chicken, vegetables, and potatoes - looked perfectly cooked, but there was something about it that made Barbara lose her appetite.

As they sat down to eat, the conversation seemed to flow unnaturally. Mr. and Mrs. Thompson kept asking her questions - simple things at first, but as the evening went on, the questions became more personal, more probing. They wanted to know about her family, her past, her likes, her dislikes. Barbara could feel their eyes on her, as though they were trying to see right through her.

"Do you ever think about the future, Barbara?" Mrs. Thompson asked, her voice strangely soft, almost intimate.

Barbara shifted in her seat, feeling uncomfortable. She didn't like how they were looking at her, how they hung on every word She said. "I - I don't know," she stammered. "I guess... I don't think about it much."

"Oh, but you should," Mr. Thompson said, his voice soothing. "Planning for the future is important. We've found that the key to a happy life is... order."

Barbara felt a strange unease wash over her, but she didn't say anything. She just nodded quietly, trying to ignore the tightness in her chest. They were both watching her now, almost too closely, and she couldn't shake the feeling that something was wrong, that this wasn't how it was supposed to be.

As the evening wore on, Barbara excused herself to go to the bathroom. She found the hallway dark and narrow with the walls lined with old family portraits. The air felt damp, as though the house was holding secrets. The bathroom, when she finally reached it, was just as sterile as the rest of the house - white tiles, white towels, everything immaculate. Except, her bedroom hadn't been immaculate, had it? It had been worn and shoddy looking, she thought as she stared into the mirror. She couldn't shake the feeling that she was being watched.

When she returned to the living room, Mr. and Mrs. Thompson were sitting closer together on the couch, their eyes fixed on her as if they had been waiting for her to come back. The silence between them seemed to stretch even longer now, and the weight of it felt suffocating.

She smiled weakly, but deep down, she knew. This wasn't right.

The first week at the Thompsons' house felt like one long, unnerving stretch of time. Every morning Barbara woke up to the smell of bacon and eggs drifting into her room. But it wasn't just the smell that kept her from feeling at home. It was everything else. The house was neat, almost too neat, with stiff couches that didn't seem meant for sitting, only for looking at. The furniture felt arranged in such a way that it was like they were living in a museum. Nothing seemed to belong, except for the people who lived there, and even they felt foreign to Barbara. And there was her room again. It didn't fit with the rest of the house.

The Thompsons - Bob and Liz - were nice enough, but Barbara couldn't shake the feeling that something was off. Bob was a tall man with broad shoulders and an easy smile, but his eyes were always darting around like he was trying to read a secret in the air. Liz, on the other hand, had soft hands and a sweet voice, but Barbara had seen the way her smile didn't quite reach her eyes. There was a distance there, an odd emptiness that was hard to explain.

When they were eating that first dinner, they told her to call them "Bob" and "Liz," but it sounded so strange to Barbara. She had always been told to call adults by their last names or some form of respect. It felt too casual, too informal for her to settle into. It didn't help that every time she said their names aloud, they echoed in her head like a whisper that never quite faded.

Barbara felt more and more uneasy with each passing day, unsure of how to behave, how to act. Liz was always so chipper and motherly, but there was a stiffness to her. She asked Barbara if she wanted bacon and eggs for breakfast every morning, as if that was supposed to make everything feel better. The first morning, Barbara had nodded, but by the fourth, it felt like a hollow gesture. She had begun to refuse, just to see what would happen. Liz would blink, a little confused, but then quickly offer something else. It was as though nothing ever bothered her.

It was Bob who unnerved Barbara the most. The way he would stand in the doorway, arms crossed, watching her as if he were waiting for her to say or do something wrong. Every time she was alone in the house, Barbara could feel his eyes on her, even if he wasn't there. It was a feeling she couldn't escape.

The first incident occurred on a Tuesday morning, the tenth day of Barbara's stay. Liz had asked her to take the trash out, a task that Barbara had done before. She grabbed the bag, walking to the back door and out to the bin in the alley. But when she reached the trash can, she felt a sudden, overwhelming need to do something rebellious.

Barbara threw the bag into the middle of the yard instead of the trash can.

She hadn't planned it. It was almost like her hands had acted on their own. The second it hit the ground, Barbara froze, her heart racing. What if Bob or Liz saw? What if they were watching? But there was nothing to do now.

She slipped back inside, trying to act casual. Liz was in the kitchen, humming softly, making a salad. She didn't even glance up. It felt as though Barbara had become invisible, an unimportant detail in the world of the Thompsons.

But Bob noticed.

That evening, as she was sitting on the couch, eyes glued to her book, Bob stood over her, arms crossed. His shadow loomed large as she looked up at him.

"Barbara," he said, his voice low but firm. "Did you throw the trash in the yard today?"

Barbara's stomach churned, but she didn't look away. "No," she lied.

Bob stared at her for a moment, his eyes narrowing. "I think you did," he said, his tone still calm, but there was a dangerous edge to it now.

Barbara's heart pounded in her chest. "I didn't," she said again, more forcefully this time, as if saying it louder would make it true.

Bob's gaze didn't soften. "I'll take care of it," he said, and then walked out of the room. Barbara heard him mutter something under his breath, but she didn't catch the words.

The rest of the evening was silent, and Barbara spent it in her room, locked away in her mind. She stared at the wall, trying to ignore the sense of unease that ate at her.

The second incident happened two days later. The Thompsons had invited a neighbor over for coffee, and Barbara was expected to behave. Liz had said, "Please, Barbara, just stay out of trouble," but it wasn't so simple. Every time Barbara tried to stay quiet, she found herself doing the opposite.

The neighbor's name was Mrs. Green, a thin woman with a sharp voice and a wide-brimmed hat that made her look like she belonged in some old movie. Barbara sat at the table, picking at the uneaten bread crusts in front of her, listening to the conversation drift from one topic to the next.

Out of nowhere, she stood up, knocking over her chair. The room went silent.

"I don't like it here," Barbara said, her voice trembling. It was the truth, the only truth she knew. The words had just spilled out, like a truth too big to hold inside. "I don't like Bob and Liz."

The room stayed still. Mrs. Green blinked, clearly shocked, and Liz's face turned a shade of red that Barbara hadn't seen before.

Bob's eyes flared up. "Barbara," he said quietly. "We don't speak like that here."

But Barbara didn't care. She didn't care about Liz's wide eyes or Bob's looming figure. She just felt trapped, like a bug caught in the web of their calm, perfect lives.

The rest of the evening passed in a haze. Mrs. Green left early, and Liz hardly said a word to Barbara after that. Bob, too, had grown quiet, his smile faded as he washed up the dishes. The tension hung in the air, thick and suffocating.

By the end of the week, Barbara knew she was no closer to understanding the Thompsons than she had been the day she arrived. She couldn't tell what was wrong with them, but she knew something was. There was a wrongness in the air, something she couldn't explain, and she couldn't shake the feeling that she was walking on eggshells all the time.

And with every passing day, she felt more and more like an outsider.

Barbara sat nervously tapping her fingers on the edge of her cereal bowl. Yesterday, Liz had dropped the bombshell. She told her she had been enrolled in the local elementary school as a fourth grader and today was her first day. The thought of starting a new school was terrifying, and the idea of doing it in the middle of the school year was worse. She didn't know anyone, didn't know the routines, didn't even know how to fit in.

Great, she thought, I was just making headway at my last school.

Her mind raced with all the "what-ifs." What if the kids didn't like her? What if she didn't understand anything? What if she was the only new kid and everyone stared at her like she was some kind of a bug?

That morning, Liz walked her to the school bus stop, reassuring her with a few warm words, but Barbara barely heard them. She was lost in her own anxiety. The moment she stepped onto the bus, the loud chatter of kids made her feel small and out of place. She took an empty seat in the middle, trying to disappear, but it didn't work. A group of girls whispered to each other, stealing glances at her. Barbara kept her eyes glued to the window, pretending she couldn't hear them, even though every whisper felt like a needle pricking her skin.

When the bus finally pulled up to the school, Barbara's stomach twisted into knots. The building was big, much bigger than the school she had been to before. She followed the other kids off the bus, trying to blend in as much as possible, but it was impossible not to stand out. She had no idea where her class was, no idea where anything was. Luckily, a teacher in the courtyard noticed her hesitating and gently guided her toward the school office.

"Are you new here?" the teacher asked, smiling kindly.

"Yes, Ma'am," Barbara mumbled, feeling the flush of embarrassment creeping up her neck.

Inside the office, a woman handed Barbara a map of the school, explaining where her class would be. It felt like a blur.

When she finally found her classroom, she hesitated at the door. The kids were already seated at their desks, and the teacher, Miss Brown, a friendly woman with short brown hair, waved her in.

"Barbara, welcome! We're so glad to have you join us. Please take a seat at that desk," the teacher said, pointing to an empty one near the back.

Barbara nodded and made her way to the desk, feeling every pair of eyes on her. She sat down quickly, looking at her hands, trying to disappear into the chair. She didn't know anyone, and she didn't know how to start. The other kids seemed to know exactly where to sit, what to do, and what to say. It all felt so foreign.

The first few days were a blur of new faces and unfamiliar routines. At lunch, she sat alone at a table, picking at her food and wondering if anyone would come over to talk to her. Some kids glanced in her direction but didn't make an effort to join her. Barbara felt that familiar feeling - the one she had always felt when she was new - of being an outsider.

She tried to focus on her schoolwork, but it was hard. The lessons weren't difficult, but it felt like she had to work twice as hard just to keep up with everything, to understand the social dynamics, to learn where the bathrooms were, to figure out the unwritten rules. Each day ended in a blur of exhaustion, and she would return home to the Thompson's house, feeling more out of place than before.

But by the end of the week, something small had changed. During math class on Friday, the teacher had called on her to solve a problem on the board. Barbara's hands shook as she walked up to the chalkboard, but when she finished, she saw a few kids nodding and smiling. One girl, a freckle-faced redhead named Sarah, whispered, "Nice job." It wasn't much, but it was enough to make Barbara feel like she wasn't invisible after all.

That night, as she sat in the living room with Liz and Bob, Barbara's heart didn't feel quite as heavy as she had at the start of the week. She was still scared, still unsure of herself, but the world hadn't fallen apart. Maybe it was okay to be nervous. Maybe she didn't have to fit in right away.

"I think I survived my first week," she said quietly, almost as if she couldn't believe it.

Liz smiled, putting a hand on her shoulder. "You did more than survive. You made it through, and that's no small thing."

Barbara nodded. Maybe things wouldn't be perfect, but she was starting to realize that wasn't the goal. She just had to get through each day.

Chapter 61

Barbara hadn't been with the Thompsons more than a month when it arrived. The letter in her hands felt like a weight she wasn't sure she could carry. It was addressed to Erma Rose, and to her, Barbara, a combination of names she had not heard together in a long time. Mr. Walker had brought it and explained they had received it at the Foster Center. Now, she sat in their small, living room, staring at it.

Her eyes looked over the handwriting, the ink somewhat smudged in places, but still legible. She recognized the name at the bottom: Charlie Zimmer. Her Dad's best friend in Europe. Her Dad had shared with them about this special person in his letters.

She held the letter against her chest for a moment, the words not quite sinking in. The silence of the room seemed to stretch around her, as if the house itself was holding its breath. She had heard so little about her Dad and his time in the Army - the stories, the memories she should have had but didn't - and now here was a letter that seemed to reach out from the past. She could almost feel the weight of the years pressing down on her as she unfolded it carefully.

The first few lines were formal, the handwriting neat and clear. But as Barbara continued reading, Charlie's words took on a more personal tone.

I hope this letter finds you all well. I know it's been a long time, and I deeply regret that it has taken me this long to write. Please forgive me for not reaching out sooner, but I've been trying to find the right words... the right way to explain what happened. It's not easy to put into words the loss of such a good friend, especially when I promised him that I would look after him.

Barbara's fingers trembled slightly as she continued.

Vince fought with us in North Africa, Italy, and finally, in France and Belgium. I don't think there was a braver man on that battlefield. He had this way of lifting the spirits of everyone around him, even in the darkest of moments. We'd all joke, even in the middle of the worst days, and Vince could joke with the best of them. Vince kept us grounded. He kept us human. He was a friend, a brother in arms, and I will never forget him.

The words blurred in front of her eyes as the tears began to well up, but she pressed on, knowing that what came next would be important.

I'm sure you have already been notified that Vince didn't make it. He was one of the last to fall, during the final push in Belgium. We were pinned down, and Vince - well, he didn't hesitate. He was ordered to move further in and I guess he got disoriented by the extreme snow. He got separated. It took me a long time to find him and he wasn't dead when I found him, but he died soon after in my arms. I made sure his body was returned behind the lines. I kept my word.

Unbroken Hope

Barbara had to pause, her breath catching in her throat. She wiped her eyes with the back of her hand before continuing, each word feeling like it was coming from someone who had lived through the same heartache.

I can't apologize enough for the delay in sending this letter. It took time to get the necessary paperwork through the military channels. But I wanted you to know that Vince wasn't alone at the end. I was there. And when I could, I made sure he came back home, in a way, to you.

The letter ended with a simple line:

I'll always miss him, but I'll never forget the man, the soldier he was.
Charlie Zimmer

Barbara let the letter fall gently to her lap. The room was still. She felt the weight of his words settling over her, the loss, the grief that had been so long buried, now fresh again. Her dad was gone. She had known that, of course, but hearing it again, hearing Charlie's final tribute to him, brought the depth of it all crashing down in a way she hadn't expected.

Beside her, Liz sat with Barbara, watching her closely. She could see the strain on Barbara's face, the way her hands had gripped the letter so tightly that the edges were starting to curl and then let it fall away.

"Do you want to talk about it?" Liz asked softly, her voice a comfort in the heavy silence.

Barbara took a deep breath and shook her head. "I don't know if I can just yet. But I think… I think Charlie did something for my dad. He was a good friend to my dad. That means a lot."

Liz nodded. "It must have been hard for him, too, to have waited so long."

Barbara looked up at Liz, her small hands clasped in her lap. "I'm glad he wrote, though. It feels like he hasn't been forgotten."

The letter, now resting between them, felt like a bridge to the past - a final gift from a man who had done his best to honor a fallen friend. For Barbara, it was both a burden and a blessing, a reminder of what had been lost, but also a testament to the strength of the bonds formed in times of war.

In the silence that followed, they all seemed to understand the weight of it. And yet, somehow, it felt like Vince's story had found a way back into their lives, as if he had never truly left.

It had been almost three months since Barbara had received Charlie's letter. The first few months, she thought, were some kind of mirage - a fleeting dream where she was caught between the peace of a family and the storm inside her, a storm she couldn't let go of. The Thompsons were kind, if not exactly perfect, and Barbara wasn't sure she even knew how to be part of something that wasn't broken.

Mr. Walker, the caseworker, had visited four or five times. Each time, he arrived with his calm demeanor and usual patient questions, attempting to gauge the progress of the arrangement. He'd always ask Liz and Bob how she was doing, and they'd smile nervously, recounting Barbara's good days and the more challenging ones. The good days were becoming less rare, even if Barbara often found herself second-guessing them. The bad days, however, came in waves - an increasingly violent storm that pulled her away from everything good, from everything she knew she should feel.

Unbroken Hope

Then in late May came the news that shook Barbara to her core. As the crackling voice of the radio announcer cut through the tension in the Thompson household, Barbara's breath caught in her throat. The announcement of VE Day - the day when Nazi Germany had finally surrendered - was met with the excited cheers of the gathered crowd. She sat still in her chair, the sound of jubilant celebration from the radio somehow clashing with the storm of emotions building inside her.

Her father, a man she had loved dearly, had died less than five months ago. Now, as Europe celebrated the end of a long and brutal war, Barbara couldn't stop herself from thinking - He could have lived to see this. He was so close! If he had lived her mother would not have gone crazy and they would all be together.

Her fists tightened in her lap, nails digging into her palms as tears threatened to fall from her eyes. If only he could have held on for a little longer, she thought bitterly. If he had just lived to hear those words on the radio. To know that his sacrifice, his suffering, had been for something... that the war was finally over for Europe.

The joy and relief in the voices on the radio felt like a mockery. Her father, a man who had fought so valiantly, had never gotten to experience this peace. All she could feel now was the sharp sting of loss and frustration, gnawing away at her insides.

"Barbara," a voice called softly from the other side of the room. It was Liz, looking at her with concern. "Are you alright, dear?"

Barbara snapped her head up, her eyes burning with unshed tears. She opened her mouth to respond, but the words caught in her throat. What could she say? Could she explain to Liz the aching, hollow grief that clawed at her heart in that moment? How could she tell her how unfair it all seemed, how her father had fought almost to the very end, only to miss out on the one thing that could have given his sacrifice meaning? The end to the war.

Michael Wells

Instead, Barbara stood up abruptly, pushing her chair back with more force than necessary. The scrape of it against the floor seemed to echo in the room, but the radio announcer's words - still full of hope and victory - drowned it out. She turned to face the window, trying to collect herself, though her hands were trembling.

"Barbara," Liz said again, more gently this time, "We knew your father was a hero. He fought bravely, and he died for a cause much greater than any of us. His sacrifice helped bring peace to the world."

But Barbara couldn't hear it. She didn't want to hear it. "It's not the same," she whispered to herself. She wanted to scream, to rail against the injustice of it all. She wanted to ask why her father couldn't have held on, why he couldn't have been spared the agony that took him just a few months too early. The hurt was now replaced by fury.

In the distance, the sound of fireworks popped in the night sky, the noise almost mocking. Outside, the streets were alive with the celebrations of VE Day - people hugging and laughing, the air thick with joy. But in the Thompson house, Barbara felt nothing but an overwhelming emptiness. Her father, the man she had adored, the man who had given everything for the fight against tyranny, would never be able to join in the celebrations. And her mother was lost to her too. Oh how she wished her mother was with her now.

And what made it worse, Barbara realized with a stab of guilt, was the knowledge that the war wasn't over. The war in the Pacific was still raging. Her father had fought for Europe, and yet the United States was still at war with Japan, soldiers still dying, families still waiting for the end. The victory in Europe was only part of the picture. The full peace she longed for - the real peace - was off in the distance.

It all felt suffocating. Her anger boiled to the surface once more. Her father was gone, and his sacrifice felt - just for a moment - meaningless. The world was rejoicing, but Barbara was trapped in the

Unbroken Hope

shadows of grief and frustration, struggling to reconcile her pain with the reality unfolding around her.

She let out a shaky breath, trying to steady her pulse, but it was impossible to quiet the storm inside her.

"Barbara?" Liz's voice was gentle again, but Barbara shook her head. She couldn't talk. Not now. She had to leave, to get away from the noise, from the voices of victory and celebration. There was no place for her in that world. Not tonight.

Without another word, she walked briskly toward the door. The cool night air began hitting her like a sharp slap as she stepped outside. She needed space to think and to be alone with her thoughts.

She couldn't let herself fall apart - not yet. Not with the war still happening in the Pacific. Not with so much still left to be done. But she couldn't stop herself from feeling the way she did. Not tonight. But she felt eventually the rage would leave her. It didn't.

In the beginning, she would leave dishes unwashed, retreat to her room when it became too much, and glare at Bob when he asked her to help out. But it didn't stop there. She began to lash out - small insults, loud outbursts, and then, there were the moments when she lost control, saying things she knew would hurt Liz or Bob. It seemed like nothing could reach her, and her anger only grew stronger and deeper.

Liz always tried to be patient. She would sit down with Barbara, offering advice or a listening ear. Sometimes Barbara would sit there, arms folded across her chest, pretending to listen, but her mind was a million miles away. At times, she'd snap at Liz, the words sharp and venomous. "I don't need your help!" she'd shout. "I didn't ask for this. For any of this. I still have a mother and I want her!"

It was those words, repeated in different forms over the months, that cut the deepest, especially for Liz. She had opened her home to Barbara, expecting the hard work of fostering a troubled child to be a gradual process. But it wasn't. No matter how much Liz tried to create a safe space, Barbara's walls grew higher. There was no way to break through, and the harder Liz tried, the more Barbara recoiled.

Bob, usually quiet and less confrontational, did what he could to keep the peace. He'd offer to take Barbara out for ice cream, or to the driving range, where he could teach her how to swing a golf club. But each time, she would pull away, her sharp, defensive attitude kept him at arm's length. "I don't need your stupid golf lessons," she'd mutter, her voice hard, betraying the hurt she carried inside.

Mr. Walker came for his scheduled visits, and each time, Barbara made sure to be distant. He'd ask her how she was adjusting, and Barbara, ever the expert in deflecting, would give him short, guarded responses. She'd say things were fine, though they were anything but. She knew the system well enough by now - she knew how to play the game. Tell them what they wanted to hear, and they'd leave you alone for a while.

But the strain was beginning to show. Her hostility was no longer just an occasional flare-up; it had become an almost permanent part of her presence. She grew irritable, unpredictable. One afternoon, after a particularly heated argument with Liz over a small issue - Barbara had been asked to clean up a spill in the kitchen - she Barbara had slammed a plate down, shattering it on the floor. Liz had flinched, her face pale with shock.

"Barbara, please," Liz had pleaded, her voice gentle yet firm. "You can't keep doing this."

But Barbara didn't care. In that moment, she felt a sick satisfaction in the way Liz had flinched, in the way Bob had quietly retreated to the other room, leaving her alone with her anger. It felt like power - something she hadn't had in a long time. Power over people who were just trying to care for her, even though she knew they weren't the enemy.

Unbroken Hope

She would scream and cry sometimes, not because she wanted to be heard, but because she didn't know any other way to make the noise in her head go quiet.

At school, she tried to keep it together, tried to be the student Miss Brown wanted her to be. But the frustration would leak out in bursts, often when she was least prepared for it.

It wasn't a loud kind of anger, not the kind that would make her shout or storm out of the classroom. Instead, it was more like pressure, like steam building up inside her until it spilled over. Maybe it would be when a classmate made a careless comment or when Miss Brown asked her to focus on a math problem she didn't care about. That was when the anger would flare up - small, sharp moments that would catch her off guard.

Miss Brown, kind but firm, noticed it almost immediately. She saw how Barbara's eyes would darken, how her hands would tremble slightly before she pushed them down flat onto her desk, trying to contain the storm. She tried to reach out, offering quiet words of reassurance during lunch or after class, but Barbara wasn't ready to open up. She felt too vulnerable, too exposed.

One afternoon, during an English lesson, things reached a boiling point. Barbara was struggling with a worksheet, her pen scratched angrily against the paper. She wasn't even sure why she was so upset anymore. Her mind was a whirlwind of emotions - confusion, sadness, anger - just a storm of feelings she couldn't name.

"Barbara," Miss Brown whispered in her ear, and it cut through the noise, calm and steady. "I can see you're having a tough time today. Would you like to talk about it?"

Barbara's heart skipped a beat. Talk about it? No, she didn't want to talk. Talking meant explaining herself, and there was no way she could explain this bubbling mess inside her.

"No," Barbara snapped, her voice sharp before she could stop it. "I don't want to talk."

Miss Brown didn't flinch. Instead, she sat down next to Barbara's desk, her presence steady like a lighthouse. "I understand. But you don't have to carry this all by yourself. I'm here if you change your mind."

The silence that followed was heavy, and for the first time, Barbara realized Miss Brown wasn't just trying to make her feel better. She was giving her space to be angry, to feel lost, and to not have the answers.

But Barbara wasn't ready yet. Not for the softness of understanding, not for the calm that Miss Brown was offering. So, she just sat there, her fists clenching and unclenching on the desk, as her mind fought against the waves of emotion crashing inside her.

By the time Mr. Walker had come for his last visit, it was clear that things had deteriorated further. He sat down with Liz and Bob in the living room, where the air felt thick with tension. Liz sat forward, her hands clasped tightly together and spoke with a quiet desperation in her voice.

"She's just... she's so angry all the time, Mr. Walker. We've tried everything, but she won't let us in. She's pushing us away, and we don't know what to do anymore."

Mr. Walker, his brow furrowed, took notes as he listened. "It's clear that Barbara is struggling," he said. "She's holding onto a lot of pain. And sometimes, that means pushing others away. But we have to think about what's best for her - and right now, it seems that the environment here might not be the right fit."

Barbara sat by the window in the dim light of her bedroom, her gaze distant, her mind a quiet whirlwind of memories. The room around her still felt unfamiliar, with its muted tones and the occasional creak of the floorboards, a place that was supposed to be a refuge but had, instead, become her prison. For the past six months she'd lived here, drifting between a sense of displacement and the haunting echoes of the life she had once known. A life that was defined by the road that had brought her and her mother across the dusty plains of Oklahoma and into the bustling streets of Los Angeles.

Her thoughts always seemed to return to her mother, Erma. The woman who had once been a force of strength and resilience, whose face had weathered the storms of the Great Depression with the same determination that had seen them through the long, difficult journey west. Barbara could still remember the constant cloud of dust that hung in the air, and the way Erma never once complained. It was as if she knew the hardship was something they had to endure for a better life, even if Barbara – then only four, at times, doubted that such a life would ever truly come.

They had traveled together, mother and daughter, for what seemed like an eternity, through the searing heat of the desert and the endless expanse of the plains. The trek from Oklahoma to the Burkey's farm had been grueling, Judy and Clem's love for Erma and her daughter had brought them a sense of family.

Then there was Vince, her stepfather, who had entered their lives like a new chapter, one that was supposed to bring stability and warmth. Vince had been a quiet man, steady and reliable, a stark contrast to the volatile world they had once known. His presence had been a comfort for Erma, a pillar that she leaned on after so many years of hardship. But Vince, too, was claimed by the war. He had gone off to fight in Europe, like so many others, and Barbara remembered the day the letter came - the one that told them he had died on the battlefield. She still recalled the way her mother had collapsed, tears flowing freely, for a loss that would never truly be healed.

Now, as Barbara sat in the foster home, surrounded by the sterile walls of a place that offered no sense of home, she thought of how much she had lost. The months had stretched on, each day blending into the next, as she tried to come to terms with the absence of those who had once been her anchors. In the quiet moments, when no one was watching, she could almost hear her mother's voice calling to her, a voice that had always been there to soothe her fears and guide her through the darkest of times.

But the world had changed. Her mother was gone, and her father's absence had left an empty space in her heart that no one could fill. Still, in the recesses of her mind, Barbara carried the strength of their journey - the hardship, the love, and the sacrifices they had made along the way. Even here, in a foster home that felt more like a cage than a sanctuary, Barbara felt the echoes of that strength within her. It was the one thing that remained constant, a tether to a past that would never fade, no matter how far she had come.

For Barbara it was becoming clear that things couldn't go on much longer. The strain on Liz and Bob had become too much. They had opened their hearts, but Barbara couldn't let them in. She was too broken. Too angry.

That night, after Mr. Walker left, Barbara stood at the window in her room, staring out at the darkening sky. The moon was barely visible, hidden behind thick clouds, much like she felt inside. She had to leave. It was inevitable. Maybe she had made it so that she had no other choice. Maybe she had pushed too far, even for the Thompsons to keep her.

The thought didn't comfort her - it only made her feel smaller. It felt like one more door closing on her, one more thing she had broken.

But she couldn't stop herself. She couldn't let them get close enough to see the wreckage of who she had become.

The next morning, the decision was made. Barbara would be removed from the Thompson home. She didn't say goodbye. She couldn't bring herself to. Instead, she simply packed her few things in her little cardboard suitcase, the cold weight of finality settling over her like a shadow. She walked out silently following Mr. Walker.

Liz and Bob were at the front door when she left, their faces drawn and weary. Neither of them spoke. There was nothing left to say. The door clicked shut behind her with a quiet, finality that echoed louder than any words could. And just like that, Barbara was gone.

Mr. Walker drove Barbara back to the Foster Care office. The car's interior quiet except for the soft hum of the engine and the occasional rustle of papers on the passenger seat. He glanced at her, her arms crossed and her eyes fixed on the window, clearly lost in thought.

Breaking the silence, Mr. Walker spoke gently, but with a firm edge. "Barbara, you're going to be 11 in a few months. You're not a little kid anymore. You can't keep acting out like this. You're getting older, and things are only going to get harder if you don't start trying to make it work."

Barbara didn't respond, her jaw clenched.

Mr. Walker's voice softened, but his words did not. "The Thompsons aren't the bad guys. They're just trying to help you, Barbara. They're not your enemy. I know it's not easy, and it may feel like they're picking on you or that it's not fair, but they're doing the best they can. They don't want you to fail. They want you to feel safe and cared for."

He took a breath before continuing, his tone becoming more serious. "If you think you don't like it there, be careful what you wish for. Things could get a lot worse. You're in a position where you have a chance to turn things around, but if you keep pushing back, you might find yourself somewhere you never wanted to be - somewhere far worse than anything the Thompsons could offer."

Barbara remained silent, her expression neutral, but somewhere in her eyes, a flicker of realization passed by. Mr. Walker knew it wasn't easy for her to accept, but sometimes, hearing the truth in such blunt terms was the only way to make a difference. He hoped she would understand - before it was too late.

"So, do you want to continue to stay with the Thompsons?"

"No."

Mr. Walker simply shrugged and kept driving.

Chapter 62

Barbara left the Thompsons behind after only eight months and now here it was early September and Barbara sat on the edge of the worn-out couch, clutching her knees to her chest as she stared out the window. The cold afternoon light filtered through the curtains, casting long shadows across the room. She could hear the muffled sound of Phyllis and Steve Daniels moving around in the kitchen, their voices low but sharp, like the edge of a knife. She had been in their home for a month.

The radio was on and she could hear," Bye, Bye Blackbird" playing. She was so hardened though that hearing her mother's favorite song didn't even impact her. Then the song abruptly stopped playing.

A voice from the speaker crackled again, a little clearer this time.

"We interrupt this broadcast to bring you this official announcement from the United States Government. We have just received word that the Empire of Japan has formally surrendered to the Allied forces, ending the Second World War. The decision came after the bombings of Hiroshima and Nagasaki, which, combined with the ongoing military pressure and the Soviet declaration of war, left Japan with no other choice but to accept the terms of unconditional surrender."

Barbara's breath caught in her throat and she could feel her heart racing.

"Now, after years of hardship and loss, peace is within our reach," the voice continued, a tone of solemn pride lacing the words. "The fighting will cease, and the world can begin to heal."

Barbara's mind swirled. The weight of the announcement, the finality of the war's end, seemed almost unreal. It was a world that had been torn apart - her own life blown up by the loss of family, friends, and neighbors - and now it would change, irrevocably. But how? What would life be like after the war? What would it mean for the soldiers, for the families, for the countries still grieving their losses?

As the words echoed in her mind, she found herself staring at the faded curtains in the living room. The silence that followed the announcement seemed deafening. But beneath the overwhelming quiet, there was a sense of relief, of hope. The war, the years of fear and uncertainty, had come to an end.

And yet, Barbara couldn't help but wonder: What now?

She could hear Steve and Phyllis talking excitedly about the broadcast, but they never came in to see how she was doing.

The house was silent most days, save for the occasional sound of an argument or the rattle of dishes being washed too loudly. It was a house of emptiness, despite the clutter. Phyllis always had a way of making the place feel cold. To her, everything had a purpose, even when that purpose didn't make sense. Such as the broken cuckoo clock hanging limply on the wall.

Unbroken Hope

Barbara's stomach growled, but she didn't dare go to the kitchen. Not after yesterday. Phyllis had looked at her with those cold, calculating eyes when she'd asked for a second helping of food. Barbara could still feel the sting of her voice, the way it twisted her insides.

"No, you've had enough. Don't get greedy, Barbara."

She had wanted to protest, to tell Phyllis that she hadn't eaten much the night before, but the words stuck in her throat. Steve was there too, sitting at the table with his greasy fingers on a half-empty beer can, watching the interaction with a kind of detached amusement. It made Barbara feel small, invisible in a way that hurt in her chest.

"Let her be," Steve had said, as if he were offering some sort of mercy. But it wasn't mercy. It was just another way of putting her in her place.

Her eyes moved to the worn frame of a photograph sitting on the mantel, the only thing in the house that had any semblance of warmth. It was a picture of the Daniels before she had come into their care - Phyllis and Steve smiling, arms around each other, looking like a family. A family that didn't include her. But even in the photo, the smiles looked fake.

A knock came to the front door, and Phyllis answered it. The door creaked open, and Barbara's heart skipped a beat. It was Mr. Walker. His presence was always a reminder that, for all the pain, someone might eventually help her. But she knew better than to expect any real change. Mr. Walker only ever came when it was scheduled - pre-announced, always. He never saw the house for what it truly was. He never saw what Barbara saw. Never experienced what Barbara experienced.

Phyllis stood there, her face painted with that false smile she wore only for people like Mr. Walker. She ushered him in, her voice too sweet, too high-pitched.

"Mr. Walker! How nice to see you! Come right in."

Michael Wells

Steve was nowhere to be seen, probably hiding out back or locked in his room, avoiding any real interaction. Phyllis, on the other hand, was all smiles and polished manners. It made Barbara sick to her stomach.

Barbara could hear their voices now, muffled as they drifted into the living room. Phyllis was talking about how well Barbara was doing in school - she wasn't. She wasn't allowed to go to school that often, not since she'd been staying here. Sometimes, Phyllis would say that she was sick, or that there were family "matters" that kept her home. The school never seemed to mind. Barbara would sit at the table with a workbook, pretending to do something, anything, to keep busy, to *not* be noticed. She loved to read, but there were no books.

And now, she had to listen to Phyllis lie to Mr. Walker, painting a picture of a happy home, a family thriving in all the ways they were meant to. Barbara could hear her saying things like "Barbara is a joy to have around," and "She's settled in so nicely, Mr. Walker."

Barbara could almost hear the case worker nodding politely, pretending to believe it. She didn't trust him either. He would never see the bruises that weren't visible or hear the words that were meant to hurt. Never see what happened in the middle of the night. He would never understand what it felt like to walk into a house full of smiles that were as fake as the flowers Phyllis kept in a vase on the table.

The conversation was only getting worse as Phyllis continued her charade. Barbara tried to block it out, her mind wandering, focusing on the soft hum of the refrigerator in the corner, the ticking of the old clock near the stove. She knew it was only a matter of time before the visit was over, and Mr. Walker would leave, convinced that everything was fine.

And then Phyllis would go back to being herself - cold, distant, like a shadow that never left. Steve would return to his usual routine of grunting and barely acknowledging Barbara's existence. But he knew she existed, particularly when he came creeping in her bedroom almost every night, pawing at her and then ultimately putting that thing of his inside her. She knew it was wrong and was disgusted by it. But who could she tell? Who would believe her? She simply suffered it in silence.

They would resume their cruel games, their punishments, their nighttime antics, until the next time Mr. Walker came to check on her, when they had to scrub their lives clean for an hour.

Mr. Walker's voice interrupted her thoughts, suddenly louder.

"Well, Barbara? Would you like to come say hello?"

Barbara froze. She knew what would come next - Phyllis would guide her into the room, put on a show of "caring" for the caseworker, as though everything was normal. But Barbara wasn't normal. She wasn't like the other kids who had come and gone from this house. She was a problem.

Taking a deep breath, Barbara stood slowly, her legs weak beneath her. She shuffled into the living room, forcing a blank expression onto her face, not allowing any emotion to show. She didn't want to give Phyllis the satisfaction of knowing she could make her uncomfortable, even if that's exactly what Phyllis was trying to do.

"Hello, Mr. Walker," Barbara said, her voice barely above a whisper.

Mr. Walker gave her a warm smile; the kind of smile people give when they don't know what to say to someone they can't quite understand.

"Well, hello, Barbara! How are you doing?" he asked, sounding almost hopeful.

Barbara wanted to say something - anything - that would make him see the truth. But she knew better. Instead, she nodded silently, avoiding his eyes.

Phyllis stood beside her; her hand pressed lightly against Barbara's back as if she were somehow guiding her. It was an empty gesture, one that had no meaning. She wasn't comforting her; she was showing Barbara that she had control.

"I'm sure Barbara has been just fine," Phyllis said smoothly, her voice sickeningly sweet. "We're so happy to have her here, aren't we, Barbara?"

Barbara forced herself to nod. She wanted it to end, wanted Mr. Walker to save her, to not believe the lies Phyllis spun. But as the minutes ticked by, Barbara knew that it would all be the same when the door closed behind him.

Phyllis would turn cold again. Steve would disappear into his own world, and Barbara would be left alone, invisible. She would survive as best she could, pretending that the world outside the house didn't exist.

Because that was all she had left - pretending.

Barbara had never known peace in the foster home of Steve and Phyllis. When she had been there six weeks, she had believed that the sexual contact between Steve and herself was something isolated - something that she could endure or perhaps even escape. She wasn't really sure what it even was. But it didn't feel right. She was fearful of bringing it out into the open. Steve had warned of the consequences if she did. And those consequences weren't good. But as time wore on, the abuse shifted, becoming more unpredictable and terrifying.

At first, it was Steve's harsh words and rough handling. He would yell at her for the smallest of mistakes, his temper flaring at the slightest provocation. Then he would come to her at night, whispering softly into her ear. Barbara was confused and frightened by his unpredictable outbursts. He would push her, slap her, and throw things in fits of rage during the day, and at night, he was a different person. She had no idea how to protect herself or what she had done wrong to deserve all of this. She was kept off balance constantly. Phyllis would often remain silent during these moments, as though she was indifferent to intervening.

But then, as the months went by, the violence and abuse escalated. Phyllis, once a distant but passive figure in the household, began to play a more active role in the sexual abuse. Barbara's once-sheltered world grew darker, more oppressive. Phyllis would join them in the bedroom, many times helping Steve restrain her, so he could have his way with her while Phyllis sat back and watched. The physical and sexual violence left Barbara feeling helpless, humiliated, and terrified of what might happen next.

There were nights when Barbara would lie awake in the small, dark room she was forced to sleep in, dreading the sound of footsteps in the hall. It wasn't uncommon for Steve to burst into her room, angry over something that seemed trivial, sometimes even something Barbara hadn't done at all. He would shout at her, and sometimes Phyllis would follow, standing by the door with a distant look, as if she hadn't a care in the world.

Or on other nights, they would both creep in, rousing her from sleep, both having their way with her. She never knew what to expect.

On the worst nights, the violence reached unimaginable extremes. Barbara, small and fragile, would cower in fear, trying to protect herself from blows and insults. Sometimes, Phyllis would hold her down while Steve raped her. The physical pain and the shame of sexual abuse were bad enough, but it was the emotional toll - the feeling that there was no one who cared, no one who would protect her - that was the hardest to bear.

Barbara began to lose hope, and she didn't know who to turn to or if there *was* anyone out there who could help. Mr. Walker had seemed to disappear. The days blended into a haze of fear and shame, each one worse than the last. It wasn't just the physical violence; it was the cruelty of being treated like she didn't matter, like she was less than human.

As the abuse continued, Barbara found herself withdrawing more and more, her spirit breaking bit by bit. She wondered if anyone would ever come to her rescue, or if she would simply be lost forever in this nightmare. The thought of escape seemed impossible, the future uncertain and grim. All she could do was survive, clinging to whatever hope she could muster, even as her world became increasingly dark.

Despite the constant fear, Barbara still held on to a tiny flicker of hope. She knew she couldn't stay much longer, but she was terrified of the consequences if she were to speak out.

Then, in the dead of an October night, when the house was quiet, Barbara managed to sneak away to the old rotary phone tucked away in a corner of the kitchen. She had learned Mr. Walker's phone numbers from a business card she had discovered. His daytime and nighttime numbers were on it. Mr. Walker, through small glimpses of the kindness he'd shown her during visits to the house, seemed to appear that he was on her side. He had been a calm, steady presence on the few times he had come here and with the Thompsons, unlike the chaotic, oppressive environment Steve and Phyllis created. Barbara had hesitated at first, unsure if reaching out would only make things worse, but desperation had driven her to act.

With shaking hands, she dialed the number. The phone rang several times before Mr. Walker answered, his voice sounding like he had been asleep. "Hello?" he said quietly. His voice was soft, a reassuring sound in her ears, but Barbara could barely speak. She was too afraid.

"I… I can't… I can't take it anymore," she stammered, trying to steady her voice.

"Barbara?" Mr. Walker's voice softened even further. "Barbara? What's going on? Are you alright?"

Unbroken Hope

Through sobs and broken sentences, Barbara explained everything. The beatings. The cruelty. The isolation. The sexual abuse. She had nowhere to turn. Mr. Walker continued to listen quietly, asking only a few guiding questions to help her articulate her fear. Once she had finished, there was a long silence on the other end of the line.

"I'm going to help you," Mr. Walker finally said, his voice firm with conviction. "You're not alone. I'll get you out of there."

He wasted no time. Over the next few hours, he coordinated with local authorities and arranged for Barbara's immediate removal from Steve and Phyllis' home. The timing was crucial, as he knew if her foster parents had found out she had reached out for help, the consequences could be dire. Mr. Walker was determined and by morning had shown up. Barbara didn't say anything as she stood with him on the front porch. She simply rolled up her sleeves to show him the massive number of bruises. Mr. Walker gasped and took her by the hand. He vowed that she would be safely placed in a new foster home, one that promised her kindness, safety, and a chance to heal.

As for Steve and Phyllis, the fallout was swift. Despite the undeniable evidence of abuse, the legal system was slow to act. The police had been involved, and there had been some evidence, but in the end, they wanted to spare Barbara from testifying. So, the couple's names were placed on a list barring them from accepting any future foster children. They were allowed to continue their lives, but their actions, though exposed, went largely unpunished. Their punishment was not jail time or even a fine; it was the irreversible consequence of being blocked from fostering again. This, however, felt like a small consolation compared to the pain they had caused.

Barbara, meanwhile, began a long, difficult journey of healing. She saw Mr. Walker several times after she was placed in her new home, and each meeting gave her more confidence in her own ability to rebuild her life. She slowly began to trust again, learning that kindness and love were not impossible, even though she'd been denied those very things for so long.

Though the scars of her past would never fully disappear, Barbara found a new sense of strength within herself. And she never forgot Mr. Walker, the case worker who had believed her when no one else had.

Chapter 63

The sky was a dull, smudged gray, just like the memories Barbara tried to push down. She sat on the sofa in the living room of Bill and Shirley Hodges's house, the quiet hum of the refrigerator the only sound in the otherwise still room. The clinking of cups and the occasional shuffling of feet created an uncomfortable silence. It was only a few days since Barbara had arrived here, but it felt like much longer. She rose and said, "I think I'll go to my room for a while."

The couple seemed nice enough - kind, though distant. There was something about their politeness that made Barbara uneasy. She wasn't sure how to describe it, but it reminded her of the masks people wore when they didn't really want to get too close. She had already learned how to read between the lines of people's kindness. It was the only way to survive in a world where trust was a luxury.

Bill, with his thick black glasses and graying hair, was an accountant and had a quiet, unassuming demeanor. Shirley, on the other hand, was brash and lively, with a sharp laugh and enthusiasm that clashed with Barbara's more reserved nature. They lived in a modest, two-story home on the outskirts of the city, one of those cookie-cutter houses that seemed to be popping up all over Los Angeles since the war.

Barbara's bedroom was actually the guest room, a cramped, sparsely furnished space with a single bed and a window that overlooked a small backyard. The room, though plain, was a significant improvement from the places she'd been before - particularly her second foster home. That was her worst nightmare, where the tension felt like an iron weight hanging in the air.

She still couldn't shake the feeling of not belonging. Every foster home had been a step further from the life she once knew, a reminder of what she had lost - of who she had lost. Her parents...She tried not to think about them too often. The ache was still too raw, the memory of the past a painful shadow that seemed to follow her wherever she went.

"Barbara, honey, how are you doing today?" Shirley's voice broke through her thoughts.

Barbara looked up to find Shirley standing in the doorway, her hands perched on her hips. She was dressed in a floral print dress, the edges frayed from years of use. Despite the warmth in her voice, Barbara couldn't quite shake the sense that Shirley was watching her a little too closely.

"I'm fine," Barbara replied curtly, not meeting her gaze.

Shirley didn't seem put off. "Bill and I thought we'd take you out this afternoon. Maybe a trip to the beach? Get some fresh air, have a little fun."

The beach. It sounded nice, almost like something out of a dream. Barbara could remember trips to the coast from when she was younger, before everything had fallen apart. But that felt like another lifetime, one that had slipped through her fingers like sand in the wind. She forced a smile, not wanting to upset Shirley's well-meaning offer.

"That sounds nice," she said, her voice flat.

Shirley seemed pleased. "Great! I'll get ready, and we'll head out in an hour. It'll be good for you to get out of this room."

Barbara nodded as Shirley disappeared into the other part of the house.

She looked around the room again, taking in the pale walls and the soft floral curtains that Shirley had chosen. It was all too new, too unfamiliar, like she didn't belong here. There was something about the way the house smelled - lemon-scented cleaner mixed with the faintest odor of tobacco. It was a small, cozy house, nothing extravagant, but it had a cleanliness to it that made her feel like an outsider, like she was intruding.

She stood up and walked to the window. Below, Bill was in the backyard, fumbling with a lawnmower, his movements slow and deliberate. A cigarette dangled from his lips. He seemed to have a level of patience that Barbara envied. Maybe it was because he had no expectations of her. At least, that's how it seemed so far.

Bill and Shirley had been kind, but they weren't family. And they weren't the kind of people who could make the world feel safe again. Nothing could.

She thought often of her mother and missed her terribly.

She had tucked away in the pocket of her jacket, the note her mother had written to her years before. She took it out and unfolded it. The note was creased and dirty from years of handling. The handwriting was familiar and made her warm inside. She looked at it for the thousandth time...a short shopping list. She felt the tears forming. The last time she'd seen her mother, there had been nothing in her eyes, a complete blank. The woman who had once been her protector became a stranger, a shadow of who she once was.

Barbara hadn't asked Bill or Shirley about her mother. They hadn't asked her anything either, which she appreciated, but she couldn't help but wonder if they knew more about her mother's situation than they let on.

"Barbara! Time to go!" Shirley shouted up the stairs, startling Barbara from her thoughts. It was time. She quickly straightened up, pushed her hair behind her ears, grabbed a bag containing her swimsuit and a towel, and went to join Bill and Shirley. The idea of going to the beach, of being in a place that reminded her of the good times of her past, was too much to pass up.

As she walked down the stairs, she saw her reflection in the hallway mirror. Her eyes were still too tired, her face still too young to bear the weight of everything she had endured. But she straightened up, giving herself a quick, tentative smile, as if to reassure herself that she was moving forward, step by step, even if the path ahead was uncertain.

When she stepped outside, the sun seemed brighter, almost mocking in its warmth, but she didn't mind. She was going to try. She was going to try to belong in this strange new place.

Bill smiled at her as she stepped onto the porch. "Ready to go?" he asked.

Barbara nodded, offering the closest thing she could to a smile. "Yeah. I'm ready."

For the first time in a long time, she allowed herself to hope that this home, this strange new world, could be a place where she could begin again.

But school was a different world. Barbara was often the target of taunting. Her classmates were relentless, calling her names like "orphan," "nobody," "useless, and "Oakie." She thought she had put all this behind her. They would glare at her every chance they got, especially during lunch when she sat alone at the back of the cafeteria. It was as if she didn't belong to any group. The popular kids made fun of the way she dressed - hand-me-down clothes from Shirley, which were fine for home but not for the constant judgment of her peers.

Barbara tried to keep her head down, focusing on her schoolwork, but the cruel words stung every day. "You'll never amount to anything," one of the boys named Derek would say with a smirk. He was the worst, always leading the charge when the others picked on her. His words echoed in her mind, always lingering there, making her doubt herself. What if they were right? What if she wouldn't amount to anything?

She would come home, her head full of taunts, and try to hide her sadness. But Shirley could always tell. She noticed the way she walked through the door with her shoulders slumped, her eyes not meeting theirs. Shirley would make her favorite meal, spaghetti and meatballs, and try to talk to her, but Barbara kept it all inside. She didn't want to burden them with her pain.

One day, as she walked home from school, Derek and a few others caught up with her. They surrounded her near an old oak tree by the park. "What's wrong, Barbara? Afraid to be seen with us?" Derek taunted, flicking a piece of mud at her. It splattered on her dress, leaving a stain. Derek laughed and was joined by the group of kids.

Barbara looked down at her dress, her favorite. She clenched her fists, trying not to cry, trying not to let them see how much his words hurt. But something inside of her snapped. She wasn't sure where the courage came from, but she stood up straighter, walked over to him, and looked Derek in the eye, and said, "Maybe I don't want to hang out with people who stink." She held her nose with her fingers. "No, I mean it. You literally stink."

There was a brief moment of silence, and for the first time, Derek didn't have an immediate comeback. The others looked at him, unsure of how to react and they laughed nervously. Derek made a slight move toward her. Barbara stepped up and got right in his face.

"Want to make something of it, or do you want to go home and take a bath?" she said firmly, hands still in fists. The other kids laughed again. This time it seemed like they were on her side.

Derek looked at the others and then back at Barbara and sneered, said something under his breath, and walked off. The others stayed behind. Then they gathered around Barbara talking excitedly. Someone had stood up to the bully. It was clear that the other kids were with Derek, pretending to be his friend only because they were afraid of him. Barbara stood there for a moment surrounded by her classmates, her heart racing, but there was a tiny spark of pride inside her. She hadn't let them push her around that day. And now she had made some friends.

That night, as she sat at the dinner table with Bill and Shirley, she found herself telling them a bit about her day. She didn't go into great detail, but she shared the part about standing up for herself. Bill gave her a proud smile, and Shirley patted her hand gently. "You surprised yourself, didn't you?" Shirley asked softly. "Don't let anyone make you feel small. You're capable of so much more than they realize."

Barbara smiled weakly, but the words sank deep into her heart. Maybe she *was* stronger than she thought. Derek didn't know everything about her. It was possible she would amount to something. She wasn't sure how or when, but she promised herself she would prove him wrong.

The next day, she walked into school with a little more confidence. The taunts rarely came, but when they did, Barbara refused to let them hold power over her. She reminded herself of the courage she had shown by standing up for herself. She might be alone sometimes, but she was not worthless. She had value. Slowly, classmates became friends.

A year had gone by in the blink of an eye, and Barbara's comfort with Bill and Shirley deepened. She had come to see their home as a haven, a safe place where she could shed the weight of her worries, even if only for a little while. Shirley, with her warmth and understanding, was always there to lend a listening ear. But it was Bill, with his calm demeanor and thoughtful responses, who ended up becoming her sounding board. His easygoing nature allowed Barbara to feel that her thoughts, no matter how jumbled, were always welcome.

It wasn't like Barbara had never opened up to anyone before, but it had been a long time since she'd trusted someone enough to truly let her guard down. Bill's gentle encouragement made it easier, though. One evening, after dinner, they were sitting on the porch, with the sounds of crickets filling the air as the sun sank below the horizon.

"How are you *really* doing, Barbara?" Bill asked, his voice soft yet steady. It was a simple question, but coming from him, it felt different. She found herself staring into the fading light, as if it might help her find the words.

For a moment, Barbara hesitated. She had been carrying so much inside for so long, and she wasn't sure how to let it all out. But Bill didn't rush her; he simply sat beside her, patiently waiting, offering his presence as a kind of reassurance.

Finally, she spoke, her voice quieter than she intended. "I've been... trying to deal with so much for so long. It's hard to explain. I thought I could handle it all on my own, but I'm realizing that I can't anymore."

Bill nodded, his eyes filled with understanding. "You don't have to handle it alone. Whatever it is, I'm here."

And just like that, something inside Barbara unlocked. She started to talk, and it felt like the floodgates opened. She told him about the struggles she'd faced, the losses, the regrets. And for the first time, she talked about her mother and father. How important their memory was. She had never done that before, with anyone. It was as if she was finally allowing herself to feel everything she had been pushing down for so long. Bill listened without judgment, his quiet presence a steady anchor for her unraveling thoughts.

As the conversation flowed, Barbara felt a weight lifting off her shoulders. She hadn't realized how much she had been holding in; how much she had been afraid to let go of. But Bill's kindness and his willingness to listen without pushing allowed her to release what she had been keeping buried for so long.

And for the first time in years, Barbara felt a spark of hope - hope that she could heal, that she could move forward, and that she didn't have to do it alone. But there were more surprises ahead.

As the sunlight filtered through the stained-glass windows, casting soft hues of red, blue, and yellow across the wooden pews, Barbara sat quietly, listening to the soothing cadence of the minister's voice. Bill and Shirley had been coming to this church for years, and they went faithfully every Sunday while Barbara was with them. They tried to quietly nudge her into coming, but she had always resisted. But this time, Shirley, after discussing the issue with Bill, had insisted on bringing her to this church, knowing that she had been struggling with a deep sense of sadness since moving in with them. This time, Barbara had relented.

But here, in this small church nestled on a quiet street, there was a sense of peace. The minister, an older man with a gentle smile and kind eyes, spoke of faith not as a set of rules, but as a path to healing, compassion, and understanding. "We all carry burdens," he said, his voice resonating through the stillness of the sanctuary. "But the journey toward peace is not one we must walk alone. In this church, we are here for each other, as a community, as a family."

Barbara felt a weight shift within her, something she hadn't realized she was carrying. It wasn't that she had expected this church to solve *all* of her problems, but in the minister's words, there was a thread of hope, a whisper of something she had been longing for but had never been able to articulate. A place where she could begin again, where she could lay down the pieces of herself that had been fractured by her circumstances. Those pieces she could then assemble into a new her.

After the service ended, the congregation lingered in the pews, chatting softly, exchanging smiles and warm embraces. Bill and Shirley, ever gracious, introduced Barbara to a few of the members. Each person was kind, not in a forced or overly eager way, but with a genuine warmth that reached out to her. Barbara found herself participating in conversations, offering small smiles, and even sharing a few words with the people she met. She felt, for the first time in a long time, that she belonged.

The minister, Reverend Elliott, approached her with a quiet, welcoming smile. "I hope you found peace here today," he said. His voice was calm, and Barbara felt the sincerity in his words. There was something about him that reminded her of the gentle assurance Bill and Shirley had always shown her, though in a different way. She nodded, surprised by the tears that welled up in her eyes.

"It was…" she hesitated, unsure of how to explain what she was feeling. "It was exactly what I needed."

"I'm glad to hear that," Reverend Elliott said, his gaze softening. "Sometimes, all it takes is a moment of quiet to begin to see things more clearly. If you ever want to talk or need a place to reflect, my door is always open."

Barbara smiled at him, grateful for the offer. She felt no pressure, only an understanding that perhaps, this church could be a place where she could lose the tension inside her, a place where she could breathe, listen, and heal.

Over the following weeks, Barbara continued to attend the services, each one leaving her feeling lighter, more centered. Bill and Shirley checked in on her often, but she could see that they were pleased with the way she was involved with the community. They had always hoped that Barbara would find something here, something beyond the quiet desperation she had arrived with. They saw the change in her before she even recognized it herself.

One morning after another service, Shirley and Bill invited Barbara to join them at a small café down the street. As they sat across from each other, steaming cups in hand, Barbara found herself opening up again about the parts of herself that she had buried for years. She spoke of her childhood, her mom, the loneliness she had carried with her for so many years, and the uncertainty that had followed her every step of the way. She ended by sharing the horror of living with the Daniels. Shirley was stunned but listened patiently, her eyes never leaving Barbara's, offering the kind of listening presence that was rare and precious.

"I've never told anyone that," Barbara admitted, her voice a little shakier than she intended. "It feels strange."

Shirley smiled gently. "Sometimes, all we need is a space to be heard. And, more importantly, to hear ourselves."

Barbara felt the weight of Shirley's words settle inside her like a blanket, warm and comforting. She knew she was still in the early stages of becoming herself again, but for the first time in a long while, she could see the possibility of peace on the horizon. Maybe this church, these people, this place - could be the beginning of something new for her. Not a complete transformation, but a gentle shift that might allow her to heal, step by step.

And as they walked back to Bill and Shirley's, she realized that she had finally found what she had been missing…a family.

One afternoon, Barbara watched from the porch as Bill mowed the lawn. She could see the puffs of grass popping up behind the push mower. Bill, the ever-present cigarette perched on his lips, was sweating and looking like he was struggling.

"Bill!" You need to take it easy. It's really hot!" Barbara yelled at him.

He looked over at Barbara with a smile, and then suddenly his hand went to his chest with a loud gasp as he winced in pain. He fell to the ground. Barbara's heart raced as she dashed across the yard, her legs feeling like they were made of lead. The sight of Bill lying motionless on the grass sent a surge of panic through her. His face was pale, his mouth slightly open in a strange, unnatural way. The mower, abandoned, sat idly beside him.

"Bill! Bill!" she screamed, kneeling beside him. She didn't know what to do. Her hands trembled as she gently touched his shoulder, trying to shake him awake. But there was no response.

She bolted toward the house, her breath coming in ragged gasps as she cried, "Shirley! Shirley! Come quick!"

The door was open, and she could see Shirley inside, tending to something on the kitchen counter. Barbara's words barely left her mouth before Shirley's face shifted from calm to alarm. She rushed toward the door; her expression full of concern.

"Barbara, what's wrong?" Shirley asked, her voice full of worry.

"It's Bill! He - he fell! He - he grabbed his chest!" Barbara's voice broke, and the tears began to well in her eyes.

Shirley's face paled at the mention of the chest pain. Without another word, she rushed past Barbara, kneeling beside Bill. Her hands were steady, despite the panic that Barbara could see in her eyes.

Shirley pushed the lit cigarette away and stepped on it. She immediately checked for a pulse and then pressed a hand against Bill's chest, trying to assess the situation. "Stay here, Barbara. I'm calling for help. Don't leave his side."

Barbara nodded quickly, too scared to speak. She stood frozen for a moment, watching Shirley as she ran into the house. Barbara could hear Shirley's voice, shakier now, as she called for an ambulance.

"Please, Bill, don't leave me," Barbara whispered, her hands wringing together, her heart pounding with fear. She didn't know how much time had passed, but it felt like hours. The air around her seemed still, too still, as if the world had paused to hold its breath along with her. Shirley came back and knelt by her side.

A few minutes later, the sirens could be heard in the distance. Shirley never stopped checking on Bill, and Barbara couldn't keep her gaze from him. He didn't seem to be breathing. She didn't want to believe it - didn't want to accept what could be happening. This wasn't how it was supposed to be!

The ambulance arrived, and its attendants quickly jumped into action. Barbara stood back, helplessly watching. She clenched and unclenched her hands as they worked on Bill, tears streaming down her cheeks. She couldn't understand everything they were doing, but she could tell that this wasn't something small.

"Barbara, honey, we need to give them space," Shirley said softly, her voice now calm but filled with concern. "They're going to help him."

Barbara nodded, but inside she felt like her world was crashing down. She had only just begun to feel safe here, in this home with Bill and Shirley, who had taken her in when she had nowhere else to go. Now, she wasn't sure if anything would ever be the same again. Would Bill be okay? Would *they* be okay?

As the attendants lifted Bill onto a stretcher and rushed him to the ambulance, Barbara couldn't help but follow, her feet heavy but determined. Shirley stayed by her side, offering quiet comfort, but her mind was a whirl of worry, just like Barbara's.

Unbroken Hope

The ambulance doors slammed shut, and with it, a part of Barbara felt like it had been closed off, too. She was left with nothing but fear and the uncertainty of what would come next.

As Barbara and Shirley sat anxiously in the hospital waiting room, the sterile, fluorescent lights above seemed to hum louder with each passing second. Barbara's hands fidgeted in her lap, the cold steel of the chair beneath her offering no comfort. She glanced over at Shirley, who was sitting beside her, her eyes hollow, staring into the distance, lost in a cloud of worry and fear.

Every few minutes, a nurse passed by, but no one spoke to them...offered no information. Shirley's hands trembled in her lap, and Barbara could see her silently counting the minutes that stretched between the soft beeping of the hospital monitors and the occasional shuffle of hospital staff. It all felt surreal to Barbara - this wasn't the way it was supposed to happen.

Bill had always been so strong. He had been the kind of man who would fix anything - cars, fences, broken hearts. His laugh, loud and contagious, would fill their small home. Shirley and Bill were the closest thing Barbara had known to stability since her mother, and now, that felt like it was slipping away.

Finally, after what felt like an eternity, the door to the waiting room opened. A tall, weary doctor walked in, his expression somber. His stethoscope hung loosely around his neck, and his eyes seemed weighted with the heaviness of the news he was about to deliver.

Shirley's eyes snapped up to meet his, and Barbara watched as her foster mother's breath caught in her chest. There was no doubt in Shirley's face that she knew what was coming.

"I'm afraid I have some difficult news," the doctor began, his voice gentle but firm. "Your husband didn't make it. We did everything we could, but..."

The words felt like a body blow. Barbara felt as if the ground beneath her had shifted. She looked at Shirley, whose face had gone ashen, her mouth was opening and closing as if searching for the right words, but none came. And then, the dam broke.

Shirley's shoulders shook as a guttural sob ripped through her chest. She pressed her hands to her face, as if trying to stop the tears from falling, but it was no use. She collapsed against Barbara, crying uncontrollably. Barbara wrapped her arms around Shirley, her own chest tightening with the weight of the moment. She didn't know what to say or how to comfort her foster mother, but she knew she couldn't let go.

The doctor stood still, his eyes lowered to the floor as he watched the grief unfold before him. After a long moment, he nodded, almost as if giving them the space they needed to process the heartbreak before he stepped away.

Barbara felt her own eyes fill with tears, the loss heavy and profound. She was too young to fully understand the fragility of life, but in this moment, everything felt so delicate. Shirley's grief felt like it could shatter her, too.

Shirley's crying became quieter, but her body shook with the force of it. She pulled back slightly from Barbara, wiping her tears away in vain.

"I... I can't..." Shirley whispered; her voice hoarse, raw. "I can't... live without him."

Barbara didn't know how to respond. She just held Shirley tighter, unsure of what else she could do.

They sat in the silence, only the sound of Shirley's quiet sobs filled the space between them. Barbara felt truly helpless. She wished she could do something - anything - to ease Shirley's pain. But all she could was stay by her side, offering whatever small comfort she could in this moment of unspeakable loss.

Time moved on, but for them, it felt as if it had stopped.

Shirley sat in the dimly lit living room, her hands folded in her lap, her eyes still red from crying. Across from her, Barbara, her face streaked with tears, stood rigid, her fists clenched at her sides. The silence between them felt suffocating from the weight of the events. The weight of loss.

"Why couldn't they save him?" Barbara's voice trembled with frustration, her gaze fixed on the floor as if searching for some kind of answer there. "Why does God always do this to me? Every time I need him, it's like he's just... gone!" She shook her head, her voice rising in anger. "He just leaves!"

Shirley swallowed hard, trying to push down the lump in her throat. It was so hard to watch Barbara struggle, to see that anger in her eyes. She had been so young when her own father was killed in the war, then the loss of her mother, and she remembered all too well the pain, the confusion, the way her faith had been shaken to its core. She couldn't blame Barbara for feeling this way. She had felt it too.

"Barbara," Shirley said softly, her voice gentle, "I know it hurts right now. And I know you're angry. It's okay to be angry. I'm angry too, but we can't let that anger control us."

Barbara's eyes snapped up, fierce and raw. "Control us? How can you even say that? Bill's gone, and no one could save him! No doctor, no medicine, and not even God could help him. How can you deal with that, Shirley? How?"

Shirley's heart broke all over again, the weight of her own grief threatening to collapse on top of her. She reached out, resting a hand on

Barbara's trembling arm, her grip steady and warm. She could feel the girl's pain radiating off her, and she understood every ounce of it.

"You're right," Shirley said, her voice thick with sorrow but steady. "I don't understand why it happened. I don't know why Bill was taken from us so suddenly, so... without warning. But I do know that we don't have to face this alone. And I know, deep in my heart, that God isn't gone. He's with us in the pain, even if we can't feel him. He's here. Right here."

Barbara let out a sharp breath, stepping back from Shirley's touch, her arms crossed tightly over her chest. She shook her head again, stubborn, unwilling to accept what she couldn't comprehend.

"I don't feel him here," Barbara whispered, her voice cracking. "I feel empty. I feel like he's turned his back on us, just like he's done every other time."

Shirley's chest tightened, the words catching in her throat. "Barbara," she began again, more softly this time, "I know that's how it feels. It feels like he's abandoned us. But you have to trust me when I say that we can't always understand why things happen." She paused to let her words sink in. "It comes down to faith...it's about trusting even when we don't get answers. Even when we're left with nothing but pain and questions."

Barbara's lips quivered, but she said nothing. The anger was still there, though softer now, buried beneath a wave of hurt.

Shirley took a deep breath, feeling a tear slip down her cheek, but she didn't wipe it away. "I've asked God the same questions, Barbara. I've screamed at Him, I've been angry with Him, and I've felt lost. But I also know that somehow, in the darkest of moments, He finds a way to carry us through. Maybe we don't see it now. Maybe we never will. But He's here. I have to believe that."

Unbroken Hope

Shirley sat on the front porch step, Barbara beside her, staring down into the grass. Her hands were pressed against the smooth wood porch, fingers trembling. The weight of the last few weeks had been suffocating. Barbara was still very young and had been touched by death far too often. With Bill gone, the house felt colder now, quieter, as though his laughter and his energy had left with him.

Shirley watched Barbara for a moment, the deep love for her foster daughter mingling with the exhaustion that had taken root in her bones. She had tried. She had tried to be strong, to be the mother Bill and she had wanted her to be, to carry on as if everything was normal. But it wasn't normal. And it hadn't been for weeks now.

"Barbara," Shirley's voice cracked as she cleared her throat, trying to steady herself. "We need to talk."

Barbara didn't look up at first. She had become quiet, withdrawn. Since the funeral, there had been moments of wide-eyed curiosity, but mostly, it was as though she was holding her breath, waiting for something. Waiting for Bill to come home. Waiting for the world to make sense again. It seemed all she had ever done in her entire life was wait.

Shirley could see the hesitance in her movements as Barbara's blue eyes lifted, and they locked on Shirley with a mix of confusion and trust.

Shirley's hands twisted together, her nails biting into her palms. "You know how I've been trying to do everything for you, right? I've been doing my best... But I think I need you to know something."

Barbara frowned. "What do you mean?"

Shirley took a deep breath, her chest tight. She had been running as fast as she could, trying to make sure Barbara was okay, making sure the house was running smoothly, making sure she didn't break down in front of her. But now, it was impossible to ignore the truth any longer.

"Sweetheart, it's been really hard for me. Since... since Bill died," she said, forcing herself to meet Barbara's gaze. "And I know it's been hard for you, too. But I need to tell you that I can't do everything alone. I can't raise you by myself the way you deserve."

Barbara blinked, clearly missing the point. She cocked her head to the side. "But you are doing it. You make my lunch. You help me with my homework. You tuck me in."

Shirley's heart ached. This young girl was still trying to hold onto some semblance of the old routine. It was a routine that had been shattered. "I know, sweetie," Shirley said softly. "But I'm not okay. And I don't want to keep pretending that I am. I can't keep holding it together for both of us when I'm falling apart inside."

The words were like stones, heavy and real. It wasn't just a conversation about responsibility; it was the painful acknowledgment that Shirley had reached her breaking point.

Barbara pushed her chair back slowly and stood. "Are we going to be okay, Shirley?"

Shirley's eyes burned with unshed tears. "I don't know, honey. I don't think so."

There was a long silence. Barbara took a step forward, her hands clutching the edge of the Shirley's chair. "I don't want you to be sad. I just want you to be happy like before. With Bill."

Shirley closed her eyes briefly, the sting of her words almost unbearable. "I wish I could promise you that, Barbara. I really do."

Shirley had never imagined it would come to this - admitting that she couldn't do it all. But it was a reality she had to face. She had to ask for help, even if it meant breaking the image she had always held of herself as the perfect mother.

Barbara reached up, touching Shirley's arm gently. "Do you need me to help? I can help."

Unbroken Hope

Shirley smiled weakly, trying to hold it together. "You're already helping, sweetheart. But... I think we both need help from other people too. We need to be okay, and that means we can't do this alone anymore."

Barbara thought for a moment, then nodded solemnly, as though she understood something bigger than her years allowed. Shirley pulled her into a tight embrace, the scent of the girl's hair soothing in the most fragile way.

"I love you, Barbara. But I think it is best that we find a better place for you to live. I talked with Mr. Walker," She whispered, more to herself than to Barbara. Barbara broke down weeping on Shirley's shoulder.

In a few days, Mr. Walker showed up again.

Chapter 64

Barbara loved the peacefulness of the Martin's house. It had a comforting familiarity - quiet, steady, and safe, filled with the sounds of an old clock ticking in the hall, the soft hum of the kitchen, and the occasional laughter from Belle and the other children. The Martin's house, Lock and Ethel's house, wasn't just any home; it had a charm all its own. Mr. Walker had introduced her to the Martins in June of 1947, and they took to her immediately.

Fortunately for Barbara, the peace she had been able to discover with the Hodges, Bill and Shirley, had stayed with her and she was able to build on it with the Martins.

Standing seven feet four, Lock was one of the tallest actors ever. He held various odd jobs before his debut on the silver screen. He worked for Spike Jones and his City Slickers, Ardens Dairy as a Cowboy for Public Relations, and at Knotts Berry Farm.

It wasn't just his size that made him stand out; it was his presence, his warmth, his ability to make everyone feel important - even if they were just a passing moment in his world.

By the 1940s, Los Angeles was home to an explosion of new genres, from the dazzling musicals of MGM to the rising interest in science fiction and fantasy. Martin's large size, once an anomaly, began to serve as an asset to a city constantly searching for new and unique talents to bring its fictional worlds to life.

He had married Ethel Mae Noonan in June of 1946. Because of his size, he was classified 4F and didn't serve in the war.

Michael Wells

Ethel was another story altogether. Living in Butte, Montana, and married at 12, and divorced a year later. She had a child out of wedlock when she was 14.

In December 1931, she married again. In June of '34, she gave birth to twin daughters, Audrey Delia and Arvilla Effie, whom they called Belle. But she was divorced seven years later.

Ethel worked her way down to Los Angeles. She would stop in various towns to pick up work. It wasn't easy toting the children with her. It was in Los Angeles where she met Lock at the height of the war.

For Ethel, the challenges of life with Lock were many, but not as challenging as her life before him. Their relationship was one built on deep affection and respect, but there was also a shared understanding that their life would never be ordinary. Ethel, a petite woman compared to Lock's giant frame, would often accompany him to premieres and public events, her presence grounding and stabilizing, a reminder of the life they had together away from the limelight. Lock loved the children and loved fostering them in short order.

He remained a humble man, focused on his family and his craft. In those quieter moments at home with Ethel, Lock would often talk about his dreams beyond the movies, his interest in art and architecture, and the occasional frustration he felt at being typecast.

Ethel, for her part, was supportive but always kept their lives grounded. She loved the simple pleasures: long walks around Los Angeles, local diners, and spending time with friends. In the evenings, they would sit together at home, sharing meals and enjoying each other's company, away from the hustle of Hollywood.

While Lock had no children of his own, he loved Ethel's unconditionally. Along with their children, their home was often filled with visitors and, more importantly, Barbara, whom they began calling

Unbroken Hope

Big Bambi, because she was older than the baby, Barbara, who became known as Little Bambi.

The children were drawn to him, each of them fascinated by the stories of Lock's career. He was, after all, a movie star, but it wasn't the fame or the movies that made him special in their eyes. It was his kindness. He didn't throw his weight around - figuratively or literally. He just... cared.

"Do you mind, Daddy?" Barbara had asked one evening after dinner when she noticed the other kids gathered around him, eager for another story. Lock smiled down at her, his eyes warm and understanding. He encouraged all the children to call him Daddy.

"Of course not, sweetie. Sit down." His voice, low and rich, made Barbara feel like she could ask him anything without fear.

She sat beside him, a plate of apple pie in hand. Belle was across the room, her brown eyes sparkling as she listened intently, a grin playing on her lips. Belle and Barbara had become inseparable over the past few months, growing closer than either of them had expected. Belle, with her quick wit and easy laughter, was more than just a friend. She was becoming a sister in the truest sense of the word. Belle, would always be close to her twin sister, Audrey, but it was with *Big Bambi*, that Belle found an uncommon bond and a shared spirit.

Barbara had never really had a sister. And now she had three! But it was Belle, who really won Barbara's heart. There was something about Belle's fierce loyalty, her understanding, that felt different. Belle had a way of listening, of offering a hand when Barbara was unsure, and a laugh when she needed it most. They'd spent hours exploring the Martins' giant yard together, picking wildflowers in the garden, or lying on their backs, staring up at the stars, their fingers tracing the constellations as they talked about everything.

"Belle!" Barbara had shouted just the other day, "Look at this! It's like the stars are smiling at us tonight!"

Belle had sat up, brushing grass from her shirt, and stared up with a soft smile. "I think they are."

Lock often told stories about the days when he'd first come to Hollywood. How he'd been a part of the movie business, but never a star. But it was the stories about his personal life that really intrigued Barbara. He told her about the struggles of being such a large man in an industry built for the typical leading men - shorter, leaner, more "average." He told her how he had found comfort in the odd roles that allowed him to be more than just a giant in the background. He'd played odd characters but always with dignity and grace.

"That's how you get through, Barbara," he said one night as they sat in the living room, the soft yellow light from a lamp casting shadows on the walls. "No matter who you are, what you look like, what they do to you. You just keep going. You find your place."

Barbara smiled. The words echoed in her mind long after the conversation had ended, and she often found herself thinking about them when she doubted herself.

But it wasn't just Lock who made the house feel like home. It was Ethel too. Ethel, who was always at the stove, always baking something sweet, always telling Barbara she needed to eat more or she'd float away. Ethel had a nurturing spirit that made Barbara feel like she had always belonged. It wasn't just about feeding you - it was about caring about you. When Barbara had first come to the house, she had been shy, reserved, but now, thanks to Ethel's gentle insistence, she had grown confident. She was no longer just the girl who didn't belong anywhere; she was someone with a place, with a family, with a home.

And then, of course, there was Belle.

Unbroken Hope

Belle was different from the others. She didn't just live here - she thrived here. It was as if the home had been built just for her, and she fit perfectly into the rhythm of it all. Belle had a natural charisma that drew people in, made them feel like they were the most important person in the room. And it was that same warmth that made Barbara feel so comfortable in her presence.

"Bambi, have you ever wondered what it would be like to be famous like Daddy?" Belle had asked one night, her eyes twinkling mischievously as they sat on the porch steps, wrapped in blankets against the cool night air.

Barbara thought for a moment before responding. "Not really. I think… I think I'd rather just have a quiet life. A peaceful one."

Belle's grin softened into something more thoughtful. "Yeah. I get that. Eh…Fame's overrated anyway."

Barbara laughed, but it wasn't the typical laughter that came from a joke. It was the kind of laughter that was born from understanding, from a shared truth between them. They were both here, in the Martins' home. They were safe and they were valued.

As the months passed, Barbara's bond with Belle only deepened. The connection between them felt like something from a fairy tale, as though the universe had conspired to bring them together at this exact moment in time. What had started as a friendship blossomed into sisterhood, a bond that transcended the boundaries of their pasts. They weren't just two girls living in the same house - they were each other's family now. They were a team, facing the world together.

One evening, as Lock tucked them into bed, Barbara whispered, "I think I finally understand what it feels like to belong, Daddy."

Michael Wells

Lock smiled down at her, his voice steady. "That's because you do. You always have, Barbara. You've always had a place here."

And for the first time in her life, Barbara believed him. She wasn't just a visitor in a stranger's house. She wasn't just a foster child. She was part of something bigger...part of this family and this home.

At that moment, Barbara knew she was exactly where she was meant to be.

Barbara and Belle's bond had always been strong, but it only grew deeper when they entered eighth grade. Despite their differences - Barbara's calm, introspective nature, and Belle's fiery, extroverted spirit - they complemented each other perfectly. Their relationship was one of those rare, effortless connections that made everyone around them see how much they truly meant to each other.

One afternoon, a few weeks into the school year, they were both in the school library, studying for a history test. Barbara had always been good at focusing. Belle was distracted, flipping through a movie magazine and doodling on the edges of her notebook.

"Belle, you're going to fail this test if you don't focus," Barbara teased, glancing up from her notes.

Belle rolled her eyes, but her grin betrayed the annoyance she pretended to have. "I'm absorbing the information... just at my own pace."

Barbara raised an eyebrow, laughing quietly. "Uh-huh. The only thing you're absorbing is the latest gossip from Hollywood." She motioned toward the magazine in Belle's hand.

Belle sighed dramatically and dropped the magazine, leaning across the table toward Barbara. "Okay, fine. Teach me. How do you do it?"

Barbara smirked and pulled her notes closer, pointing to a few key sections. They spent the next hour studying together, Barbara explaining the material in her calm, methodical way while Belle asked questions and added humor to lighten the mood. By the end of the session, Belle had actually learned a lot, even if she wouldn't admit it.

"Alright, alright, I have to say you're actually good at this," Belle chuckled, packing up her things.

Barbara smiled, proud of herself for being able to help, but also knowing Belle was always more of a visual learner. "You'll do fine. Just don't forget your study guide tomorrow morning."

The next week, when they both walked into the classroom for the history test, Belle gave Barbara a thumbs-up, signaling that she felt prepared - at least, enough to pass. Barbara gave her a knowing smile, thinking she might have underestimated Belle's ability to pull things together at the last minute.

Belle had dragged Barbara to a school dance, much to her reluctance. Barbara wasn't big on dances, preferring the comfort of her books or a quiet evening at home. But Belle had insisted, practically pulling her into the gymnasium despite Barbara's protests.

Once there, Belle immediately disappeared into the crowd, weaving between friends, laughing and chatting. Barbara, meanwhile, hovered on the outskirts, leaning against the wall, feeling out of place. That was when she noticed Belle's eyes darting across the room. Without saying a word, she walked over to Barbara and grabbed her hand.

"Come on, Bambi, you're gonna have fun," Belle said, pulling her toward the center of the floor.

Barbara hesitated but followed, and soon she was laughing and dancing along with Belle, the awkwardness melting away. The music, the lights, the energy - it wasn't her type of place, but with Belle beside her, it felt different. Belle had this way of making things feel okay, even if they weren't.

Later that night, when they were sitting on the steps outside, catching their breath, Belle turned to her.

"I told you," She said with a grin, "dancing's not so bad when you're with me."

Barbara rolled her eyes but couldn't help smiling. "You're impossible."

It was then that they both knew - they had each other, no matter what.

Barbara and Belle's relationship was rooted in the kind of sisterhood that went beyond blood. They understood each other's quirks, embraced the challenges life threw at them, and knew that, no matter how much they bickered or teased, they would always protect each other. Eighth grade had only strengthened that bond, laying the foundation for the rest of their lives together.

Chapter 65

Barbara found herself on the edge of going to high school and she was flourishing. She, Belle, and Audrey were all going to be freshmen!

Belle greeted her that morning with a bright smile. She was wearing her first day of school outfit and looked splendid.

It wasn't long before Barbara found herself walking to Van Nuys High School with Belle. Audrey had decided to walk with other friends. Barbara was the same age as Belle, but Belle always watched out for her. They would cut through the neighborhood, Belle with her dark long legs swinging confidently, Barbara's shoes dragging a little behind. Belle didn't speak much about school - she never did, really - but there was something in the way she moved, like she had already decided that life had a rhythm to it, and you could either follow or get left behind. Barbara was learning, slowly, that she could follow and lead when she had to.

The school itself was a sprawling complex, the kind of place where the sounds of lockers slamming and voices echoing through the hallways could make anyone feel small if they didn't have someone to walk with. Barbara wasn't the kind of girl who easily made friends, and she didn't have to. Belle had a way of drawing people to her, and soon enough, Barbara found herself included in conversations, at lunch, in moments that used to feel out of reach. There was a grace in Belle's way of moving through the world, an ease that made it look effortless.

At first, Barbara stayed on the edges, sitting with her back pressed against the brick wall, watching the other girls with their bright laughter and smooth skin. She tried to listen, tried to make sense of their words, but mostly she felt like a shadow in a room full of light. Belle would sit beside her then, swinging her legs over the side of the bench, and without a word, pull Barbara into her orbit. Some days, they wouldn't talk at all, and it was just the quiet that settled between them, but Barbara knew - somehow - this was what she had been waiting for.

The weeks turned into months, and the days began to look the same, though Barbara felt something inside her changing. She started to laugh more, even if it felt foreign. She started to think about things like who she wanted to be when she grew up, and whether or not the old world was ever coming back. She found herself looking forward to the sound of Belle's voice calling her name, the warmth of Daddy's soft voice, and Mama's soft hands as she served dinner, and the way Mama never spoke about her past, only about the books Barbara was reading, and Barbara did love to read.

Sometimes, in the quiet of the evenings, when the last rays of sun slid over the hills and the streetlamps flickered on one by one, Barbara would lie on the grass with Belle, her hands clasped behind her head, staring up at the California sky. It was a different kind of sky than the one she remembered - clearer, less troubled - and it felt like the kind of sky that could hold her future, if only she could find the courage to reach for it.

"Do you ever think about leaving?" Barbara asked one night, her voice barely above a whisper. Belle didn't answer right away, but Barbara knew she was thinking.

"Sometimes," Belle said after a long pause, her voice like a sigh carried by the wind. "But then I remember, there's always something to stay for, you know? Something small, like a moment that's just yours."

Barbara turned her head toward Belle, their eyes meeting in the soft dusk. It wasn't the first time she'd heard Belle talk like that. But Belle

Unbroken Hope

answered as she always did, as if she had already figured out what the rest of them were still trying to grasp.

"What about you?" Belle asked, turning the question back on Barbara, and for the first time in a long time, Barbara knew that the answer didn't feel so far away.

"I think," she said slowly, feeling the words take shape in the quiet of the night, "I think I've already found something here that I don't want to give up. it. But it gives me the courage to see what happens next. You know what I mean?"

Belle just nodded.

The bond between them deepened in that moment, an unspoken promise that no matter how much the world might change, no matter how far they might go, there would always be this place - this house, this street, this school - and there would always be Belle. And for Barbara, that was enough to make the days ahead seem less uncertain.

Chapter 66

Barbara had never been one for routine, but there was something about *Phillipe - The Original* that always drew her in. It wasn't just the French dip sandwiches - though, of course, they were legendary - or the fact that the restaurant had invented the dish itself. It was the way everything felt steeped in history, a world apart from the bustle of Van Nuys High School, where she spent her days drifting between classes and trying to make sense of the disjointed patchwork of teenage life. Phillipe's was a place where time seemed to slow down, as though it were frozen in a moment long before she'd ever existed. The deli's long counter, the bright red vinyl stools, the faded photographs of old Hollywood legends on the walls, all gave the sense that you were walking into a slice of Los Angeles history - a time capsule with a side of extra au jus.

One afternoon, Barbara and Belle were tucked into one of the vinyl booths near the counter. Their sandwiches sat in front of them and both of the girls were nursing Pepsis in bottles, sipping through a straw and waiting to dig in. She had been going to Phillipe's for a little under a year now, ever since she'd first tasted the tender beef on a fresh roll dipped in jus that warmed her soul. It was a weekday, a rare break from the chaos of school, and she relished the quiet moment of solitude. Her history test that morning had been a breeze, but still, she was thankful for this small reprieve. Belle and she had agreed to come here to downtown Los Angeles by riding the bus after school.

A man clearing the tables walked by. He must've been working there for decades. Barbara nodded at him, a small smile forming on her lips, as she greeted him with her usual, "Hi, Mack." Mack didn't say much, but there was something comforting about his steady presence, as though he had seen generations of customers come and go.

Belle laughed, "You always say hello to him."

Barbara didn't respond.

Barbara's gaze wandered around the room, as it often did. The place was almost always busy, with families, businessmen and couples, all coming for the same thing: a taste of tradition. She was starting to daydream about the bite she'd soon take of her sandwich when, suddenly, she saw *him* and her heart skipped a beat.

He was very tall and he looked sort of like one of those motorcycle gang members and was effortlessly handsome. Barbara knew he would tower over her, but that just reminded her of Daddy who did the same thing. He fit the bad boy type, black hair, slick with Wildroot Creme Oil in a duck tail, easy grin, and the kind of laid-back confidence that made you wonder if he even tried. He wore jeans but he was so tall he couldn't roll the cuffs up like the other boys did. But he could roll his Camel cigarette pack up into the sleeve of his white t-shirt.

She watched, frozen, as he went up and placed his order at the counter. For a moment, she was sure he hadn't seen her, but then their eyes met, and something clicked. A second of magic, a slight raise of his eyebrow, as if he thought he knew her. She looked over at Belle who just shrugged, implying you're on your own. Barbara had forgotten about her sandwich.

Grabbing his sandwich he sauntered over to the girl's booth. "Well, well," he said, his voice warm with an easy charm that made her skin tingle. "What are you girls doin?"

Barbara blinked, her mind scrambling to find the right words. She hadn't expected him to actually talk to her, let alone so casually. She had been preparing to pretend she didn't see him, to keep her head down and hope she wasn't noticed. But now, the moment had come, and there was no escaping it.

"Oh, nothing," she said, keeping her voice steady. "Just eating. Don't you love these sandwiches?"

She shrieked inside, Don't you just love these sandwiches!!? You sound like an idiot. Belle looked at her as if to confirm it.

He laughed, the sound like a gentle breeze. "I'll eat anything, really. But there's something about the original French dip that just calls to me." He paused and took in the scene with a slight grin. "It's like a relic of the past, don't ya think?"

Barbara laughed, and for a split second, they were just two people talking in a deli, a momentary connection shared over the rich history of a sandwich. But she could feel her heart racing in her chest, trying to keep up with the unexpected direction her day had taken.

"Well, if you're going to eat here," she said, trying to sound nonchalant, "you've gotta get the dip. The roast beef is the best in town.."

"I like the pork," he replied dryly. "But no one's gonna quibble over it. Think I'll try the beef though on your recommendation.".

For a moment, the world around them seemed to disappear. The clatter of dishes, the buzz of conversation - everything fell away. All that existed was this strange, surreal meeting between two people who had never known each other, yet were suddenly thrown into the same small universe. Even Belle was lost in the haze.

Barbara realized, with a small sting of self-awareness, that she had been staring at him. She quickly averted her eyes, her cheeks hot. "Right. You should."

He seemed to notice, but he didn't press. He held up his sandwich, "Maybe next time. Well, I guess I will see ya around." And he moved toward a table on the other side of the restaurant and then turned before he got there. "Say what's your name?"

"Bar…Barbara," she stuttered, "Barbara Rose. This is my sister, Belle"

"Well it's nice to meet you, Bar…Barbara and you too, Belle." He turned to leave again and then as an afterthought turned back, "Rod…Rod Wells." He then took a seat at the distant table.

Barbara couldn't help but steal glances at him from time to time, as though she were watching a character in a movie, trying to figure out what was going to happen next.

And then, as though the world had come back into focus, Belle was there. Barbara turned her attention back to her sandwich, trying to regain some semblance of normalcy. She had no idea what to make of this encounter - or of Rod Wells.

As she took a bite of her sandwich, savoring the familiar, juicy flavors, she couldn't shake the feeling that today would be the start of something unexpected. And somehow, she wasn't sure whether that was a good thing or not.

But then again, life had a way of surprising you when you least expected it. Just like this moment at Phillipe's.

Belle just stared at her and then laughed softly.

Chapter 67

Barbara was no longer the girl who had stumbled through her teenage years unsure of where she belonged. At sixteen, she'd grown into someone who knew what she wanted and wasn't afraid to chase after it. And what she wanted now, more than anything, was Rod.

Rod had a smile that took over his whole face whenever he talked. He was seventeen when they first met. And he had become her best friend, next to Belle, He was one person she could imagine walking beside her in a life that had always seemed too big, too unpredictable, until now. He was now eighteen and had recently graduated from high school.

They had started dating a year ago last summer after she had gone back to Phillipe's, and lo and behold he had been there. He even admitted later he had been coming regularly in the event he would meet up with her again.

It felt natural - like they'd always been meant to be together, like a door they hadn't known was waiting had suddenly swung open. He had gotten a job at Ted Cannon's machine shop in North Hollywood, not far from where he lived with his parents. Ted built racecars as well. And it was in Ted's shop that Rod learned about auto mechanics.

After work Rod would pick Barbara up and they would drive through town in his old, Ford roadster, a car he had built himself. They would drive laughing at inside jokes and talking about their dreams like they had nothing else to lose.

One lazy afternoon, while they were parked at a lookout spot, Rod turned to her with that serious look he sometimes got when he was thinking about something important.

"Barbara, have you ever thought about... running away?" he asked.

Barbara laughed, but it was a nervous laugh, because she knew him too well. Rod had a way of saying the wildest things like they were simple truths, things you could just decide and make happen.

"You're joking, right?" she asked, looking over at him.

"No. I mean, what's stopping us? You, me, Tijuana. We could just go. Get married, make it official. You and me."

Her heart skipped a beat. The words hung in the air between them, impossible and perfect at the same time.

"Rod..." she whispered. "I don't even know if we're old enough to do that."

Rod just grinned, that boyish charm that always made her feel like anything was possible. "Who cares? We've got everything we need - us. And maybe a couple bucks, but we'll figure it out."

Barbara looked at him, unsure whether it was impulsiveness or something deeper, but there was a pull she couldn't resist. She felt it, too - the desire to break free, to escape from the expectations and limitations that always seemed to hover just above her head. She loved Belle and the Martins, but this was suddenly a new way of life opening up before her.

She turned her gaze back to the sunset, her mind racing. "And what happens after?"

"After?" Rod shrugged. "We start our life. The real one."

That night, they made a pact, as reckless and full of fire as their love. They would go to Tijuana, cross that invisible line into another world where they weren't just a sixteen-year-old girl and an eighteen-year-old boy from North Hollywood. They would be more than their pasts - more than anyone could tell them they were allowed to be.

Unbroken Hope

A week later, Barbara packed a small bag. Clothes she didn't care about, a few dollars hidden in her jacket pocket, and her heart full of an audacity she hadn't known she was capable of. She snuck out of the house with no one seeing her.

Rod was waiting for her outside. His car made a soft rumbling sound as it idled. They didn't talk much on the way down to the border, but the quiet felt comfortable, like they were in on a secret.

When they finally made it to Tijuana, the city felt like a living thing - vibrant, chaotic, alive with possibilities. They walked through the streets hand in hand, the noise of the city surrounding them, but for the first time, Barbara felt like she was exactly where she was supposed to be.

Once in Tijuana they visited one of the local civil registries, known as "Registro Civil," where they applied for a marriage license. They were told that normally they would have to wait a day or two before they could get married, but the clerk took pity on them and arranged for the ceremony that afternoon. After eating a meal at a local restaurant, the two trundled back to the office. The judge who acted as the officiant, read the vows in broken English. Barbara and Rod exchanged vows in front of strangers who didn't care about their age or their pasts, only about what they were willing to promise right then and there. The strangers even witnessed the signing of their license.

Barbara felt the weight of it all, but it was a weight she didn't mind. They were married. They were free.

As they stepped out of the office, the weight lifted, leaving only the warmth of the evening sun and the soft hum of the world around them. Barbara looked at Rod, her new husband, her heart thumping in her chest, and everything else fell away.

"Where to now?" she asked, grinning.

Rod took her hand and led her into the crowd, their steps light and sure. They didn't know exactly where they were going, but that didn't matter. They had each other, and Barbara realized that was all she really needed.

"Anywhere," Rod said. "As long as it's with you."

And together, they walked into the night, their future unspoken but full of promise, the world ahead of them waiting to be discovered - just as wild, just as free as their love.

Chapter 68

The years slipped by like pages torn from a book no one meant to finish. Seasons blurred - summer's heat mellowed into autumn's hush, winter cold slipped into spring rains, and each time it happened, it felt both new and strangely familiar. Faces changed. Some grew lines, some disappeared altogether. The house creaked a little more with each passing winter, and the trees out front leaned farther toward the ground, as if bowing under the weight of memory. Life didn't move in leaps, just in quiet shifts - until one day, without warning, the past felt further away than she ever imagined it could.

Barbara and Rod had a good life. Three children, Michael, Judy, who was named in honor and to the memory of Judy Burkey. And finally, baby Steven. And yet, Barbara always felt somewhat unsettled.

And then one day, everything changed.

Barbara didn't usually check the mail. Not right away, anyway. It had a habit of bringing bad news - past due notices, bank statements, reminders that things like stability were a luxury she'd never had. But today, something nudged her. A feeling, maybe, or just a break in routine.

She came in from the hallway holding a small stack of envelopes, flicking through them with practiced disinterest. Belle was sitting on the couch with an old blanket wrapped around her shoulders. She came over often while Rod was at work and Michael and Judy were at school and the baby was napping. The two women were almost always together, virtually inseparable.

"Anything good?" Belle asked about the mail, without looking up.

"Bill, bill, something in Spanish that's not ours…" Barbara muttered, flipping. Then she stopped abruptly with a soft inhale of breath

Belle looked up at her quizzically, "Bambi?"

Barbara's fingers had tightened on a thick white envelope. The return address made her freeze.

Los Angeles County Department of Children and Family Services. She stared at it.

"Bambi?" Belle had turned around now, sensing the shift. "What is it?"

Barbara didn't answer. She sat on the edge of the couch, carefully tearing it open. The paper inside was heavy and official. She unfolded it slowly, each crease feeling like it held its own kind of truth.

She read the first line and then read it again.

```
This letter is to inform you that your biological mother,
Erma Rose, has contacted the Department and requested to
be reunited with you...
```

The rest blurred. Her heart beat so loud she could hear it echo in her ears.

"She found me," Barbara said, barely above a whisper. "She… found me.

Belle's eyes widened. "Wait - your mom?"

Barbara nodded. "She wants to meet. She asked for me. After all this time…"

Tears welled up, uninvited but unstoppable. Belle was beside her in an instant, pulling her into a hug. For a long moment they sat there, the quiet of the apartment filled only by the sound of Barbara's breathing as it cracked and caught.

Unbroken Hope

"She left me," Barbara whispered. "I waited for so long. And then I stopped waiting. I thought she was gone. Dead, maybe. Or just done with me."

"You don't have to see her if you don't want to," Belle said gently. "But... maybe she didn't have a choice. Maybe she's been looking for you this whole time."

Barbara wiped at her face, the letter still trembling in her hands. "I need to know," she said. "How she is...even if it hurts."

The air smelled fresh that morning and the lake in MacArthur Park shimmered under the bright blue sky. Barbara sat on a worn bench, her fingers twisting in her lap. She'd worn her denim jacket - the one she'd had since high school, frayed at the sleeves - because she didn't want to look like she was trying too hard.

Then she saw her. Barbara stood and began walking toward her. As she got closer, she could see the pained expression on the woman's face.

In her late 50s, with dark brown hair streaked with grey, pulled back in a nervous bun, and blue eyes mirrored Barbara's own blue eyes.

They stared at each other for a moment. Neither moved.

"Barbara?" the woman said, voice shaking.

Barbara stood slowly. "Erma?" then, "Mom?" then, "Mama?"

The woman's hand went to her mouth as her eyes filled with tears. "You're so grown. So beautiful."

Barbara tried to speak, but her throat was thick with feeling. Her mother stepped forward, unsure, then opened her arms.

Barbara didn't think. She just moved. And when they embraced, the years collapsed.

All the nights in strange beds. All the birthdays that passed without candles or cake. All the questions that never had answers - they rose and broke like a wave between them.

"I wanted you," Erma whispered through sobs. "I swear to God, I never wanted to let you go. I was broken, and I didn't know how to fix it. I thought you would hate me. You don't know how many times I started to call the foster people. Years, baby. I just couldn't face it. I was embarrassed and…I thought you would hate me," she repeated.

Barbara clung to her, her face buried in the soft fabric of a stranger's coat that somehow already felt like family.

Barbara whispered, "I thought you forgot. I could never hate you!"

"I never forgot," Erma mumbled. "Never."

They stood there in the park, mother and daughter, surrounded by strangers and the sweet songs of birds, both holding on to each other, crying like the world had cracked open and let in something holy.

And after all the years, Barbara finally felt it, knew it, in her heart.

Her mother's love.

Chapter 69

Barbara stood at the edge of the Pacific Ocean, the wind whipping through her hair, the vast expanse of ocean stretching endlessly before her. She could almost feel the weight of the years, the battles fought, the heartache endured, like a distant echo in the back of her mind. It had taken so long - so much longer than she ever imagined - but here she was, standing on her own, free of the shackles that had once bound her.

The scars - both the ones she could see and the ones she couldn't - no longer defined her. They were simply part of her story, but they weren't the ending. She had written her own, and it was a story of resilience, of fighting with everything she had, even when it felt like the world was trying to crush her.

Barbara turned and looked behind her - at the path she had walked to get here. The memories were still there, vivid as ever. The betrayal, the loss, the countless sleepless nights, the moments of doubt that had almost broken her. But she had endured, and somewhere along the way, she had learned that it wasn't the pain that shaped her, but how she chose to rise after each fall.

A figure appeared at the top of the trail, moving toward her with purpose. It was Rod, her friend, her confidant, her husband of six years. The person who had believed in her when she hadn't believed in herself. He reached her side, his eyes meeting hers with an unspoken understanding.

"You did it," he said, his voice barely above a whisper. There was awe in it, but also something deeper. Something that said, *I always knew you would.*

Barbara smiled, her heart full, the weight of everything she'd been carrying lifting just a little more. "We did it."

They stood together, looking out over the horizon, where the sun was beginning to dip, painting the sky in hues of orange and pink. The beauty of it all felt almost unreal, like something she had never dared to dream of.

Then a movement on the rise caught their attention and they turned to see Erma trundling forward, carrying the baby, Steven, with little Judy and slightly older Michael, walking beside her. She waved. The two children mimicked her and waved too.

And for the first time in a long time, Barbara felt it. That overwhelming sense of peace and of, finally, being whole.

There were no more questions, no more regrets, no more wondering if she was enough. She *was* enough. And the happiness she had found wasn't some fleeting, fragile thing - it was hers, solid and unshakeable, because she had fought for it every single day.

The future stretched before her, full of possibilities she had once thought were out of reach. But now? Now, Barbara knew she would meet each new chapter with open arms. She had already faced the hardest battles. The rest of her story was hers to write.

And this time, it would be nothing short of beautiful.

She took a deep breath, letting the salty air fill her lungs, and finally, with a quiet laugh, she whispered to the wind, "I'm home."

Epilogue

The dust had blown itself to nothing, but it had taken so much with it. Erma had come west, clutching a threadbare hope in her chest, her little girl, Barbara Jean held close to her side, like some shield against the world. It wasn't the world that had made them wander, but the hunger for the kind of life that people in the stories lived, the kind that didn't choke on dirt and sweat and broken promises. She followed Clay, her man, west, believing that California would be their salvation, their new beginning. But the dream turned sour when they found him, the man she had trusted with her heart and her future, dead on a farm at the edge of nowhere in California.

So, Erma kept living as mothers do, through grief, through loss, through the aching silence. She accepted the love of the owners of the farm. She came to rely on the grit that holds a person together when there's nothing left to hold. And yet, there was always the emptiness, always the horizon that promised something more than the dust, but never quite delivered it.

Then came Vince, a man made with a hard edge. In Los Angeles, she loved him, in a way, but it wasn't the love of promises made in daylight. It was the kind of love born from necessity, born of survival. And it didn't survive. When he died, somewhere in the frozen trenches of Europe, shrapnel finding him before he could find the way back, Erma's world crumbled again. The war didn't just take lives; it took whole ways of being. It took the fire from her bones, until there was nothing left but a body that moved by habit.

Michael Wells

Barbara Jean became just Barbara, still too young to understand much, but old enough to know that the world wasn't a safe place. And the world wasn't kind. Eventually, that small, aching family of two - mother and daughter - was torn apart. Erma's mind gave way like a riverbank too worn to hold the flood, and Barbara was taken, not by death, but by the cold, indifferent hand of the system.

The years dragged on like the wind through a broken fence. Barbara had been in four different homes by the time she was twelve, one a home trying to help but not knowing how, a second that was a horror, and the last two of them good and kind. She had learned to keep her head down, to hide behind the walls of her heart, to become a shadow in a world that barely noticed. One foster home had broken her in ways that couldn't be fixed, the cruelty a brand that never quite healed. But she survived. The heart of her, the part that her mother had once protected, fought through. And there was one thing Barbara had learned from the hard dust of the world: you keep going. You keep moving forward, even when you don't know where you're headed.

But it was with Bill and Shirley where she found the beginning of love. But then Bill, so full of kindness, was stripped away by the failure of his own body.

Finally, it was with the Martins that Barbara, now affectionately known as Bambi, found something like peace. They were good people, kind in their own quiet way. Ethel and Lock took her in when she was older, a girl shaped by years of hardship but still carrying the remnants of something soft and warm inside. They gave her a place to stand, and in time, Barbara stood tall. Lock went on to the most famous role of his career, playing Gort, the robot in *The Day The Earth Stood Still*. And yet. It never changed him. He was ever kind and Barbara forever looked on Ethel and Lock as Mama and Daddy.

Unbroken Hope

Then there was Belle. Belle, who with her pushy ways, prodded Barbara to explore the world, and Barbara blossomed. Belle. who became more than a sister, helped Barbara imagine a bright future.

In that quiet place where the Martins had let her rest, she found Rod, and he was gentle. Gentle in the way that Barbara had long forgotten tenderness could be. They married, and she gave him all the love she had left, the love that had been hidden for so long.

In the end, the path was long, and it was hard, and the pieces of it scattered like the wind scattering seeds in a field. The dust had taken so much, but it hadn't taken everything. Some things were left behind, buried deep, and Barbara learned, as she had to, to pull them out, one by one. And then, she would finally be whole.

And somewhere in her heart, where Vince and Clay and Judy still lived, she heard the quiet, soft promise of a life yet to be fully lived. A life where, perhaps, she would not be defined by the winds that swept across the plains, or by the men who had taken so much from her. No, Barbara would be defined by what she had made of herself - what she had built, despite the odds.

And perhaps that's all there is in the end. Believing in oneself and taking that and building it into a life. Believing in the kindness of others and using that to get through each day. But finally, and perhaps more importantly, believing in the promises of unbroken hope.

Author's Note

Because there exists no record, this novel is a *fictionalized* account of my mother's early life. As fiction, many of the names have been changed, or people have been totally invented. The names of some key people were used, but fictionalized versions of them have been created.

I have tried to remain true to the spirit of the 1930s, 40s, and 50s.

Acknowledgments

Many people have made this book possible. I would like to recognize Brian Bradley, Norma Kaufman, Patti Detwiler, Chuck Vizzini, Bob Kaufman, Dennis Frodsham, Cindy Styron, and Roxanne Bradley who all read early drafts and offered great feedback and outstanding encouragement,

I want to recognize my children, Ryan Garl, Lauren Wells, and Grant Wells for their support.

Finally, to my beloved wife, Dede—

Thank you for being my constant light, my quiet strength, and my truest companion through every chapter of this journey. Your love, patience, and unwavering belief in me have been the foundation upon which this story was built. Every late night, every word written, and every moment of doubt was met with your grace and encouragement. This novel would not exist without you, and in many ways, it is as much yours as it is mine.

"Bye Bye Blackbird" (1926)
Written by Ray Henderson (music) and Mort Dixon (lyrics)

This work is in the public domain.

"Over There" (1917)
Written and composed by George M. Cohan
This work is in the public domain.

About The Author

MICHAEL WELLS is the author of several books on the television and film industry. He has produced over 200 video, film, and multimedia titles. He was named as one of the Top 100 multimedia producers in the world by Multimedia Producer Magazine. His previous novel, *Keeper of the Light* was published in 2012. He lives in Hernando, Florida with his wife, Dede.

www.ingramcontent.com/pod-product-compliance
Lightning Source LLC
LaVergne TN
LVHW091653070526
838199LV00050B/2164